ACCLAIM FOR JOANNE ~~BISCHOF~~

"Bischof's effortless prose and e̶ ̶ ̶ ̶ ̶ ̶ ̶ ̶ ̶ ̶ ̶ ̶ ̶ ̶ ̶ ̶ate the reader from beginning to end̶ ̶ ̶ ̶ ̶ ̶ ̶ ̶ ̶ ̶you begin to believe they are. The Norgaard bro̶ ̶ ̶ ̶ ̶their families will steal your heart. Beautifully eloquent, this grace-filled tale is one not to be missed."

—Catherine West, author of *Where Hope
Begins,* on *Daughters of Northern Shores*

"Laced with lyrical prose, *Daughters of Northern Shores* is a story of redemption that gripped me from its first moments. I savored every gorgeous detail, and the characters continue to live with me even now. Bischof is a master at enfolding readers in her story world and bringing them along on a journey of the heart."

—Lindsay Harrel, author of *The Heart Between Us*
and *The Secrets of Paper and Ink*

"*Sons of Blackbird Mountain* is a quiet gem of a historical romance. Refreshingly real and honest in its depiction of flawed but lovable individuals, it introduces characters readers will want to meet again."

—*CBA Marketplace*

"Christy and Carol Award–winning author Bischof (*The Lady and the Lionheart*) creates endearing characters and a heartwarming story line in this unforgettable novel about the power of family, love, and the true meaning of home. Fans of Kristy Cambron, Julie Klassen, and Susan Meissner will love this one."

—*Library Journal* on *Sons of Blackbird Mountain*

"Bischof (*The Lady and the Lionheart*) transports readers to late 19th-century Appalachian Virginia in this moving historical romance . . . With fine historical details and stark prose that fits the story, Bischof skillfully weaves a tale of love and redemption in rough Appalachia."

—*Publishers Weekly* on *Sons of Blackbird Mountain*

"Beloved author Joanne Bischof doesn't disappoint with her latest beautifully written, heartrending tale, *The Sons of Blackbird Mountain*. Her lyrical style is carefully woven together with authentic faith and unique characters that won't soon be forgotten. It will be a quick favorite for historical romance readers."

—Elizabeth Byler Younts, author of *The Solace of Water*

"The sights, sounds, and people of a turn-of-the-century circus come alive in this novel that captivates from word one. Every sentence is pitch perfect, while the characters embed themselves soul deep. Charlie Lionheart is the hero of heroes and a reflection of the fairy tale 'Beast.' He is so brilliantly multidimensional that he could easily live outside the pages. The romance between Charlie and Ella is heartachingly beautiful, and the redemption organically sewn into the story's tent flaps will linger with readers for years."

—*RT Book Reviews*, 5 Star TOP PICK!,
on *The Lady and the Lionheart*

"From the moment he bursts onto the pages, Charlie Lionheart splashes color across Ella Beckley's drab, confined world—and along the way he stole my heart."

—Lori Benton, Christy Award-winning author of
Burning Sky, on *The Lady and the Lionheart*

"The best stories are ones where you are torn between the desire to linger or read it all in one sitting because you simply have to know what's going to happen next. *The Lady and the Lionheart* put me into that delicious agony and held me there until that final page."

—Sigmund Brouwer, author of *Thief of Glory*,
Christy Award book of the year 2015

"Absorbing. Emotional. Colorful and clever . . . Bischof brings the world of the vintage circus to life in *The Lady and the Lionheart*, with vibrant scenes and deeply poignant characters. It's a masterful portrait of redemption—with faith and hope deftly woven in—that grips the reader until the final page. I was swept away and didn't want to return."

—Kristy Cambron, author of *The Ringmaster's Wife*

"When it comes to depth and originality, Joanne Bischof delivers, and this unique historical is no exception. If you're wanting a story that satisfies heart and soul, this richly woven novel is for you—a keeper you're sure to recommend to friends. Beautiful!"

—Laura Frantz, author of *The Mistress of Tall Acre*,
on *The Lady and the Lionheart*

"*The Lady and the Lionheart* isn't a book to read so much as it is a world to inhabit, a story to relish, a love to cherish. It is lyrical, achingly beautiful, and larger than life. This novel is Joanne Bischof at her very finest."

—Jocelyn Green, award-winning author of the
Heroines Behind the Lines Civil War series

"One of the best works of historical fiction I have ever read, Bischof's alluring prose perfectly relays the heart-rending stories of Charlie, Ella, and a populous of characters who leap from the page. Strewn with threads of redemption not unlike those found in *Les Misérables*, Bischof perfectly pairs an accessible and engaging historical romance with a deft nod to the classics."

—Rachel McMillan, author of *Murder at the Flamingo*, on *The Lady and the Lionheart*

"Only a handful of authors craft stories that leave an indelible mark on my heart—Joanne Bischof is one of them . . . guaranteed, every single time. *The Lady and the Lionheart* is simply stunning, from the provocative beginning to its exquisite conclusion, this story is mesmerizing."

—Rel Mollet, Relz Reviewz & INSPY Award advisory board member

"Breathtaking and drenched in grace, *The Lady and the Lionheart* will sweep you away with the magic of the circus—and the miracle of redemption. This tale is one for the ages; Charlie and Ella will dance into your life with a story to settle deep within your soul."

—Amanda Dykes, author of the critically acclaimed *Bespoke: a Tiny Christmas Tale*

DAUGHTERS OF NORTHERN SHORES

OTHER BOOKS BY JOANNE BISCHOF

DAUGHTERS
of
NORTHERN
SHORES

A NOVEL

JOANNE BISCHOF

THOMAS NELSON
Since 1798

Library of Congress Cataloging-in-Publication Data

Names: Bischof, Joanne, author.
Title: Daughters of Northern Shores / Joanne Bischof.
Description: Nashville, Tennessee : Thomas Nelson, [2019] | Series: A Blackbird mountain novel
Identifiers: LCCN 2018044022 | ISBN 9780718099121 (softcover)
Subjects: | GSAFD: Christian fiction.
Classification: LCC PS3602.I75 D38 2019 | DDC 813/.6--dc23 LC record available at https://lccn.loc.gov/2018044022

To all the women who have loved and believed,
even in the winds of uncertainty

DEAFNESS ON
BLACKBIRD MOUNTAIN

FOR EACH DEAF PERSON, INCLUDING ONE OF
the characters in this novel, communication methods evolve through
unique skills, preferences, and environments. For the characters of
Blackbird Mountain, their understanding of this is shaped by their
bond to the husband, brother, and friend that is Thor Norgaard, and
as a Deaf man in nineteenth-century Appalachia, Thor's communication was shaped by the very lives around him.

As a boy who could neither hear nor speak, he walked shoulder to
shoulder with his brothers in the wilds of their mountain, where the
shoving of a shoulder denoted the same comradery as calling out a hello,
and the tossing of a pebble garnered as much attention as a whisper.
When opportunity brought him to a new language altogether, Thor
came to know American Sign Language (ASL) through the teachings
of a private school in North Carolina.

This language was carried home with him and shared with his
family, as well as, eventually, his bride. As you read, you'll find these
diverse forms of communication at hand, including the use of ASL
marked by italics—a visual, three-dimensional language distilled into

the two-dimensional written English. Melding these two distinct lin-guistics was not only a unique challenge for me as an author but a true delight, as both languages are dear to my heart.

For those of you who met the Norgaards within *Sons of Blackbird Mountain*, your compassion and enthusiasm for their way of life alongside Thor was a true joy to witness. Thank you for voyaging with me into their world once more among these pages of *Daughters of Northern Shores*. Just as with his brothers during the summers of their youth, and all the willing souls he's met since, Thor is ready and honored to show the way.

PROLOGUE

DECEMBER 3, 1894
EAGLE ROCK, VIRGINIA

AVEN LOOPED A HAND AROUND HER HUS-
band's strong forearm, holding tight to Thor's steadying strength. She
glanced across the train platform, searching the crowd for the doctor
they'd driven the morning to meet. A midwinter's day stretched in
billows of gray and blue overhead, but the beauty was lost to her as
rising nerves tamped down even the peace of their life in these mountains. Aven peered up at Thor, who lowered a look her way—one
wrapped in his gentle courage and silent fortitude. Generous since it
was his own comfort at stake today.

Behind them the train station stood shuttered on both sides by
parked wagons and waiting horses, including the four muddied wheels
and faithful team of mares that had brought them here. Travelers
milled about on the boarded platform where a line of boxcars curved
around the bend and out of sight through towering woodlands. Soot
and pine spiced the air, as did the chatter of travelers, most seeking a
stretch of legs and a breath of crisp mountain air before their journey
led away from this rural Appalachian town.

Aven stayed close to her husband's side amid the commotion,
and hearing, "Mr. and Mrs. Norgaard?" she glanced toward a nearby

passenger car where a man waited just in front. The cropped hair beneath his bowler hat was as red as her own. With shirtsleeves rolled back and a slim pencil wedged behind his ear, he appeared to be more about business than travel. Just what they'd come for.

"Aye. Doctor Kent?" Her nervousness quieted as Thor led them nearer.

"Yes, ma'am." A cool, December gust underlined Dr. Kent's deep southern drawl as he swept the bowler hat from his head. He thanked Aven for her attendance today, then offered a handshake to Thor.

Thor's forearm tensed with the grip. The leather suspenders that strapped his broad shoulders were thick and well worn compared to this man's fine tailoring.

"A pleasure to meet you, Mr. Norgaard," Dr. Kent said. Few people addressed Thor with such ease of comfort, and Aven glanced to her husband, who appeared to read the man's lips with ease. "I've been looking forward to this since learning of your participation in the study."

Thor gave a polite nod. Most men would have voiced a response, but Thor couldn't speak a greeting even if he wanted to. The very reason they were here, meeting a physician on this wooden platform.

"Do come inside. The train isn't scheduled to leave until quarter after. We'll begin the interview straightaway, but with the question-naire brief, there should be sufficient time." After glancing up the line, the man climbed three metal steps into the nearest passenger car.

At Aven's hesitation, Thor gave her a smile so sober it could barely be seen within his thick brown beard. He motioned for her to go next, then followed behind, strong fingers bracing the small of her back. Her belly blossomed with their child, and while she could still wear a loosely laced corset and get around with ease, his protective care was tender and constant.

When they entered the train car, he took hold of her hand. In his other he gripped the letter that had summoned him here this day. Sent

2

to their farm by the Bureau of Research and Resource for the Deaf and Dumb, it requested an interview with him as well as a brief medical examination and blood draw. Thor admitted to being unfamiliar with the organization, but while the bureau declared themselves a small venture, he'd shown approval at their mission to advance the understanding of the Deaf in the United States.

As a farmer who kept a vast acreage of orchard land, Thor had little time for a day away, but he'd made an exception, expressing to Aven that if his involvement could help others understand his kind better, he would go. If it could benefit future generations of Deaf children to be less misunderstood—perhaps their own son or daughter included—he would commit to the procedure. A noble choice since neither Thor nor Aven had been certain how blood was drawn.

She had heard of bloodletting before—of a physician making an incision in a patient's vein. Might the process be similar? Thor had concurred, and the summons declared the research a most promising endeavor. For that, he had been willing to brave even this unknown. Participation also offered a small cash compensation for travel, and while the three dollars was generous, Thor would have come regardless.

After stepping down the narrow hallway of the passenger car, they were led to a private compartment where a makeshift office boasted organized chaos. Two cushioned benches faced one another in snug fashion with a medic chest resting on the far end of one. Beside it sat a lap desk that lay flung open to reveal papers, some of which were piled across the seat. Just beneath the window overlooking winter-brown hills hung a small table, folded down from the wall and braced level with a bracket beneath. The narrow surface supported a basin of water and folded towel. Just below stood an icebox of polished oak.

"Do come in, please." The doctor motioned for them to be seated.

"Thank you, sir," Aven said as Thor moved to the bench opposite the cluttered one.

Thor waited for her to sit, then took the place beside her. His grip

3

on her hand never wavered. If she wasn't mistaken, it grew firmer. Strong and strapping, Thor kept two knives on him at all times and could land a stag from four hundred yards with a rifle. He'd survived ruthless fistfights and even endured a marginal stabbing. But the process of his blood being offered up had him tenser than the springs of the cushioned bench beneath them. Though nervous herself, Aven gave his fingers a squeeze of comfort.

"I understand this is rather unusual." Dr. Kent rummaged through his wares. "But due to the nature of the study and the varied locations of the participants, I find it easiest to conduct the interview here as opposed to setting up an office in each town visited."

Accustomed to speaking on Thor's behalf with strangers, Aven looked to her husband and, sensing his lack of concern, offered such assurance to the doctor. "'Tis just fine here, thank you."

The doctor handed over an envelope with the payment. Thor pressed it into his shirt pocket, followed by the folded letter from the bureau.

Medical tools glinted in the late-afternoon light when Dr. Kent opened a drawer. "There are several other physicians assisting with the program across the East. I am overseeing the regions of Tennessee, Virginia, and most of Kentucky. Your participation in the study, Mr. Norgaard, is most appreciated."

Thor's brown eyes didn't waver from the man's face as he spoke.

"First we'll begin the interview, then proceed from there." He lifted a blank form from a satchel. Thor's name was already written on top along with the location of their farm in Botetourt County. A fountain pen was uncapped and the date added to the top of the paper. The doctor signed his name at the bottom, then touched the pen tip beside the first question. "Tell me, Mr. Norgaard. Were either of your parents Deaf?"

Thor shook his head.

"What is your nationality of origin?"

Thor's hand moved in a blur as he fingerspelled the answer. *N-O-R-W-E-G-I-A-N.*

"Forgive me, I'm not well trained with Sign Language. If you'll do that again slowly . . ."

Thor formed the answer once more, this time molding each letter with his hand in unhurried procession.

Pen scraped against paper. *Norwegian.* "Here I'd assumed you Irish as your wife. If that is indeed what I caught in her voice." His smile was amiable as he added to Thor, "Have you had any success with speech?"

Thor shook his head, and the doctor marked a box on the form beside *Oral Failure.*

Aven pursed her lips to keep from chiming in. While the few verbalizations her husband managed wouldn't be heard as words by others, they were most precious to her, especially the brief hint of her name that he attempted at times. Deep and husky from his lips, it always made her warm all over, and awed by the fortitude of this man whom God had blessed her with.

"On a scale from one to ten, with one being a complete void of sound, how would you rate your lack of hearing?"

Thor closed rounded fingers in the shape of a zero.

More notes were taken. "And what is the cause of your hearing loss? Was it the effect of an illness? Accident? Or a defect from birth?"

Reaching over, Thor touched the box on the form to be checked beside *Birth,* then, borrowing the doctor's pen, crossed out the word *Defect.*

Aven smiled.

"And have you any children? Besides the one on the way, that is."

Handing the pen back, Thor shook his head.

The questions seeming at an end, Dr. Kent brought a canvas strip with a metal attachment out of a drawer along with an ear scope. Upon standing, he used the small scope to examine one of Thor's ears. After quiet study, he angled Thor's head to inspect the other. He jotted additional notes and, after capping the pen, rolled up Thor's right shirtsleeve. "Now for the blood draw." Practiced hands secured the strip of canvas around Thor's solid upper arm, turning the metal crank in a tourniquet. The man examined the thick veins in the hollow of Thor's elbow.

Looking uncomfortable, Thor flexed his hand, then relaxed it. His other, still wrapped up with Aven's, grazed the side of her rounded stomach as if he sought all the comfort he could get. Dr. Kent's gaze settled on the exchange as he opened a small leather case to reveal a metal vial. Two needles lay against the black velvet lining on either side, each fitted with a tiny screw cap.

When Thor cleared his throat, the doctor's ginger mustache lifted cordially. "It's known as a hypodermic syringe and I assure you is quite undemanding." He lifted one of the needles and screwed it onto the ribbed tip of the syringe. "Though intimidating on initial glimpse, I reckon. The first man I saw here today didn't express any discomfort, although he admitted to having been exposed to the instrument before. You should find it a minor prick."

The doctor gripped the underside of Thor's bicep with one hand and pressed the sharp tip into his skin with the other. Thor drew in a quiet breath.

Aven stroked her thumb against his palm. "There was another Deaf man here?" she asked, hoping conversation might settle Thor's nerves.

"Yes." A slow tug on the syringe pulled crimson liquid into the glass vial. "About a quarter of an hour before you arrived." As he spoke, the doctor's focus stayed fixed on his task. "It was quite the chance meeting."

She hadn't known of any others in the area, but perhaps the stranger had traveled from a neighboring county. What a pleasing notion—the possibility for Thor to make the acquaintance of another soul who understood the intricacies of living life in silence.

But Thor didn't seem impressed by the possibility. Instead, he stoically watched his blood being siphoned. Aven gave his hand another squeeze. When he looked at her, she flashed him a reassuring smile and inquired further on his behalf. "'Twas a gentleman, you said?"

"Correct." The physician slipped the needle from Thor's skin, then removed the vial of blood from the brass syringe, which he set on his small desktop. "He mentioned his acquaintance with your husband, in fact, and asked me to extend his thanks to Mr. Norgaard for alerting him to the study."

Puzzled, Aven glanced to Thor, but he seemed as confused as she.

"His name eludes me." Dr. Kent shuffled through nearby papers. "But he was a tall sort of fellow—one who looked accustomed to hard labor. Light hair and coloring. Full beard rather like Mr. Norgaard's."

Aven thought of who might match that description, but she knew of no other Deaf men.

Something wasn't right. She could see it now in Thor's pinched brow.

After tying a strip of bandage around Thor's elbow, Dr. Kent rinsed his hands in the basin of water, then dipped the bloodied end of the needle into the same dish. "He was perhaps mid-forties. One of the finest lip readers I've encountered. Understood every word I said without mishap." He sloshed the needle around, then swiped it dry with a rag. A careful polish made it sparkle.

The physician set the syringe back in its case.

Thor squinted over at the needle now lying in its velvet cradle, then looked back to the doctor and signed, *Man name?*

Before Aven could voice the question, Dr. Kent spoke. "Fascinating, isn't it?" He closed the case on the ornate tool. "It came to me through my father, who fought for the Confederacy during the War. It's served a great many purposes."

Shaking his head, Thor inquired again.

"He's asking after the gentleman," Aven clarified. "I'm afraid we don't understand, Dr. Kent."

Closed and then latched, the small leather case was slid aside. "He was a rather stern sort of chap. Rough around the edges . . . burly and a bit unkempt, if you will. He was silent, as yourself, Mr. Norgaard, but his father was here and spoke for him. An old general with a war injury."

Alarm rose within Aven.

Dr. Kent lifted the lid on the top of his medic case, where a faded Confederacy emblem was pasted in the underside. "The gentleman was missing three fingers on his left hand, but he's still got a rebel yell in him, if you ask me."

Thor's gaze locked on the physician's face as the crimson vial was labeled with a tag and string. Thor inquired with the sign for *father* and then gestured the appearance of a patch by covering his right eye.

The doctor implored Aven for assistance. She relayed the inquiry though the only man she knew who matched that description was Jed Sorrel. One of the ruffians who'd been the cause of so much harassment in these parts. Men with their white robes and masked hoods who had tormented the Norgaards for harboring former slaves. Jed and his son were criminal men, banished from the region by Thor and his brothers during a perilous battle of gunfire and bloodied fists four years ago. One fought between neighbors for two different views on freedom.

"His father did indeed." The doctor opened the icebox and set the vial in. He glanced over his shoulder as he clicked the door closed. "And he'd been most adamant you were acquainted. Fallen on hard times, he'd declared, so the cash was welcome."

Thor stared at his interviewer as if unable to believe what was being said. *Name H-A-R-L-A-N.* Then six more letters, just as rapid, and ones that sealed the direness. *S-O-R-R-E-L.*

Aven's fingers went numb, the tingling spreading through her body. Not only because Jed Sorrel was Thor's archenemy, but because his son, Harlan—a man of cunning ways and loose morals—was no more Deaf than she. She needed to express this to the doctor; Thor's eyes pleaded for it.

"Sir—"

"Come to think of it, he also made mention of some young boys. I had assumed them yours, but perhaps they are relatives."

Aven could scarcely speak amid a grip of fear. "We have two nephews." One was three and the other only learning to waddle about.

"Yes. The older gentleman said they'd conversed with the boys just the other day. That they had a rather amiable visit in the yard. He complimented what fine neighbors you all are."

Thor's face flushed. He looked around the train car as his brow dug in. Last, he stood.

"Sir, there is a grave problem." Aven rose as the Klansmen's hatred and destruction assaulted her memories.

Thor nabbed his paper from the desk and began to dig for another. Not finding what he sought, he shoved the stack aside and stepped away.

"I fear you have your information wrong," Aven rushed out— hoping to bring voice to Thor's distress. With the boys having been mentioned, he surely wanted to make haste back to the farm.

Catching her worried gaze, Thor stepped to the door.

"How did these men find you?" Aven entreated.

"They expressed to me that it was through a connection with Mr. Norgaard."

Having turned to watch, Thor hit the wall so hard the basin of bloodied water shuddered. *Not connected!*

Aven touched her husband's waist, hoping to calm him, but truly her own panic rose that these men were not only returned but rousing trouble.

After ensuring he had his form in his grasp, Thor rammed open the door of the train compartment.

"Sir," Aven said as he coaxed her out with a gentle hold at her side. "I'm afraid that whoever you just met with was not who he said he was. That vial of blood will be no use to you. That man you saw is not Deaf."

Thor stomped to the doctor's desk. He flipped over a blank form, uncapped the pen, and wrote the names of the men, where they had once lived, and what their crimes were.

Thieves. Murderers. The doctor read while Thor added several other crimes, all describing them as the felons they were.

In hurried scrawl, Thor indicated that he would alert the authorities of their whereabouts, then motioned for Aven to step down the narrow hallway. Glancing back, she saw the doctor fold Thor's note and pocket it.

Aven reached the platform in a gust of chilly air. Thor trudged behind her, furious and rightly so.

Had the Sorrel men come for the money? She *prayed* that was the reason.

Aven looked to the paper pinched in her husband's fist, then to the bandage wrapping the hollow of his elbow. A wound that, while small, now bridged the gap between him and an enemy that hadn't been crossed in years. A blotch of crimson that would be identical to one Harlan Sorrel bore this very day from the same physician.

Last, she thought of her young nephews, who often played in the yard. Though under careful watch, there were moments when the children wandered around the side of the barn—chasing kittens or searching for frogs as little ones did. Was that how Jed and Harlan had come upon them? What if the Sorrel men meant to do it again? Aven quickened her pace to match Thor's.

The land they called home was too remote for the guardianship of law officers, so for years Thor had surveyed the edge of their woods, and for years his brother Jorgan had done the same. They kept careful stock of ammunition and firearms, with a subtle tending to door locks and a frequent sharpening of knife blades. All while the absence of their third brother and the most cunning fighter weighed on each of their hearts. But though the youngest Norgaard man owned a portion of the farm, and though he had outsmarted the Sorrels that fateful day four autumns ago, no sooner could Haakon protect the land and family than the missing of him could heal hearts yet wounded by his choices. If Haakon meant to be a prodigal son, 'twas best he be one that didn't return.

With all these tragedies drawn quiet, Blackbird Mountain had become so peaceful that Aven often wondered if their caution was for naught. If there was no need to fear. That perhaps the Klansmen had truly departed this region for good, perhaps even been secured by national authorities. But as Thor led her to the wagon, keeping a keen eye on the rural outskirts of the crowd and a careful grip on her waist, she knew she'd been wrong.

ONE

BUILT OF BOARDS AS BROAD AS A MAN'S BACK, the cidery had stood at the edge of this wooded farm for as many years as Thor Norgaard. That was thirty-two among knowing souls, but to others it meant countless summers and winters that this massive building had endured winds and rains on the northernmost reach of Blackbird Mountain. Much like the Norwegian men who had worked the press and jarred the drink. First Da. Then the three sons who had followed.

Yet gone from within these walls was the sweet aroma of fermenting drink. In its stead were apple butters, pie fillings, and vinegars. Another side of the business that could be dated back to Thor. So long as he'd been sober—four years and counting—the Norgaard family operation of making liquor had ground to a halt.

Straddling the highest peak of the cidery roof, Thor rammed a metal scraper beneath a sun-rotted shingle. It snapped loose, and with gloved hands he pitched it toward the ground. Just below, Jorgan gathered up the shards and tossed them into the bed of the wagon that three months ago had been parked aside the train station—the day Thor and Jorgan had vowed to keep a closer watch on everything in their domain.

Thor tossed down two more broken shingles. He would have aimed better toward his older brother, but it took all his effort to rip and balance. Knees clutched to the peak, he shoved the metal tool down and broke off another old shingle. The splintered fragments slid down the backside of the roof and hit the dirt.

Just beyond the nearest trees, Thor's wife and sister-in-law kept the children busy at play near the spring. He glimpsed them through the budding branches, ensuring they were safe. Behind him rose the house that was as massive as the cidery.

Finished with this section of roof, Thor crammed the handle of the tool under the back waistband of his pants. He brushed dust from his beard, ignoring all that covered the upper half of his winter underwear. The air was heavy with warming light and drying land, so he'd already shoved back the sleeves and unfastened the buttons at the top of his chest. A mild spring day that made for easier work.

Needing a swig of water, he released a sharp whistle, one he felt in the roof of his mouth instead of hearing.

Jorgan looked up and shaded his eyes from the sun.

Using three fingers to form a *W*, Thor tapped them to his lips in the hand sign for *water*.

Jorgan retrieved a jar from the wagon seat and started up the ladder. His shirt was as sweat stained as Thor's own, and while his hair was a lighter brown, it hung tied back in the same rough knot, the cords cut from the rawhide of the elk Thor had downed that autumn. The meat was all cured or canned and stored in the springhouse thanks to the hard work of their wives as well as Ida, the aged freedwoman and faithful housekeeper who had raised Thor and his brothers since birth. Though her wrinkled, dark skin shone in stark contrast to their own, she'd been as a mother to them. A woman they'd defend with as strong a zeal as the others.

Thor sidestepped to the lower portion of the roof, bent down, and gripped the metal lid on the water. His side had bothered him of late, and although he reached gingerly, a pain lanced through his middle. He winced and pressed a firm grip to the spot, but the pressure did little to help as he fumbled the jar. Jorgan steadied it, and as Thor braced against the throbbing to reach for the jar again, Jorgan eyed him with confusion. If he sensed Thor's discomfort, he didn't let on. Thor tried to improve the situation with a lopsided smile before gulping water down.

Having gutted enough wild game to know where a liver was, Thor rubbed the tender spot that had troubled him the last few weeks and that, as of right now, was a dish cloth wrung tight. The same kind of pain Da had suffered before Thor and his brothers dug his grave and marked it with a cross. One Thor might have seen from the cidery roof had he searched westward for the family plot. But he kept his focus diverted from that place, and when fear tramped through him, he shot out a slow breath and capped the lid on the water. This was no time to lose his calm. As it was, anxiety already stole his sleep. As fierce as this growing ache was a bewilderment, because unlike Da, Thor had sobered from an addiction to hard drink. He'd restored his health as best he could, so why was this spot bothering him now?

Jorgan tapped him for his attention, and Thor watched his brother's mouth move amid a beard streaked in silver. "Let's switch places. You come on down."

Thor shook his head, understanding an act of kindness when he saw one. It lived in a person's eyes more than any words expressed. Something he wouldn't have learned had he been born with ears that were for more than decoration.

Thor clambered back to the peak, glad his brother couldn't see his grimace as he settled again. Jorgan returned to the ground, where he gathered more shingles. The man never probed too deep, but he was always there—sure and steady. An older brother who was as temperate and honest a leader as they came. As for their younger brother . . .

Thor made it a point to think of Haakon as little as possible.

It was for the best that the runt was gone, but every so often the missing of Haakon hung around this farm like a blanket of memories and regret that would never be shed. It tried to drape itself around Thor now as he worked atop the building where he and Haakon had played as children and worked side by side as men. Determined not to let the past rear its head, Thor rammed his tool down and snapped off another worn shingle.

He had better things to do than think about Haakon. If he gave in, he'd only recall what Haakon had done to Aven. How he'd tried to force himself on her in a way no woman deserved. She had been Thor's bride-to-be four years ago, but Thor would have defended her whether her heart had been his or not.

At a flash of color in the distance, Thor viewed the lane where the women strolled with the children in tow, all damp and happy from the spring—a bit of fun with warmer days on the rise. More important, near enough to the homestead that the women were within hollering distance. Something Thor and Jorgan had insisted upon since that winter's day when the doctor from the train depot had declared the Sorrels' return. No one had seen hide nor hair of the Klansmen yet, but it didn't mean they weren't around.

When the women wished to venture off, they agreed not to go so far that Thor and Jorgan couldn't come to their aid. While Thor wouldn't be able to hear them call, no one kept a better ear out for the family than Jorgan. And for Thor . . . Well, there was a reason he'd stationed himself up on the ridgeline of the roof.

Aven waved as she crossed the yard with the others. Her copper-colored braid was as noticeable as the swimming ensemble she wore of boy's knickers and an old shirt. The belt she used to cinch around her waist had been abandoned now that her belly swelled full with child. Her bare ankles and feet were nearly as fair as the snow that had melted from the yard just weeks back. Thor smiled at the sight of his Irish bride and unborn babe.

Fay walked beside Aven with eleven-month-old Bjørn on her hip and three-year-old Sigurd skipping along. Dressed in a bathing costume that Aven had given her, Fay's white-blonde hair was as light as Bjørn's curls. The babe clung to his mother, chubby legs showing from beneath his soggy nightshirt. Energetic Sigurd held tight to Aven's hand, skipping beside his aunt beneath a clear, blue sky. He appeared to be laughing, and it must have been loud because the chickens startled in their coop with the same liveliness.

Below, Jorgan stood as unmoving as the pines, watching his family with pride. Thor didn't blame him. If he had young sons such as Bjørn and Sigurd, the same contentment would be hard to contain. He felt it even now—but it was of an unknowing anticipation. Due to be born later in the summer, boy or girl, it mattered not to him. He only wanted to hold and know the life Aven had made with him and that the Lord had seen fit to bless them with. A life they had longed for during years of uncertainty, made more heartrending by Aven's tears and his own silent longing that he'd tried not to burden her with.

And now, even though the babe could be born Deaf as he had been, Aven only asserted that she would love the child with all her might, as she loved him.

With Aven heading inside, Thor descended the ladder. He tugged off his gloves and followed Jorgan across the yard. Soil crumbled fertile beneath their boots, land that just asked to be tilled and planted, but they farmed little. His orchards—now that was another matter. Of the 327 acres that spread before them, a third sustained apple trees. Several varieties already budded with unfurled blossoms across acreage that was not only Thor's haven and sanctuary but the family's livelihood.

In place of the hard cider that had supported the family for decades was now fresh, unfermented drink that they sold around the county each fall. That which couldn't be distributed in short fashion was crafted into jams and jellies by the women who teased that their innocent concoctions made more than the liquor ever had. But Thor kept the ledgers and knew they spoke in jest. His liquor had been fine, and he and his brothers had lived like kings. But although the money box didn't hold the surplus it once had, he and Jorgan were richer than they'd ever been as bachelors.

In a flash, three-year-old Sigurd darted nearer, pinning his tiny form around Thor's leg. Thor caught the boy up and locked the child in a playful hold while Sigurd squirmed and giggled. Thor felt the vibrations from the scrawny chest against his forearm. Small hands pulled at the very place, but Thor's strength was no match for his captive. He hefted his nephew over his shoulder like a sack of grain and toted him toward the house. Sigurd was laughing so hard Thor worried he couldn't breathe, so he set him right side up on the porch. The boy pleaded for him to do it again, but Bjørn lunged from his mother's arms. Thor caught the pudgy babe and, resting him in the crook of his arm, nuzzled a creamy shoulder like a hungry bear.

There was that same sensation again—the unmistakable feel of a child's laughter. Except this time it was smaller and squishier.

Feeling a chuckle rise in his own chest, Thor handed Bjørn over to Jorgan. The moment he did, pain squeezed his side. He regretted every drop of liquor he'd ever drunk as the spot throbbed. If he could do it all over again—starting with his first indulgence at twelve—he would. He would tell that boy from long ago to put the pint of cider down, vowing that liquor wouldn't drown out despair. It would worsen it, because not only had he spent nearly two decades enslaved to the bottle, he now faced down a whole new agony.

As his side unclenched, Thor knew he'd have to mind the

roughhousing. With Jorgan observing him, Thor gave a final pat to his nephew's diapered bottom and strode into the kitchen. Ida was there, seated at the table in the center of the snug space where she sorted the latest arrival of mail from town. Nearly seventy, the house-keeper was slight of frame, but scrappy enough to have raised him and his brothers from boyhood.

With the mail sitting beside her plate of half-eaten spice cake, Thor rifled through the envelopes, searching for a response to his let-ter for the Bureau of Research and Resource for the Deaf and Dumb. Instead, he unearthed only bills and a few new orders for their cider products.

Ida offered a smile of assurance. "Somethin'll come soon." She squeezed his hand in her knobby one, driving home that hope.

Thor nodded his gratitude and stepped into the great room feeling a heaviness that this wait brought. While he didn't know what he'd receive from the bureau, he had penned a letter to its return address, requesting it to be forwarded to Dr. Kent. Inside had been an apology for his abrupt demeanor along with a request for any additional infor-mation the doctor could recall about the Sorrel men that day.

After climbing both flights of stairs to the third-floor attic that was his and Aven's bedroom, Thor found his wife toweling her hair. The spring had to be freezing, and while he doubted she meant to get so wet, Bjørn could splash like nothing else. It was no surprise when Aven paced to him and slid her arms beneath his own, pulling herself close to his chest. Thor wrapped her up and, at her shiver, bound his arms tighter. When she settled her forehead against his shoulder, he tipped his head down and kissed her damp hair.

He felt her brush fingertips against his sleeve where engrained into the skin of his upper arm lay a scar that marked their first days of knowing one another. The beginning of this life together. With no way to speak such thoughts, he smoothed a thumb across the back of her neck, pressing the long, wet locks aside. What the doctor had marked on the form was all truth. *Oral Failure.* Except at times, here with his wife, Thor put voice to the first two letters of her name.

"Av—" He sensed the fragment was scant compared to what she was meant to be called, but he breathed it between them when his tenderness for her overruled even his incapacity with speech. That he'd spoken it now had Aven pulling away enough for him to see that her cheeks were rosier.

Thor smiled. She did as well, and with her needing to dress, he drew the curtains. While once a bunkhouse for him and his younger brother, this room had been refashioned to suit a bride's needs, now housing two mismatched reading chairs beside a stand of shelves laden with books. The family cradle rested beside the bed, and framed pictures sat about thanks to Aven's thoughtful efforts. But four pinholes on the far wall would always remind him of Haakon and the dusty map of the world that had once hung there.

After Haakon's fleeing, Thor had boxed up everything from the far half of this room and stored it away to bring Aven added peace. It had seemed to work, but Thor wasn't certain. Rarely did Aven speak of his younger brother, and she seemed to prefer it that way.

Having discarded all but her damp shift, Aven fetched a dry one from the dresser. As Thor watched her, memories of the past fell away. In their stead lingered the comforting presence of his wife. A chill shuddered her frame, so he fetched a blanket from the foot of the bed and draped it around her and her wet shift, pulling the knitted yarn snug beneath her chin. She smiled and rose onto her tiptoes for a kiss. He rubbed his hands up and down her arms, then touched the firm curve of her stomach. A tiny foot or knee pressed against his palm. Aven's eyes brightened with the sensation, and Thor savored it all. Savored everything God had blessed him with.

But as he did, he was overwhelmed with the need to sit down. Seeming puzzled, Aven watched him settle on the edge of the bed. Thor ran a hand across his forehead and had to work hard not to think of Da's cross on the distant hill or the pain setting up camp in his gut. Of the growing ache in his joints and what seemed like a trace of a fever.

Aven touched his beard, tipping his head up before she spoke. "Are you feeling unwell?" The worry in her eyes deepened.

Need rest better. He'd been working too hard was all. Once the roof was done, he'd slow his pace and be right as rain again. Parched, Thor made his sign again for *water*, entreating Aven for help. He followed it with the word for *eat* by pressing closed fingertips to his mouth.

"Of course." With a trace of alarm, she fetched a humble gown from the back of the chair and began to dress.

He'd go down himself, but the thought of two flights of stairs was more than he could handle right now. That frightened him more than he wanted to admit. Thor swallowed a dry taste in his mouth and prayed with all that was in him that this ache was just temporary. And if it wasn't, that God would see fit to help him through.

TWO

"HAAAKKOOON NOORGGAAARRD!"

At the faraway shout from his best friend and fellow seaman, Haakon opened his eyes to find that he wasn't on the ship. He was in a barn. Though the boarded walls creaked in March's winds, there was a pair of goats staring at him from the left while on his right lay the warm, soft form of a Norwegian woman. Mind still foggy about the night before, Haakon turned his head to see young Widow Jönsson blessedly asleep, her blonde hair barely visible above the supple furs she had carried here under starlight.

A situation that would normally conjure pleasurable memories, but this maiden was different because, if he wasn't mistaken . . .

He lifted a corner of the coverings and saw a hint of her plaid blouse. The humble collar was buttoned snug against her cream-colored skin. For weeks, he'd tried to woo her, disregarding half a dozen other women for the sole wanting of this one with her deep-blue eyes and hair so lush and golden he hungered to run his fingers through it again even now. As it was, her crown of braids had come unraveled in the night, but that had less to do with him and more to do with the fact that they'd stayed up late to watch over a newborn goat.

Though perhaps he might imagine that the golden tendrils falling loose against her pillow of sack grain had been a restlessness shared. One of both their knowing that even an interlude so innocent as last night would be the nearest they would ever be in the dark.

Though time was of the essence, Haakon watched her sleep for a precious moment more. Never would he forget the boldness she'd demonstrated the first time he'd seen her. She'd been on the hillside with her small children about her skirts, rounding up a herd of goats before a storm. Clouds had churned nearly black overhead as she'd aided the creatures in her charge. He'd stood there on the ship's deck, ice tongs in hand, struck dumb by her bravery and longing to help.

His memory was muddled about the night before, but it took little effort to recall that he still hadn't succeeded in winning her, no matter how much he'd pursued her these three weeks ashore. So tender she'd been the hours past, only wanting to talk with him late into the night, that she'd drifted off in his arms before he'd even kicked off his boots. The new goat had slumbered in a pile of hay, just as content looking.

Not quite the gratifying send-off he'd hoped for.

Haakon scratched his thick beard and, with sunrise barely lightening the air, ached to go back to sleep, especially with the honeyed scent of this woman and the way she sighed in her sleep. Yet he needed to get to the ship—and now. Part of him wanted to ask God to aid his silent exit, but he didn't spend much time talking to God these days.

Then again, after the night before, he was practically a priest.

It pained Haakon to push back the furs, but he forced himself to brave the frigid Scandinavian morning and leave the warm mound of straw behind. He took great care to keep the bedding around his companion lest she stir. His fingertips grazed the ends of her unbound hair, and he pulled his hand away.

Over the years, he'd learned it best not to wake a woman. Otherwise they'd want to know where he was going and when he'd be back. Answers he never gave on mornings such as these or there'd be a claim on him in every port from here to London. But this was different. This woman had endeared herself to him more than he knew how to face. Yet though she was a sweet soul that he longed for more of, she could never be more than a brief encounter. Not only was he leaving but she hadn't been nearly as interested in him as he with her. It was with that fresh blow to his ego that he searched for his boots. They weren't where he'd left them. Nor were they as falling apart as he recalled. Trying to ignore the reason for that, he pushed his feet in.

The older goats chewed their cud, paying him little heed as he yanked the laces tight. When Haakon stumbled, knocking into a pitchfork that skidded against the wall, one of them let out an ornery *bleat* that fogged in the cold. Haakon held a finger to his mouth.

Even if the night had gone as he'd hoped, he knew this woman sought his companionship and not coin, but with her and her children alone, he couldn't ignore the urge to fish a few pieces of silver from his pack and slip them beneath a sack of grain. She would find them later, once the sack was emptied and taken away, and by then might have lost all memory of him. Better sense would be to leave the money in view, but he didn't want to humiliate her by insinuating that he'd meant to pay for her company.

Fighting both a shiver and stiffening hands, Haakon unlatched the barn door, winced at its creak, and snuck out.

Coastal winds hit him—dense, salty, and so cold they pierced through his shirt like ice picks. He swung his coat on, eased the door closed, and started down the hillside with pack in hand. In the distance spread the bay and its glittering waters where ships from all over the world moored. Haakon's only focus was *Le Grelotter*, the vessel that had been home for the last four years and the one that had brought him here to the Old Country. The land of his ancestors.

At a little voice calling after him, Haakon glanced back to see one of the widow's boys. Maybe six, the lad was bundled in a coat of thick hide, and so deep was the snow that he struggled with every lift of his small boots. Needing to hurry, Haakon nearly pressed on, but the boy's struggle was so severe, his call so determined, that Haakon traced his bootprints back, meeting the lad halfway.

Blinking up at him, the fair-haired boy spoke in Norwegian. Haakon didn't understand but a word or two. Not uncommon between them, but always the boy's mother had been there to bridge the gap. Now it was just the pair of them, a rising sun, and a leaving ship.

"I don't understand," Haakon said regretfully. As deep a regret was sight of sorrow in the eyes peering up at him.

A child who knew he was being left behind.

Again.

First with a da that had departed this world too soon, and now with Haakon who couldn't stay.

When the boy entreated him, Haakon took a knee. "I have to go."

"*Ja*," the boy concurred, but though the single word was an affirmation, the folded paper he held out to Haakon seemed anything but. Haakon hesitated to take it, fearing that if he did, it would make turning away all the harder. But he couldn't very well neglect such an offering, so he took the paper and thanked its giver.

When Haakon's name was shouted again from the deck of the ship, he rose. "I'm so sorry. I have to go."

Squinting against the morning light, the boy stepped back. Haakon wished he had turned away before seeing that tiny chin tremble, but he was frozen into place.

"You be safe now. Take care of your mother." The lad wouldn't understand so much English, but the words had to be said all the same. "*Oppfør deg, ja?*" Haakon added in Norwegian. The decree for *behave* came easy, so often Aunt Dorothe had used it with him while growing up.

"*Ja*," the boy confirmed in a shaky voice.

Haakon took another step aside. He *had* to go. "*Ha det bra*," he said in goodbye. Haakon hated to turn away but he had to or he'd be living here for good.

The boy called after him. "*På gjensyn!*"

Haakon winced. There was no mistaking such a farewell. He'd heard it often amid his travels to this country. *We meet again.* Did the boy actually believe that?

The folded paper in hand, Haakon tucked it deep in his pocket and gave a final wave before lumbering through a sloping, snowy field. At the bottom, he hopped a low fence and skidded around a crumbling outbuilding. He was just ducking beneath a stone archway when he saw the crew readying the mainsails.

"You're late for watch," Tate called when Haakon hurried down the wooden dock. A devout Christian, Tate Kennedy was as moral as they came, so Haakon didn't elaborate as to what motives had him ashore as he hopped over the railing. Then again, Tate wouldn't have shouted so loud if he didn't already know.

"I assure you I've been punished." Haakon pitched his pack to the nearest cabin boy along with a request for it to be stowed.

After swiping a hand down his buttoned coat, Tate straightened his spectacles. "*Punished* would be if we'd weighed anchor without you." His breath fogged with each tug on the line he was winding.

"Yet that's never happened."

"Wouldn't want to lose one of our finest," Tate said dryly. Used to Haakon's frequent onshore excursions, he thumbed him up toward the crow's nest. A gesture that might have seemed indifferent if it weren't for the narrow scar that spliced his palm. Though long since healed, the marks of their blood brotherhood were ones they would bear always. Rivals they'd once been, until the night Tate had rescued Haakon from a cold death in the Norwegian Sea.

"Flag's tangled. Right it while you're up there." So formidable was the task that Tate smirked, and it was there, within his stern mood—a flash of their comradery. As boatswain, Tate's next command was for the foredeck crew, who heaved against wooden bars that turned the iron capstan, hoisting the anchor chain. The chain clattered while the shanty they sang kept a steady rhythm and marked the beginning of the voyage.

The mainsail unfurled. It whipped until it caught wind and tightened, bowing and pulling like a lead dog in a sled race. Except instead of crossing icy vistas, that spirit would bear them far from this snowy harbor, clear of this churning fjord, and out into the open blue.

And, if he could have what he'd dreamed of in the wee hours of the night, back to Blackbird Mountain. But that couldn't be home anymore.

Gripping hold of the rope ladder, Haakon started to climb.

To not look back was wisest, but he'd come to discover a point of no return with each disembarking, so he glanced over his shoulder to the cliff tops surrounding the fjord. The boy was gone. His mother—likely still asleep. Or worse, just being woken by her son, who would have some news for her. That Haakon had left . . . without telling her goodbye.

He should have woken her to say farewell. She deserved nothing less.

Why was he such a coward?

At the shouts of crewmembers all around, he continued climbing the crisscrossed ropes and upon reaching the first set of rigging clambered higher until he'd passed the second. Wind gusted off the water, hitting him with an icy blast. When Haakon reached the crow's nest that wasn't much more than a barrel lashed to the mast, he climbed farther to a third stretch of rigging. With the ship away from its mooring, it rocked enough to suddenly make holding on his every thought.

Near the top of the mast, the mainsail flapped so loudly it drowned out even the screech of herring gulls that soared below. The patriotic colors were knotted around the highest point of the mast, and it was easier to focus on the wind-battered wool than the fact that the widow's cottage was far from sight now. No longer would he have the satisfaction of glimpsing her during his workday or sharing her table come dusk.

Haakon swallowed hard. Such a longing would fade with time.

It had to.

Over a hundred feet up from the deck, he forced his focus to rise ahead. Reaching up, he unwound the frigid cloth until the red and white of the ensign hailed this vessel as Canadian more boldly than even her name: *Le Grelotter*. The shivering.

Aptly named for this brig with its belly full of ice.

Packed tightly for the trip south, the frozen cargo was bound for England's upper class, who expressed their wealth with delicate sorbets, intricate sculptures, and chilled bourbon in the heat of summer. From Lisbon to Bath, gentry would pay well for the choice cargo—all that Haakon and his fellow crewmates had spent the winter harvesting from Norway's pristine lakes. That which wasn't needed for garden parties and the like would be sold to meat and brewery enterprises. This was their second trip to London for the season, so what the icehouses there couldn't hold would be whisked south to the Caribbean, where every last block would be unloaded until there was nothing left in the hull but wet boards and damp sawdust.

It meant the need to sail proficiently. Too long at sea and their winter of labor would be for naught. Too reckless in their navigation and the ship could capsize. A boatload of shifting ice wreaked havoc on a crew and its vessel, so with care and precision they would sail south and then west until their pockets were lined with silver yet again.

The ship dipped and sprayed. Water gusted against the sides, foamy and white. Though she was gaining speed, the last of her sails were being unfurled, running rigging pulled tight and laid over the pins. With easy foot placements, Haakon descended the few meters down to the crow's nest. In the distance the water glittered with sunrise, and on both sides of the narrow fjord rose steep mountains of slate gray and snowcapped white. The wind was ruthless, and as stunning the view, Haakon would much prefer being on deck, pulling in lines to keep from freezing.

With work-roughened hands, he tugged his coat tighter and tried not to think about the warmth he'd just left behind, but as he thought on the woman again, he knew there was no point in fooling himself. The real reason he hadn't wanted her to wake was because he couldn't bear to look into her eyes and contend with the guilt that as much as he aimed to bring her comfort, it was ultimately his own pleasure he sought. He would forget her and her children by the time he arrived in the next port.

With a three-legged stool behind him, Haakon pulled it forward and sat, keeping his eyes on the water. For most, the hours on watch were a time to ponder. For several, a chance to log the events of the previous day. But unlike those contemplative souls, Haakon didn't keep a journal. If he did, he would write that they'd hoisted sail and caught a breeze from west-southwest. A gust that was shouldering them away from southern Norway. He'd try to find the words to describe how hard it was to see that shoreline grow fainter. If they lingered, they'd watch the birches begin to open their leaves. He was yet to see Norway in the summer and had only heard of its splendor.

The practical side of him would note that there were eight hundred tons of crystal ice in the hold bound for London. That's if they survived the North Sea. If so, they would land in England four days from now.

It would take great effort to cap the inkwell then, but if he lost the battle with himself, he would add that it was getting harder and harder not to think of home.

That was why he didn't keep a journal. There was no sense in documenting such a desire. He couldn't go home. He *shouldn't* go home. And he was a fool to continually be tempted. Though time had passed, the years hadn't worn the memories smooth. In fact, it felt like just yesterday that he'd walked with Aven, her arm on his. Her brown eyes trusting as they strolled through the woods. They'd ventured to the west cabin, where she'd imagined herself safe to be alone with him, only to discover that she'd been anything but.

Haakon should have tried harder to make amends, but knowing he couldn't rightly step foot back on the farm, he'd opted instead to blow the Sorrels' barn sky-high with nearly a thousand dollars' worth of his brother's stolen liquor still inside. While it had halted a decades-old war between their families, he doubted it had been the most sentimental way to apologize.

Pulling his arms tight across his middle, Haakon bent forward on the stool and, with his gaze still on the inlet, did all he could to keep from trembling from the cold. He wanted something hot to drink. Something good and strong.

More than that, he wanted to make peace with Aven. He wanted to break free from the challenge young Widow Jönsson had given him to cease his running from whatever had him on the move for nearly half a decade. But he didn't know how to do either, so here he would stay—on this restless sea—until he finally vanished from all their memories for good. Or until he grew enough of a backbone to step back onto his family's farm and try to right what he had wronged.

THREE

AVEN COULDN'T RECALL SUNSETS LIKE THIS in Ireland when she was a child. If a rare bright day spanned the skies, the sun sank behind the stone walls of the workhouse long before nightfall. When it wasn't cloudy and rainy, cool shadows still blanketed the corridors of the orphanage where she'd lived among hundreds of other children who were as lost to the world as she'd been upon her mother's too-soon death.

But not here. How different from the workhouse this was—the Virginia sun like melted gold through the treetops, brightening everything in its warm haze and piercing through the branches of the great maple overhead. A dance of light and childhood charm where nestled within the leaves sat the treehouse that had sheltered many an adventure for the Norgaard brothers.

While Aven's climbing days were at a standstill, if she were to scale the makeshift ladder and settle against the rough trunk, she would see the three carved names. *Jorgan. Thor. Haakon.* Whittled into the living wood as boys when time and distance hadn't changed them so. 'Twas just as well that she was land bound with child. She had no desire to see Haakon's name, nor anything that reminded her of the man who had once been her friend but had proved himself anything but.

Seated below it all, Aven tugged her knit shawl closer against her shoulders and listened as Ida read to Sigurd from where they shared his blanket at the base of the great tree. A small pile of children's tales lay near, and while Sigurd leaned an elbow on those, Aven kept her hands busy with the stitches on a nightdress for the coming baby. Though she could have finished the tiny collar at home, she'd followed along with Sigurd and Ida since she was as eager for an outing as the rambunctious boy.

Aven had her own fondness for this glen where Thor had first begun to claim her heart and hand. Never would she forget sitting on the treehouse platform while he tied together a string of buttons and, with a hint of shyness, slid the gift onto her wrist. They'd been far from lovers then, but it had been the beginning of a tender unfolding between them.

At the sound of Sigurd's giggling, her attention lifted from the flash of the needle to where he sat cross-legged beside her. The three-year-old's face was a stark contrast to Ida's brown skin, but rarely were two souls as kindred as the boy and the freedwoman who stood in place as his proud grandmamma.

Just beyond, Aven glimpsed their farmhand, Peter, moving about in a far stretch of woods. The young Sorrel had trailed them, but the act was far from ominous, so loyal was he to the Norgaard family. Peter had come along today to check snares, he'd said, but she knew it was Thor and Jorgan's way of seeing them looked after. The snares having been set close to the treehouse for this very purpose.

Underbrush rustled as Peter knelt to remove a gray hare. At Ida's noticing, he held it over for her to see. She waved her gratitude, and

Peter smiled, flashing rough teeth in a handsome face. As Jed Sorrel's grandson, Peter had once been part of the underground Ku Klux Klan, so the fact that he and Ida kept such choice company was a miracle. That Peter kept guard against his own father and grandfather, whose whereabouts remained a mystery, yet another. Though Aven saw no weapon in plain view, sense told her Peter was armed.

As Ida read on, Aven placed the tiny garment against the front of her mounded womb. Had she fashioned it too narrow? Sewing was her favorite pastime and the soundest skill acquired from her years in the Limerick workhouse. She scarcely measured a size wrong. But since the object of her efforts lay curled up and out of sight, she wouldn't be too hard on herself.

"What do you think?" Aven asked, still gauging the wee gown.

Ida did the same. "Prettiest thing I ever saw, but you gonna need to let out a seam or two."

Aven chuckled. She was afraid so.

Heavens, what a child. She should have expected nothing less from Thor Norgaard, but where he was strapping, she was slight of frame. The difference amplified the size of her rounded skirt front. A trial in store come the birthing hour, but while an inkling of worry trailed her of late, her life, the babe's life, and the impending delivery were all in the Lord's hands. Cultivating worries would do no good. Aven smoothed her womb, thankful beyond measure for the gift of life inside her. She nestled the nightdress in her basket as Ida continued to read.

The woman's dictation was smooth, testament to years of study after the War. While Aven couldn't begin to comprehend the torment Ida and her sister, Cora, had endured as young slaves, Aven knew of hardship. Having grown up within the workhouse, where struggle dwelled in steady fashion, she recognized, as Ida did, the will of the human spirit and what it could conquer, be it learning the alphabet in adulthood as Ida had, staring down death with a brave countenance as Aven's mother had, or facing down a future alone as Aven had done as a girl. Though mourning her mother's death as the blackest of nights, Aven had faced the unknowns with a teary courage, going on to survive long enough to marry a Norwegian man who liberated her from the labor wards and brought her to his homeland in Norway. She'd not be sitting here today if it weren't for Benn Norgaard. He'd made her a part of this family, but while she'd meant to be his wife until the end of her days, his own end had come much sooner.

Amid their grief, Dorothe Norgaard had penned Aven an invitation to come to a place called Blackbird Mountain in America. Bidding her to voyage here to Virginia where Aunt Dorothe and the rest of Benn's relatives dwelled. Nearly two years later, Aven had braved the ocean crossing, and when the dangerous beauty of the open sea was behind her, she'd climbed these rugged hills to an all-new adventure—meeting and knowing the mountain-raised men on this farm. Aven's black mourning dress had slowed her every step even as hope budded in her heart that she might call this place home.

And home she'd found, here with Thor and this beloved family. God had led her through many trials and storms, and while none of them had been easy, the Lord had guided her. He wouldn't stop now. Of that she had no need to fear. For the future, it meant trusting in God for this growing life inside her.

Aven placed a hand to Sigurd's thin back, relishing his sweetness. The Lord knew what He was doing upon the knitting of each and every soul and was with Thor and Aven through the waiting for a child of their own. The waiting had deepened their trust and opened their hands to whatever God meant to provide. 'Twas far from easy, but it had taught her more about navigating the trials of life with grace than smooth seas ever would have.

Book in hand, Ida read. "'Darkness closed over a wild and terrific scene, and returning light as often brought but renewed distress, for the raging storm increased in fury until on the seventh day all hope was lost.'" Ida's eyes widened dramatically as Sigurd's did.

"*I* want to go there," he said.

"To the middle of a storm?"

A zealous nod.

"Oh, my boy, you'll have your fair share of those. How's about we stay here safe and sound for the time bein'?" Ida pulled him close, squeezing tight.

Peter came along and leaned against the tree. At his feet he set a game bag lumpy with the catch. He waited patiently, being paid by the farm no matter his assigned task. If Aven wasn't mistaken, he seemed to be listening as Ida read. Though Peter was near the same age as her five and twenty, she sensed he could read and write only modestly.

With dusk cooling the air, Ida rose and handed the book to Sigurd. There was light yet for the walk home, but if they didn't start now, they'd be returning to the farm by starlight. Aven struggled to stand. Just as Peter edged nearer to help, she found her feet, then threw him a sheepish grin. He returned the sentiment.

"Fetch them other books, Sigurd, and we'll be on our way." Ida folded the blanket, and Aven tucked it under her arm to help.

The boy gathered the other books to his chest and squealed with delight when Peter hoisted him up to sturdy shoulders. The farmhand took a knock in the ear from *The Swiss Family Robinson* as he did. He handled it good-naturedly, got both boy and books righted, then nabbed the game bag and headed on. Aven fell into step beside Ida— their pace a pleasing match of slow and steady. A cool breeze swept through the woods, stirring grasses that were damp but determined to stretch out in these warmer days. Being reborn the mountain was, just as it was each spring.

Sigurd clutched tight to the top of Peter's head, listening to the lay of the land that Peter described to him. Peter pointed out a squirrel's hollow, then directed the boy's focus to where a rise of blackbirds soared southward and away from Thor's orchards. Just beyond rose a lofty hill, and though Aven couldn't see the house on the other side, she'd been to the Sorrels' plantation now and again over the years. Slaves no longer worked its fields, and Peter no longer lived among its many rooms with his mother and sisters. The old mansion stood as if remembering days gone. Now it was nearly empty—many of the Sorrels having moved on, including most of Peter's male kinfolk.

Though Peter chatted with Sigurd, he kept careful survey of the woods around them.

They returned to the farm to Thor and Jorgan working atop the roof once more. The last of the shingles had come down that morning, and now the men nailed fresh slats into place with pounding force. A fierce racket it was, and with sunset hastening in, a need to hurry. Clear skies rarely lasted this time of year.

Sigurd pleaded to linger amongst the ruckus, but Aven insisted his mother first be keen of his whereabouts. Aven followed him up the front steps and into the kitchen, where they were greeted by the warmth of the cookstove and Fay's cheery smile. Her blonde hair, twisted up in a bun, was as light a gold as the steamed potatoes she mashed with butter.

In his high chair, Bjørn made a racket with a spoon on the wooden tray. His small feet were clad in leather booties, one of the shoes about to tumble off. His cotton shift was drenched down the front from his efforts at drinking from a new tin cup. Poor Fay looked near to coming undone. Ida moved to the stove and took over a pot of bubbling gravy. Aven dampened a rag and liberated the child from the mess and his mother from the bundle of chaos.

"You're both dears." Fay glanced out the window to where Peter had joined the men in the work on the roof. "Should we ask Peter to stay for supper?"

"I'll see to it." Swiping her hands on her apron, Ida left the gravy to finish thickening. She ducked into her bedroom that was just off the kitchen, returning a moment later with a heavy shawl, which she laid about her shoulders before departing.

"We should have been back sooner," Aven apologized. While each of them saw to housekeeping tasks, Aven had hardly done her share of the labor today. A reprieve Fay encouraged these days, but Aven hadn't meant to leave her sister-in-law with a herd of hungry men, little Bjørn included. "I misjudged how quickly I could walk."

Fay chuckled, and the brightness in her cheeks said that she well remembered those days.

Thinking it the best way to assist, Aven hefted her nephew to her hip—a juggling act with the unborn babe already in place. A thump came from the great room followed by a flash of gray fur. The cat, Dotti, bounded up the stairs, and her scamper was followed by the rush of Sigurd's footsteps as he raced up to the second-floor bedroom he shared with his parents and brother.

"I better see what he's after." Fay slid the gravy aside, and her wool skirts swished as she stepped that way. "Could you mind Bjørn for a moment?"

"Gladly." Aven set the squirming toddler down and followed his wobbly steps into the next room. Bjørn made his way to Thor's chess table. Once there, he gave a valiant effort to climb onto his uncle's chair. Upon succeeding, he set his sights on the small table as his next conquest.

Aven hurried to his side. "No, love. Not there." She tucked him back onto the seat.

Squirming onto his knees, Bjørn made another attempt, so Aven returned him to the floor. He peered up at her with blue eyes as striking as his uncle Haakon's and a determination near as robust. Still looking at her, he flaunted a dimpled smile.

"Oh, so now you're to try that method?" She righted his rumpled nightshirt. "I assure you it won't get you what you wish." Best Bjørn learn that quicker than his uncle Haakon had. She kissed Bjørn's downy head, and when he tried to nab a chess piece, she stopped him with a slight squeeze to his wrist. "*No.*" When the lad didn't heed, she tried in Norwegian. "*Nei.*"

Bjørn squealed and rose onto the toes of his booties as he reached for the playing piece again. With an exasperated chuckle, Aven went to tote him elsewhere when the floorboards shuddered. She looked back to see Thor trudging across the room. He hefted up his nephew by the back of the shirt and held him aloft as a bear would a cub. Bjørn's eyes went round.

"Now see what you've done," Aven said in jest to the babe.

Thor settled his nephew on the crook of his arm and made the hand sign for *no*. Next he pointed to Aven and shaped the word for *obey* by touching a finger to the side of his forehead, then bringing that hand down in a fist alongside his other. Brow stern, Thor's expression ordered the same.

Bjørn stuck two fingers in his mouth as if in vow to busy them some other way.

"That's a good lad," Aven said, then to Thor, "'Twould seem you've found the language he hearkens to."

Thor slid a large, gentle hand behind Bjørn's head, and Bjørn wriggled his tiny fingers into Thor's thick beard, babbling as he did. Thor watched the little one's mouth and, upon realizing that it was gibberish, pulled out one of the chairs and plopped the boy onto the wooden seat. Thor sat in the other, and Bjørn flapped a hand toward the pieces. With a nod of consent, Thor nudged the board closer. Bjørn retrieved the knighted horse he'd been after and rammed the bottom into his mouth. Thor's brown eyes were merry. Within moments, the little warrior had leveled the entire board, but his uncle didn't so much as flinch. Thor would begin again as he always did when the eleven-month-old visited this spot of the room.

Aven touched Thor's shoulder and spoke when he watched her. "You've a wee prodigy to teach."

Thor smoothed a hand over her rounded belly and then held up two fingers as he kissed the top of her apron.

"Aye, and another on the way."

He lifted his gaze, and while his regard of people was always steady and silent, he was keener with her. In her first days of knowing him, his frequent study of her had been startling, but she'd come to learn that it was his way of listening. Be they large or small, his noble acts confessed a love he couldn't voice. Though she'd scarcely needed rescuing from the mischief of their nephew, there had been a time when she had needed much rescuing indeed. A time that had caused a rift between two brothers that seemed unmendable. Did the memories haunt Thor as they did her?

Though she didn't think on it often, she would never forget the day of Haakon's brash advance—of the way she'd tried to get free of his hold even as his resolve had countered all her pleas. Her screams for aid had brought nothing but birdsong since Thor couldn't hear her from where he'd been in the farmyard. In those bleak moments Haakon's choice to claim her seemed a certain one, but he'd suddenly halted as though knowing his callousness was a breaking that would run through both of their souls. Moments later, Haakon's cabin had tremored with Thor's ramming of the door. His determination to break through had shattered hinges and lock—the battered door faring no better than Haakon by the time Thor was pried off him.

At the press of a tiny foot against her side, memories fell away, and Aven was grateful for the nudge from the child inside her to think no longer on the past. To look to the future instead and the newness to come.

Thor slid his broad hand over her rounded belly and looked up to Aven with a trace of worry. Since he'd lost his own mother in childbirth, and since he was the largest of the sons born, there was no wonder why his touch lingered warm and protective. He had wrangled Bjørn toward obedience, protected her from Haakon's self-ishness, and set snares in a strategic location for their safety, but he knew, as Aven did, that this coming birth was the one challenge he wouldn't be able to shelter her through.

FOUR

THE FIRST MATE TRUDGED UP THE CANON deck, spewing a slew of curses so forceful they should have lifted the limp sails. But not a breeze stirred against the few canvas sheets that hung unfurled, casting angled shadows across deck and water alike. Below, the ocean was smooth as an oyster pearl, and even the porpoises that had trailed them since the coast of Africa had vanished as if they, too, dreaded the stupor of a motionless tide.

Le Grelotter drifted, moving what felt like inches every hour. Most of the crew were upon her decks. Some lounged in slumber, faded hats resting over their eyes, while others kept busy repairing sails. Their tireless hands worked thick thread in a herringbone pattern along tears that would spread if left unattended. As for Haakon and a cabin boy, they ran pieces of glass paper along the side rails nearest the bow, sloughing away splinters and dried-out varnish, all of them earning more days at sea than dollars.

Was it now three of those days that they'd floated on lifeless waters? After depositing half of the ice they'd harvested to London, the ship had sailed south to drop anchor in the Canary Islands, just off the coast of Morocco. There they'd taken on cotton and coffee from Africa. They'd disembarked, enjoying a fair wind into the deeps of the Atlantic before the gust had dwindled like a dying breath. Now they drifted somewhere around 32° north and 25° west according to the captain's precise chart keeping. Nothing around but blue horizon and the risk of madness and mutiny. As it was, a wiry greenhorn paced the deck, wringing his cap in his hands, muttering to himself in French. He eyed the water as if it were cursed. More than once, Haakon thought the youth was going to throw himself into it. Someone was going to have to knock him out if he was to make it another day.

With the glass paper in hand worn to pulp, Haakon folded it over and thrust the rougher side along the railing with forceful strokes. Dust speckled the air. Sweat slid down his temple—a reminder of the fragile ice in the hull and the fact that over three thousand nautical miles stood between them and the Caribbean. A wad of coca leaves sat wedged inside his cheek, reminding him further of the distance, since this ration was among the last he had. Haakon spit the juices over the side, grateful for the medicine that calmed his nerves and spurred his work.

"Gonna leave some of that rail intact?"

At his friend's voice, Haakon moved the course paper to a new spot. He slanted Tate the smile he'd always used with Thor and Jorgan whenever they were right. Bedeviling was the longing to flash that smirk just once more in Ida's kitchen and see their amused grins right back, but with his family thousands of miles away and as many leagues apart from him in spirit, Haakon forced the yearning aside.

The plank Tate was seated on *thunk*ed against the side of the hull. Suspended by two ropes, it hung just level with the figurehead—a merman with a thick, curling beard all carved from dense oak. Just visible through the spindles of the bow railings, Tate used a matted brush to streak gold paint along the merman's trident, repairing what Northern storms had ravaged away. As boatswain, Tate had many duties that included overseeing the tasks of the deckhands, but never did a day go by that Tate Kennedy didn't climb up into the rigging to set sails, haul in lines, or carry out any of the other work to be done. As it was now, his shirt lay cast aside, skin browned by the sun, build as sinewy and strong as the rest of the crew who carved out their survival from water and wood, sun and ice.

Upon Haakon's first joining the crew at a cocky twenty-one years of age, he'd walked around this place insolent and sulky, irritating everyone in his wake, including Tate. Never would Haakon have imagined they'd end up friends, let alone the best of pals. And in fact, it hadn't been until the night Tate had saved his life that Haakon understood sincere friendship. He'd spent the last few years trying to be worthy of such kindness. He even irritated the crew a whole lot less.

While Haakon had his share of brothers, as did Tate, never had brotherhood been by choice. Now Haakon was something other than the runt of the litter. He was *chosen* as a brother. More potent was the way Tate often spoke of the God who could bring even the lost and the broken into His family and of how it was a calling-in more powerful than any other. Tate lived and breathed the awe of it, whiling away the hours below deck with dog-eared Scriptures in hand while Haakon lived a different kind of life, one that preferred the company of women to the Lord Almighty. Through it all, Tate was there as a steady friend and a rudder should Haakon ever decide to steer himself to holier waters.

But God wouldn't want the likes of him. No point in hoping for a wind that didn't exist.

The wiry greenhorn was still muttering to himself in French, worn shoes shuffling back and forth without aim. Someone passed him a flask of whiskey, and the youth gulped it down with a grimace.

The freckle-faced cabin boy regarded the poor soul, then leaned over the railing and scrutinized the water that didn't so much as lap against the hull. "Do you think this is a bad omen?" Perhaps ten, the boy was too small to be asking such a question. Too small to be from his parents, surrounded by a sea, but that was the life for many lads, some that Haakon had helped grow to manhood on this very vessel as they toiled side by side.

"No." Haakon crouched to scrub the underside of the railing. "It is *Jörmungandr*. The great beast."

The boy's eyes widened, and though he continued scraping, his rhythm slowed.

"A serpent so huge, it wraps the entire sea within its scaly body, biting his own tail to hold the waters at bay. The waters lurch against his side, every breath putting waves in motion."

The captain strode near and set down two pails of varnish.

Haakon angled a nod to his superior, then continued the tale for the boy. "Perhaps the great snake is sleeping too deeply. So deeply that his sighs don't even stir the air." He reached up to scrape loose a splinter the boy had missed. "What we need to do is wake him. But who would be brave enough? Especially since the serpent is so cunning that he outsmarted his archenemy, the mighty Thor, who tried to fish him from the sea with an ox head for bait."

The gritty paper in the boy's hand stilled. Haakon didn't need to glance around to know he held the attention of others. Stories at sea were more than a novelty; they were a way to pass time and maintain sanity. And they just happened to be his specialty. Even the captain leaned against the foremast and folded his arms, waiting for what would come next. The buckles on the sides of his boots glistened in the hot sun, and the shirt he wore was open at the chest, void of the neck cloth he often wore as if he, too, were fed up with the stagnant air.

"Perhaps we should lower bait into the water to see if we can rouse him," Haakon continued. "Get him to swish his tail and send a new current our way. What say you?"

The boy gulped as if he had been volunteered to be lowered. Reaching over, Haakon tousled his hair, feeling the grime of sea air and life aboard ship.

"You and your tales, Norgaard." The captain's voice sparked with amusement and challenge. "Would not a real Viking pull out an oar and start rowing?"

Haakon chuckled as he stood. "With all due respect, sir, I believe a real Viking would get one of his slaves to do it."

Grinning, the captain dipped his head in deference.

Knowing his place, Haakon did the same.

One of the crewmembers came along distributing water that was rationed more with each passing day. Haakon accepted a serving, filling his water skin partway to leave enough for all. He drank a swig, corked it, then stepped to a fresh length of railing and continued sloughing the rough wood.

The boy followed with the same hushed reverence that softened his voice. "Are you really a Viking, Mr. Haakon?"

Haakon scratched at his beard before looking over with an answer. "No. They are long gone, you see. But I admire them." Their bloodline was what gave him life. It was the raiders whom he called ancestors—the great fathers of his lineage, as Da had taught them. With pleasures of the flesh and a hunger for victory haunting his every waking hour, Haakon couldn't discount the stock he'd come from even if he wanted to.

At another *thunk*, he looked over to see Tate scale back over the side. The fellow American placed his bucket of gold paint on the deck and dropped the brush in. His hands and forearms were streaked with paint, and he tugged a rag from the waistband of his pants to scrub at them. Having saved him most of the water in the skin, Haakon tossed it over.

Tate caught it and uncorked the top. "So what happened in the end?"

"What do you mean?"

The cabin boy chimed in. "When Thor tried to fish the serpent from the water. How did he outsmart him?"

With the paper in the boy's grip void of all coarseness, Haakon took out his knife and spliced his own good portion in half. He handed a piece over. "A great giant came along and, fearing for the serpent's life, cut the line." Haakon couldn't help but think of his brother Jorgan and the way Jorgan had always walked between his rivaling brothers with wisdom and caution. Protecting them as much from themselves as from one another. Though Jorgan was no giant, he had a heart to match one.

A small voice pulled Haakon's attention back. "So in the end the serpent won?"

"Not entirely." Haakon tugged a bucket of varnish near and dipped a brush. "You see, he battled with Thor not once but three times. It was in the final battle that the serpent met his demise."

He knew that all too well.

Haakon pressed the gloss to the parched rail, saturating it to a chestnut sheen. Just as he had done to the porch of the mountain cabin he'd fled from. The cabin that was all he had in this world to call his own.

"Why?" The boy nabbed the second brush.

Haakon drew out a steady stroke. Varnish dripped down the side, oozing like drops of blood and bringing to mind a time—a fight—he longed to forget. "Because Thor was a god." He caught the droplets with the edge of his brush, smearing the sight away if not the memory of what his brother could do with those fists of his. "And the snake was only the son of one."

He'd long ago learned there was little he could do to best Thor. The inkling still walked alongside him though. A shadow of what was and what might be that remained more of an unease than a comfort. Did he *want* to challenge Thor again?

Part of him did. But Thor would always win. Always.

Haakon had been defeated long ago when as a baby he'd looked up at two boys who had lost their mother more abruptly than he had because they'd lost the privilege of knowing her. And there he'd lain in a wooden cradle, the very reason she was gone.

Haakon lowered his gaze and rubbed a thumb over his forehead.

How he longed to stand in that house again. To see Ida. Jorgan. Everyone. Even though he was terrified. Compounding his uncertainty about Thor was a greater one regarding Aven.

Haakon lifted his head, chiding himself that it had taken so long to finally glance in that direction. Though he saw nothing other than a glittering, vast sea, he squinted toward the sun, and be it a yearning for home or an exhaustion from doing *everything* the hard way, a longing for guidance sprung from the very depths of his spirit. One as battered and thirsty as the deck he stepped across.

Fresh to mind were the young widow's words—the ones that challenged him to do more. To be more. An insinuation that though he'd spent weeks cutting and hauling ice, he had more inside him yet. A duty not to be rendered through ax or ice pick, but of a harvesting much more pure. One of heart and of life. He might have disregarded the challenge but had witnessed a fortitude in Mrs. Jönsson that sprang straight from the depths of hope and brokenness. To ignore her appeal to him would be to undermine her every effort of keeping her children fed and cared for in the wake of torment, and of a faith she'd placed in a God who, by all appearances, had forsaken her.

In Haakon's foolishness he'd assumed her eliciting the makings of a husband. Now . . . he feared he'd been terribly wrong. Perhaps her insinuation for him to rise to a greater challenge had been a beseeching for him to thread wholeness and restitution into whatever wrong had sent him to the far side of the world. As selfless as the rest of her encounters with him had been. If she needed rescuing, Haakon doubted it would have been by his own strength. He'd have sunk her as soon as save her, and she'd probably known that more than he.

Perhaps it hadn't been saving she sought from him but honesty. Even nobility. All encompassed in a heart that might have fit against her own had he not left it in pieces on Blackbird Mountain.

Was he brave enough to go home and try and make things right? Did he have that kind of courage?

At a sudden shout, Haakon lifted his head to see two crew-members jogging down from the quarterdeck. More men stood at attention, some pointing up to the mainsail. The steep sheet of canvas rippled then drew still. Haakon set the brush aside and stepped nearer to the mast. He shielded his eyes from the sun and for some strange reason whispered the only prayer to fall from his lips in over four years.

The canvas rippled again . . . then bowed out . . . snapping as wind filled it. The ship heeled with the force, and for the first time in days Haakon had to right his stance along with everyone else. Cheers bellowed from all around, and he let out a sharp whistle. A deckhand raced for the helm, grabbing the spoked wheel as it spun to port.

Tate shouted orders, and at the call of his own task, Haakon rushed for the topgallant halyard. A young deckhand was already there fling-ing off turns of the rope, fumbling it with inexperience. With the need to hurry, Haakon shouldered the youth aside and threw the turn off the pin so that the yard came down with a run.

"Secure the buntlines!" he commanded.

The youth rushed to obey. Together they pulled and hauled lines, then hurried aloft and balanced across footropes to unfurl sails. The wind roared past with the waking growl of a bear.

Haakon kept an eye on the mainsail as it held the wind that bore in with a will. If it stayed fair, they'd make it in and out of the Caribbean before hurricane season began in May. Then it could be a straight shot to the coast of North America. From there just a train ride home.

Should a man want to do such a thing.

Haakon glanced to the horizon. He doubted the rise in wind had anything to do with his prayer, but then again, maybe God was trying to get his attention all the same.

FIVE

April 3, 1895
Fincastle, Virginia

BODY ACHING, THOR TRUDGED AROUND THE
back of the wagon and unloaded a crate filled with pint jars. The
modest town of Fincastle stood around him, just several hours' drive
from the farm—a journey he often made across the James River by
ferry to deliver goods to a mercantile that placed orders by mail.

Today's delivery was of twenty-eight pints of Aven's cider jelly and
twice that of the women's apple butter and pie filling. With the help
of the shopkeeper, they unloaded the first of the twenty gallon jugs
of cider vinegar.

The shopkeeper spoke as he carried the jugs inside the mercantile. Following behind, Thor had no idea what was being said, so he
cleared his throat. A gesture that was more polite than whistling, Ida
had once explained.

The balding man turned. "My apologies." His mouth, now in sight,
moved slower than need be, but Thor knew it was meant as a courtesy. "I was askin' if you've got any liquor in the works. Folks are often
wonderin'."

Though fermented brews profited more per acre, Thor shook his head. The same answer he always gave. He admired the shopkeeper's savvy persistence, but if customers hankered for something stronger, they'd have to look elsewhere. As much as Thor missed the crafting of liquor, he missed the taste even more. Since cravings hit him with little warning, he'd sold off his fermenting equipment to be safe. To his relief, the longings were far apart, but it didn't make them any less potent. In fact, they came worse at harvest time. Turns out sobering hadn't done a thing for his memory of how to concoct a mighty fine brew. Because of that, he'd found it best to eliminate even the chance.

Back at the wagon, Thor hefted out two more jugs of vinegar and slid them onto the stoop of the mercantile, careful to keep them out of the way of passing customers. He turned for more product and winced at the throbbing in his side. A flush warmed his skin, but truth be told, he'd already felt feverish that morning. He should have enlisted help from home but hadn't wanted to take Jorgan or Peter away. Aven was always eager to come along, but the long, bumpy wagon ride seemed a danger in her late condition.

Taking a breath, Thor fetched more jugs and passed the vinegar into the waiting grasp of the shopkeeper. They kept at it until the wagon was unloaded of its goods right down to every last jar of apple butter, all of which was heartily fussed over by the shopkeeper's wife.

"Oh, these labels just get prettier and prettier," she said, admiring Aven and Fay's handiwork where *Norgaard Family Orchard* was stamped on rounds of neatly trimmed paper.

Thor gave her a polite smile and would pass on the appreciation. He handed the shopkeeper the invoice, and once the transaction was complete, Thor folded the payment into his pocket. He nodded a thanks to the loyal patrons and crossed the mercantile, aiming toward the shelves nearest the front window.

Lace ribbons were displayed on wooden spools, and tiny, painted bottles caught the noon glow. Straw bonnets sat on wire stands beside a looking glass. All would be nice for Aven, but last they were here, he'd witnessed her examining something else. Thor found the very item near the floor in an enamel pail. The vessel held umbrellas and the fancier ones that women used on sunny days. He didn't know what they were called.

Thor pulled one out and turned it in the light of the window. He rather wanted to test it but checked over both shoulders to make sure no one was watching. He lowered the lacy contraption, loosened its binding, and pressed it open. It was awful pretty. And he could just see Aven and his child sitting beneath it on a hot summer day.

Thor closed it, and when he couldn't retie the tiny ribbon meant to hold it snug, a female shopper stepped in to aid him. When she'd finished forming a bow, the elderly woman gave him an understanding smile, and he smiled back.

Fishing out some of his pay, he went back to the counter and purchased the gift. The shopkeeper wrapped it in brown paper, and Thor was grateful for a way to keep the fragile lace clean until he could tuck the gift into a corner for Aven to discover.

After pulling out his notebook and small pencil, Thor scrawled a question for the shopkeeper, who then pointed in the direction of the doctor's residence at the end of the road. Thor offered his gratitude and headed out.

He drove the team of mares down the road to the two-story clapboard where a sign indicated the physician's place of residence. After leading the team and wagon around back, he set the brake and left the horses to graze on the spring grass beneath their hooves.

Thor followed a low, tidy fence around the building to a thick-slabbed door. He knocked, waited, and when nothing happened, tried again. At his third attempt, he gave a good pounding, hoping it was still a reasonable amount of sound. He didn't mean to go banging anyone's door down.

When no one answered, he moved closer to the window. The space, though filled with a desk, chair, and medical equipment, was void of human life.

Now what? If the doctor was treating a patient in the countryside, it could be hours if not days until his return. Thor could come back in a week or two, but it seemed wise to leave some kind of word. He wrote a note listing his ailments, including one he hadn't mentioned to Aven, let alone anyone else—that the content of his bladder was dark as rust and as painful to rid. At the top of the page, Thor added his name and noted where he lived before folding the page in half and slipping it under the door. Whether or not the note got lost, it seemed better to try.

He wrestled with discouragement as he climbed back onto the wagon seat, and he fought the same battle as he drove the team onto the road and toward home.

The harnesses jostled and the wheels turned. Birds darted about. All making noise, as he knew they did, but everything was hollow of sound. Instead, the world was made up of sight and color and texture. The rhythm of the horse's hooves as they lifted and lowered. The taste of the air that was earthy and rich in spring and the smell of it . . . even more pungent and fertile.

He crossed at the ferry, flipping a coin as payment to the operator, and led the team off the flat-bottomed boat and onto the road. As the miles toward home wore on, he shifted on the seat to try and get comfortable. He was hot and then chilled, and his limbs were sore as the dickens. The pain in his side hadn't worsened, but it caught him by surprise even during the most menial of tasks.

All he wanted was a warm bed and a long sleep with Aven curled beside him. She had a way of looking after him, and he needed her right now. A few days ago, Thor had tipped her off to the amount of his discomfort. Her concern garnered a visit from Ida's sister, Cora, who lived on their land, just past the orchards as Peter did. Skilled in herbal remedies, she had brought Thor a tonic, which Aven prepared as a tea for him three times daily. So why was he feeling so poorly?

Sight of his lower orchards indicated just a half mile to go until the farmyard. Thor drove along and, spying something to his right, slowed the team. Flashes of blue and brown like that of denim and wool rushed through his trees. He halted the wagon only to blink again and see nothing. Had he imagined that? Maybe it had been blue jays flitting from a running deer. Or maybe he was simply more feverish than he realized.

Yet when he entered the farmyard, he feared he'd been wrong. In the distance, Jorgan surveyed the cidery with Bjørn on his hip. Was something wrong with the roof? When he angled Thor's way, his face was the somber reserved for bad news. Gut souring worse, Thor set the brake and climbed down. That's when he halted altogether.

Slopped across the cidery were giant brushstrokes of blood-red paint in crudely drawn words.

Still wet.

We haven't forgotten.

The last letters were scrawled in such haste they were scarcely legible. Thor went cold. A chill that inked through his limbs.

Nailed below the vow was a fold of white cloth. Thor freed the wrinkled muslin. Unfolding what could only be a Klansmen's mask, his hands moved of their own accord as if in silent acceptance of what was coming upon them. Two slits cut for eyes gaped at him from beneath a peaked hood. Designed to make the wearer appear as a ghostly figure . . .

Returning from the dead to finish the fight.

Thor looked to Jorgan, who remained somber, and sparking in his eyes was the willingness to face a fight should it come to that again. No doubt now it would.

They were short a man, and Thor didn't even know how well he could raise a rifle and fire. There was something in Jorgan's expression that declared the worry over Thor's state mutual.

Jorgan surveyed the wall again—the words written there—and

Thor followed suit. After nearly forty years of feuding with Jed and his sons, this day was destined to come.

One didn't drive wolves from their den without some kind of retaliation.

The rest of Jed's men would be in tow as well. Likely one of them had done this. Jed never handled this kind of dirty work, but the old general was always the mastermind behind these acts. Recalling the movement out through his orchard, Thor scanned the portion of land but knew that if it had been the men he thought it was, they were vanished again into these wilds.

Where I-D-A? Thor signed.

Jorgan pointed to the house.

C-O-R-A? Thor stroked a thumb against the side of his beard, doing it twice to add *Girls?* While a comely shade to Thor's way of thinking, Cora's skin, and that of her two daughters, posed danger for the brave souls. Danger to be living in these parts where Klansmen had once prowled and now did again.

"They're home. Peter agreed to stay close to them for now."

Starting back toward the wagon with Jorgan, Thor fingerspelled *F-A-Y? A-V-E-N?*

"They're in the house with Sigurd."

While the Klansmen would take no offense with the color of Fay and Aven's skin, it was a different fear that plagued Thor. Almost as dangerous as being the wrong color to men like the Sorrels was being the right one.

Reaching the wagon, Thor dropped the white hood in the back, then started on the first mare's bridle. Jorgan unfastened the other, and at sight of his brother waving for his attention, Thor looked at him.

I feed horses, Jorgan signed.

Thor nodded his thanks. Did it truly show how much he needed to lie down just now? After coming around the team, he squeezed his brother's shoulder, then reached in for the paper-wrapped parcel.

With Aven's gift in hand, he headed for the house that spread before them as vast as the cidery itself. With its three stories of windows and two first-floor doors, not impenetrable. He drew in a slow breath. Even if the house sat locked and guarded, they couldn't just keep the women and children there for days or even weeks on end. But with the Sorrels getting bolder, something had to be done.

He stepped inside, his only focusing being the stairs that would lead him to bed. As Thor climbed, never would he forget the way Peter had been stunned senseless upon first seeing Aven. Him standing there in his white cloak and hood that wretched night, watching her as though she'd come out of a dream. Fay embodied what would have the same kind of appeal. Stemming from German blood, Fay possessed a waif-like beauty. While Peter had rallied his senses, becoming *friend* instead of *admirer*, there were others of Peter's kin who wouldn't be so noble.

Near the attic, Thor was too exhausted to tread with any care. An U-N-W-I-E-L-D-Y sound, Ida called it, when he was careless with the weight of his bootfalls. Making it no surprise that Aven rose from her chair near the window, looking alarmed.

She lowered her sewing to the seat, and his name came from her lips, spoken in question with her pretty eyes wide.

After giving her a smile of assurance, he leaned the gift against the cradle, hoping she'd understand that it was for the pair of them. Aven smiled softly, and while he expected her to peek inside the paper, she reached instead for his hand. Savoring the feel, Thor led her over to the bed. He touched the top of the coverlet for her to lie down there, then bent to unlace his boots. At his struggle, Aven came around to help but was as cumbersome to reach them as he. What a pair they were these days. A faint chuckle shook his chest, and Aven's eyes shone with amusement.

It was easier to focus on that than what he should be explaining to her right now: of the danger that had been painted across the cidery wall.

But such trepidation could wait for just a little while longer. He begged it from on high. After managing to work free of his boots, he claimed his own side of the bed and, once settled, relished the way she tucked herself near, so close that he scarcely needed to move to rest the backs of his fingers against her round, firm stomach. His other hand came around her own, holding it safe. Thor closed his eyes and savored the sensation. A moment made all the more right as their prayers for a child all their own lay granted between them.

Aven tipped her chin up, claiming a kiss before he could open his eyes. Thor savored it—sweet and soft as it was—and even as he delighted in the tenderness, he cupped the top of her head to tuck it safely beneath his beard. Aven started to protest, so Thor made his sign for *sleep*. Hopefully she would think him already drifting. She nestled in again, even closer. He didn't mean to discourage her affections, but if she knew the longing inside him, and how he was fighting it . . .

But until he could be seen by a doctor, something about this ailment made him uneasy for her. Something that wasn't right with him. He didn't know what it was, but he wouldn't allow himself any nearer to her until a doctor assured him it was fine. That she would be fine.

Aven lay unmoving save her fingertips, which slowly brushed back and forth against his own. A gentle lulling that was sending him into the throes of peace and sleep.

But just before he succumbed to it, he saw the warning in his mind's eye.

We haven't forgotten.

The last time the Norgaards had faced off to the Sorrels, bullets had ripped up the hillside, all aimed at Haakon, who raced toward his own disappearance. Not only had Haakon blown up the Sorrel barn to avenge the thievery, he'd done it to eliminate the choice from Thor as to whether or not to sell the last of his stock.

A freedom from the burden of the liquor that Thor *still* wrestled with.

Whether bravery or foolheadedness, Haakon had scarcely escaped over the ridgeline with his life. It was the last time Thor had seen his brother, but even as those memories trod around this sacred place, unwelcome, a stronger taunt rose up to join them. Jed and Harlan were returned to Blackbird Mountain. Twice now to this very farmyard.

Aven touched Thor's arm where the needle had pressed into his vein just as it had done to Harlan's.

Thor sighed, relieved when sleep began to claim him. A way to liberate his mind, even briefly, from the fact that so clever were the Klansmen, so full of vengeance, that they wouldn't show themselves until they were sure of victory. Now he could only pray that he would be well enough to stand against them.

SIX

APRIL 9, 1895
NORTH ATLANTIC OCEAN

DREAMS PUMMELED FROM EVERY WHICH WAY. Rolling over him as a current that couldn't be stemmed. Exhaustion and regret blurred his focus . . . making the memories bend on themselves. Cramming thoughts together and confusing him.

Hammocks creaked, weighted with sleeping sailors, Haakon's included. But louder than any shifting of canvas and rope were the screams of the little girl. Screams that were seared into his memory with as torrid a force as the explosion itself.

Just moments before the barn had burst apart, Haakon had raced down the hillside to where Jed Sorrel's granddaughter was tugging on the barn door to go inside. Reaching the child, Haakon had ripped her away from the rigged structure where inside burned a fuse that he'd already lit. His one thought had been to keep her alive but she hadn't known that. All she knew was the force with which he rushed her across the farmyard toward safety.

Her screams had pierced the air, driving fear and regret through his very core.

That's when the earth shook—a ball of fire scalding his back. The closest he'd come to hell thus far. The fireball singed his skin even through his clothes. Sweat had covered him, nearly causing him to lose his grip on the child. And that was just the first explosion. Because when his second homemade bomb went off, it took hundreds of quarts of liquor with it, shuddering the ground like a giant rising from slumber. Accompanying it was a shattering so loud, Thor might as well have heard.

Haakon had gotten the girl to safety when guns were drawn, Jed's pistol being the first. All Haakon remembered was racing back toward his hiding spot on the top of the nearest hill as gunfire pelted around him, more menacing than the falling debris of boards and sharded glass.

How he survived, he didn't know. It was the nearest brush he'd had with death. That was until the night he'd fallen from the ship into a dark North Sea. Striking the side of the vessel on the way down, Haakon hit the water nearly unconscious. He learned only later that the boatswain, Tate, jumped in after him, and with the help of a rope and the strength of a dozen sailors Haakon lived to see another sunrise.

Maybe it was God's mercy, but he sensed survival had less to do with holy sympathy and more to do with the fact that God wasn't ready to deal with him yet. It would be a long recount—his sins—and surely the Maker of the earth had better things to do than stand with him in judgement.

The ship creaked. Hammocks shifted again. The air hung still and hot. Each awareness lay distant yet strangely comforting.

"Haakon, you're dreaming."

It was the same thing the woman in Norway had once whispered to him.

When he'd scaled the hill to see her again for the third time that week, she'd stopped her chores to warm for him a meal from her already scant supply. As generous an offering as a feast in a fortress.

He'd sat down at her table, a dinner of mincemeat stew in hand, and so exhausted he'd been, so satisfying the fare, that he'd dozed there beside the fire. She'd come to his side and spoken in her gentle voice. Her calming him amid whatever heartache he'd been murmuring about in his sleep. A pain she'd probably understood even more than he.

What was her name?

She'd given it to him once, but to his shame he'd forgotten. Mrs. Jönsson, the villagers called her, and so such formality had sufficed for him as well. He'd been too ashamed to inquire again. The sound of it, he recalled, was a pretty one, yet he'd been careless to lose it. Just as he was with everything else in this life.

Sweat trickled down his temple. A groan rose in his sleep, coursing up from utter agony.

"Norgaard!"

Suddenly Haakon crashed to the ground as his hammock overturned. The memories slamming south of consciousness, he rose and grabbed the culprit by the front of his linen shirt.

Tate.

Haakon rammed him into the wall. "Why did you do that!" he shouted.

Tate tossed him off, tangling Haakon into the still swinging hammock. "Because you were shouting in your sleep again."

That wasn't what he'd meant. Haakon rammed him harder, this time slamming Tate into a barrel filled with dried peas. The racket was loud enough to stir more men from slumber. Instead of being his usually peaceful self, Tate scrambled up and shoved Haakon in the direction of the stairs. "So we could have this pleasant conversation!"

Haakon stumbled, but caught himself on a salted mutton leg that hung from the rafters, wrapped in cloth. Two mice scattered from between his boots, and the ship's cat darted after them, making more crash and clatter.

With the groggy attention of their fellow crewmembers focusing in, Haakon stomped up the stairs. At the top, he opened the hatch and climbed out into the cold night. The stench of the living quarters fell away to a gust of salty air. Overhead, stars pierced the blackness, and water lapped against the hull. A still night that was nothing like the turmoil within him.

Fatigue threatening to buckle him, Haakon pulled a dried coca leaf from his pouch. His tin of sodium bicarbonate wasn't near, so he crammed the leaf into his cheek without the powder that rendered the leaves potent enough to suppress hunger, thirst, fatigue, and even pain. He'd heard of men losing their minds for coca, and while the plant was different than those rumored to have been taken by the wildest of Norse warriors to chase away fear and even reason, he knew this dabbling was as reckless.

He meant to kick the habit, but with them sailing toward the Caribbean where the stimulant was easily traded for, the choice wouldn't be so simple. Made harder every time memories stole his sleep and plunged him deep. Deep below the surface . . . so far and so fast that he might as well have been falling again. Might as well have plummeted into the black sea so needling cold it tore the breath from his lungs. Beyond that had only been pain as he'd rolled against the hull of the ship and a distant awareness that in those waters swam whales that would tear a man apart.

Death would have taken him then, and he'd been nigh unto welcoming it, but before his lungs could give out, two hands ripped him from the blackness, tugging him higher and higher and higher until there was air again. He'd gasped for it—clawing at life as if having awoken from Valhalla itself. Instead of Valkyries summoning him to an eternal feast, it had been the grip of the gospel ushering him toward a new dawn through the bravery of a single man, the creak of rope and wood, and a Christian's prayer whispered into the cold as Haakon had fought for consciousness.

"I should have died then." The words tried to cleave in his chest, but it was time he forced them out. Haakon might have come out alive, but as for Tate's appeal to God that night, he still didn't know if he believed in such sovereignty. "The night you jumped in after me."

The night he'd jumped in himself.

Death would have been cleaner instead of the alternative, bearing yet another burden on his back. One of a second chance he didn't deserve.

Tate was hard to see in the dark, so Haakon didn't try. Instead he just listened to the voice that he had come to know as steady and wise. "Sorry to disappoint you, but I can't stand by and watch a man drown. None of the crew would. I went in because I got there first. Anyone would have done the same."

Haakon wasn't so sure about that.

Gone from mind was the young Sorrel girl. Even the woman he'd left behind in Norway. In their place rushed forward a face so familiar and so tender that Haakon nearly gasped with the ache of it. Aven— with her brown eyes and freckled cheeks. Just as staggering was the memory of her voice. Her gentle ways and her trust in him. The tender feel of her hands in his hair as she trimmed it or of how he'd kissed her in the pond that day, him hoping to awaken her to the possibility of something more than friendship.

Yet it was an encounter months later that haunted him. A rush of his desire that hadn't been welcomed by Aven no matter how much he'd tried to coerce her.

Why couldn't he have just given up after losing her to Thor?

Why had he sapped the light from her eyes—all for his own gain and to punish his brother? How hard she'd fought against him. How urgently she'd pleaded for him to let her free as he'd lowered his suspenders, him giving in to her cries only when he'd felt a jolt to his soul so icy cold he was certain he'd be barred from heaven forever. The empty, black sensation of God turning His face from him.

Which meant he had to believe. A man couldn't feel that amount of dread otherwise.

Haakon's throat clamped tight, and he looked to the sky studded with so many stars, such beauty would seem impossible had he not spent all these years discovering it was so. His gaze fell from the heavens to the abyss below. Would death have satisfied him? Even if that death led to darker shores? He didn't know, but he was more and more tormented by the answer.

"I don't know what to do." It was the first time he'd admitted such a thing. Coca always made him philosophical, but he didn't think this was the potion talking.

Tate swung on the coat Haakon hadn't realized he'd been holding. "Are you asking me?"

His most trusted friend? On a night as bleak as this? "Yes."

Eyes adjusting to the scant moonlight, Haakon saw the way Tate braced both hands to the railing and lowered his head. The man's voice rose strong over the chop of the current. "I don't know what you should do, but I can tell you what I'm gonna do."

A crisp breeze gusted against them, but to both Haakon's relief and despair, the medicine was beginning to take effect. A numbing and a strength that he craved. He didn't know how to make it through a day otherwise.

"I'm gonna go home," Tate said. "I've been gone four years now and didn't tell a soul where I was going. It was foolish and juvenile, and now I need to go back and make amends for that. There are people who are waiting for me."

Though Haakon knew little of the woman Tate had left behind, he understood heartsickness when he heard it in a man's voice.

"She may no longer be waiting, but I need to be brave enough to find out."

Haakon leaned his forearms on the railing. Moonlit water churned against the hull like ink beneath a lantern flame. "And what should a man do who has no one waiting on him?"

"You think you have no one waiting for you back home?"

Haakon surrendered a nod.

Tate thumped the toe of his boot to a post, then tipped his head back as if unable to bear Haakon's foolishness for one more league. "Then I'd say you've never been more wrong in your life." His gaze lifted to those stars. Ones that had been burning and guiding since the beginning of time. Finally he dropped his focus that was stern but threaded with faith. A hope that Haakon had long since lost but ached to recover. "Granted, they won't be very impressed with what they see—I know I'm not—but that part will . . . *as always* . . . be up to you."

Sigurd stood with his nose pressed to the window, watching a herring gull soar along the cloudy sky. 'Twas not uncommon for clouds to roll in from the coast, nor was it rare to spot sea birds on days such as these.

Sigurd hurried back to the dining table where Aven sat. He clambered onto the bench, returning his attention to the map spread between them. "And dis?" Sigurd asked as if he hadn't just been distracted by the gull's lonely cry.

"That's Australia." Aven skimmed her finger southward.

The three-year-old traced the wobbly outline of its coast. Upstairs, Fay was settling Bjørn for a nap, so Aven had offered to watch her fidgety nephew, who smelled of sunshine and who was curious enough to have found a map that morning. While searching the house for a missing marble, he'd scoured the floor in Aven and Thor's room, spotting the map beneath a bookshelf on the side of the room that had once belonged to Haakon.

The paper must have fallen and furled from sight in the wake of Haakon's leaving. With Sigurd's help, Aven had blown off the layers of time and, to the boy's delight, brought the map down here for him to explore.

While she was much less fascinated by Haakon's keepsake than her nephew was, it had captured his interest, and she needed to rest her feet.

"Where No-way?" he asked.

"Norway?" Aven guided Sigurd's small finger nearer to Scandinavia as a hint.

He touched England, and when she shook her head his search moved to Germany. "Closer. That's where your mama's parents came from." With a smile, Aven touched the northern shore that sat just below Norway. She slid her finger across waters where the Vikings had once sailed their dragon ships to raid for riches, power, and even brides from the countries surrounding the North Sea. She showed him where Ireland was, just a short boat ride away, and a land that Norse raiders had plundered for the same goods.

She told Sigurd all of this, wanting to keep the history of their homelands alive, and when his eyes widened in shock, she added, "I'm sure your da and uncles are very sorry for that."

He looked relieved. "We should tell dem dats not nice."

"Yes, we should," she said gravely, then with a wink spoke an assurance that neither she nor Fay had been plundered.

He smiled and she voyaged her fingertip to that stretch of land along the North Atlantic. "Oh . . . what might this be?"

"Da!" Sigurd cried. He touched Germany again with a tender-sounding, "Ma."

"Aye, that is where your ancestors come from."

With a shuffling that always followed her limp, Ida stepped into the great room and set aside a basket of folded laundry.

"Nanna?" Sigurd asked.

Aven nestled him closer on their shared bench. "Before being here in Virginia, your nanna came from Louisiana. Which isn't a country. It's a state. Though I'm afraid . . ." Her brow puckered. "I'm not certain where it is."

"Just down south there." Ida limped nearer and pointed a gnarled finger to the bottom portion of the United States.

"And before that?" Aven asked. "Your kinfolk?"

"Just here." Ida's voice held a touch of pride as she tapped a string of islands near the Caribbean Sea. "Long before my own mammy was born."

Aven's gaze roved the map. She studied both land and sea, and a twinge of wondering arose as to where on the surface of this printed paper Haakon roamed. Was he well? Was he alive? Had he a wife and children to bear his name and bring him joy?

Or did he live free and alone?

All those questions were compounded by a more desperate one. Did he regret his actions? She'd never seen him again after that awful hour, and even though his brothers had glimpsed him at the Sorrel farm days later, sentiments hadn't been swapped amid the chaos. The letter he'd mailed home after his leaving had indicated regret, but had been so brief and so hurriedly scrawled that it did little more than place a tiny flame under hope. It was barely enough to light the darkness of their last encounter, but might Haakon have learned a lesson of how people were to be treated? She hoped no others would be harmed by his choices. Especially those weaker than him as she had been.

Wherever Haakon was—be he a vagabond or a family man—what mattered most was that he was living wiser now.

While she might never know, that was what prayers were for.

Sigurd stood on the seat of his chair and reached for Ida.

Ida scooped him up. "We all came awful far." She kissed his forehead where a blond curl always dangled. "And look where we ended up. Here. Together."

Sigurd wrapped his arms around her neck. "I'm hungry, Nanna," he said matter-of-factly. Something he announced at least once an hour.

"Then we need to fill you up." Chuckling, Ida toted him into the kitchen. "But I best hear a 'please' first."

"Please. And thank you." Sigurd giggled.

As the pair busied themselves in the pantry, Aven rolled up the map. She climbed the stairs for the third floor. There she rifled through the box of important matters Thor kept on his dresser— coins, old keys, and other odds and ends. She shuffled to the bottom, finding a key that was slightly bent. A chill slid across her skin as she freed what had once been in Haakon's care. Wearing one of Thor's old shirts atop her mounded patchwork skirt, Aven slipped the key into the chest pocket. The slight weight of it was unsettling, so she squared her shoulders, inhaled a dose of courage, and headed back downstairs.

With Thor's insistence she not venture away from the farmyard alone, she searched for Jorgan, since Thor was looking in on Cora and the girls. She was grateful he wasn't around to accompany her. To spare him the unease of returning to Haakon's cabin made the missing of him worth it. As Aven ventured across the farmyard, the white mass of clouds tinged the air with a hint of the sea. Though sunlight was sparse today, she recalled the lace-trimmed parasol he'd brought her. Both the babe and sunnier days would be here soon, making his thoughtfulness all the more cherished.

Aven found Jorgan in the horse barn shoveling the remains of last winter's hay into the nearest pen. "Might you be able to accompany me to the west cabin?" She felt silly disturbing him for something as trite as the map curled in her hand. "'Twill only take a few minutes."

Jorgan pitched another scoop of hay into the pen, where just beyond, two of Dotti's kittens scampered along the storage loft. "Certainly." He heaved the last of the dried grass over the side, then leaned the pitchfork against a wall.

After snagging his hat from a corner of the nearest stall, he used it to swipe hay from his wool pants. Sliding the hat on, he gestured for her to step out first. Together they aimed for the narrow patch of woodland that separated the great house from the west cabin that was Haakon's inheritance. Aven meant to make polite conversation with Jorgan as they walked, but all sensibility lodged in her throat as they reached the first spread of trees. She hadn't walked this portion of Norgaard land in years. Though she was hesitant in crossing it now, 'twas time.

The last she had stood on Haakon's land, autumn winds had swept through with a promise of winter, and the man himself had regarded her with those piercing blue eyes. Now his face was one she could scarcely conjure. Instead, it was the wildflowers feathered about that filled her senses. Not the fair-haired Norseman with a smooth voice and cunning ways.

Jorgan was steady at her side as they passed through the trees. When she glimpsed the cabin in its sweeping meadow, Aven slowed. 'Twas a quaint dwelling, with a humble lower floor that, while meagerly adorned, housed the makings of a kitchen and living space— both of which had been left in progress. Above that rose a loft that she'd never been up to.

Still holding onto the map, Aven forced herself to cross the yard that spread overgrown and empty. As she climbed the porch steps, old boards creaked a welcome that might as well have been a longing for life in this place once again.

"Do you want me to go in with you?" Jorgan called from where he'd halted in the yard.

"I'll just be a moment," she called back gently. Aven freed the key from the shirt pocket, pressed it into the lock, and turned it with a click so soft that it shouldn't have heralded in memories of the man who had once been so dear. But as rusty, forgotten things had a way of doing, it sounded an alarm that she hadn't anticipated. With a trembling hand she pressed her way into his cabin.

The air inside was dim and stagnant. Ripe with the scent of musty wood. A fresh leak had blossomed in the far corner, and sunlight hadn't been kind to the curtains hanging on the windows. Aven stepped to them and fingered a hem just as she'd done when Haakon had stood beside her. He'd raised the curtain rod into place, giving her that boyish smile as he did, then the back of his hand had touched her arm. A coaxing—a pleading—for her to choose him.

A would-be lover who had lost her to Thor, losing his own way in the aftermath.

With a shuddering breath, Aven set the map on a wobbly table and turned away. Not wanting to linger, she stepped out and bolted the door before pressing the key back from sight.

Turning, she spotted a flash of white overhead and shielded her eyes to spy the lone herring gull dipping beneath the spread of clouds. She walked back toward Jorgan, still watching the sea bird that arced down to soar over the treetops of this land. It let out an urgent call, a cry for waters to rest upon, as it curved in a slow circle above towering pines.

"You are far from home, little one." Chilled, she wrapped her arms around herself, thankful for the earthy scent of Thor's shirt as she stepped farther down the lane. "But I do believe you'll fare just fine," she whispered.

As Aven neared Jorgan, the bird dipped and turned back the way it had come, wings spread sure and steady. Not so much as a falter in the steady *pump, pump, pump* as it rose higher. A determination. A steady climbing. And a reminder that just like a bird seeking a haven, the lost would do all they could to find their way home.

SEVEN

THE CREW STOOD ON DECK AS THE PORT warmed with a Caribbean sunrise. The round glow burned on the horizon—streaking the rolling sea that spread around their anchored ship. Water glittered as liquid gold, and freshly stained decks glistened, filling Haakon with a warmth that promised to thaw the ache in his bones if not his soul.

Just minutes ago the business agents had convened on the dock for the paying of port charges and to price the crystal ice. They would argue anywhere from ten to twenty-five cents per pound. With summer up ahead and with the extensive households of wealthy Englishmen and plantation owners on the island, not to mention a ship full of men needing to be paid, the bartering in British currency was already passionate.

Behind the businessmen stretched white-sand beaches where palms leaned at water-reaching angles. Locals roused for another day of trade and labor amid colonial buildings and rustic huts. Their voices filled the air as English in the island cadence. A welcome and familiar sound, so often the ship returned here.

Haakon leaned against the main mast and waited for the signal to unload. His stomach grumbled despite their early-morning meal of hard biscuits and salt pork. What he wouldn't give for fresh fruit. With the opportunity only hours away, he tried to ignore the way his stomach complained over the stale breakfast. It didn't help that a dark-skinned woman treaded along the dock with a basket of such wares on her head, her manner of dress not unlike Ida's sister, Cora, or her niece, Tess, who often wore such head wrappings.

With thoughts of home haunting him more and more, Haakon forced the noticing aside and watched as the businessmen bartered—this, one of the most unnerving parts of the voyage. It wasn't un-common for a winter's worth of work to be sold below market value out of sheer desperation to unload. Worse yet, to anchor in port only to learn that a different company had arrived just days prior, filling every icehouse to the brim. Haakon had seen it before. An entire ship forced to unload its cargo into the bay. Tons upon tons of ice heaved overboard into warm waters to protect ship and crew from the dan-gers of melting ice on their return voyage.

Restless, Haakon shifted his boots and flicked at a bug that buzzed around his head. Beside him, Tate sighed. With the bartering taking longer than usual, even the boatswain stood tense. A rare thing.

Finally, the signal was given. A deal had been struck.

Tate issued orders, and the crew hustled into action, spirits ris-ing as the sun did. Below deck, a pulley hung anchored to steel hoisting tongs, and men grunted as they hauled up the first block. Standing atop deck, Haakon used a large set of hand tongs to clamp the slippery ice and shove it across the deck. While he worked quickly, he took care with aim and force because a sliding three-hundred-pound block could crush a man's bones. Every sailor knew the dangers, and it kept the work efficient as they pierced the ice with picks and passed the blocks down ramps to waiting wagons. The drivers would take the frozen cargo to icehouses long since built to laugh in the face of the hottest summer months.

Haakon secured another block and shoved it forward. He kept at it while his muscles loosened and his breath quickened. It was wet work, and while the ice stung his hands even through his gloves, they would soon be numb, and he'd forget about the cold. Clamp and drag. Hold and shove. He did this over and over, sliding the dense blocks across the boards to the next crewmember. Every muscle in his arms and back strained to keep the blocks in control, but he didn't falter so much as once. While chunks of it littered the deck, crunching beneath their boots like snow, they all took care not to damage or crack the valuable product as each piece was hoisted up, slid toward the ramp, and skidded down where it was loaded for transport—each crewmember laboring as a well-oiled machine.

He worked alongside his fellow men for the better part of the day until the last block had been hoisted from the hold and slid across the deck, down the ramp, and hefted into the final wagon. Though exhausted, the wet and weary men celebrated with whoops and cheers. As crewmembers set about swabbing up water and laying away tools, the captain strode along the decks, tipping his hat to those who served beneath him. He shook hands with anyone in reach, even the youngest of cabin boys. An honor and one they had worked hard to earn.

Haakon shook the captain's hand, beholden to this man for allowing him on board as a lost young buck long ago in the port of Norfolk, Virginia. The bruises Thor had pounded into him hadn't even been healed when he signed up to join this crew, and now he'd seen the northern hemisphere half a dozen times over. An adventure he'd only dreamt of as a boy.

While he didn't wish the last years away, there was one thing he would trade them for.

That he never would have given Thor cause to break down the door that day.

When a deckhand came by with a sopping mop, Haakon moved aside and joined his fellow mates in search of pay and papers. Funds were distributed, each man receiving in full what he was due. Whenever they sold cargo in port, the crew was paid half of their earned balance, but with the voyage at an end finances were squared away—this the completion of their service on the ice trade for the year.

While most of the men inked their names into the ledger for another season of service, Haakon couldn't get his hand to press the tip to the line.

Though some would seek positions aboard ships bound to new regions, Haakon didn't wish to sail for any vessel other than the one that had become his home. With such loyalty rallying, he nearly signed his name in that breath, but instead set the pen aside and shot out a sigh. He exchanged a look with the first mate who oversaw such transactions and then with the boatswain who was waiting to go ashore.

There were days yet to decide, so Haakon stepped away. He could come back later and commit once he had a chance to stretch his legs and clear his head. Now, with his wages in pounds sterling, he had a mind to satisfy that craving at the markets. He'd be wise to resupply on clothing and boots worn thin with hard labor and briny air, but the shirt on his back was sound yet, so he'd splurge on other wares.

For a few days, the crew would relish life at port while the captain and first mate procured the next round of cargo to be hauled to distant lands. Then the time would come to load the ship with sugar and spices. Once that was delivered across the deep, *Le Grelotter* would be chartered for new trades as she always was until winter winds hailed her back to Norway.

Enjoying the stretch of freedom, Haakon strode with his crewmen down the dock. Bobbing along the bay were several small vessels with fishermen towing in nets. On shore, baskets of fish filled carts to be hauled to the marketplace—the same direction Haakon and Tate aimed. Neither of them evoked attention to their fresh pay, Haakon's coins having been stored in a leather satchel around his neck. The small bag hung beneath his shirt, safely out of sight, and while he'd had thugs bully him about it before, they'd only ever come to regret it.

Just past the beaches, the market spread between balconied buildings and humble shanties. There, air flowed ripe with the smell of spices and fresh foods of the most exotic kinds. Tate secured a handful of roasted bread fruit, and Haakon bought some kind of grilled meat, nearly scorching both fingers and tongue to wolf it down. He got a second for Tate, then purchased a dram of rum, throwing the aged liquor back in one shot. As Haakon returned the wooden cup, Tate admired a colorful ladies fan. He opened and closed it with care.

Haakon eyed him. "*Really?*"

Tate chuckled. "Was thinking of it as a gift." He set the fan aside.

"You're honestly planning on going home, then?" Haakon bought his own roasted bread fruit and ate the soft flesh as they started on again. It was hardly sweeter than a potato but was easily the best taste he'd had in weeks.

Tate tore off a piece of the spiced meat. "Just as soon as I can procure passage to the States from here. I'll ask around tomorrow. I spoke to the captain last week and offered my resignation. He was disappointed, but he understood."

Haakon halted. "You're being serious."

"Did it sound like I wasn't?"

"You're actually going home?"

"I can't say it any more plainly."

"What about your brother?" For a season, Timothy Kennedy had sailed with them, but preferring the Scandinavian lands, Tate's brother had joined a crew on a well-paying Norwegian vessel in the

North Sea. They passed him now and again when they were in that stretch of ocean and had seen him but weeks ago.

"He's content." Tate bit another piece of meat, then licked the tip of his finger clean.

"You didn't try to talk him into coming with you?"

"He's a grown man. He knows what he's doing."

Probably why Tate wasn't trying to talk him into it either.

It would be so much easier if he did.

Having halted in front of a tavern without realizing, Haakon heard a feminine voice beckoning them from above. The busty islander leaned over an iron railing. Her skin was the color of melted chocolate, a sharp contrast to her painted lips of cherry red. She waved at them, and soon several more women came onto the balcony to garner interest from the newly arrived sailors milling about the market. Tate glanced at the women, then back to the path. Frustration flickered in the tightening of his eyes. He sniffed and crammed his hands in his pockets. Though he appeared collected, his composure always became more strained under such attentions.

Haakon grinned as he followed Tate farther down the street. Why his friend was determined to remain chaste these years at sea was something he couldn't begin to comprehend. As for himself, he made it a point to secure female company whenever he wished. For the rest of the crew who partook of such comforts, they sought it at taverns upon arrival into ports, but Haakon put off pleasantries of that nature until closer to departure. He bided his time, and it was during the days ashore that he browsed potential conquests.

Though tavern wenches were a tempting lot, he'd chosen to steer clear of them to avoid the disagreeable aftermaths that plagued some of his fellow men, and since he rather liked a challenge. Because of that, it was young women of the surrounding farmlands he sought. His pursuit of them was far from easy, but that was half the appeal.

As for Widow Jönsson, she hadn't so much as inferred an indulgence would happen between them. He sensed she had cared for him, which made her reasons awfully noble. That humbled him more than he wanted to admit. The fact that he kept thinking about her humbled him further.

He'd spotted her at a distance, during the beginning days of their ice harvest there. Seeing no man on her farm, Haakon had suggested to the captain that they procure some of her goat's milk. With the captain's agreement, Haakon had volunteered to hike up to her small farm and trade coin for jugs of the fresh milk she gleaned each morning. She said little to him that first day, but upon the second he learned that her husband had been buried only months before. On the third day Haakon motioned to a break in her fence and inquired as to if he might repair it for her.

And so had passed nearly three weeks of trying to court her. While the familiarity didn't produce what he'd wanted, she'd endeared herself to him in such a way that it vexed him that he couldn't remember her name. He'd always made it a point not to remember names, and as much as that shamed what was left of his soul, there was little he could do about it now.

He sensed she'd known that too. The night in her barn, as she'd bundled up the newest addition to her small herd, she'd looked at Haakon, and with the new life beating within her touch, whispered that she'd never seen a man so far away in his eyes. It was as though thousands of miles separated them, despite the fact that they sat side by side that snowy night. He'd hated how close she'd gotten to the truth. It was one of the reasons he'd risen that morning without waking her. He wasn't used to near strangers seeing more than he meant. Though he doubted she was naïve to the way he'd been living, she couldn't have been aware of Aven or his shame there.

While he wished for some way to amend that—he didn't know who he needed to speak to the most right now: the woman from

Kristiansand or the woman he'd left behind on Blackbird Mountain. Both were on distant sides of the Atlantic, one much nearer than the other. A reality that prodded him toward what he needed to do. Was he really ready, though? He had to be.

With some help for the journey in sight, Haakon slowed to a stop before an old man seated on a stone stoop. The man was hunched, legs so thin they didn't look like they would bear his scant weight. A knobby crutch sat beside him, but what captured Haakon's focus was the basket of coca leaves beside it.

Haakon freed several shillings from his pocket and dropped them in the merchant's hand. The man stacked six leaves and placed them on a shred of coarse cloth. Dissatisfied, Haakon shook his head. He pointed to the man's basket and gestured for more. The man babbled at him in words he didn't know.

"Can you help, please," Haakon called over to Tate.

Though having picked up languages well enough to secure the position as boatswain, Tate glanced to what Haakon aimed to buy, then shook his head.

"Please?" He was rather desperate.

"Sorry, no."

Perhaps a different approach, then . . .

Haakon thought of the four French words he knew and used them in random succession. With all of them quite colorful, the old man went wide eyed, then angered. He spat a slew of words back.

Tate rushed over. "What is wrong with you?" he huffed at Haakon, then to the vendor, "*Je vous demande pardon.*" He went on to explain something more—probably describing that Haakon was ill in the head as a way to appease for whatever it was he'd said. Tate finished with another apology. "*Veuillez m'excuser.*"

"*Veuillez m'excuser,*" Haakon mimicked and motioned to the basket. At least he'd gotten Tate over here to help.

But his friend just pulled off his spectacles and used the hem of

his shirt to polish the first eye piece. "He says that's all you get." He
started on the second round of glass.

Irritated, Haakon pulled out enough coin to feed a Barbadian for
weeks. The merchant's eyes widened again. "Tell him this is his if he
does a proper job." In the coming weeks he was going to need all the
courage he could get. More courage than he'd ever needed in his life.

"I'm not helping you with that," Tate said.

"*Please*."

"I guess you should learn to make more friends." Backing away,
Tate started off again.

Biting back a growl, Haakon crouched and lowered the money for
the merchant to see. With unhurried movements, the man counted
out two dozen leaves. Haakon waited and the merchant added four
more. Satisfied, Haakon nodded.

The purchase was bound up, tied with a length of grass, and
handed over. The leaves inside were valued like gold in some parts of
the world. Even buried with the dead. So with care, Haakon stashed
the package in the pouch he kept around his neck. Later, he'd hide
some in his pack—stitching them inside the canvas as a reserve that
even his fellow seaman didn't know about. If he rationed this, it would
last for a few months. He tried not to think about what would happen
when he ran out. In that moment, he recalled Thor's suffering upon
quitting the bottle. That had been voluntary, but it had been a fierce
withdrawal all the same.

Haakon straightened the cord around his neck and stepped away.
Coca wasn't something that could be procured in the states, let alone
Blackbird Mountain.

It made him crazy to be thinking of going home.

Doubly crazy for jogging through the marketplace to catch up
to his friend. Downright insane for gripping Tate's arm, halting him,
and with a struggle to catch a breath, asking him to secure passage
home not just for one . . . but for two.

EIGHT

MAY 5, 1895
BLACKBIRD MOUNTAIN, VIRGINIA

THOUGH THE MEMORY WAS AS THICKLY HAZED
as his delirium had been that long ago day, Thor could recall a time
when he had clamored down the hallway of the house, both Jorgan
and Haakon trying to hold him down with all their might. It was
shortly after his twenty-eighth birthday, and he'd spent days locked
in the attic as a way to keep others safe during the hallucinations that
quaked him from a loss of alcohol. From the choice he'd made to try
and let the bottle go.

It was because of that delirium that Thor had broken out of the
attic, forgetting even his resolve to stay shut away. Knowing the dangers, Haakon had chased him down the hallway, tackling him against
the wall so hard they'd nearly ripped a hole through. Jorgan put up
as good of a fight, and even Ida's nephew, Al, had rushed in to help.
Crazed, Thor dragged them all forward, desperate and bewitched by
his cravings. He punched and thrashed, doing everything he could to
get free, surrendering on the stairs only when he'd blacked out from
sheer exhaustion.

That had been three to one, and still Thor nearly beat them.

So this? The fact that it was with a trembling hand that he removed a box of bullets from the gun cabinet in the cidery?

Thor set the box aside, then withdrew Haakon's brass-receivered Winchester and laid the levergun beside it. His skin was flushed, but the task was mellow enough that at least he wasn't out of breath. Still, this wasn't who he was. Never had something stood in his way that he couldn't put up a fight with. But whatever ailed him . . . It wasn't frightened.

Quite the opposite. It was a bully, this illness, and if it meant to break him, it was doing an awful good job of it. But like that day in the hallway, it was going to have to beat him. No surrender here. There had to be another way . . . Something he hadn't thought of yet.

Thor checked that Haakon's rifle was empty. Built in 1866, the Winchester Yellowboy was one that Haakon had saved up for. While Thor wasn't interested in using Haakon's things, the levergun was a sure shot and handsome enough to be stolen should the cidery be broken into again. Thor fetched a box of .44 rimfires. While he and Jorgan kept plenty of firearms in the house, he'd use this one should the need arise.

Forehead clammy, Thor ran his sleeve over it. He couldn't shake the urge to sit down but didn't want to give in to this growing weakness.

In a brush of her patchwork skirt, Aven entered the vast workshop, joining him as she often did. Upon reaching his side, she touched his arm. A gesture that most folks did to secure his attention. As for Aven, she had his focus the moment she was near . . . and for most of the time that she wasn't. Thor gave her a gentle smile and while she smiled back, her eyes were awash with worry.

"How are you feeling?"

He tapped a thumb to his chest for *fine*, then, knowing that he ought to be more forthright with his wife, he touched his fingertips to his lips, then pressed that hand downward for *bad*.

In her face lived the depth of her concern. "Is there anything I can get you?"

Stay, he beseeched her.

Aven squeezed his hand, and when he reached back into the cabinet, she edged around him, remaining near all the while. A common sight it was to find her or Fay dusting shelves, counting jars, or planning a fresh batch of goods to restock the product shelves. For today, Aven set to the task of tidying, and he more than appreciated her company. Today it brought a bolstering he desperately needed.

In a way that bespoke her years at his side, she fetched a broom and swept dried apple leaves from behind a stack of crates, releasing the faintest aroma of autumn into the air. When she finished, she moved a pile of greased rags from beside the cider press that, while the most dominating contraption in this barn, wouldn't be used until the apples were picked that autumn.

Aven beckoned for his attention, and he watched her mouth. "We ought to choose a name for a girl."

Was that what she had come here for? One side of his mouth lifted in a smile. *Idea you?* he signed.

"A few, but I don't know that you would fancy them. How about you?"

Same. He requested she share hers.

"Well, I was rather thinking of flowers. Perhaps Rose or Daisy. Or maybe Iris."

He was making a sour face, he could feel it. Norgaards stemmed from a lineage of solid Norse names. Even their old dog's name had hailed from the motherland. He didn't want to name anybody Iris.

She flashed a winsome look. "I can tell just what you're thinking."

You not know. Thor softened his expression as he removed two boxes of buckshot from the cabinet.

"Oh yes I do." Aven gripped her hip and stood as tall as possible, face stern. He really hoped that's not what she thought he looked like. "All

Norgaards must have good strong names. Viking names." She formed a fist, holding it in the air with gusto. "Names like Ulf and Torstein."

He chuckled, not about to admit that she was right. But . . . something was coming to mind ever since her mention of flowers. Thor fingerspelled it. *T-U-S-E-N-F-R-Y-D.*

Surprise registered in her face. "What was that?"

He shaped each letter more slowly.

"Tusenfryd?"

He nodded, formed a fist, and using two pinched fingers from his other hand, mimicked the plucking of petals in hopes she would understand the sign. *Daisy. N-O-R-W-E-G-I-A-N.*

"Oh." Aven spoke the name again, seeming hesitant. Perhaps it sounded strange to the ear? He didn't know. He only knew that he liked the way the letters moved on his hand. The way it felt to shape them. It felt whole and right and pretty.

Her skirts swayed as she hung up another picking bag. "Tusenfryd. Little Tusie," she said to herself. "Tusie-Daisy."

He grinned, pretty sure she was going to try it every which way before answering.

She continued her pondering, her belly round and high, their child folded in there like a bud. No wonder she had flowers on her mind. With it being spring, Aven's skin was still winter pale, making the freckles across her nose and cheeks more pronounced. As vibrant an amber as her hair that tumbled to her waist, where the ends brushed against a figure that was shapely in a softer way these days. It struck him—as it often did—a wanting for her to know his affection. How he longed to please her somehow. For her to know that there wasn't a dullness in his heart for her. Not even close.

How long had it been since he'd enjoyed her company as marriage vows encouraged? It had been weeks now. His worsening ailment and her own need for rest had more and more nights serving only the purpose of sleep.

When he cleared his throat, Aven smiled over her shoulder.

Maybe just for a moment . . .

Thor strode to his wife, set down the boxes of bullets on the workbench in front of her, and had just eased her hair from her neck to lower a kiss there when the door slid open.

Of course.

He sidestepped Aven as more light spilled into the workspace. Someone entered, and so bright was the day that Thor couldn't tell who it was until the person neared. Peter.

The young man slowed and glanced from Thor to Aven, whose cheeks were flushed.

"This a bad time?" Peter asked.

Thor tried to conjure up a response, but all he landed on was a scowl.

Peter's shirt was stained from his work in the orchards, and he fetched up the hem to run it over his forehead. The hint of a smile he'd shown faded as he spoke. "I've come to speak to you about Pawpaw . . . and my pa."

Jed and Harlan. Important enough that Aven gave Thor's hand a squeeze and excused herself. Thor watched her go, then turned to his farmhand. It had been four years now since the Sorrel family had split down the center: those loyal to Jed's beliefs and those who weren't. The ones who'd stuck around had been peaceful neighbors in the time since. Now, with matters astir, there couldn't have been a more accurate messenger than Jed's own grandson. Thor would be lying if he didn't admit that there were moments he wondered if Peter could betray them, but season after season, Peter had proven his loyalty.

Any doubts were unjustified.

"None of my folks have seen or heard a thing, but that don't mean they're not here." The cadence of Peter's mouth was somber but his eyes were unwavering and unafraid. "Ma doesn't think Pa'll come back around—Pawpaw neither—but we all know those two are awful good at doin' what you least expect."

After the decree painted across the side of this shop, Thor didn't doubt that Jed's remaining men were just a stone's throw away, camped out in the woods somewhere.

In fact, he wouldn't be surprised if they knew that Aven had walked here alone.

The thought sickened him, but all that was within his and Jorgan's power was to protect the farm and keep their families close. If there were men of crueler make prowling this mountain, they wouldn't stay hidden for long. While Peter had already been informed of his father's falsified meeting with the doctor, there had been nothing more to do but send the letter to the bureau and prepare for the next incident. This time they wouldn't be taken by surprise.

Muscles aching, Thor pulled a stool near and sat. Peter's mouth set to moving again. Vision unsteady, Thor blinked quickly and signaled for the young man to repeat himself.

"You feelin' alright?"

Since being vulnerable was easier with his wife, Thor tipped his hand from side to side to indicate *somewhat*.

Peter didn't look convinced. "Pa's wanted in two counties, and Pawpaw's wanted in a heap more. There's a list of charges against them a mile long. A sheriff came in from Roanoke and with his men searched our property high and low. They're searchin' roundabout a ways too. Don't know that they're gonna find much, but if Pa and Pawpaw Jed are watchin', they'll think twice about raisin' trouble."

Thor hoped so. But he doubted it. Peter gnawed the side of his lip as if doubting it too.

Wanted or not, Jed Sorrel didn't seem the type to shy away from revenge.

It was the very reason Thor had unlocked the gun cabinet today. The sheriff and his men would soon be gone, and the men who lay hidden would have less cause to stay that way. Needing to know what Peter's kin was wanted for, Thor freed the small notebook and stubby pencil from his shirt pocket. He wrote the question, and Peter scrawled a response. The man's silence only underlined the dire situation. As he waited, Thor removed his shotgun from the storage space and the extra barrel that was rifled. After closing the cabinet, he locked it well.

When Peter finished writing, Thor accepted the notebook back. He struggled with Peter's rough spelling, but understood enough to dread what these men were capable of. Heartsick for those who had been injured and worse, Thor tore out the sheet and folded it up tight. He'd show Jorgan, and together they would express to all those in their care just what kind of evil lurked in these woods.

Thor handed Peter the boxes of ammunition, then the rifle. He longed to rid the cidery boards of the Sorrels' tarnishing, but needing to rest, he went back to his workbench and grabbed the business ledger as well as the latest rounds of invoices and receipts. Just the way to settle at the table until dark. Thor was just stacking all the documents together when Peter came near and shook his shoulder. Looking to his farmhand and friend, Thor saw that Peter was pointing to the doorway.

Ida stood there, eyes wide and her words so quick, Thor struggled to understand. "Someone's come for you, Thor." She pressed a hand to her heaving chest.

He formed the sign for *who?*

"A doctor. From Fincastle." Ida swallowed hard. "He's come over in a rush. Came soon as he got your note, he said." She glanced behind her and hustled aside as a young doctor hurried into the cider barn. The tailored man looked around the dim space, finally spotting Thor, and it was there in the physician's face . . . a panic. One that sealed Thor's every fear.

NINE

'TWAS DEATH THAT LOOMED IN TOO MANY memories. First, her mother's frail body waning within the stone walls of the workhouse. Then it was Benn, who had taken his own life— surrendering both his breath and his marriage vows in one wretched choice. So when Ida came to fetch her in the garden, saying a doctor had just arrived from Fincastle, Aven couldn't get the willow gate unlatched quick enough. More so at sight of the sweat-drenched stallion that Peter was brushing down. Sparse droplets of rain fell, but she scarcely felt them as she hurried down to the house.

That Ida didn't chide her for nearly running in her condition made this reality all the more grave.

"Where are they?" Aven panted as she rounded the side of the house, Ida limping along behind. Aven slowed to aid her but was waved off with a sharp hand.

"Leave me, I'm comin'. The doctor took Thor upstairs," Ida called. "You get there."

Clouds churned gray overhead—a spring storm just beginning. Aven rushed into the dim house, up the first set of stairs, down the long hallway, then climbed the curving stairwell that led to the attic. There, Jorgan and a second man stood in the doorway.

Aven meant to squeeze by, desperate for Thor, but the young doctor gripped her arm before another step fell.

"Please, my husband." She pulled at his hold.

"Ma'am, I need you to remain here."

Aven looked to where Thor stood in the center of the bedroom. He held up a hand, urging her to stay put. What was happening?

"He may be infectious." The doctor slowly released her. Perhaps no older than herself, he flashed a sympathetic petition from wide-set eyes. "I am Dr. Abramson, and I've come to aid him. Please, remain here."

"What do you mean?"

"Allow me to examine your husband and I'll have more answers." Breathless and speckled in road dust, the physician removed his black hat. He crossed the room in determined strides, where he greeted Thor, set his bag on the end of the bed, and opened it with a snap. "Can someone please ask him to be seated?"

Jorgan stomped a foot, shuddering the floorboards to garner Thor's glazed focus, and made the sign for *sit*. Thor moved to the bed and heeded his request.

The doctor tipped Thor's head back to study his eyes, then with the same ease of movement took Thor's pulse. Not a sound was made in the room until the man lowered Thor's wrist and rifled through his bag. "Your pulse is slow, but steady."

Thor looked to Aven for help.

"Slow but steady," she repeated, then to the doctor, "If you can face him when you speak, he'll understand better."

"My apologies." His straight brows slanted to Thor even as he slid a hand into place to apply a mild pressure to Thor's abdomen. This time he aimed his question directly. "Does this hurt?"

Thor shook his head.

"Any vomiting?"

Thor fingerspelled *N-A-U-S-E-A-T-E-D*, and Jorgan explained.

Sliding a hand to Thor's other side, the doctor pressed again. With a gasp, Thor shoved the man's hand away.

The doctor took two steps back. "Tender. My apologies."

With a note of trepidation in his eyes, Thor nodded. His sharp panting rattled the room.

A kind hand touched his shoulder. "Take a moment to catch your breath."

As Thor struggled to do so, the physician requested water be brought up.

"'Tis just here." Aven nearly moved to the pitcher on its stand, but the doctor intervened. He filled a tin cup and offered Thor the water. It wasn't until the cup was returned to the nightstand that he spoke.

"As stated, my name is Dr. Abramson." He surveyed all in the room. "I've recently taken over the physician post in Fincastle where I received Mr. Norgaard's note and list of symptoms. The missive brought me here straightaway."

He spoke toward Thor again. "I regret to make your acquaintance under such circumstances but offer my services." He lifted the back of Thor's shirt and examined his skin there. After lowering the hem, he angled for Thor to see him speaking. "I can't yet offer a diagnosis, but must insist you stay abed. Rest may restore your strength—but I don't believe it will cure you."

"Have you no inclinations?" Aven asked, desperate for answers. Grief pooled in her chest.

"We'll begin with this . . ." He spoke directly to Thor. "I suspect this is an ailment involving the liver. There are only a few causes for that. To be honest, Mr. Norgaard, your reputation has preceded you, but I'm not here to diagnose you on hearsay. If you've consumed hard drink in your life, may I inquire as to what degree?"

Thor nodded regretfully, then looked to Jorgan for help.

"Yes, sir," Jorgan began. "He's had more than a man ought to in the past and would say the same."

"And are you drinking still?"

Thor shook his head, and Jorgan spoke for him. "Four years sober now."

The child in Aven's belly kicked, and she pressed a hand there.

Dr. Abramson's eyes moved in Jorgan's direction. "You're certain?"

"Quite."

The earnestness in Thor's expression declared all that Jorgan had. Except it was then that Aven realized Thor's silent appeal was to her.

Did he fear her belief in him and his word? Having been wedded to Thor's cousin until his death, Aven knew what it was to have lain beside Benn in their tiny flat on the Norwegian coast and, instead of smelling the crisp sea air or the fish markets up the dock, to have noticed the spiced liquor he was so fond of. It had lived on his skin and in his every breath.

But with Thor?

She had witnessed him surrender the bottle during her first weeks here, and it was with a cautious unfolding that their friendship had formed and then deepened. When Thor had outlasted the worst of his drying-out, he proved it to be a vow he stood by. She had witnessed Benn surrender his will, but 'twas Thor who demonstrated that a man could turn his back on the bottle should his determination run deep enough. He had spent the seasons that followed proving it to be so. She knew it in the gentle touch he had with her, the sweetness of his kisses, and the desertion of a trade that had been sacred to him.

Aven stepped forward, so overcome with a need to comfort Thor that she forgot the doctor's insistence until it was Jorgan who halted her this time.

Compassion flooded the doctor's face. "In this instance, then, the liver should no longer be declining, but it appears it may be." He accepted the chair Jorgan carried over and sat facing Thor. "This leads me to a second theory, which may answer your question, Mrs. Norgaard. During the War, an outbreak of jaundice and abdominal pain afflicted soldiers. It produced joint discomfort and, in some cases, vomiting. The illness affected tens of thousands of soldiers on both sides of the Mason-Dixon Line. Causes of the jaundice remain disputed. Most agree that unsanitary conditions were a culprit. That doesn't seem to be the case here, which indicates a different cause. I cannot say for certain what that might be."

He rose and with care studied the whites of Thor's eyes, which in this light seemed to bear a yellowed tint. Aven took a small step closer—certain her own sight was deceiving her.

"If you have consumed no alcohol in the last several years, you may be suffering from this illness that infected your liver as opposed to wearing it out. How you've come by this infection will be worth investigating. How to restore your health and prevent spread of the disease is of even greater importance."

"Are you saying it's contagious?" Jorgan asked.

"If this is the same plague rampant during the Civil War, it is imperative that Mr. Norgaard be quarantined. With no certainty of how it's spread, caution is vital. I do not know the full nature of Epidemic Jaundice, but I'll begin inquiries at once. As for now, all of you may be at risk, and with children in the house—not to mention your delicate state, Mrs. Norgaard—your husband needs to be quarantined immediately. Be on the lookout for any developing symptoms amongst yourselves." He rose from his chair and placed his medic bag on the seat. "While this may be discouraging news, take heart that soldiers with proper care made regular recovery."

He closed his bag, then moved to the washstand, where he soaped and rinsed his hands. "I've a colleague in Vermont. A friend and mentor who once worked on the front lines." Dr. Abramson shook droplets from his hands. "He will undoubtedly know more, so I'll send a telegram and continue my own study. For now, I advise we find Mr. Norgaard a more secluded location."

Thor lowered his face—something he never did. 'Twas as though he wanted to see no more of what was said. Or worse, what he already knew.

"What if it's not this epidemic?" Aven asked through a tightening throat.

The doctor drew in a heavy breath. "With that type of drinking history, if his liver is instead failing of its own accord, he will have a short while yet to live."

At that, Aven could scarcely see beyond Thor. Even as she peered upon her beloved, there was a wrenching in her heart so deep she feared it might harm the baby. Such grief that she barely knew how to stay standing. For when Dr. Abramson returned to his bag and took hold of the leather handle, he added, "If this ailment is not Epidemic Jaundice, then your husband, Mrs. Norgaard, is dying."

TEN

THOR SAT ON THE EDGE OF THE BED IN A
room so hollow it may as well have been a tomb. He was alone now,
per the doctor's advice, but if he knew anything about his family, he
wouldn't be alone for long. He imagined everyone downstairs discuss-
ing what should be done. He didn't need to be there to guess what
would be said. Aven would be the most adamant to be allowed to care
for him, but it was paramount she see reason.

Next he thought of Jorgan, who had cared for him when he
sobered from hard drink. Jorgan had sat with him through the worst
of it. Through the terrors and the vomiting and every misery in
between. If anyone was capable of seeing a body through the furthest
reaches of awful, it was Jorgan. But with a wife and two children,
Jorgan didn't belong anywhere near him either.

Then there would be Ida with her heart of gold and a grit that
defied her age. She'd volunteer without pause, but Thor would no
more burden her with caring for him than he would anyone else. So
with a settled resolve he rose and reached for his coat. Sliding it on
took great effort, but if he was going to do this, he needed to be able
to fend for himself. He made slow work with the buttons but was too
chilled to let it hang open. He ached for more water, but overriding

all thirst was the pain it caused to empty his bladder. Worse than that discomfort was the lump in his throat that became harder and harder to fight.

A sweet ache it was, loving Aven, because life would part them some day. Sheer agony overrode that tenfold at the knowledge that the day could be soon.

The doctor's optimism offered a hope that he suffered only from this strange epidemic. But so dreadful were the symptoms, and with children about, Thor couldn't pose his family further risk. There would be time in the coming days to ponder the alternate outcome, but for now he stepped gingerly toward the dresser and opened his lidded box there. He had need of a key that had sat forgotten for years. All the more bewildering to find it not on the bottom of the box as expected but on the top of everything else. Had it been used recently?

There was little point in wondering, so Thor opened the door. Use of the handrail got him down the steps, and he took his time across the second-floor hallway. When he descended the bottom flight of stairs, it was to find the family deep in conversation. Fay sat in a chair near the window. Jorgan stood behind her, both hands on his wife's shoulders. His thumb worked against the fabric of her blouse collar, grazing a curve of lace. The doctor stood nearest the windows, backlit by a sun so low Thor couldn't make out his face and moving lips. But by his mannerisms, he was in grave discourse with them all.

Thor didn't try to interrupt and instead waited until one by one they drew still. He saw it only in his peripheral vision as his focus had shifted to Aven. She cradled both arms beneath her stomach—eyes on him and him alone. He wanted to pull her close with an assurance that all would be fine. He wanted to believe it himself, which made sight of her and their child all the more sobering.

Jorgan gestured for his attention, and Thor shifted to see him better. "I'm gonna go with you."

Ida limped nearer, capturing Thor's focus next. "Nonsense. I raised you since you were just a tyke, and if you think you's goin' anywhere without me, you got another thing comin'."

He loved her for it—both of them—but Thor stepped aside. Jorgan hedged his path and spoke something that Thor couldn't make out as he moved around his brother again. It was hard to sign at the same time, but Thor managed. *Cabin.* He took another step toward the kitchen. *Alone.*

With both arms, Ida waved him down. "Who's gonna help you?"

He touched his chest, made the sign for *help,* then touched his chest again.

Aven stepped forward, garnering his attention. "And what of care? What of meals?"

They could leave food just outside. Thor implied as much, and needing to pull himself away from his wife, he strode through the kitchen, and opened the door. The cool of dusk brushed against his neck, and he raised his collar as shivers broke loose inside him.

Once beneath the gray sky, he glanced back to make certain no one followed. He didn't look back again until he'd reached the stand of trees that separated the great house from Haakon's cabin. His steps were slow as pain wormed up his side. Darkness that had nothing to do with the coming night edged around his vision as it had done in the few days prior. Lightheaded, he braced a hand against a tree. This was no time to pass out. He took steadying breaths until his vision righted. The scant daylight that remained was enough to see by, and there, in the distance, stood the outline of Haakon's cabin. Thor stepped into the yard, and only then did he glance back again.

Everyone was coming, though the distance between him and them meant they'd been arguing. Aven was the farthest along, with her skirts clutched up in a hand and her small feet nearly running. No doubt she'd won. Jorgan was rushing to catch up to her. Despite the intensity of Jorgan's speech—a pleading for her to see reason—Aven didn't acknowledge him. Nor did she heed the doctor who was fast to reach her other side.

Thor forced himself to move quicker so she wouldn't catch up to him. His gait was a bitter limp, and a groan scraped up his throat. Grief sank its stone into his chest, and he nearly stumbled. Just a short distance to go. Thor knew he lacked the strength to make it, so was walking on borrowed mettle, shutting his mind off from all pain as he trudged onward. Haakon's cabin grew bigger the nearer he drew.

How he hated this place.

But it was the only fitting spot he could think of. Secluded, secure, and near enough to the house to be practical. Thor pressed on, though his mind was beginning to lose its grip on determination. Pain flamed, demanding he slow. As he did, his boots skidded over a mass of south-bound tracks made not by animals but by men. From the different sizes and makes of bootprints . . . perhaps half a dozen of them. Not only did they cross this way through the yard, they circled the cabin like a pack of wolves.

Sorrels.

They'd been here and weren't being shy about it.

Suddenly someone was in his side vision. Thor nearly stumbled again but it was only Jorgan. His brother spouted off alternate ways for Thor to rest in safety, and Thor snapped off the hand sign for *no* as he backed farther away. Holding his palms up peaceably, he tried to get them both to stop. For pity's sake, at least Aven.

When she kept after him, Thor growled her name. "Av—" The only part he could ever manage. Except he'd never spoken it so roughly.

While he knew not the sound, it had to be as sharp as he'd intended because Aven halted at the force.

How sweet her name was to him. Always said as a cherishing. In this moment it was the same cherishing that drove his determination to protect her. He prayed she knew that.

With Jorgan having yet to notice the tracks, Thor considered not pointing them out. It only deepened the danger of this place and would be yet another reason for Jorgan to urge him elsewhere, but with the likelihood of Aven or Ida now crossing this wooded grove to reach Haakon's cabin, he had to do something to warn them.

Thor snapped for Jorgan's attention, then pointed to the ground. Jorgan's gaze trailed along the tracks all the way around the side of the cabin. The gravity of what this meant wasn't lost in Jorgan's paling face, and when he looked back at Thor, there was pleading in his eyes.

"You can't do this."

He had to. *Guard A-V-E-N, you.*

"Thor, don't do this."

Thor repeated the word for *guard*, then pointed back to his wife.

"Of course, Thor. I promise."

He made the signs for *gun* and *bring*, then pointed to himself.

Finally Jorgan nodded. "I'll fetch you two."

Shivers quaked him so hard that Thor could scarcely extend his gratitude. Beholden to his brother, he backed away. The last person he saw as he climbed the porch steps was the doctor. The young man gave him a nod of understanding, and if Thor wasn't mistaken, there was hope in his steely gaze, as if the doctor believed there would be good at the end of this.

With his strength sapped, Thor harnessed that force of assurance as he climbed the last step. His hands shook as he fished the key from his pocket. He pressed his way in and didn't look back as he entered walls that housed the final, bleak memories of Haakon. He surveyed the far end of the room where they had brawled, then, pulling his eyes from the past still tainting the first floor, Thor bolted the door shut behind him, fixed his gaze on the stairs, and determined to climb them.

ELEVEN

THE FOG MAY AS WELL HAVE CLEARED JUST for them. Upon nearing the United States coast, the sea air no longer spread as thick as their breakfast of overcooked oats. Now the sun could be seen just shy of noon over buildings that wove along the South Carolina coastline. Church steeples rose above the knobby roofline, their height and majesty trumped only by the masts of the ships that anchored there.

Though the plantation system had collapsed, taking down this seaside economy and its shipments of slaves, Charleston was once again a booming hub as one of the busiest cargo terminals in the American Southeast. It was that energy and familiarity that Haakon wished he could sidestep, but this was just the first taste of home. The illustrious Charleston was a shy reckoning to what stepping foot on Blackbird Mountain would be.

Days ago, Haakon and Tate had disembarked *Le Grelotter* and, with salutes from their crewmembers, watched the vessel sail away from Barbados until it was only a speck on the horizon. A farewell as hard as all the others. With a homeward current calling them, he and Tate had joined the small crew of a two-masted schooner bound for America, bunking down in the hold among sacks of rice and cakes of indigo. Their labor above deck had paid for the nine-day passage, and now they bid their thanks and started down the narrow gangway.

When Haakon reached American ground, it felt as weighty as when he had raced along such a dock . . . running from his past and toward a future that, while taking him far and wide on this great earth, had brought him back to the very same coastline.

Workers milled about, some stacking heavy sacks, others moving loaded wagons by horseback. Men bellowed commands to one another, while interspersed throughout the chaos were women and children who had come to greet the seamen. Some ladies stood on tiptoe as though awaiting husbands. Others shielded their eyes, scanning the tanned and grizzly faces in search of who might have been brothers or fathers.

Haakon did his best to weave around passersby, but all at once he saw a woman in the distance looking his way. She was a petite thing, straining to try and see over the crowd gathered. Her smile was as bright as the sun shining on her coal-black hair, and never had Haakon seen such anticipation.

Did she know him? He'd encountered enough women along his travels that faces were hard to recognize.

Then one of the crewmembers he'd recently met burst past Haakon with a jolly "'Scuse me, mate!"

Upon reaching the woman, the sailor pulled her into a hug so tight that her laugh slipped out breathless. Her eyes glistened as she beheld the man who must have been her husband, judging by the ring Haakon now saw on her finger. A gentle banding upon the same hand that reached up to loop around the man's neck.

Lowering his sight, Haakon stepped past them. He pulled his

pack forward and dug around for his pocket watch. Finding it, he scanned the time as a way to busy himself. Some way to strip away thoughts of home and who he'd left behind. A moment to regain his wits and be prodded by the reminder that the woman he desperately needed to make amends with was not only wed but wedded to his brother.

Beside him, Tate hitched his pack higher up his shoulder, flashing a newly earned bandage that wrapped his forearm. They walked on as investors discussed pricing and exchanges while travelers gauged their whereabouts. Mariners of every size and color filled out the rest of the crowd, some exchanging wares with one another, others destined for new vessels and crews. Striking his way through the thick of it all, Haakon had never been so uncertain about who he was or where he belonged. Here he walked, foreign and lost in his own country.

"I think this is the way," he called to Tate before edging between a loaded cart and a brick building.

A coach clattered by, and his ears warmed against the tinkling laugh of a southern belle and the low, smooth drawl of her gentleman. Had Haakon really spent most of his life here? While Charleston was a few days south of the Norgaard orchards, these folks were American through and through, making him only a short train ride to the backwoods he called home.

Searching for the train depot, Haakon headed farther from the waterfront, and beside him Tate took in the sights. As they walked, Haakon realized there would be no more sea shanties. Never again would they stand on the forecastle as the four-hundred-ton brig dipped and crashed over the swell. No more nights sitting beneath stars while winds cold enough to shape icebergs cut through their coats, even as laughter and stories kept them merry. There would be no more glow of the Northern Lights or dorsal fins beneath a rounded moon. He would never forget the stormy nights belowdecks or the creak of rope and wood as they worked alongside a crew so noble Haakon had scarcely known how to watch their home ship sail away.

In the distance, a train whistle blew.

He was stepping away from a life molded and shaped by survival and comradery . . . bound for a life that had once held the same.

Pretty sure his next days would be bent more on survival than comradery, Haakon wondered why he'd thought any of this going-home business was a wise idea. Maybe he should skip the part of his plan that involved walking into another pummeling by Thor Norgaard. Maybe he could settle here instead. Find a wife and make a decent living in this portside town. The world was a big place, and there was nothing that had to draw him back to Blackbird Mountain.

Nothing but his own conscience that would continue to haunt him.

Tate knelt and opened the top flap of his pack. "There's something I want to give you." He rose again, his Bible in hand. He opened the black book, licked his thumb, and sifted toward the middle, where he slowed his search, ending it by tearing out a sheet.

Haakon's eyebrows lifted, but Tate just folded the paper in half. He handed it over.

Uncertain, Haakon accepted the offering.

"There's the answer to your question, and it's also the reason why you didn't need to jump that night."

So Tate had seen him pitch himself overboard after all. No wonder Tate had dove in first. It was a debt Haakon could never begin to repay.

Rising, Tate inhaled a deep breath, and he squinted in a way that had nothing to do with light. "It's been an honor, my friend."

Haakon nodded, hating the swell of sadness that tightened his throat. "Why are you saying all this? We're getting on the train." He started in that direction but Tate didn't budge.

"No. I've got some business to do at the bank."

"What do you mean?"

There was a hint of regret in Tate's face as he asked, "Did you get paid in coin?"

Haakon nodded. Gold sovereigns and sterling shillings—the currency of Barbados and tender he was in no rush to exchange. Gold and silver would speak the right language in Appalachia, and as for the train ticket he needed, there were a few US dollars in his pack for the occasion.

"Well, I got paid in British banknotes."

"Oh."

As boatswain, Tate made much more aboard ship than Haakon did as an able seaman. He should have realized Tate would receive paper slips instead of a mound of coinage.

"I'll wait with you," Haakon offered. "While you switch it to dollars." He was in no hurry.

"Nonsense. The bank won't be open 'til Monday, and this train is leaving soon. You'll be home by the time I'm done. There's no sense in waiting."

Haakon looked down the street one way and then the other. Last, he glanced over his shoulder toward the depot, wishing for answers.

"Haakon. Go on."

Whether alone or with his friend, he didn't know how to get on that train.

"I can get home from here without your help." Tate consulted a brass pocket watch. "More notably, you can get home without mine." He smiled again.

Haakon shook his head. Tate didn't understand the hulking force of Norwegian revenge awaiting him back home. "I think I might . . ."

At thought of his brother, memories and worries collided in his brain, making a mess of his vision, his plan, his hopes. Everything. Maybe he would just stay where he was standing for a while. Give this day a chance to sink in. It was happening too fast.

Then again, maybe four years had been plenty long.

Haakon swallowed hard, scared senseless of standing before Thor again, but whether or not he stalled a few more days, he would still be facing his brother alone. Maybe there was no point in prolonging the event.

How different this was than the maritime orders he'd grown used to following. Haakon hadn't realized how accustomed he'd gotten to such a way of life until this moment when his very own boatswain held no authority over him anymore. Now Tate was just a farm boy again, and so was he. They were on the North Atlantic no longer. The surface beneath his boots didn't rock and creak, and there was no work to be done. No wind to catch save the one that would carry him home.

It was time. And he needed to be the one to make the choice.

Haakon ran a hand over his face. He had to get on that train. The locomotive was about to depart, and with the line at the distant ticket window over a dozen patrons long, he took a step forward and extended a hand to Tate. Season after season they'd traveled together, and now he had nothing to offer but a handshake. "It's been an honor."

Tate gripped it tight in a way that spanned every adventure. "Likewise."

Haakon stepped back. Though too much of him felt the weight of yet another farewell, there was no sense in getting any more sentimental. He stepped farther away, flashed Tate one final wave, and hurried toward the train on its tracks. Without a ticket he'd just have to cram in and pay later. Ill-advised for a body to do, but he'd broken bigger rules than this before.

Haakon smirked as he jogged along because there he was again— the man who took the turbulence of life by the horns and roughed it up right back. It was such a freeing feeling that he latched onto the hope that he could do this.

He had to do this.

With a final whistle, the engine groaned forward, steel wheels churning a slow rotation along the tracks. Still yards shy of the rolling freight, Haakon quickened his jog and paced alongside the nearest passenger car. The speed was slack yet, but it would pick up quickly. He gripped the handle beside the open doorway and swung himself onto the step and inside.

After blinking against the dim light, he found himself in a car so packed it offered not a sliver of sitting room left. He didn't mind standing, but there wasn't any room for that either.

At a shuffling on his right he noticed a large family making space for him. The father pulled a young girl onto his knee to free up the end of their bench. Haakon nodded his thanks and worked his way down the aisle. He sat and crammed his pack on the floor between his boots that had been repaired with thick, waxed thread. The canvas bag seemed too small to hold what he had left in the world, but there it was: A change of clothes. Some hardtack. An old compass and a tin of soda bicarbonate. Last of all the drawing given to him by the widow's middle boy.

The whistle sounded again. People cast him curious glances. He must look a sight. His face hadn't seen a razor in years, and though his hair was pulled back in a short tail at the nape of his neck, he was as gritty and briny as the piling of a pier. His eyes were tired, his heart sore, and he probably stank to high heaven. More than anything, he was exhausted. Both in body and soul. Although a hoard of people filled this car, each one was a stranger, making him more alone than he'd been in a good long while.

Leaning forward allowed him to see out the nearest window where the Atlantic glittered with coming sunset. This was the bitter end of his journey—the end of the rope. There was nothing left to tie off or cut away. It was just him and home now.

Another day, two tops, and he would see Thor. Even harder, he would see Aven.

What would his family do when he arrived? Would he just knock on the front door, or would he find someone in the yard first? He wondered if his old dog would sound the alarm. Or was Grete no longer living? What of Ida? She'd been up there in years when he'd left. What if he returned to find her already gone? He didn't want to fathom it.

Tate's Bible passage still in hand, Haakon balanced it on the top of his thigh, and though people watched on, he pulled a leaf from the pouch hanging around his neck. He was going to need all the courage he could muster to face what was ahead, so he fetched the tin of soda bicarbonate from his pack and sprinkled white powder onto the coca. He wadded it up tight to mash the elements together. With practiced fingers, Haakon crammed the concoction into his cheek. An older woman across the aisle widened her eyes, and he tried to appear as nonchalant as possible. With others still casting him curious looks, he lowered his gaze to the folded slip of paper on his knee. Too tired to read a word of it right now, he folded it smaller.

While the train gained speed, he loosened the top of his leather pouch that kept his coca leaves and money safe. The Word of God wasn't something he put much thought to, let alone stock in. So maybe it was the goodness in which it was given, or maybe it was because of the first true friend he'd ever really had, but for some reason Haakon carefully slid the folded page inside the pouch along with the rest of his most valued possessions and yanked the cord tight.

TWELVE

MAY 6, 1895
BLACKBIRD MOUNTAIN, VIRGINIA

MORNING LIGHT SPILLED THROUGH THE
upstairs window as Thor sat up. He'd passed the night on the floor, using two rolled-up gunny sacks as a pillow. While someone had placed an abundance of folded bedding on the porch before dusk, he hadn't been willing to unbolt the door to retrieve it. Aven would have a time of it if she knew the state he'd slept in.

Thor struggled to a stand and moved to the window, which he lifted. Fresh air rushed in, heavy and moist from the rain that had damped the air in the night. With a low mist the only thing in the meadow, he made his way down the stairs and pulled the items inside, as well as two pails of good clear water that had been placed there.

His movements were slow, stiff, and, frankly, agonizing.

Everything hurt.

His joints, his abdomen, and parts of him that he didn't want a doctor checking on.

Lacking the strength to lift a crate of items, he dragged it in, and by the time he'd secured the door again, sweat beaded on his brow.

Sinking to the floor, he wedged himself into the corner for support. He leaned his head against the wall and longed to close his eyes, but braved a reach for the nearby crate and pulled it closer.

Inside rested a small sack of shelled pecans and a jar packed with jerked elk meat. Beside it sat a lidded crock—still warm. He raised the top to find stewed apples. Last was a loaf of braided Norwegian bread that smelled of cardamom. Baking day was earlier in the week, and this hadn't been in the kitchen the night before, which meant his wife had stayed up late making it. She was the only woman in the house who baked this bread. Thor ran his thumb against the soft, golden crust. He hadn't an appetite yet, but the notion that Aven had been on her feet at odd hours just for him was a comfort that went beyond anything a bite might have provided.

At movement in his peripheral vision, he looked up to see Jorgan at the window, tipping his head as a request to be joined outside. Jorgan held two steaming cups of coffee. It took Thor a while to rise and move to the glass, but when he did, he watched as his brother set one of the cups on the top banister. Nabbing an old chair, Jorgan toted it a few paces into the yard where he turned it to sit backward. He sipped coffee as if this were the most normal morning of their lives.

Despite everything, the side of Thor's mouth lifted in a smile.

After sliding on his coat, he unlatched the door and stepped out into the cool air of dawn. He picked up the tin mug, sat on the top step, and took a gulp of good, strong brew. When he raised the cup to his brother in thanks, Jorgan dipped a nod. There didn't seem much to say, and in Jorgan's mellow presence Thor was thankful.

With his stomach unsettled, Thor managed another drink before he decided to set the coffee aside.

When he looked back to his brother, Jorgan spoke. "How did you sleep?"

Thor gave a one-shoulder shrug that didn't even come close to the truth.

Jorgan must have known. "Is there anything I can fetch? Anything that might make you more comfortable?"

There was an old rope bed upstairs, but no rope to weave across the slats. Thor thought about asking Jorgan for some, but maybe later. Right now he wanted to know how his wife was doing.

Thor turned the mug in his fingers. "Av—" He never spoke that to Jorgan, but had said it so firmly the night before he'd been aching to soften the force of it ever since. He only wished she were here to know that.

Jorgan's brows tipped up in surprise. "She's, uh, doin' alright. About as you might imagine. She's distressed, Thor, but she's only thinkin' of ways to help you get well. She'd be the one sitting here if I hadn't insisted on coming by first. She scolded me, but I'm sure she's cooled her heels by now." Jorgan grinned.

Thor smiled again, and it was the full kind. He would expect nothing less from Aven but that stout courage of hers.

Jorgan went on to explain that she was on her way to Fincastle to talk to the doctor some more and had elicited Peter to go with her.

Now it was Thor's turn to be surprised. It was a long morning of travel to Fincastle by wagon, including a ferry crossing at the James. While an inkling of worry rose, he had no choice but to tamp it down. Aven would have made a careful choice, determined or not, and he'd come to trust Peter even as much as Jorgan.

Focus having drifted along the mass of Sorrel footprints, Jorgan rose and examined them again. Thor cleared his throat to garner his brother's attention, then inquired as to what should be done.

"I don't know. I don't know what they're about, but it doesn't sit well."

No, it didn't.

"I'll inform the sheriff." Jorgan said. "Let them know we have fresh whereabouts."

Thor nodded. He doubted the sheriff and his men from Roanoke could do much, but it was worth a try. And in the meantime, Thor would do his best to help. Providential, perhaps, that he was here. If he could stay well enough, he could keep watch over the farm from a different location. One the Sorrels seemed to frequent. Yes, he was in more danger here alone, but he wasn't afraid, and thanks to Jorgan, Thor's shotgun and Haakon's rifle were now propped up against the porch railing. Leaning there side by side as though they belonged there together all along.

Teaching her to drive a team and wagon was something Aven had asked of Thor years ago, so it was with ease that she drove the wagon off the long boarded platform of the ferry. Stabilized by a stretch of ropes from one bank to the other, the sturdy ferry shuttled passengers and carts across the James River for a small fee. In a clatter of harnesses, the team of brown mares lunged up the shallow embankment, leaving the churning water behind. The horses had been calm for the short crossing, but had they been restless, 'twas assuring that Peter sat beside her.

Ever since the doctor's visit the day before, Aven had stumbled upon more and more unanswered questions, so after breakfast, both Jorgan and Peter had listened slack jawed to her scheme to venture to Fincastle. Undeterred, Aven had fetched her straw hat and shawl, and while Peter finished his morning chores, she implored Jorgan to help her hitch up the team. He'd obliged with a spark of good humor in his eyes, and no doubt Thor was now abreast of her whereabouts.

The wagon jostled when a wheel hit a rut. Aven raised the reins higher as if that would smooth things out. She felt Peter slide her a sideways glance that had been one of many.

Whether or not Peter was worried about her modest proficiency with the team, he spoke of nothing more than the weather and the work Jorgan aided him with on his cabin—a dwelling just a stone's throw from Cora's own that Peter leased by way of labor to the farm. While Peter earned his way through the sweat of his back, the brothers never sought recompense from Cora. Instead they provided a safe place for her to live with her daughters just past Thor's orchards, where she could remain close to her older sister, Ida.

In return, Cora offered wisdom and medical aid. The faithful midwife's own form of goodwill. Ever since Cora's husband's passing some ten years prior, the Norgaard men had insisted she and her daughters make their land home for so long as she wished. The brothers' way of caring for the two beloved freedwomen—one who had tended their mother amid three trying births and the other who had raised them since their mother's passing upon Haakon's first breaths some twenty-five years ago.

When Peter spoke again, Aven's thoughts slipped from the dangers of birthing and back to this curving lane.

"Two glass windows in now. They let in an awful lot of light. I can read now in the daytime there."

"Is Tess still tutoring you?" The wagon hit another bump, and Aven pulled one hand from the reins to rub the side of her rounded belly. 'Twas far from comfortable, but she wasn't going to complain.

"Yes'm." His eyes, which were trained on the road, softened some. "We practice over at Miss Cora's in the evenings, and little Georgie's awful amused that I gotta use her primer."

At ten years old and spunky to boot, Cora's youngest was no doubt giving him a time of it. "I'm proud of the progress you're making, and I'm sure she is too."

He smiled. "Tess says the same thing, but I'm awful slow."

Aven thought of Tess with her cheery ways and how she always encouraged Peter in his ventures. "Your diligence is paying off."

"Thank you, ma'am." Taking off his hat, Peter motioned up ahead. "As is yours."

There stood in the distance a sign marking the way to Fincastle. They drove on, and as the morning warmed, they passed sprawling farms and patches of woodlands where cabins sat tucked away, announcing their presence by the smell of cook fires or rugged lanes.

Brown heads bobbing with each step, the team of horses ambled through a stretch of grassland, and upon spotting buildings that stood closer together, Aven craned her neck to better see the town. Its shapes and sounds were familiar due to her having accompanied Thor on deliveries a few times a year. Brick buildings cast dense shadows across the road, and clapboard houses stood tall and bright under the nearly noon sun. Children played in the yard of a schoolhouse, and two men lifted a slabbed door into place on a newly built barn. Just past the pounding of their hammers, Aven spotted the sign for the doctor's establishment.

She bit the inside of her lip, so nervous the busy road made her. Peter gripped the seat. More than once, she sensed him nearly reach for the reins, but she somehow got the team off the main street and stopped beneath a tree beside the doctor's home. Aven set the brake and pulling off her straw hat, tucked it in a corner of the wagon bed. Peter hopped down and came around as she righted the bun wound atop her head. Still keeping a watchful study of their surroundings, he helped her climb down, then offered her the lead in stepping on.

Aven wasted no time in reaching the door where she gave three sound knocks.

After a shuffle and a clatter, the door opened and there stood young Dr. Abramson. His tweed vest was rumpled, and the ink stain on his hand still damp. "Good day, ma'am." He opened the door wider, and upon seeing her in full, his voice rose an octave. "Are you in labor?"

Aven touched the side of her stomach again. "Goodness, no."

At his sigh of relief Peter coughed into his fist, suppressing a chuckle.

"My apologies. I've just . . . never . . ." Dr. Abramson angled both hands toward her womb in a manner that suggested he wasn't sure which direction the baby was to come out.

Peter arched an eyebrow as though knowing more about such matters.

"Er . . . um . . . do come in, Mrs. Norgaard." The physician opened the door wider.

"Thank you." Aven crossed the threshold into a parlor, where she introduced Peter, who closed the door.

Dr. Abramson shook his hand, then motioned to a folding chair for Aven to sit. "Please." The doctor offered to fetch another chair but Peter politely declined.

After sitting, Aven looked over the contents of the secretary desk beside her. The front lay folded down to balance a stack of books. Just beyond it rose a tall glass cabinet filled with polished tools, bottles of medicines, and rolls of bandages.

Peter stationed himself beside the window on the opposite side of the room where he observed quietly.

"I've come to inquire as to what you may have discovered." Aven loosened her shawl and nestled it in her lap.

Dr. Abramson turned his desk chair and sat facing her. "I sent the telegram to my mentor this morning and should hear word soon. Perhaps a few days, perhaps longer." He gestured to the stack of books, his hand landing atop the one that was opened. "But I am doing further reading as promised."

"I thank you. Have you discovered anything?"

"In the ten minutes I've been at the task? Well, I was just perusing the index when there came a knock at the door." His smile was amiable.

Aven tugged on one cuff of her blouse sleeve, righting it absently. "I don't mind waiting. Until you make progress."

His expression went slack. "Wait here?"

She nodded. "I'm in no hurry. Though . . . may I ask how long you've been a physician?" He seemed no older than herself and much more flustered.

"Mrs. Norgaard, it will take some time, if not *days*, to draw a conclusion."

"Sir. The last physician who examined my husband administered more distress than comfort. I wish I had done more then and intend to now." While she knew not how she might have improved that experience, she wasn't about to sit at home while Thor lay untreated. The doctor before her was so young that her worry deepened. To pose that question again . . . "May I ask how long you've been practicing medicine?"

"Two years, ma'am. Though only a few weeks in Fincastle. I worked for a surgeon in Boston for most of my apprenticeship and am well practiced in the surgical field, even for someone of my age." He went to cross his legs but tipped back in his chair, which had some sort of spring mechanism. The young man planted both polished shoes on the floor. "As for my hesitation . . ." He motioned to her unborn child. "I have no experience with childbirth, so any reservations expressed were solely for your well-being. I'm sure the time approaches when I'm indoctrinated into the world of child delivery, but I admit, I am glad it is not this day."

Aven gave in to a smile. 'Twas a mutual relief.

At a soft *thump*, she looked over to see that Peter had stepped to a nearby shelf, scrutinizing a human skull that rested there.

Dr. Abramson continued. "I understand your concern. It's no easy thing to witness a loved one suffer while we ourselves feel helpless." He swiveled his springy chair toward the desk and nabbed a pencil from a narrow porcelain vase. "I'd like to inquire as to this physician your husband saw previously? His name, please, and also, what was the purpose of Mr. Norgaard's visit? Did something occur to bring your husband distress?"

"Aye. Doctor Kent was his name, and he was working for the Bureau for the Deaf. I'm sorry that the exact name of the organization eludes me, but I can retrieve that information for you straight away from some paperwork at home. I wish I had thought to bring it with me."

Nodding, the doctor scribbled his notes, and Aven continued.

"Thor and I were troubled by what seemed a lack of vigilance." With little choice but to trust this young surgeon, she went on to describe how the doctor from the train had·been conned by Jed and Harlan Sorrel. With Peter listening on, she regretted describing his family's bad form.

But not only did Peter show no offense, he added a testimony of his own. "They're a dark sort, sir, and were given undue trust in a way that reckoned poor judgment on the doctor's part."

Looking troubled, Dr. Abramson nodded at Peter's description and flipped to a new page in his notebook. "Describe the manner of the examination. What was the nature of the assessment?"

"'Twas an interview about his lack of hearing," Aven said. "It involved several questions as well as an examination of the ear canal and a blood draw for study, which I believe was to occur at a later date. The study, that is."

The doctor lowered his pen tip and jotted down quick thoughts. "How invasive was the study of the ear canal? Was it a deep probing?"

Aven watched as he scribbled more notes.

Breakage of the eardrum? Would cause nausea. Also trouble with balance. Walking?

Research symptoms of vertigo.

She lifted her gaze to his face, and while his brow was unlined, it furrowed beneath the weight of his wonderings.

"'Twas not very invasive. The ear examination seemed more a cursory glance."

"And when did this all occur? Was your husband yet showing

signs of the ailment?" He pulled a book from the stack and flipped to the index.

"No, he was in excellent health." She pondered the exact time and offered up the date, which he scribbled to paper.

The young physician studied his notes, confusion lining his face as though he were missing a clue that remained hidden. He skimmed the index of the book and added a new word to his wonderings. *Labyrinthitis*? "Please explain to me again what you observed in as much detail as possible."

She did, going on to describe that the purpose of the blood draw was to better learn about the anatomy of the Deaf, especially those born with the condition as her husband was. "The blood would be examined under a microscope, or so the letter said. While we were at the depot, blood was taken from Thor's veins by way of a needle. I cannot remember what it was called. I wish I had brought his paper-work. I can do so tomorrow—"

"Microscopic study, hmm . . ." Dr. Abramson slid his pencil behind one ear and, lifting up his notes, examined them by light of the window. His brow puckered in confusion, then he rose, strode to a shelf of books, and perused the titles. After selecting one, he set it on his desk, then went back for another, which he also added to his growing stack. "This needle you describe . . ." He moved to the cabi-net and opened it. "Did it look like this?" With a crouch, he reached to the back of the lowest shelf, then rose with a small leather case in hand. He opened the lid and showed Aven the contents.

There among the velvet padding lay a glass syringe and glinting needle.

From where he stood, Peter bowed his head.

"Aye, though his vial had a glass center." This one was metallic all around.

The doctor angled the tool to the afternoon light. "I've only recently acquired it, and confess that I know little of the methods of application. The surgeon I studied under used it infrequently, opting for alternate administrations of medication. My predecessor here in Fincastle left it to me upon his retirement. He served as a surgeon for the Union and, from what I gleaned, used it to administer opiates to soldiers via injection."

Peter interjected. "But the doctor didn't put anything *into* Thor's veins. He was taking something out."

"Yes, a difference there, of course. Still . . . I wonder . . ." Dr. Abramson studied the tool with its sharp tip a few moments longer, then, closing the case, set it on his desk. "I lack the answers we need, Mrs. Norgaard, but I promise you that I'll do all I can to secure them. As soon as I discover something further, I'll return to you all. Please also gather those documents you mentioned. I have a feeling they'll be of use to us."

THIRTEEN

HAAKON ENTERED THE FARM BY WAY OF the small graveyard. If any of the family had been surrendered to the earth, he wanted to know now. To have time to prepare himself for who would or would not be there upon arrival. Birds squawked at him from branches overhead as he edged around the fenceless plot. His steps sank in the soft dirt while his heart hammered with the same urgency as their song. At the count of only three crosses, he shot out the breath that had been caught in his lungs. Da and Ma and Aunt Dorothe. As it had been when he'd left.

That meant his brothers were still alive. And their wives.

No children—if born—had been lost.

Relief swelling inside, Haakon sidestepped down the slope. Dirt trickled and tumbled. This wasn't a path already cut, but he meant not to be spotted yet. Much better to avoid the main road so as to know just who he'd be coming upon first. Depending on the person, it would alter his approach. While each of the coming introductions would be apologetic, some meetings were about to be more grievous than others. As it was, he'd kept to the shadows and woodlands on his hike up this mountain. He'd passed through underbrush, trod through cow fields, and even stumbled past an abandoned camp in the woods where he knew better than to pause and gather his wits.

Haakon worked his way along the high side of the creek bank and let out a low whistle for Grete to come running if she could. Water gurgled below, so clear and inviting, that he stepped lower and crouched. With a wad of spent coca leaves in his cheek, he turned his head to the side and spat them out. Leaning lower, he filled his hands with the mountain water and couldn't recall a taste so keen. It was just as he remembered—all of it. Even the air draped deep and heavy as it had been since his first taste of it.

Haakon rose and slung his pack onto his shoulder, then stepped down a stretch of rutted deer trail. He clambered back up a small hillock to see—for the first time in over four years—the meadow that was his. At the far end of the grassy hollow stood his cabin where overgrown grasses swayed in the spring air . . . and it dawned on him then that Grete was gone.

The brown hound hadn't come running. Unless she was too old to leave the porch, she had died. Never once in his upbringing had she been away from his side. Not until the day he'd left this place. An ache he didn't want to acknowledge broke inside him as he waded through waist-high weeds. Swallowing down his grief, Haakon stepped over a low wire fence that hung askew. The losses could have been much greater, and as much as he longed to see Grete bounding across the farm to him, it was a loss bent with time. A consequence to his choices that she'd had to pass without him at her side.

Haakon fought against the heartache as he walked along the thin stretch of woods that separated the two pieces of land. While both sides pulled at his intentions, he caved nearer to safety, veering toward his own cabin where he might gain his bearings for a few minutes. Maybe even wash up, though he doubted the family cared much about how he appeared. It was something much deeper they would be caring after, and he feared he lacked what they deserved. Only a testing of the waters in his soul would tell, and truth be told, he was uncertain as to what might be found.

At sight of movement, Haakon slowed. Someone was walking from the direction of the great house. He squinted that way, trying to make sense of the snatches of color that moved through the leafy branches. It was a woman. While he could glimpse little of her manner through the foliage, those were bare feet beneath a lace hem and hair the shade of the cinnamon tea she'd favored.

Aven.

Haakon froze. Perhaps thirty yards off, she headed crossways over Norgaard land. If he wasn't mistaken, toward his own section of the farm where his cabin stood empty and awaiting him. She carried a basket at her middle and seemed bent on her destination. With Aven venturing that way, a sudden northeaster may as well have gusted against his sails, all but capsizing him to alter course. The last thing she needed was him walking up to her without warning.

With her attention elsewhere, he went unnoticed, but for him there was suddenly nothing between them but his own agony. Even the trees that had stood there were gone from sight. The meadow grasses but a blur. It was just him and Aven, and he was losing his breath to it.

He blinked quickly, and the world returned—every green leaf of it. It was then he noticed a man walking at Aven's side. Thor? It had to be. But no. While the fellow was tall, he was lean. A watchtower of a man that could be no one other than Jorgan. Melancholy and homesickness stirred Haakon forward, but he braced a hand to the nearest tree, forcing himself to remain put. He was too much in the clearing to go unnoticed much longer, so he stepped deeper into the nearest thicket . . . only to crunch underbrush beneath his boots. He froze the same moment Aven and Jorgan did.

The rifle Jorgan carried was suddenly aimed his way. Jorgan ducked lower, his eyes meeting Haakon's own. Haakon waited for the rifle to lower but it didn't.

Fair.

Haakon took a slow step forward, and that's when Aven did the last thing he expected. She stepped forward as well, a hand shadowing her eyes. When she halted, it was so sudden that she must have seen him good and proper. Heart thundering in his chest, Haakon swallowed hard.

Like the firing of a shotgun, several things passed through his mind at once.

First—she was stunning. As lovely as he remembered, shoulders squared, showing no fear of him. Her brown eyes were doe wide, though, diverting all assurance of her calm. A spirit of fortitude that had been shaped by the distant shores she'd come from as well as the faith that dwelled within her, and in this moment he remembered as vividly as last he'd stood here that she was more than he ever deserved.

The second realization was that she was with child. And far along at that. Not only had Thor made her his wife, he had made her a mother. Haakon tried to make peace with that—and quickly—but it settled inside him in a place not so easily atoned for. While he meant to repair that, a third awareness rose above all else. This one jarred him like no other. She had every reason to despise him, and yet in her expression dwelled no trace of hate. Shock, yes, as well as quiet trepidation that bespoke her memory of their last encounter. But what he saw more than anything else was pity.

Dropping his gaze, Haakon fought to rally his capacities, and then someone moved in the shadows of the porch. He knew not who it was until he heard footsteps so heavily placed they could only be one person's. The urge to take a step back was so riotous that Haakon shifted his stance.

Thor stepped into the sunlight and Haakon saw his brother for the first since that wretched day on Sorrel land when Thor had fought to save his life.

Gaze riveted to Haakon, Thor leaned against a post. His towering build was just as sobering, yet an arm encircled his abdomen, sturdy hand gripping that side. Thor's expression was stoic, but something else was there. Pain. Had he been injured?

Focus torn between Thor and Aven, Haakon knew not how to address them. Aven made the choice all the simpler when she set her basket aside and turned away. Haakon watched her go, wishing he hadn't when she cast a glimpse over her shoulder that held every brokenness he had inflicted upon her. The sheer sight of it nearly buckled his knees. Why had he thought coming home a good idea?

When she was gone, Haakon searched for words, but his mouth wouldn't move. His hands wouldn't either—save a slight tremble that was far from Sign Language. Thor seemed to notice, just as he always did since the language was one of movement and observation, be it a grand sweeping phrase or something as subtle as Haakon's frayed nerves and the rush of blood through his limbs.

Haakon wracked his brain for some semblance of what to do, and it was standing here, looking at a slightly older Thor, that had him recalling their da. They shared the same wide shoulders, that strapping brawn. How similar the two were, yet while Da's coloring had been sun and wheat, Thor's hair and beard was the dark of the earth.

That story Haakon had told the deckhands hadn't been one he'd conjured on his own. No, it was one of the Nordic sagas Da had passed down to them. The sea serpent really was fabled to have battled with Odin's son, Thor. While the man before him wasn't as fierce as the Viking god depicted in the legends, his brother was powerful enough to have earned the name, even on the hour of his birth.

Looking at Thor now, Haakon could all but hear the stories from their childhood. Those that Da wove for them by the warmth of the fire and the sweetness of his pipe smoke. Tales of might and courage, of valor and battle.

If this were a battlefield, a gesture of peace would be to lay down a shield. Haakon had only a pack, so he eased it from his body and lowered it to the ground.

Thor glanced to the frayed canvas, then back. Perhaps he read it as a declaration of being here to stay. Desperate to clarify, and too humbled to even attempt communicating in Sign, Haakon lowered himself to one knee and then the other. He unsheathed his knife next and laid it flat in the dirt.

Thor's brows pulled together, confusion carving every stern feature.

Did he not recognize him? Yes, Haakon's skin was more weathered and his beard full. Hair that had once been cropped short was long enough to tie back. His boots were as dusty as ever and more patched than Ida allowed under her kitchen table. But he was still him, and the longer Thor looked his way, the more Haakon realized that Thor hadn't doubted it for a moment. It wasn't misunderstanding in Thor's expression but disbelief.

"I'm sorry for coming without warning," Haakon said. "I need to sort some things out with my land and, more important . . . with you all." In particular, Aven. He didn't say that because he didn't need to, and he doubted Thor would appreciate him so much as *mentioning* his wife just now.

"Care to tell us where you've been?" Jorgan asked calmly.

"I was at sea."

Nodding without the slightest shred of surprise, Jorgan looked to Thor. After watching Haakon for several moments, Thor made the sign for *stay* by dragging his hands down toward the ground, then moved them from side to side above the earth for *here*. His brow was tipped up in question, and it was a gracious one at that. More than Haakon ever deserved, and even then it wasn't kindness he saw in Thor's face but a desperation to make sense of what to do.

Knowing he would need to be closer for Thor to read his speech, Haakon rose and paced forward some. "If you don't mind," he said. "Just until we sort things out. If you'd rather, I can stay elsewhere for the time." He glanced toward the sun that had already dipped behind the trees with coming dusk.

It was getting late in the day, but he doubted either of his brothers cared. Their only care would be not to let him anywhere near Aven. Nor Fay for that matter. Maybe they'd let him stay in a shed or an outbuilding? He could certainly keep to himself and would make it a hard and fast point not to be a bother. Then again, if they chose against him remaining here, he could camp out elsewhere, just until they all decided how to proceed.

How he wished it wasn't this way, but to his disgrace, what was done was done. Now all he could do was work to make amends. He was scarcely sure where to begin. More confusing were his uncertainties about Aven. Haakon had cared for her once. Very deeply. But that care hadn't been a love as Thor's had been. Instead, he'd let longing fester into something much too dangerous.

Would he have the chance to apologize to her?

Even more worrisome, did he know how to make sense of this root inside him that still belonged to her? It was a sentiment stronger than he cared to admit and was part of the reason he had stayed away for so long. He had hoped time would obliterate his tenderness for Aven, but perhaps the ocean hadn't been as big as he had thought.

Gripping tight to the handrail, Thor went to move down the steps but only descended two before stopping. He bent over some, fist clenched tight at his side.

What was going on?

Jorgan watched without speaking. As much ground as Haakon had to make up with his oldest brother, this moment was between him and Thor, and they all knew it.

Breathing as loud as an ox, Thor moved another step, and grimaced again. His knuckles turned white from his grip on the railing. Haakon had witnessed ailments of every make on his travels. From the gaunt faces of starvation to the delirium of dysentery, he knew he was looking upon a misery as grave. Thor's eyes found Haakon's, skin bearing the yellowish hue of jaundice, and there lived within his gaze the undeniable sorrow of a man about to dig his own grave. A near assurance that both intrigued and terrified Haakon. Thor Norgaard was dying.

FOURTEEN

AVEN'S FINGERS TREMBLED AS SHE SEARCHED along a row of Thor's books in their bedroom. Finding the one she sought, she pulled it out, but her unsteady grip sent it tumbling to the floor. Sinking down, she reached for it even as her vision blurred. Her hands stilled, ceasing their chase for understanding. For sense of this . . .

That Haakon was home.

For years she had wondered if he was alive, and now the answer jarred her as unfettered relief against a wind-battered heart. How she wished she didn't care, but the same man who had broken her trust had once been her friend.

She should seek naught but penance, but while that was the most needed of mendings if he were to linger, within her tromped a menagerie of emotions that she didn't know how to give order to. Could restoration ever come to that man and her heart?

'Twas no wonder she'd left them under lock and key all this while.

Having retrieved the book, Aven laid it aside, then reached up again to where Thor's thickest volumes resided on the uppermost shelf. She sought no particular text, but instead had freed the space to better reach what rested between the dusty titles. Rising as high as she could manage, she wedged two fingers into the empty spot and felt a pinch of the envelope Thor had tucked there long ago. Well from sight, as had been her request. Aven pulled it down now, aching for Thor beside her.

She grazed her thumb against the jagged envelope where he had slit it open, then freed the letter Haakon had sent them after his vanishing. 'Twas brief, a few roughly scratched lines on wrinkled paper, but each sentiment stirred her now as they had then. In her hand lay hint of his remorse and an appeal for forgiveness.

'Twas just like Haakon Norgaard to have sent such a note with no return address.

At a gentle knock on the door, Fay's voice called through. "May I come in?"

Aven swiped at her eyes and lowered the letter. "Aye."

The door creaked open, and Fay slipped around it. In her arms, Bjørn lay deep asleep. One of his pudgy wrists hung limp, and his blond curls were askew. "I thought you were up here." Fay allowed a few moments for Aven to swipe once more beneath her eyes. "How are you faring?"

"Oh . . ." It was all she could say, and with tears pooling afresh, Aven returned the letter to its home.

Fay moved nearer and pulled Aven close in a one-armed hold. Bjørn nestled between them, warm, sleepy, and soft. Aven touched the back of his wee head for comfort.

"You brave dear," Fay whispered.

Sniffing, Aven stepped back. She didn't feel brave, but there was a solace in Fay's manner that said otherwise.

"I don't understand why he's come," Aven finally said.

"He told Jorgan that he's been at sea. Something about the ice trade and Norway. It seems as though he's sailed around the Atlantic many times."

Haakon at sea all this while? Aven thought back to the last

conversations they'd shared when he'd described his wish to see the world and, later, even pleaded for her to go with him.

"Has he no other family? No home?" Four years was a long time.

Fay shook her head. "I don't believe so. Just here."

Wonderings colliding into one another, and when Aven's fingers began to worry themselves, she clasped them at her sides. She tried to think of what to say but could no sooner come up with a concise response than she could make sense of the truth that Haakon had returned.

"I've just spoken with Jorgan and came up to let you know what passed between them and Haakon," Fay said. "I know not where to begin, Aven, or how to make this as gentle on you as possible. Would you most wish to hear of matters of business or matters of the heart? I will only say that which you wish to know of. While some urgency is at hand with Haakon's presence now, there is no rush in these matters. Things need not be done according to his timing, and I believe we can all agree that it would be better for them not to."

"I thank you." More than she could express. Not knowing how to proceed or even what to say, Aven went with what felt safest. "What is the business that Haakon has come for?"

"He has admitted to returning for his land and cabin."

With it his only inheritance, that surprised her not.

Fay brushed the side of her cheek against the top of Bjørn's head. "Be it to live in or to sell away, I don't know, but Jorgan was most adamant that Haakon's right to making that decision is forfeited."

Aven knew little of the arrangement between brothers for the sharing of this land, but she doubted they had official documents stating their agreements. She couldn't begin to imagine how they would settle any disputes there.

"Haakon has also expressed a wanting to try and make amends for his wrong to you. I'm not sure what his intentions are, but Jorgan sensed that penance was a sincere desire."

Aven looked out the window where dark was falling. For so long that had been her hope, and now that it was here she felt a wash of trepidation in place of comfort. While she'd glimpsed him only a moment, 'twas enough to observe the workings of time. On the outside, at least. So different he appeared from the reckless youth who had wounded her, and while she longed for such change, it took a lot more than a toughened bearing to make a man.

Fay's skirts swayed as she shifted to keep Bjørn asleep. "With there much yet to be discussed and decided, I've come to assure you that both Thor and Jorgan are adamant of Haakon keeping his distance as they assess the situation."

Aven's eyes blurred with tears again, and she could scarcely whisper her gratitude. "And what of this night?" Cradling a hand beneath her stomach, she felt afresh the long day and the coming need for rest. "Where will Haakon be?"

"That is why I've come to seek your input. Jorgan thought he might stay elsewhere—with Peter, perhaps, if Peter agreed. There's also no reason Haakon can't sleep in the woods."

Aven considered the Sorrels who might also be out there.

"Or, if you were to agree, he might stay in the horse barn or the cidery. Tomorrow will be a new day, and different arrangements can be made. Sometimes a night's sleep is best medicine for all, but not if your own peace is robbed by Haakon's presence on the farm."

"What of Thor?"

With a slow hand, Fay patted Bjørn's diapered bottom. "He is resting." Fay's eyes glistened with wetness. Aven had seen firsthand how frail Thor had been this evening. She'd meant to sit with him, keep him company even if at a distance, but then Haakon had appeared. Her throat cinched tight with the grief of it all. More heightened than any fear of Haakon was a fear of Thor's well-being—both in body and in spirit.

"Oh, Fay. I don't know what to do."

Reaching out, Fay squeezed Aven's wrist. "Be assured that Thor is well and safe this night and that his rest will be as peaceful as it can be. Jorgan has assured him that you will be safe. As for Haakon, I'll tell Jorgan to send him elsewhere for the night, and they can reconvene tomorrow." Fay gave her a tender smile, then stepped toward the door. "I'll be back to check on you in a bit. Ida's fixing you some tea. Rest all you can." She eyed Aven's stomach as if knowing the weight of it ached at this late hour.

Aven glanced to the northernmost window where tarnished across the cider barn were the words the Sorrels had painted. A stark contrast to the weathered boards that could bear any tempest and the peace this farm had rested upon. And here Ida cared for this family without hesitation, dwelling in this land where danger stalked around these very buildings in the night.

With a chubby cheek pressed to his mother's chest, Bjørn sighed in his sleep. Aven couldn't help but think that Haakon's dwelling near might keep these souls safer. She reached for Fay, halting her departure. "The cidery would be fine. For Haakon."

"Are you certain?"

"Aye." With dusk settling in, there seemed no cause to send Haakon off just now. He was well apart from her, and while she knew not the cause of his return, she didn't sense harm. 'Twas not tears of fright that had just spilled from her cheeks, but of a raw uncertainty and splayed-open soul. "Please tell Jorgan?"

"Of course. I'll do so now."

Aven thanked her, and when she was alone again, she drew the curtains over each window. The room was too quiet without Thor. The floorboards didn't quake under his heavy steps, and her shoulder wasn't warmed with the touch of his broad hand. He wasn't here to pull her near to kiss, for she felt neither the strength of his arms nor the brush of his beard. Instead she was alone and the attic empty of his comfort.

Beside the bed sat the wooden cradle he had shouldered up from Fay and Jorgan's bedroom when Bjørn outgrew it just a month ago. How many Norgaard offspring had this cradle held since being crafted decades ago for this very house? Five now, soon to be six. Haakon included.

At the dresser, Aven removed her nightgown and draped it over the footboard of the bed. 'Twas with an extra measure of care that she pulled each curtain snug. The room dimmer now, she worked free of her gown and pulled the nightgown overhead, then fastened each sleeve cuff snug. Now for prayers. They'd endlessly filled her heart, but in the hour since Haakon's arrival, Aven's heart had gone silent.

Holding the edge of the mattress, she knelt and sank lower to sit back on her calves. Resting this way, her womb forced down pressure, but in truth she'd felt the low ache even in standing. This babe wasn't long in coming. Less than a month now. Would Thor be well for the birth? Would he know the face of his child? Would Haakon still be traipsing around in their lives? The answers to that were as far off as her husband, so Aven folded her hands and bowed her head, but in place of prayers, there were naught but tears.

FIFTEEN

SHE'D BEEN DRESSED IN BLACK THAT DAY. Widow's black that reached from hem to throat. Like the feathers of a raven, the fabric of her mourning gown had caught the sun with a soft sheen as she'd walked the final steps onto Blackbird Mountain. A color so striking against her pale skin, even the crows had stilled to watch her. A beauty that might as well not have been real. That was the first true glimpse Haakon had ever had of Aven as he'd pushed his way past the kitchen door to see the woman who had sailed to them from the north.

There had never been a newcomer on this farm in all of their lives. And then there she'd come, just walking up to them, probably as uncertain of them as they were of her.

She was twenty-one, he'd learned that day. Same age as him, and he'd rather thought that a nice fit. Haakon had watched her from the kitchen porch while Thor stood across the yard, seven years older and, if Haakon wasn't mistaken, a touch protective. He'd looked at Haakon then, and there was a knowing stretched between them so coarse and taut Jorgan might as well have had to duck under it to make introductions.

As much effort as Haakon had put into staying collected, he knew

Thor had labored doubly hard. Because unlike Haakon's inquisitive fascination, Thor had loved her in that moment. It was impossible not to know. Impossible to miss the way Thor used to slow in front of Aven's photograph that hung on the wall in the great room. Her essence captured there in a small portrait beside Benn. Upon their cousin's untimely death, Thor had taken the picture down and kept it. At least that's what Haakon assumed when the photograph went missing.

Haakon had always imagined those memories long past spent, but being returned home, they were as vivid now as they'd been then.

The last cords of slumber falling away, Haakon stirred awake. He opened his eyes to blinding sunlight in the cidery and the creak of a rope swing. That made no sense because he never slept past dawn and the rope swing had been taken down years ago. Groggy, he rubbed his eyes and sat up to see that he was wrong on both accounts. Late-morning light flooded the building, and lashed to the center rafter hung a knotted rope. Riding it was Jorgan's oldest boy.

The lad swung forward, arcing in a broad sweep the width of the massive workshop. The boy let go, landing in the low dregs of the haystack beside where Haakon had slept. The child crawled over and spoke in a lispy voice.

Haakon didn't understand a word of it. "Huh?"

The boy inclined his focus toward the well-risen sun. "You swept too wong."

He supposed he had. And he was mighty thankful for the place to have bunked down. At his brothers' permission, Haakon had entered this sacred place the night before to the smell of apples and dried leaves, so heady it had been marched through these floors for decades, lingering in cracks and unswept corners along with the memories of countless harvests.

Unable to recall the name of this little ciderkin, Haakon inquired and was soon well informed. "How old are you, Sigurd?"

Sticking his tongue out in concentration, Sigurd held up four fingers, then worked hard to push one back down. Lean and long limbed, he resembled his da, though that little head of white-blond hair was definitely Fay's. Another trait he had of his mother's were those wide-set eyes. Noble and gentle beneath pale brows.

Reaching over, Haakon shook his hand, then, as Sigurd beamed at him, Haakon rose. He brushed straw from his thin cotton shirt and wool pants. He hadn't meant to sleep this late but had stayed up keeping watch through the night. No one had asked him to, but he couldn't help it. Not with what was written just outside.

Jorgan had told him yesterday that it was Sorrel doing, so it was beneath the stars that Haakon sat outside of the cider barn with a rifle across his lap, listening for anything out of the ordinary. A habit he'd learned at sea and one as hard to break. He'd picked the lock on the gun cabinet to discover that his Winchester was gone. He'd ask about that soon but had helped himself to one of the less impressive firearms left to appease robbers such as him.

Starving, Haakon pulled a square of hardtack from his pack. It was the last thing in the world he wanted to eat, but he wasn't about to knock on the kitchen door to inquire about meals. The shelves running the length of the longest wall that had once housed hard drink were now covered in jars of goods, from what looked like apple pie filling to jugs of vinegar. His mouth watered at sight of apple butter, but he didn't dare touch one and instead snapped the hardtack in half and handed some over.

"Here."

Sigurd nibbled the pallid biscuit with delight.

"You'll get over the taste real quick."

At a sudden scuff, Haakon looked over to see Jorgan trudging in. Jorgan bent to survey the dark recess beneath the workbench. Sigurd raced over and wrapped slender arms around his da's neck in a hug. After a friendly pat to Sigurd's back, Jorgan urged him to run along and find his ma.

"Somethin' wrong?" Haakon asked.

Without speaking, Jorgan stood and continued his search.

"I'm sorry about Sigurd just now. I didn't know he had come in here." Perhaps he shouldn't have spoken to the boy without Jorgan's knowing.

"It's not that." Jorgan shoved aside an empty barrel. "It's Thor."

"What about him?" Haakon hadn't asked, and Jorgan certainly hadn't confided.

Jorgan took so long in responding that Haakon almost asked again. "Aven brought over his breakfast this morning to find that he hadn't touched his supper. It's all still outside the door. We've waited two hours since, and he hasn't appeared."

Aven would be beside herself.

Haakon rose. "What's wrong with him?"

"It's a sickness. One the doctor is trying to figure out—but all we know right now is that it's best Thor stay where he is, alone."

Haakon doubted that idea had gone over well with the family. More pressing, with Thor's lack of hearing, there'd be no amount of knocking that could draw his attention. "Did you try ramming the door?"

Though Jorgan didn't answer, Haakon knew enough of his brother that the door would have already been rammed within an inch of its life. That amount of force tremoring through a wall always drew Thor's focus. If he could have come down, he would have. No one missed meals unless they had to or were out of their mind. At the state he'd seen Thor in yesterday, either could be the culprit.

"Thor's got the door locked, but an upper window is ajar." Finding a ladder, Jorgan dragged it out into the open.

"You don't need a ladder." Haakon tossed his pack aside and started out. A huddle of crows scattered from his path.

"What are you doing?"

"Showing you that you don't need a ladder," he called back. He expected Jorgan to stop him and would have halted had he been asked to, but Jorgan seemed more worried about Thor than him.

Haakon had scarcely reached the cabin's yard when he spotted Aven gauging the open loft window. She turned, and he nearly stopped dead in his tracks but instead strode well around her. Behind him, Jorgan was gaining ground with the ladder in tow. Haakon passed by Aven and her eyes widened. He surveyed the structure, then sidestepped along the edge of the porch, walking on the outside of the railing, which he gripped for balance.

"What are you doing?" Jorgan called.

"Making sure Thor's alright."

The logs of the cabin were each a foot in width, and with the chinking scraped flush between them, there were no places for a foothold. A big jump up let Haakon grab hold of the first-floor eaves. His grip threatening to slip, he swung a leg up. Jorgan tried to call him back, but it was too late. Haakon leaned forward onto a forearm and heaved himself higher until his chest pressed to the shingles, and then his whole torso. He dragged himself farther up and managed to stand.

After several steps, his footing slipped with the sharp slope. Aven gasped. Old leaves and pine needles tumbled, but to his relief—and probably her disappointment—he didn't fall. Using an old drainage pipe for leverage, Haakon steadied himself along the side of the house and would have a few bruises to show for this, but it was a fine trade-off considering he was now a reach from the open window.

He climbed beneath the raised sash. Despite the light of day, the room was dim, all curtains drawn, including the one he had to get untangled from. Instinct nearly had him call for Thor, but he hadn't been gone so long to forget what it was like searching for his Deaf brother.

Yet this was far from boyhood games or announcing that supper had come. Knowing that Thor was somewhere in here brought an eerie sensation as Haakon stepped across the room toward a stack of old crates. Haakon stomped several times to send a shudder through the floorboards as he used to do. It worked when Thor appeared, drawing a knife as he did. Any hope of this being a peaceful meeting vanished. Haakon hadn't lost a knife fight in his life, which was why he'd never gone into one with Thor.

Hands up, Haakon took a step back. Thor's grip on the birch handle was sure, but his eyes were glazed with fever.

There didn't appear much space for reason, so Haakon chose his first words with care. "Everyone's worried about you."

Thor turned the handle in his palm.

Maybe a different approach. "Aven's troubled that you haven't eaten. I've come to help."

Thor glanced to the open window then back.

"There's food on the front doorstep. One of us needs to fetch it. I've come to do that, do you understand?" He had no idea if Thor could read what he was saying.

Sweat glistened on Thor's brow, and he blinked in confusion.

Haakon took a step nearer to the stairs. "I'm going to bring it back up so you can eat." Haakon pointed down the stairs, then made the sign for *food*, followed by the gesture that he would carry it back up here.

Brow digging in, Thor took a step forward. A rush of air escaped his lungs, and though he seemed to be fighting it, he sank down to one knee. The knife never left his grip, but while this was Haakon's chance to wrench it loose, he didn't move. Thor was strong, yes. Livid—for certain. But deep down, Haakon didn't believe his brother would cut him. It was because of that long-remembered trust that he waited.

Still breathing hard, Thor finally sheathed his knife. His skin was yellowed, glistening with a fevered sweat, and if Haakon wasn't mistaken, delirium was as rampant as everything else.

He made the sign for *bed*, then indicated to Thor that he needed to lie down. With a bed in the corner, Haakon finished by pointing that way.

In response, Thor shaped an oath declaring what he thought of Haakon's concern.

Maybe he wasn't so delirious after all.

"Well, the feeling's mutual," Haakon muttered as he moved closer to the stairs. If he could get down and unlock the door, he could reach the provisions. Thor needed water in him right quick. Dehydration only sped along sickness. Haakon had witnessed that too many times.

Thor looked about to collapse and, reaching out a hand, braced himself to the floor.

Determined to help, Haakon paced back to him, crouched, and reached under his brother's arm. Thor slammed him away, and the effort cost them both. Haakon when he crashed into the wall and Thor when he doubled over. Having bitten his tongue, Haakon swallowed the taste of blood and wiped his mouth. When Thor pushed him away again, Haakon shoved his shoulder. It was enough to lift Thor's gaze.

"Aven's waitin' on you. She needs you, and I'm the only one who can help you right now. So knock it off!"

He lifted Thor's arm across his shoulder and gripped him around his side. A vulnerable place to put himself, but he didn't think his brother had the strength to crush him just now. Haakon fought hard to rise and with a mountain of effort got Thor standing. His stance wobbled, and he was certain they would go down again, but Thor managed a step and then several more. Haakon led him over to the corner of the room where the bed stood only to see that the old rope frame was empty. No wonder Thor hadn't wanted to do this.

Even as he chided himself, Haakon crouched and helped lower the poor man to a sit. Leaning his head against the wall, Thor looked up at the ceiling with fever-glazed eyes. The water. Haakon wanted to kick himself for not having fetched it sooner. Rushing down the stairs, he unbolted the door and was met with Aven, who looked as worried as he was starting to feel. He knew he wasn't supposed to be standing here, facing her this way, but sometimes desperate times came knocking. The fact that she was anywhere near him of her own accord confirmed it.

Haakon tugged the crate in, and when she went to speak, he shut the door again. He didn't mean to be rude but was afraid she'd push her way through to get to Thor. He wouldn't put it past her, and seeing now how ill Thor was, Haakon bolted the latch for the sake of her and the baby. He hurried back up the stairs with the goods. After setting the box down, he knelt and pulled out a jar of water. In these hills, a quart of clear liquid could mean a number of things, so shaping a *w* with three fingers, he tapped it to his mouth so Thor would know that this was far from white whiskey. Thor gulped it down. Next Haakon pulled out a bowl of fried potatoes. They were cold now but plenty good. He fetched the fork and passed both over. With unsteady hands, Thor accepted the meal and managed a bite.

Remembering the others waiting, Haakon returned to the first floor, unbolted the door, and opened it to their stunned faces. "He's still very alive."

"Where is he?" Aven rushed forward.

"No!" Haakon nearly braced her back but Jorgan did it first. "You know what the doctor said."

Grief flooded her face, and the moment it did, he knew he'd spoken out of line. He owed her an apology for that and so much more, but right now something was more urgent. "I need at least fifty feet of strong rope," he said to Jorgan, who stood just behind her. "And as quick as you can, a straw tick."

"What are you gonna do?" Jorgan's brow plunged as he urged Aven farther away from the door. Or maybe just from him.

"I'm gonna fix the bed. I'm also gonna stay with him until he's able to come home. We all know Thor won't risk any of your lives for his, but we also know one thing for certain . . ." Haakon stepped back until he was on the inside of the threshold and finally gave in to a smirk at the lunacy of what he was about to do. "He won't put up much of a fight over riskin' mine."

SIXTEEN

THE FEVER WAS SUBSIDING, BUT AS THOR had discovered over the last few days, it came and went with abandon. Now nausea staked a claim. He smoothed a hand over his abdomen, all his joints hurting at once. The doctor said that if his liver was indeed infected with the jaundice, these symptoms would subside. If his liver was instead failing, he'd have months of worsening pain, just as Da had, and then death. Had Thor really hoped for a different outcome? Had he dared to sidestep the odds? He was the one who had glutted his body with so much alcohol folks had probably placed bets on when he might die.

Thor shifted on the pallet. There was really no way to get comfortable, so he finally sank his head back into a pillow and closed his eyes.

Thoughts of Aven were his one comfort, so as he lay here, he said a prayer for her. If he knew anything about his wife, she was beside herself with worry. Perhaps he could rally enough today to pen a note, some way to offer her assurance. If she wrote him back, it would give him something to hold while he lay here.

Thor had neither paper nor pen, but he'd request some. At memory of who that someone would be, he opened his eyes. His wrist knocked into the rifle that was on the floor at his side, and his hand closed around it with the same agonizing slowness that he sat up with. Across the room, Haakon worked to unwind a length of rope, pausing at a knot.

Stiff, Thor settled against the wall.

His brother's profile was lit by the sunrise spilling in from the window, and for a moment Thor thought they were on a ship. But the swaying he felt was only his faintness. The man across from him just fixing an old bed. Thor had never been to sea. Now or ever. This mountain was his home, and the only land he'd ever roamed had been the place where his heart had been its lightest . . . and its worst. This place where he had laughed with his brothers as a boy and sat at his ma's bare feet while she peeled apples—it was the same place where his mother had been surrendered to the earth and where Haakon had broken Aven's heart.

The very man shifted and looked at Thor. Those weathered hands that were too much like his own slowed in their work. "You're awake."

It was just like Haakon to declare the obvious.

"You feelin' alright?"

Blinking, Thor didn't answer.

There was so much to be said between them. So much to be addressed and set to rights, and while Thor wished this moment could house those regrets and, of utmost importance, the justice that needed to be tended to for Aven's behalf, he hadn't the strength. All he had the strength for was to brace against the rising sun and the fact that it was Haakon's silhouette against it. That it was Haakon here, in this room, and that this wasn't a dream, as Thor had determined in his sleep.

This was real.

Haakon had dragged the bedstead away from the wall to fashion a mattress support from rope. Bent over the century-old footboard, he pushed an end of rope through a hole in one of the side rails and pulled yard after yard of line through. Rather like weaving, he pushed the end into the next hole and continued the pattern. Thor watched, and if he wasn't mistaken, the job was being done wrong. Not in the mood to extend advice, he just waited. Haakon would figure it out eventually.

All at once, Haakon stood and went downstairs. He came back up a minute later with a steaming tin cup. A kettle must have sounded. Haakon set the offering next to Thor, then fingerspelled *C-O-R-A*. That's all that needed to be explained. It would be herbs of the midwife's bringing. Thor closed a hand around the hot tin and sipped. It was a rough swallow, but if Cora advised it, he'd get the brew down.

Even more bitter to swallow was Haakon's presence, but for the sake of others, maybe it was best that he was here under this roof. There couldn't be a better way to keep an eye on him, uncomfortable as this hour, and those to follow, would be. Was there hope at the end of that? Was there hope even now? Thor had no idea.

Haakon made several more lengths of webbing, then examined his handiwork. He scratched the back of his head and looked over at Thor. "I think I'm doin' this the hard way."

At least they agreed on something.

He unlaced his efforts and looking at Thor again, spoke. "I've got a few things jotted down on that slip there." He tipped his head toward a scrap of paper with a pencil beside it. "If there's somethin' you want, just list it, and Jorgan will make sure it gets here."

Not sure how to respond to that, Thor picked up the paper and studied the items Haakon had already written. There was much he needed but little that could be remedied by way of paper and pencil. With Haakon's focus back on the bedstead, Thor rapped a knuckle on the floor to get his brother's attention. When Haakon paused, Thor motioned the pattern, showing that the frame needed to be woven the long way first.

"Oh." Haakon tried the method and made progress. He stepped in and out of the maple frame as he formed the pattern. When he skidded the bed sideways, vibrations rattled the floor. Haakon pressed the fibrous end of the rope through another hole and pulled the length hand over hand until it was snug. Again and again he did this, working in a manner that sanctioned his time aboard a ship. He plied the line with ease, shaping it and tucking the rest out of his way with swift authority. A telltale sign of carving out survival.

When the long lengths were finished, Haakon turned the piece of furniture to fashion the shorter portions.

Thor wondered what his younger brother might have done and seen in the years passed. What continents had he visited? How close had he come to death and what commissions had filled his months and days? Had things been different between them, Thor might have hunted down a story or two, but not now. What he needed instead was to address the ghost of trouble still in this very house.

Haakon stood and pressed on the slack webbing. It required a rope key but they didn't have one. The kid searched the room until he found a small piece of wood that had long ago snapped from the edge of the nearest windowsill. Sitting, he braced his dusty boot against a leg of the bed, wedged the wood inside one of the loops of rope, and tugged hard. The interior line tightened as the outside slackened. He braced the tension with his free hand, and stepped around the bed where he created stiffness on the opposite side. Time after time he did this until the slack was gone from the middle and there was more rope to tie off. Haakon pressed on the center section again. Tight as a spring.

"I'm gonna go check on that straw tick." He tossed the wood back into the corner, then brushed at his hands. "You know, before I haul it up, are you sure you don't want to be down on the first floor? It'd be a lot easier."

Thor just stared at him.

Haakon explained the same sentiment in Sign.

Right. He'd caught that.

"I ain't carryin' a privy pot up and down the stairs for you."

Again Thor stared at him, except this time it was to clarify just how much he cared.

Shoulders lowering, Haakon coiled up the remaining rope. He blew out a slow sigh, taking his time with the task. Finally, he spoke. "Look, Thor. I'm really sorry. I'm sorry for everything."

About time. But was it enough? Thor shaped the letters of Aven's name, then motioned between him and Haakon. Did his brother understand?

Did *he* understand?

Haakon knelt back. "Thor . . . I'm really sorry about what I did." He lowered his head and scratched the top of it again. His mouth moved, but whatever he said was lost at this angle. Thor tapped the wall for help. Haakon lifted his face and repeated himself. "I don't even know how to say how much."

Slowly, Thor nodded. He'd thought through this moment for nearly every day that Haakon had been gone. For nearly every night that Thor had lain beside his wife, determined to keep her safe and prayerful for her to find peace. All the while wondering that if Haakon were to come back—and if he were able to truly prove himself—that healing might come in the fullest sense. Was such a thing possible?

Speak A-V-E-N, you?

Pulling out his knife, Haakon spliced off the loose end of the rope. "Not unless you and she were agreed."

A-V-E-N agree? Yes. But only if she did. Thor pointed to himself. *I ask.*

Haakon turned the scrap of curling rope in his hands, and it was surely easier to make sense of than all of this. "Thank you." He gave a small smile, but while Thor felt the first risings of hope, there was an undercurrent of worry there as well. One that reminded him just how unpredictable his brother could be. To what degree these days, Thor didn't know, but he was bound and determined to be the one to find out.

SEVENTEEN

HAAKON WOKE IN THE BARN ONCE MORE, cross with himself for oversleeping again and so exhausted still that he wouldn't have noticed the little ciderkin standing there had the three-year-old not reminded him that he'd *swept wong* again.

Rising, Haakon scrubbed at his face with dry, calloused hands and wished for a swig of rum. He'd settle for coffee, but wasn't sure how to go about it. He was just going to have to down some water and hardtack and be grateful for it.

He longed to sleep longer, but the sun was more than risen. Once again, he'd stayed up into the night, keeping watch over the farm and scanning the distant hills for any signs of a campfire. The Sorrels were out there. He just knew it. Not only because Jorgan had informed him of their recent activity but because Haakon had seen his own share of evidence on his walk up this mountain. Less than a stone's throw away from the farm he'd found the cold dregs of a campfire, broken jars that still smelled of moonshine, and one drained bottle of morphine. He mightn't assume that Sorrel business if it weren't for the number and size of the bootprints in the dirt. Few men ran in packs so fearsome, and even fewer knew how to inject pain medication right into their veins.

Though Haakon had spotted no dangers to the farm last night, he sensed he was missing something. The realization that Jed and Harlan were somewhere in these wilds pestered him in a way he couldn't shake. Tomorrow night he'd try a different approach.

He'd outsmarted Jed and his men once and aimed to do it again.

Through the window, Haakon saw the kitchen door open. Fay came out and fetched a pail of water from the pump. Before she returned to the house, it opened again as Jorgan headed off to the horse barn for the morning chores. Though Sigurd bounded into the entry of the cidery to wave at his parents, neither of them seemed concerned for Sigurd to be in here with him. The boy must have known to keep his distance since he always lingered off a ways.

Kneeling in the straw, Haakon fished out the bundle that was the last of his hardtack. He broke it in half again before realizing he couldn't offer any over. Not now that he had been in close contact with Thor. Beside him, Sigurd climbed atop one of Thor's old wine barrels and sat. Long since emptied, blackberry stains tinted the wood in drips down the front. A barn cat crept out from behind the barrel with a stretch. The boy went to hold the scrawny bundle but wasn't quick enough.

Haakon looked around, wishing again for Grete. For so many years, his dog had kept pace beside him, never far from his feet. Now this place was empty of her, and he regretted again having not said goodbye. That the little boy sat at his side softened, for a spell, the sharpness of the loss.

With a heavy sigh, Haakon brushed at his hands as he rose. "Tell me, ciderkin, you have a brother, right?"

Sigurd nodded. "He dust a baby. Da says he walks wike he dwank too much. He dwinks a wot of milk."

"I'm sure he does." Haakon chuckled. "What's his name?"

"Bjørn."

"That's a fine name. Like yours."

"Aunt Avie's baby gonna be Jarle. Same as Granda."

The purring kitten returned and rubbed against his pants leg. Haakon bent to scruff it between the ears. "And if it's a girl?"

Sigurd scrunched up his face in confusion. Apparently they weren't expecting it to be a girl. Since no daughter had ever been born on this farm in nearly four decades, Haakon didn't blame them. Then again, maybe it was time.

Thinking to keep busy, he perused the box of tools beneath Thor's workbench. Not finding what he sought, he checked along the far wall where more tools sat waiting to be used in crates beside the massive cider press. Grabbing up a rasp, he checked the heft of it, then found one that was lighter. He handed the second to Sigurd and gripped the first for himself.

"Let's see if we can't get the outside of this building looking like it should again." He knew Jorgan or Thor would have covered over the markings there, but both of them were busy. As for him . . . He had time.

Once outside, Haakon squared his stance and placed the rasp to the tainted wall, then scraped it forward over the coarse boards. Shavings and dried paint fell away.

"Why are you doing dat?" Sigurd asked, squinting up.

"Because it's not supposed to be here."

"Can I help?"

Realizing that the boy couldn't reach, Haakon skidded a metal box into place and patted the rusted lid. Sigurd climbed onto it and could just reach a portion of the writing.

"Now . . ." Haakon said. "Get after it like I'm paying you."

Tongue sticking out in concentration, Sigurd did just that.

Haakon followed suit, and soon much was scraped away. Still exhausted from scant sleep, he rubbed the heel of his palm against his forehead. His stomach grumbled for a solid breakfast, and when he couldn't put off breaking into one more portion of hardtack, he returned to his pack. He'd just snapped another stale piece in half when he saw Ida entering with a tray. Her mouth was set tight—her disappointment in him clear—and yet those thin, knobby hands were the same ones that had swiped his tears as a lad and helped him see that there was hope in the world even when it was bleak.

As Haakon rose, he could scarcely lift his eyes to her face, but he forced himself to.

Ida was silent as she set the tray on the edge of Thor's workbench.

He brushed crumbs from his hands. "Thank you." Lowering his head, Haakon pulled out the list of items for Thor and set it aside the tray where she could reach it. Ida tucked the folded list into the pocket of her worn apron.

She gave a sure nod and instead of turning away spoke in the voice that filled all the places his mother hadn't been able to. "There's someone here to speak to you."

Despite himself, the back of his throat stung with emotion. After a nod of his own, Haakon cleared his throat. "Thank you, Miss Ida."

"You best treat her with kindness. I'll be near, and so will Jorgan, ya hear?" Though not tall, Ida lifted her chin, giving him a heady dose of challenge. "I's awful glad you came back, my boy. Best not make me wish I wasn't."

Though his throat tightened further, Haakon made himself speak. "Yes, ma'am." He pulled up his suspenders and adjusted his shirt, tucking it well despite the wrinkles. He ran a hand over his beard to make sure it wasn't in shambles, then tied back his hair to be as respectful as possible for this.

When Ida moved to Sigurd's side, Haakon stepped out into the sunshine.

Aven stood there with a shawl drawn tight around her shoulders.

Beyond her, Jorgan sat on the porch swing with his own breakfast in hand. Haakon gave his brother a small nod, then slowed to a stop at least a dozen paces from Aven. Everything about this filled him with fear, but he'd more than earned the discomfort. He blinked against the brightness of the morning, shielding his eyes only to see her better. Aven moved crossways into the dimness of the cider barn's shade, bringing him an ease of comfort that he didn't deserve.

Though Ida had said Aven wished to speak to him, Haakon could tell that he was going to need to be the first to say something. But all he could do was look at her and regret. On the chance that was making her uncomfortable, he dropped his gaze to the patch of ground between them.

Glory, he could use some coca right now, but it was too late.

"I . . . uh . . ." He wet his lips and braved a look at her again. "I'm awful sorry, Aven." He winced at how futile that sounded. "I'm more than sorry."

She clasped her hands and rested them together above her unborn child. Thor's child.

"Sorry's for somethin' you didn't mean to do," he added. "For breakin' something that's on accident. But my behavior that day wasn't an accident, so I know it'll take more than a word to make it right."

Aven's eyes filled with a sheen, and she set her mouth tighter as though to keep her chin steady. As for Haakon, he was thankful for his beard and hoped it concealed the fact that he was a mess inside.

"That I'm standing here now is a kindness, and I thank you. Thor too. And the family." Anxiety rising, he fisted his hands at his sides and worked his thumbs against his fingers. "I want to promise you that I'll never again try to bring you harm. I understand that my word doesn't hold any weight, and that's fair. If you'll allow me, I'll say that I mean it all the same and will do what I can to make that evident."

Aven didn't so much as move. Nothing stirred on her person save the twisting of her shawl's edge and a bit of hair that brushed against her cheek in the breeze.

"If it's best for you that I move on, I'll do so right away. But please take my apology and my assurance that I'm more sorry than I can say."

Dagnabit, he was going to cry. Haakon coughed into his fist to fight it. Made harder that Aven was tearing up enough for the both of them.

"Will you forgive me, Aven?" He asked through a throat so tight, it was scarcely a whisper. "I mean—might you consider it some day?" This wasn't coming out right.

She dropped her gaze then, seeming to focus instead on his boots. They were as patched and awful as he felt, and he had to force himself not to shift them. When a cloud drifted in front of the sun, the land dimmed. Air cooling. He couldn't read her expression so well, but he didn't dare move closer. To his shock, it was she who took a small step nearer. Not so near as to be friendly, but near enough that he could see the splattering of freckles across her face and the deep brown of her eyes. Eyes that had once regarded him in panic—driving a wedge into his soul that he was yet to pull free.

Now they were soft and so filled with grace, he lost the battle with himself and had to swipe a hand over his eyes. Though he couldn't see her in doing so, the voice that spoke then was as small as his own had been.

"You're forgiven, Haakon."

EIGHTEEN

WITH A FEW MINUTES BEFORE AUNT CORA was due to visit, Aven lifted a wicker basket to the center of the mattress. Beside it rested a list brought to her by Ida—one written from Haakon and containing items requested for Thor. 'Twas strange to peer upon Haakon's penmanship after all this while, but with his apology this morning, she was able to lift the scrap of paper in a steady hand. While the first bricks of possibility had been laid, bringing the first traces of newfound peace, uncertainty still dwelled within her, so she would seek Cora's counsel during their visit today.

Beginning with the initial items on the list, Aven fetched fresh sheets of paper for letter writing as well as several new pencils. Next she gathered up Thor's pipe and pouch of tobacco along with other sundry items listed for him. Aven placed everything in the basket, grateful for a way to help, small as it was.

But what wasn't easy to lower into place was the framed photograph that Haakon had requested last of all. A wedding picture that Thor kept. How Haakon had known about the photograph bespoke his years of living in this very attic before Aven's arrival. That the framed memory would soon be in Haakon's care left her unsettled— but with these things bound for Thor, Aven pulled the photograph from its place among her husband's most treasured items and laid it in the basket.

A gentle knock on the door frame had her turning to see Cora with medic bag in hand.

"Oh, do come in." Aven waved her nearer and pushed the basket aside.

Cora entered with a cheery greeting and set her black bag on the edge of the bed. A few strands of the midwife's graying hair peeked out from beneath the cotton wrapping she always wore wound around her head as other freedwomen did—her chestnut-brown skin a pretty contrast to the soft blue of the cloth.

"Now, how's about you lie back and we see how this little one be faring?" Having served as midwife to the Norgaards for over thirty years, Cora moved to the window and pushed the curtains farther open, spilling in brighter light. Dotti, who had been asleep in the sunny corner, lifted her head, whiskers twitching in soft greeting. Cora gave the cat a gentle rub under the chin before tying back the drapes.

With the coverlet now cleared, Cora helped Aven lie back and 'twas a relief to pull her feet up. Always did she look forward to Cora's visits. Not only did they offer cause to rest a while, but Cora's sage wisdom and kind ways were as cherished as Ida's. Perhaps a few years past fifty, Cora bore the same sprightly way as her older sister—caring and kind, while never one to shy away from the truths of life or the delivery of them to body and soul.

With skilled hands, Cora felt along one side of Aven's mounded abdomen, then switched to the other side and did the same. Often during these visits, Georgie's laughter carried from the first floor, but today Cora's ten-year-old daughter hadn't come along to play with the boys. The absence of the child was likely due to Haakon's presence and the fact that he'd always held a special spot in the girl's heart. Cora's way of guarding that heart, perhaps, until time and answers eased the strain of his presence.

Cora pressed along the underside of Aven's belly where she declared the baby's head well settled. "That good." Cora lessened the pressure. "Be just where we hope."

She tugged up Aven's blouse and chemise so that her stomach was exposed. Aven followed Fay's lead in not giving corsets a second thought in the final months of pregnancy. 'Twas freeing, and as Cora readily confirmed, much healthier for the growing babe. In the late afternoon light, the skin of Aven's belly was as tight as a drum, and as of right now, the little one inside kept a cheery rhythm of the wiggling sort. Cora must have felt it beneath her hands because she lifted her eyes to the ceiling with a tender expression.

"Have you and Thor settled on names? Last I came, you was thinkin' on one for a girl still."

"Aye. We have." Aven described the uniting of her and Thor's ideas and Cora smiled.

"I rather like that. It suits you both." Having fetched her tool for listening to the baby's heart, Cora bent and pressed it to the underside of Aven's belly. "Have you pains?" she asked.

"Soreness here and there, but mostly just a heaviness. Do you think it will be soon?"

"By our count, it be a few weeks off, though the babes know when it time. The waitin' be hard, but you doin' a fine job." After affirming a good, steady heartbeat, Cora smoothed her hands around Aven's stomach, shaping a secure circle as she made her assessments.

"What do you think of the size of this next Norgaard?" Aven asked. So substantial had Thor been upon his birth that she was preparing herself for a testing like his mother had had.

Cora smiled. "If you's worried because Thor the biggest baby I ever attended, then let me tell you that the papas don't have all the say in the size of their babies." She winked. "It might just be feelin' so big 'cause of your own small stature. But I wouldn't worry after it too much."

Aven nodded, relieved.

Cora lowered Aven's chemise and blouse back down. Though a scraping sound came from the yard, Cora's focus didn't leave Aven's face. "No matter what, little ones come into this world just as they ought. Just as God arranged. It ain't easy, but your body'll know what to do, and you're to trust in that." Cora righted a button of Aven's blouse that had come undone. "I'll be there to guide you. Whatever might be asked of you during those hours . . . trust that there be purpose behind it." Her eyes were wise and kind. "I promise that God knew just what He was doing when He knit this life inside you, and I also promise that I won't walk from this room without having spent all I got to see you both safely along."

"I thank you." At a pinch of tears, Aven tried to cling not to worry but to the hope and assurance Cora offered. She sat up some when the midwife moved to help her. The task might have been a welcome distraction, but the struggle of it all only sent more tears welling. Aven sucked in a breath as sorrow broke in waves now. "I . . . if Thor . . ." For so long they'd dreamt of this time—of a child. And now that it was here, he was elsewhere fighting for his life. Fear crashed around her, blotting out even the joy of all that might be.

Cora's expression softened, and she lowered her gaze to the basket of things for Thor. "Take heart, dear one." Her grip on Aven's hand offered assurance. "Since the start of time, soldiers done marched to the front lines and men set out on voyages, even as their women labor back home—bringin' life into this world. You'll not be the first to give birth on the shores of *missing him*, and you'll not be the last." Cora lowered her head so Aven could look straight into her gentle eyes. "I say that to bolster. You've no need to fear. It a gusty place to stand, but it only mean that the Lord be all the nearer."

Aven nodded as a soft breeze drifted in from the open window. The same gentle rush lifted her shawl that was draped on the bedstead, filling it with air as though a sail. It swiped against the cradle, trailing against the smooth wood that Jarle Norgaard had carved with the curving filigree that harkened back to Norwegian ships of old.

Cora lifted the window higher, inviting in more of the sweet air. When the shawl slid loose of its smooth knob, she folded it with care. "Wherever Thor be both now and on the day of this one's birth, he'll be lovin' you fiercely." Cora's smile was as warm as her words. "Now you rest here a spell longer, and I'll be right by your side. No need for either of us to rush off."

Settling back against the raised pillows, Aven thanked her. Wanting to hold tight to Cora's sage wisdom, she fingered the soft sheet where Thor always lay and closed her eyes.

Cora moved about and by the sound of it was shifting bottles in her medic case. Her footsteps crossed the floor, followed by the gentle rattle of the chains that belonged to the hanging farm scale. Though most oft used for weighing bags of apples, it had been hung into place near the newly arrived cradle—both rituals belonging to the time just before a new Norgaard babe.

With the scraping sound still in the yard that was much less familiar, Aven glanced out the window.

Haakon stood in front of the cidery and with a rasp in hand ran it against the weathered wood, causing a portion of the vow written there to fade. Same as he'd been doing that morning while she'd rallied the courage to face him of her own accord. The shirt between his suspenders was dark with sweat, his boyish confidence gone, and in its place was a raw and real ability that bespoke years of sea and survival.

Cora's own gaze moved to the window. A shadow passed over her eyes—brief but telling. The woman wasn't pleased with the youngest Norgaard, that was certain. Cora watched as Haakon worked—the very woman who had helped bring him into the world. Perhaps in this very room. So close was Haakon in age to Cora's daughter, Tess, that Aven had a sense Cora might have been his wet nurse. A motherly bond that she couldn't yet begin to fathom. 'Twas a broken heart shining in Cora's eyes, and it made Aven's own chest ache even more.

At the washstand, Cora poured a glass of water while she watched Haakon scrape at the nearest board. "He due to have a time of it if he aimin' to make that writin' go away." As Haakon continued his work, so softened Cora's countenance. With the markings made by secret leaders of the Ku Klux Klan, Aven realized just how potent Haakon's actions were to Cora.

Yet 'twas a motherly protection for Aven in Cora's voice. "How you farin' with him home?"

"I'm not certain. At first I was stunned to see him. He came with no word or warning."

"Ain't that just like Haakon?"

Aye. "I don't know what to think or believe. There has been time enough to prepare for that, but I don't know that I'm as ready as I might have been."

"I say you're doin' right fine. More than fine."

"We've spoken briefly, and he asked me to forgive him."

Cora's hands that had been busy adjusting a pillow stilled. "What had you to say?"

The scraping continued—muted by distance but steady with determination.

"I told him that I forgive him, but I'm not sure of what to do. I don't feel any different, Aunt Cora. I'm still uneasy."

Cora patted a cool touch to Aven's arm. "There be no shame in unease. Not when it be of such a nature as you've known. Your trust been broken, and he must bear the consequence."

"But how can that be? If I've forgiven him . . . am I not doing something wrong?"

"Forgiveness be a gift taught to us by the One who forgave first and who forgave the most. You took that to heart when Haakon done asked you, and I'm right proud of you and your answer. Mighty proud. But that you's unsettled around him be the cost of his choice. Unlike forgiveness, trust be a cost only *he* can pay."

Aven watched him through the window as he stood there, speaking to Sigurd, who was helping. In this moment, she could see a trace of the kindness she'd once known was in him.

"It be trust he need to earn, and that's what sin does. Forgiveness . . . it pure and good, but it just the start of it. Offering one don't mean the other be remedied as well. When a person be hurt, there need be a minding to both hope *and* sense."

With Cora the faithful soul to have delivered most of the infants in the region for decades, she'd surely seen her share of injustice when it came to the ways of a man with a woman. How many trembling hands had she laid newborns in? How many misty-eyed mothers had she spoken these words of comfort to?

The side of Cora's mouth tipped up in a smile that bespoke a faith as bright as the sunshine streaming in. The shawl still in hand, she lay the soft folds over the footboard of the bed. "Overcoming such hurts ain't so different than what that man be aimin' to achieve out there." Her eyes shifted to the window once more. "All that been painted there may soon be scoured off, but the grooves of their doin' will remain. Those hollows will serve as a reminder that iniquity be possible. And the scraping away is what the restoring does. Our hearts ain't so different than the side of that barn. And we not so different in the hands of our Maker."

NINETEEN

STANDING BEHIND A STACK OF APPLE CRATES
at the back end of the cidery, Haakon buttoned up the top half of
his winter underwear. It felt mighty fine to his skin that was equally
as clean. The distant barking of dogs broke the silence, but while he
glimpsed a view of the surrounding hills through the windows, he
could see neither the sheriff and his deputies nor the hounds that
they'd loosed into the vast timberland of Blackbird Mountain.

Haakon might have helped in the search for the Sorrel men, but
he had a different kind of plan, and it hinged on staying as far from
the sheriff as possible.

He grabbed his pants and shook them out. Earlier, he'd unearthed
the boxes of his old things from the cabin loft, and grubbier than
was decent, he'd marched to the spring and drenched himself, thinking it a good way to scrub everything he had to his name—himself
included. Now he bent lower behind the barrel and crammed one leg
into place and then the second. The massive door slid aside just as
he'd fastened the waistband of his pants, and Peter stepped in.

After lifting a hand in greeting, Peter headed his way. So large
was the cidery that the man's footsteps echoed throughout the soaring
space. As children, he and Peter had always been in the same school

grade and often shared a bench and slate, but rarely had they gotten along. In fact, they'd only managed to tolerate one another just days before Haakon had left, which made it strange to step forward and extend a hand to Peter Sorrel for the first time in their lives. "Jorgan mentioned you've been working for the farm."

Peter swiped a hand down the front of his threadbare coveralls and accepted the shake. "Your folks are good people." He looked so much like his father, Harlan, it was uncanny. If it weren't for Peter's lack of beard, Haakon would have gotten a start at sight of him standing there.

Haakon reached for a cotton shirt, the white cloth having sat folded for years. When Peter waited there, he looked back to the farmhand. "Did you need something?"

"Just wanted to let you know that I'm comin' with you."

"I don't know what you're talking about."

"You know exactly what I'm talkin' about. You've been on the lookout for my pa and pawpaw, and wherever it is you're goin' tonight, I'm goin' with you."

The hounds barked again, farther away this time.

Haakon shook out the shirt. "How do you know I'm goin' somewhere?"

"'Cause it's plain as day."

"It ain't *plain as day*."

"It is to me." Peter folded arms across his chest and leaned a shoulder against the nearest wall. Though his stance was easy, his face was all business. "Things are grim, and we both know it. Tess won't wander ten paces from their cabin these days, and she'll scarce let Georgie past the door."

Near to their own age, Tess had grown up like a sister to Haakon, and while Georgie was a fair deal younger, he cherished her the same. That Peter was outshining him in both regards spoke volumes.

Peter continued. "Cora ain't scared to wander out none, but she oughtta be. I guarantee you that PawPaw Jed and my pa are not alone.

There's half a dozen of them, or I don't know my own kin. They done busted into one of the outbuildings up on the plantation yesterday, and still they're on the loose. We both know those dogs won't find nothin'. If Pa was a man to be found, he'd have been caught long ago. That sheriff's gonna have to give up like all the others have."

Haakon conceded the point. Peter's uncles and cousins who'd gone off with Jed and Harlan those years back hadn't avoided the law all this while by being careless. Haakon swung his shirt on. It wasn't lost to him that once upon a time, Peter had aided Jorgan in pulling Thor off of him. A man had to be strong, crazy, and loyal to wrestle back a furious god of thunder.

He could use a man like that.

Haakon righted his collar. "Fine. I'm not goin' anywhere 'til dusk, so you're gonna have to come back."

Though even taller than Haakon, the former Klansman stood a mite straighter. If Haakon was walking into trouble, he wouldn't for one moment mind having the mountain-grown Sorrel at his side. "I can do that."

Haakon buttoned one sleeve cuff and then the other. "You got a soft spot for Tess."

"I live near their cabin and owe them a whole heap. They been kind to me, so I care about their safety. All of them, not just Tess."

"If you say so."

Peter was sober, making the fact that he hadn't denied it all the more honorable. While words were potent, a man's caring ran through deeper waters. It dwelled right there in what he was willing to do. Haakon knew all too well that Peter had once taken a beating for Tess. A way to protect her from his own kin. If anyone was ready to face an uncertain future against Jed and Harlan, it was Peter.

Haakon belted his knife sheath around his hip. "Come an hour before dark."

"I'll be here." Peter ran a rough hand up and down his forearm,

chafing at an old scar. "I also came to tell you that my sister . . .
Sibby . . . She's married."

"Is she?"

"Sorry to disappoint you."

Haakon grinned. "I'm not disappointed." Though he had a few fond
memories of Sibby Sorrel. While little more than a handful of secret inter-
ludes, and rather innocent ones at that, it was best he and she had gone
their separate ways. Their last names would never have gotten along.

"She was sweet on you, ya know. Sulked for months after you
were gone."

Haakon shoved the crate of clothes aside. "She's better off, I'm
sure."

"She is," Peter quipped with a slanted smirk. "Married to a moonshiner over on the other side of the crest. Got twenty acres of rough
land, but it don't matter 'cause he don't farm none. Makes whiskey
that even Thor would've taken a likin' to."

"That good?"

"Real good. He's a right straight shot too. That's where I wanna
take you."

"I don't know that it would be the best time for—"

"No, you don't understand. Sibby's fella, he seen my pawpaw.
Two nights ago."

Jed? "What about your sister?"

"She weren't there. Jed don't know she got married, so he didn't
know who he was buyin' from. Orville's his name. Decent fella, and
he thinks Jed'll be back in a night or two."

"You sure."

"More than sure."

"Sheriff know?"

Peter shook his head. "It'd blow the whole point—sending a slew
o' lawmen up there with a pack of dogs."

It sure-fired would. Best to keep it to themselves for now. The sheriff knew how to manage himself, and while Haakon respected that, he also needed the same leeway to handle this in a different fashion. One that didn't announce itself all over these hills.

"Pa might even be with him," Peter added. "He wasn't last time. Pawpaw Jed made mention that he was laid up for some reason."

"Jed?"

The haystack near, Peter fetched a short piece. "No, my pa." He slid it into the side of his mouth.

Well, whatever ailed Harlan Sorrel, he'd be on his feet again soon. There wasn't much that could get a man like that down. "So you think they'll be at this fella's still?"

"Supposed to be."

Why hadn't he thought of it sooner? Pirates . . . They always went where the treasure was. And he'd learned aboard ship that pirates weren't just for fairy tales. He need only look into Jed Sorrel's unpatched eye to know that the man was made of darker stuff than most. The war general's two-fingered hand was as much of an iron fist as any other leader's, maybe even more so.

The Sorrel patriarch had a reason to be angry. Not only had he lost his livelihood in the War, he'd lost pieces of himself in battle as well as control of over thirty slaves, including Cora and Ida. Really, he'd lost control of this mountain. It had slackened further when Thor refused to sell his hard cider to them, then, when Jed had stolen nearly a thousand dollars' worth of brew, it was good and gone when Haakon snuck into their barn and blew it to blazes.

"He'll want to get even with me," Haakon said. "And I don't want that comin' down on my brothers."

Peter turned the straw and slid the end back in his mouth. "I don't think he cares a lick about you."

"But I'm the one who blew up his barn."

"I think he's owin' that to somebody else. Somebody who put you up to it."

"Who?"

"Who else but the one who wouldn't sell to them in the first place? Who stopped makin' it altogether."

"Your grandpop's after Thor?"

"Seems that way. It's why they broke in here and stole all his stock in the first place. To teach Thor a lesson, wouldn't you think?"

Overwhelmed, Haakon rubbed his forehead with the heel of his palm, barely noticing the way Peter's attention shifted to the house. Haakon leaned that way and through the open doorway saw Aven stepping onto the porch with a basket.

Haakon swiped his Yellowboy rifle along with the box of ammo. "Come back tonight." He was already halfway to the open door. "I'll be ready."

Aven was probably searching for Jorgan to escort her Thor's way, and not wanting to make her uneasy or insinuate that he could do the task, Haakon kept his head down and aimed straight for the stretch of trees that blocked his cabin from view. Pulling out his pouch, he freed a coca leaf, dusted it with powder, and crammed the folded square far back into his cheek. A small enough portion that he could talk around it with ease, and while the leaves were brittle now, making them less palatable, by hour's end all these troubles would be easier to manage.

At the cabin, Thor sat on the porch steps as downtrodden as Haakon had ever seen with his face tilted down and his forehead braced with a hand. Haakon hadn't given much thought as to what was ailing Thor, and while he had a hunch it was a result of too much drink in years past, the doctor seemed to think otherwise. Haakon had meant to inquire more but supposed it really didn't matter so long as he did what he'd promised to do for his brother. As for catching something rough, it was too late to worry now.

There was no way to get Thor's attention like this, so Haakon stepped wide in a way that sent his shadow into his brother's line of sight. Thor lifted his head.

"You alright?"

Thor signed a response as if Haakon were the last person in the world he wanted to reply to. *Breakfast not stay down.*

Glad he'd missed it. "There's not a mess upstairs is there?"

Thor shook his head. He wet his lips, and his skin was as sallow as ever. Never, not even in Thor's most saturated days with alcohol, had Haakon seen him this bad off.

"You sure you don't want me to move the bed downstairs? It would be a lot easier on you."

When Thor looked away, that was answer enough.

"Stubborn ox," Haakon muttered. Leaning the rifle against the banister, he stomped into the cabin. Time to make some sense of the mess on this lower level. If he had it tidied up, then maybe his brother would see reason. Haakon picked up a broken chair and, with the door still open, tossed the heap past where the porch swing used to hang and over the far railing. He did the same with a rusted-out pail and some old paint cloths. All reminded him of a distant time, so he tried to turn his mind from that as he gutted the place of rubbish and cobwebs.

It worked fine until he shoved back an empty barrel where ruddy droplets stained the floor, windowsill, and lowest panes of glass. Long since dried with time. Haakon didn't need to look any closer to know the sight of his own blood. Even now the back of his skull throbbed at memory of colliding into this window from the violent storm that had been Thor.

So this was why his brother didn't want to stay downstairs. How had Haakon not noticed? Because Thor was more observant—always seeing what others missed. At some point Haakon was going to need soap and a rag. A little patience and an iron will. To his shame, it wouldn't be today. His stomach churned, and determined for Thor to be the only one to lose his breakfast, Haakon stepped out and further away from the past, certain beyond doubt that a hundred barn walls would be easier to scrub clean than his own wretchedness.

Outside, Thor struggled to rise.

Haakon tapped his shoulder. *Stairs. Need help you?* he signed the language. How natural it returned.

Thor shook his head and lumbered back inside. His steps were slow and heavy, and Haakon listened as they grew higher. In a minute it was silent.

Haakon turned to rid the cabin of more debris, but in passing the door again, the lock drew his attention. Dropping to a crouch, he fingered the keyhole. The brass was scarred and dented. It had to be from a metal tool of some sort, and a bold effort at that. But why was someone picking the lock? Haakon studied it more closely only to realize the gut-churning answer.

No one but the Sorrels would have cause to try, and since this hadn't been here yesterday, the gouges could only be from the night before. Pulse rising, Haakon stood and moved to the nearest window where the outside sill was battered as well. Some kind of tool had been used to try and loosen the frame from the wall. Why hadn't they just broken the glass? It wasn't as though Thor would have heard.

Haakon stilled. They thought Thor wasn't alone.

That meant they knew Haakon had come back. It also meant they didn't realize he was bedding down in the cider barn. If they knew that there was no one to hear a break-in, Thor might have already been a goner. While his brother was a sure shot and fast draw, this would have been many men against one, and so long as they walked gentle, they'd have taken him by surprise.

Haakon knelt again and surveyed the Sorrels' handiwork. He needed to warn Thor and Jorgan. Of equal importance, he was going to need to stay here now.

At sound of someone coming, he turned to see Peter striding this way, Aven at his side. Haakon dropped his hand from the battered lock and rose. He crossed the porch, meeting them both in the yard. Peter stayed back, and Haakon gave him a cordial nod. He didn't know if Peter had come along to guard Aven from the Sorrels or from him, but on both accounts it was justified.

Aven freed her arm from the basket handle, holding the woven wicker down beside her patchwork skirt. Scarcely as tall as his shoulder, and far along with child, she was womanly and fragile. Every curve of her would be tempting to men on the lookout for vulnerability. Haakon glanced back to where he'd left his rifle and longed to fetch it. She shouldn't have come here.

The eyes that turned to him were hopeful. "Is Thor awake?"

He checked his warring concerns. "I can go up and find out." Turning, he kept pace with her toward the cabin and was all the more glad for Peter's watchful eye.

"How is he today?" Aven asked.

"He's still pretty beat."

"Has the doctor come yet?"

"Not yet. If much more time goes by, I can ride out with a message for you."

"Thank you."

At the cabin, she slowed beneath an upstairs window as though to call out. How easy that would be for her. To simply call her husband's name so he would come, or tap a pebble to the window. But that's not how it worked with Thor.

"Listen, Aven. I don't think you should come here anymore. Not even with Peter. It's not safe."

Her glance to Haakon was wary.

Should he explain his suspicions? Or would he only cause unnecessary fear? It seemed best she be well informed, but he needed to sort through some uncertainties first. Besides, she already knew this farm was surrounded. No sense in reminding her one more time. Haakon considered Peter, and while he trusted the farmhand, something was still making him uneasy. It would be better that she not come here at all, guardian or not.

"Haakon?" Aven asked. "About Thor . . ."

Oh, right. "I'll go check." Haakon strode to the porch, crossed in three long strides, and ducked inside. He stormed up the stairs, took note of his brother's status, and went back down, this time grabbing the rifle before returning to the yard.

Aven's eyes widened with anticipation, making his words taste bitter.

"He's out cold still. I could wake him, but he was fit to be tied last time I did."

The hope flitted away, replaced by hurt at what would seem like a snub from her husband. Eyes downcast, she handed over the basket, then from her skirt pocket withdrew a sealed envelope. "This is from Washington, DC," Aven said softly. "It came by post this morning."

Haakon accepted both. "I'll see that he gets it. And Aven. It would be best if you stayed with Jorgan. Stayed close. Even better than Peter." He feared that with Peter's past with his family, that posed its own kind of risk. By denouncing his loyalty to the Klan, Peter had a mark on his back about the same size as Thor's. Haakon had his own kind of target. But not Jorgan.

"I will," she said, and he could see that she meant it. Still looking crestfallen, she cast one more look toward the cabin, then turned away. As she left, her head tilted toward the graying sky. To summon a few more hours of strength from heaven?

She needed to stop coming here and knew not what she was up against. Knew not what the men in these parts were capable of or how far they would go for the revenge. What she'd endured with him? It was but a tip of the iceberg to the terrors she could face. As for turning her away, he'd done it for her and the baby's sake. Even for Thor.

Aven needed to stay where Jorgan was because it wasn't Jorgan who had stopped making the liquor the Sorrels craved. It certainly wasn't Jorgan who had blown up their barn. This place—where Thor was, and now Haakon—it was the last place Aven needed to be.

Turning her away hadn't been an unkindness, but guilt stabbed him for the deceit regardless. It drove in hard and deep, making him sick. She truly didn't know what she was up against . . . not even with him. She didn't know that he'd been lying back there. Lying straight through his teeth. It had taken a mere glance from the top of the stairs to confirm that Thor had been wide awake and waiting for her.

TWENTY

THOR WOKE TO MORNING LIGHT AND HAAKON asleep in the chair. Beard crushed to his chest, Haakon must have dozed off sometime in the night. Why was he sleeping here in the cabin? He always bunked down in the cidery.

A lantern sat beside him on the floor, and an almanac lay abandoned beneath his seat, perhaps dropped when he'd lost consciousness. His levergun rifle leaned against the wall beside him. Still resting on the bed, Thor reached over the edge and caught hold of one of his boot laces. He tugged the shoe up, gripped it good by the sole, and chucked it at his brother's head.

It slammed into its target, and Haakon jolted awake. With a scowl, he rubbed the side of his face. "What is wrong with you?"

You send wife away again? I break your neck.

Haakon's eyebrows shot up. He stared at Thor, then bent forward and picked up the dropped almanac. Propping an ankle over his opposite knee, he slouched in the chair, opened the pamphlet, and continued reading. Thor reached down for the other boot.

Haakon lurched upright. "Alright, I'm sorry!" He rubbed the side of his head a second time. "I won't do that again. I promise."

Thor pointed at his brother, then tapped the side of his finger to

his lips before bringing it down to his other hand to form *Promise.*
Have no value.

Haakon squinted, and a sentiment that was rarely seen in his eyes
darkened the blue of them. Regret.

Thor wasn't one for eavesdropping, but it hadn't been difficult to
glimpse the pair of them yesterday through a window. He certainly
hadn't missed the way his brother had appeared here at the top of the
stairs only to rush back down just as quick. Thor had watched through
the window to where Aven had stood waiting, braided hair as coppery
as a field in autumn. Even from the distance, her eyes had been a stark
contrast to her cream-colored skin, and her freckles had made him want
to be able to cup the side of her face and brush his thumb there.

Though he couldn't touch her, Thor had risen to fetch his coat,
but before he'd even slid it on, Aven had been sent away. Anger had
boiled in him, but weak still, there had been little he could do since
Haakon hadn't returned. Finally, and to his frustration, Thor had
fallen asleep in the night. He'd woken to find Haakon in the chair
and the light of a new morning spilling in. That's when he'd reached
for his boot.

Not only had Aven been turned away, but she'd given Haakon
a letter. In the twelve hours since, Thor hadn't seen so much as a
trace of it, and with it Sunday morning, Aven would be off to church
instead of coming to visit him. He wouldn't be able to inquire with
her until later, let alone see her.

Letter. Furious, Thor snapped off the sign.

Haakon's brows shot up again, this time as abruptly as the rest of
him did. He rushed down the stairs, then returned with a grimace, a
basket, and a letter. "I'm really sorry—"

Thor snatched the letter from him.

Haakon set the basket near. "Listen. About yesterday—"

Ignoring him, Thor dropped his attention to the envelope.
Alexander Graham Bell. Washington, DC.

Haakon tapped him for his attention, and Thor shoved his hand away.

Undeterred, Haakon communicated in Sign, which was harder to ignore, explaining that he needed to tell Thor something important. Haakon nudged Aven's offering aside and had the audacity to begin to sit. Just as he did, his head turned toward the stairwell and he stepped that way, saving Thor the trouble of kicking him off.

Haakon headed back down the stairs, and Thor lifted the cloth on Aven's offering. Inside lay sundry items that would be of use. Haakon's doing? Since he'd made the list, it had to be. Which likened Haakon as the cause for the photograph resting beside Thor's pipe and tobacco pouch. A photograph taken some eight years ago when Aven had married their cousin in Norway. This had been the very first glimpse Thor ever had of her. The first he'd ever known of her existence—a tender face and what seemed a gentle soul. Both that had proved more than true upon her arrival here.

Thor doubted Aven would have been so direct as to offer her likeness as comfort, but the sight of her so near and lovely was a bolstering that eased the sorrow. Leave it to his brother—a man who had lost much and given up much—to know that.

The house lightened in what had to be the front door opening. It dimmed, and Thor felt the shuddering of it close. He started to rise, but before he got far saw that it wasn't his brother coming up the stairs but the doctor. Haakon followed right behind.

Young Dr. Abramson set his black satchel on the empty chair. "I'm glad to see you upright, Mr. Norgaard. I had a very interesting conversation with your wife not too long ago, and now I come bearing new developments."

Oh? Thor set the unread letter on the windowsill, keeping it within sight.

"How are you feeling?"

Little better.

When Haakon spoke for him, the doctor smiled. "That's good to hear. I had a hunch you might be. I believe rest is what you've been needing." He came nearer and set his bag aside. He bent to better study Thor. "Your eyes, I see, are still yellowed. But if you'll hold out your hands, I'd like to try something." The physician demonstrated for him to hold his palms out as though to place them flush to a wall. When Thor did, the doctor pressed, causing Thor's wrists to angle back. The doctor held a good strong pressure for several seconds, then let go. Nothing happened.

The young man's brows shot up. So accustomed was Thor to reading people's faces that he knew relief when he saw it.

"What of nausea?" Dr. Abramson asked.

Thor made a slicing motion across his palm with his opposite hand.

"He said 'some,'" Haakon clarified. "It seems to come and go."

Dr. Abramson nodded. "Will you lie back for me, Mr. Norgaard?"

Thor did as asked, and the man tugged up one side of his shirt. "I'm looking for bruising." He examined Thor's flesh on one side and then the other. "Any pain?"

Thor made the same motion again and the doctor inquired. "Some?"

Thor nodded.

"Well, you didn't try and rip my arm off this time." He smiled again, setting Thor more at ease. It hurt, yes, but no he hadn't. "I don't feel any swelling, and with a lack of bruising, that's a sound indication that your liver is not failing. Also when I examined the reflex of your hands, they didn't behave as is common with failure of the liver. I confess, it's taken me some further study to identify these traits."

Returning to mind was a memory of Da's hands having a jerky motion. Like the flapping of bird's wings in his last days of life. Thor had never experienced that condition, but it might still come. He signed the worry to Haakon, who spoke again.

"He's wondering if it might be too soon to tell."

"Possibly, but in truth I now sense that something else is at work here. I've done further reading, and based off your symptoms, and in conjunction with your wife's added information and some assistance from my mentor, I have a hypothesis." Dr. Abramson took care to stay angled toward Thor as he spoke. "Your liver may not be fatally diseased. Granted, it's too early to be certain, but I'm of a mind that what you have is indeed Epidemic Jaundice."

Though that meant he was contagious, it also held the hope that he was going to live.

Relief hit him with such a rush that Thor drew in a sharp breath. A sting in his eyes, he tried to fight it.

The doctor shifted Thor's shirt back into place and motioned for him to sit up. "You've every reason to be relieved. I'm optimistic that what you're facing does not place your life at risk. If it is indeed Epidemic Jaundice with which you suffer, you'll need to stay away from the others for a while yet but should soon be recovered enough to return to your family."

Thor shaped the phrase with his hand.

"He said thank you," Haakon relayed. Then, speaking of his own accord, asked the question that Thor meant to pose next. "How soon?"

The doctor moved to the washstand, where he rinsed and lathered his hands. He answered as he washed, and unable to see it, Thor waved for his brother's help.

Haakon waited, apparently listening, then spoke in Thor's direction. "He said a few weeks more at most based on your steady recovery and the time since you met the doctor at the train." Haakon's brow furrowed. "What doctor at the train?"

Thor shook his head. He'd explain that later. As for right now, what did this have to do with that day on the train?

Dr. Abramson shook droplets from his hands, then glanced back to Thor. "Do you recall the blood draw you received?"

He nodded.

Lines of confusion lifted Haakon's forehead.

"It may be the cause of your ailment. Having looked into the matter more, I have further discoveries. You see . . ." He pulled a cloth from his bag and dried his hands. "During the War, some seventy thousand soldiers were affected with Epidemic Jaundice. Astounding numbers. Yet what made it so rampant? Some believe it was due to the soldiers' poor living conditions and a diet of food that was often contaminated. I have a hunch this may be correct, yet there might be another culprit." He folded the towel and stuffed it away. "Officers were given injections of morphine for pain, administered as a way to promote calm amid the horrors of war. Often of their own gangrene and amputations. Such an antidote was even given to the lowest ranking soldiers if their injuries were dire enough. For these administrations, physicians utilized the use of a needle syringe, much like that which you became familiarized with some months back."

Thor watched the doctor intently, but when Haakon shifted, he gauged what his brother had to ask.

"I don't understand what this has to do with Thor being sick," Haakon said. "He wasn't even alive during the Civil War."

The doctor's demeanor was patient. "Correct." Then to Thor, "What I mean to imply is a link between needle administration and the epidemic itself. Since needles were routinely used among surgeons, and Epidemic Jaundice was rampant, there's speculation of a connection. When I sent my mentor the additional information that I procured through your wife's visit to my office, he concurred the likelihood. That these needles, which were injected into countless soldiers, might have *transferred* the illness. If this is indeed a possibility, might your own case of the epidemic have come by way of the blood draw?"

Thor thought back to the day of the interview, recalling first the prick and then the knowledge that Harlan Sorrel had returned.

"During my time as a surgeon's apprentice, I studied much on the works of a Dr. Joseph Lister who developed a principle of the use of an antiseptic in surgical methods." Dr. Abramson went on to explain that this was an organic compound used to kill low forms of life that caused infection in injuries and wounds.

Thor hadn't a clue what that meant, but he focused in to try and understand.

"The antiseptic prevents decomposition of the flesh and promotes survival in patients. Based on Lister's research, death and illness can be greatly lessened if these methods are employed. Of this, I speak to the sanitization of surgical tools by route of the antiseptic, as well as careful cleansing of the hands and any other involved surfaces."

Haakon's brow puckered in confusion. "I don't understand."

"Which is why the research is so controversial. Many physicians hold to the belief that a blood-encrusted surgical apron is a mark of expertise and efficiency, but having studied under my mentor, who was a firm advocate to Dr. Lister's demonstrations, I'm convinced that cleanliness is most advantageous, if not critical."

Rubbing dirt-creased hands together, Haakon scrutinized the young physician but said no more.

"Simply put, should organic matter be able to live in the blood . . . causing infection . . ."

Exhausted, Thor blinked quickly, losing some of the words. He waved to the doctor to stop, then, holding out an arm, dragged a hand up the length of it to indicate *slow*.

He could read lips, yes, but these were phrasings he wasn't accustomed to.

Haakon spoke. "He's asking if you can talk slower."

"Of course." Dr. Abramson eased the pace of his speech. "My apologies. What I'm inferring is that infection might linger on a surgical tool such as a scalpel or—in this case—a needle." He paused as though to let Thor process that. "Optimal cleansing methods could eliminate the issue. There is a growing number of the medical profession convinced on the matter, particularly those who have had success with Lister's methods. While it's too late for you to benefit from such caution, Mr. Norgaard, I offer this not as a cure but as a diagnosis. Did you witness the needle used in your blood draw sanitized in any way?"

Thor entreated Haakon for help on what *S-A-N-I-T-I-Z-E-D* meant.

His brother only shrugged.

The doctor stepped forward. "Did you ever boil any of your equipment when you produced liquor?"

Yes, some of it, so the drink wouldn't sour. Thor passed that answer on by way of Haakon, and the doctor looked pleased.

"That's it exactly. Did you in any way witness the needle be so well cleaned?"

Polished with cloth. Water. That was all.

Haakon relayed that.

"Then that is what I fear may be the culprit of your illness."

His brother pointed at him. "But if Thor's eyes are yellowed and he's in pain, how does all of *that* get on the needle in the first place?"

"It's microscopic, sir. I could explain it to you, but perhaps simply trust me on this: I'm convinced that the most likely reason for such a contamination would be that someone who had the same illness came in contact with the needle first."

Thor stared at the doctor, breaking his scrutiny only to study the hollow of his elbow. He pressed against the softness of his flesh, and it was then that Dr. Abramson sat on the edge of the bed, pulled something from his bag, and set it on the rumpled blanket. A small case. The young man opened it, showing a needle and syringe against a red cloth.

"One of these, Mr. Norgaard, is what I believe made you ill. And that someone who was in contact with the needle prior to you harbored this same illness. Likely unwittingly since the epidemic lies dormant for a period of weeks to several months." His face was taut with regret.

Thor ran a hand through his unbound hair, stopping to grip the back of his head.

Harlan had gone before him.

"I'll go over the documents from your visit that day to investigate this doctor you were seen by. It may be a dead end, but it may also save lives."

Save lives? He thought the epidemic wasn't fatal.

"There's one matter more. It may not be linked, but it's worth addressing." The doctor pulled a fold of paper from his bag. "My mentor sent his insights by express post, including this. It's a record he transcribed of a lecture from more than twenty years ago where the teaching physician described an ailment that was believed to be Epidemic Jaundice. There have been many such recountings of this illness over the centuries, but this one is most critical to the situation here." There was sorrow in his eyes, but to Thor's relief, he spoke slowly. "I'm sorry to say that this particular outbreak occurred among women who were with child."

Chills covered Thor's skin.

"This account was some years ago on the island of Martinique, and the outbreak afflicted thirty pregnant women." He unfolded the paper and handed it over. "Twenty of them died, and the babies were lost."

Thor shook his head, confusion now warring with panic. *Aven not touch needle.*

Looking panicked himself, Haakon quickly relayed that.

The doctor nodded soberly, turning grieved eyes back to Thor. "No. But she was in close contact with you, her husband who had the illness."

Everything else he said was patchy as Thor's focus blurred, mottled with despair.

". . . so far along in her pregnancy . . . bode well for your infant . . . If the baby were to deliver now, survival for the child would be likely . . ."

Thor blinked, forcing himself to follow the doctor's moving mouth.

". . . while still in the womb. Mr. Norgaard, I'm wretchedly sorry to have to ask you this, but has the heartbeat been confirmed lately?"

Haakon spoke in a rush. "A few days ago, I think."

The doctor nodded, shoulders settling with relief. "We'll check again right away. I've had no practice with childbirth as of yet, but what I can tell you is that her well-being will remain uncertain for a while."

Thor blinked back a white-hot fury for Harlan Sorrel.

"This is an illness we lack answers on, but I vow to exhaust every effort in unearthing more. Since your symptoms are still pronounced, you must remain quarantined, though I sense that neither I nor your brother here are at risk, nor would the rest of your extended family be. Regardless, with the illness being most affecting to young children, it's wise we retain limited contact. I'll discuss this with Mrs. Norgaard's midwife so she can assess your wife and child. In the meantime, I'll offer up my prayers for protection for your wife and infant."

Haakon snapped off a response but Thor saw only his angst then the doctor's answer.

"Yes. I do resort to prayer . . . even as a physician." The young man picked up his papers and slid them away, eyes rising to Haakon. "Please know, sir, that I've seen a fair number of diseases in my apprenticeship and have sat with souls as they've departed this world. I've seen firsthand how finite humanity is, and while I uphold the power of science, I would be a fool not to also seek prayer. When it comes to the safety of a woman and her unborn child, I should, in truth, have already taken a knee."

TWENTY-ONE

A TENDERNESS THROBBED LOW IN HER BELLY as Aven opened her linen fan to stir the air. Beside her on the pew, Fay reached around both sons and closed the finished hymnal. The shift offset Bjørn's balance, and he squirmed as if this were his chance to escape his mother's arms and perhaps the crowded church altogether. Across the way, Jorgan and Peter sat in the men's section, which spanned two sides of the room, same as the women's—each group joining to form a hollow square in the center. How Aven longed to look across the way and see her husband sitting there. She prayed the day would come. And soon.

When Bjørn fussed, Sigurd leaned over and whispered. "Stop wiggling, ciderkin." From his pocket, he pulled out a tiny carving of a Viking ship. Its sides and dragon headpiece had been knifed with such detail it might have been found among the ancient ruins of Norway. One of the many wooden toys Jorgan had fashioned for his sons.

As Bjørn turned the vessel in his pudgy fingers, Sigurd patted the top of his head. "Dat's a good wittle swash-buckwer."

Aven and Fay exchanged smiles. Across from them, Peter looked amused. He straightened his posture, and there seemed to be a lightening in him. The poor man carried a burden with his menfolk's return, standing—in truth—between two different worlds. One of blood and one of belief.

'Twas hard to recall that there had been a time that Peter's presence filled her with fear. It seemed a million nights ago that he'd smashed his way into the Norgaard house, clad in a white robe and hood alongside his male kin, who had shattered windows and torched the wood crib to ashes. Peter had stood mere feet from Aven as well as Cora's daughters—Tess and little Georgie—observing them through his slitted hood. An ominous foreboding far from the peace his presence brought now. He was a good man, Aven had since learned, and one who wanted nothing to do with his grandfather's way of life. Instead, Peter showed a tenderness of soul and, if she wasn't mistaken, had a protective way about Cora and her daughters. In particular Tess, with her sunny smile and fawn-wide eyes. A young woman he always seemed to watch as if waiting for her to need him.

The reverend rose to stand in the center of the square, opened a dense Bible, and began a reading in the fifteenth chapter of Luke. Uncomfortable, Aven shifted on the bench. A low pain in her womb slipped in and out of her awareness like an hourly sigh. Nay, now that she was thinking upon it, the tightness came much more often this morning.

To keep distracted, Aven took careful notes of the sermon, something she always did for Thor—a way to recall the teachings to him afterwards. So little could he see of the reverend's speech as the clergyman addressed each side of the room that Thor missed much of the sermon. Yet he always sat here, somber and reverent, as if the sheer notion of being in God's house was solace enough. With him ill, perhaps the notes would encourage him in like fashion. Perhaps she could beseech Jorgan to walk her over after the service, though she feared she'd not have the strength.

She wrote quickly, meaning them for Thor one way or another, and the reverend was just to the parable of the lost son when the door creaked open. A bright shaft of light fell across the center of the square, followed by a gust of breeze. A couple stole inside and closed the door. Aven recognized the fair-haired young woman as Sibby Sorrel. The lass had grown up on the neighboring farm and had just married. At sight of his sister and new brother-in-law, Peter gave a cordial nod.

Sibby took a place in the women's section, slipping in like a mouse and looking to weigh as much. Her long, flaxen braid fell over one shoulder when she bent to tuck a wayward hymnal away. Across the room, Sibby's husband joined the men's section. Aven knew almost nothing about him. Only that he had a way of keeping his head down and eyes averted. As of now, his gaze lay fixed on the floor, lifting only to glimpse the reverend, who extended his own measure of study. The stranger's dark hair hung to his shoulders, black and stringy beneath a faded hat that he promptly tugged from his head.

The reverend continued at an easy cadence. "'And the younger of them said to his father, Father, give me the portion of goods that falleth to me. And he divided unto them his living. And not many days after the younger son gathered all together, and took his journey into a far country, and there—'"

Aven dropped her pencil when Bjørn pulled on her arm in an effort to squirm nearer. With naught but an inch of space in front of her round belly, she shifted over enough to wedge Bjørn on the bench beside her. Sigurd hopped down and fetched the pencil while Aven draped an arm around the younger tot, who kept busy fiddling with the button bracelet on her wrist. She wore it on such days as a diversion for tiny fingers during long church services.

The sermon continued in the reverend's ardent voice. "'And am no more worthy to be called thy son: make me as one of thy hired servants. And he arose, and came to his father. But when he was yet a great way off, his father saw him, and had compassion.'"

Aven couldn't help but think of Haakon. Not only his leaving but his longing for the inheritance that had once been set aside for him. A share of his father's land.

The reverend expounded on the text with fervor. Equally as fervent was Bjørn's complaint. Aven tried to ease him, but Bjørn stretched grumpily, nearly tumbling from the bench. Fay flashed him a stern look as she pulled him into her lap. He squealed, and after a sigh Fay carried him outside. With the service near an end, she wasn't the only mother quieting a fussy babe out of doors.

Another low pain began, this one strong enough to garner all of Aven's focus. When it passed, she felt no more in labor than she had before it began, but something told her this was just the start. She was just blowing out a soft breath when folks rose and their chatter clapped around the building, lifting high to the peaked roof and rafters. Aven viewed her notes, wishing she'd finished, but perhaps the story alone could be a comfort to Thor. Maybe . . . maybe even Haakon.

She folded it with care, trusting that the Lord would do His work—both in the hearts of those two men and in her own.

With the family gathering outside, Aven collected her shawl and with a few smiles to familiar faces joined Fay in the sun. Wind swept across the churchyard, stirring old leaves and new flowers. Jorgan paced across the lawn to where the boys were romping with others their age. To his sons' dismay, they were herded toward the wagon. Perhaps Jorgan meant not to leave Thor and Haakon alone any longer than was necessary. She was grateful herself, for as another twinge came, she was more than ready for a lie down and a strong cup of tea. Aven whispered her suspicions to Fay, who nodded assuringly.

"Let's get you home," Fay whispered, sliding a comforting hand to Aven's back.

Jorgan assisted his wife and sons into the back of the wagon, then helped Aven up to the front seat. The climb proved an effort, and when she was settled, Jorgan pushed her hem clear of the wheel and went around to the driver's side.

Across the churchyard, Peter stood deep in conversation with his sister's husband. The dark-haired man made no movement as he spoke, as if a statuesque appearance would make his presence less noticed. Peter spoke with much more passion. Whatever they discussed was a sensitive subject because even Sibby looked worried.

She had more than cause to with hounds having searched the hills surrounding both the Norgaard orchards and the Sorrel plantation. After speaking to the sheriff, Jorgan had announced over last night's supper that the search was spread out for nearly twenty square miles—a vast amount of land to cover—and while the lawman's efforts brought prospect, it had also afforded nothing other than weary dogs and empty trails.

Wind tugged at Aven's shawl, and she tucked her hands snug against her skirt folds.

Peter exchanged a few more words with the man, bid his sister goodbye, then headed for the wagon.

"Thanks for waitin'." He climbed into the back.

"Sorry to be in such a hurry." Jorgan tapped the reins, and the wagon lurched into motion. "I don't want to leave my brothers alone for too long."

Peter pulled up a knee, resting his forearm there. "I'm bettin' my money on Thor. I say he'll be the last one standin'."

Jorgan chuckled. "I dunno. A buck says Haakon's pretty scrappy."

"Fellows," Fay said with a touch of amusement. "Ought you to be placing bets on the Lord's Day?" She shared a smile with Aven.

While the ride home was a breezy one, it was a refreshing kind of wind. One that brought in change and newness. Jorgan cradled the reins with an easy, one-handed grip, and Aven noticed that his other arm draped over the back of the bench seat to hold Fay's fingers in his own. Aven smiled again. Now and again she felt the sober tightening in her womb, but each occurrence was so spaced out and manageable that she sensed the day would be a long, uneventful one.

When they reached the farm, Haakon was crossing the yard, aiming for the orchards. Behind him followed the doctor from Fincastle. The man called after Haakon, and they both halted in their tracks as the wagon approached.

Was something the matter? Was it Thor? Aven gripped the seat as Jorgan slowed the team with a strong tug of the reins. Haakon circled the wagon bed, and she spoke before he'd reached her side.

"Where is Thor?"

Haakon blinked quickly—visibly jarred. "He's uh . . . He's fine. Thor's just fine."

The doctor reached them, the brisk breeze whipping the side of his tailored coat. "I was able to give your husband a favorable diagnosis, Mrs. Norgaard. I expect him to be recovered before long, and already he's showed a marked improvement."

Gripping tighter to the wagon seat, Aven closed her eyes and bowed her head. Relief made her every limb warm with release—all fear over losing Thor gone as quick as it had come knocking, making her nearly tremble with the rush of it.

The doctor spoke on, and while she could scarcely comprehend anything beyond joy unfurled, she listened with care for want of Thor's whereabouts. "While I'm here, I would also like to check you and your child. Your brother-in-law was just heading off to retrieve your midwife for the same purpose."

"Is there concern?"

"Let's get you down." Dr. Abramson reached up to assist her, but while Aven accepted his grip, she couldn't move from the seat. A new tightening was taking hold of her womb. "Sir—" She let out a low breath. "I just need a moment."

"Are you in pain?" the doctor asked.

"Aye. Only slightly, but 'tis more frequent than in days past."

He looked to Haakon, and with a sure nod, Haakon stepped forward and spoke to Jorgan. The next moments were a blur as Fay and the boys climbed down. Haakon stepped nearer as the doctor gave him space. With a mark of regret, Haakon reached up, looping a sturdy hand around Aven's waist as though to lift her down. She wavered from his touch, but the doctor spoke.

"He'll bring you no harm, Mrs. Norgaard. It would be impossible for him to."

Haakon's eyes held a longing for that to have been true. "He's speaking of the illness," he said, as though unable to accept such a generous statement to be latched to his name. He stepped aside and called for Jorgan.

"Something I can explain in more detail during my exam," the doctor added.

Jorgan came to her side, and overwhelmed, Aven slid an arm about his neck. He lifted her from the wagon. Wind gusted against them, all but tugging her twisted bun loose of its pins. Jorgan braced her to his chest and she went weightless, her heart anything but. He lowered her to her feet, not pulling away until she was steady.

Aven spoke against the shield that was his shoulder. "I need Thor." If she could only see him. Some way to harness a final dose of courage for what was to come.

"I'll get him." Haakon started that way.

After steadying her, Jorgan reached for the bridle of the nearest mare, promising that he would hurry in getting Cora. He drove away, the horses breaking into a run as the wheels clattered down the lane to Cora's nearby home. Fay stepped to the doorway of the kitchen with Bjørn in her arms and a promise to return straightaway. Sigurd raced along behind her.

Aven turned to the doctor, aching for answers. "What is happening? You said Thor is recovering. Is something else the matter?"

"I'm quite certain his recovery is sure and steady. But we need to tend to you and your baby. One of the reasons I've sought your midwife's aid." He adjusted his grip on his handled bag. "While I

184

wish I could declare it simply a routine examination, it's a matter of more urgency." With gentle calm, he relayed what he'd announced to Thor: that her life and the babe's life were at risk from the epidemic of jaundice—even more than Thor's own had ever been.

Aven heard the words but knew not where to place them. She wanted to bundle them up and toss them far and away and let the peace of his earlier news wrap her up in safety and rest. But this? "What—what do we do? I don't feel unwell. What of the baby?" The words came tumbling out, each more panicked than the ones before.

"I'm greatly relieved to hear it." He went on to describe Thor's symptoms in detail, and as he described the obstacles her husband had been enduring, none of the discomforts or symptoms were famil- iar to her own body. A marked relief and one she announced with utmost certainty. But . . . "What of the baby?" she echoed.

"I'd like to have a listen to its heartbeat. Though your midwife will have more ability there, so if we can await her arrival, I believe it will—"

"Can you not check now?" her plea was urgent.

"Of course. I can try if you wish it. Let's get you into the house."

"No. Right now, please." Aven pulled her shawl clear, clutching the folds in nervous hands.

With a look of compassion, the doctor nodded. "Of course. Let's see what we can do." He set his black bag on the ground, snapped it open, and pulled out a funneled ear scope much like Cora's own. He bent at the waist, pressing the tool to one side of her womb and then to the other. He moved the fluted end to the top of her stomach and with his eyes closed listened intently. "Ma'am, I assure you that your midwife will be much more able to locate the position of the baby's heart than myself. I can keep trying but fear bringing you more worry."

"Aven!"

At the call of her name, she saw Haakon and Thor crossing through the grove. Thor's steps were slow, and he had an arm braced over Haakon's back, his brother supporting him with each stride. Lifting up the hem of her skirt, Aven hurried that way—feeling more like she was wading across a river than stepping over solid ground. A current pushed against her, one of growing pain and fear.

Haakon ducked as Thor pulled his arm loose. "He was already comin' this way."

Reaching Thor, Aven longed to take hold of his hands. Instead, she fisted the fabric of her skirt as she spoke. "Thor, I believe the baby may be coming soon." She gripped the underside of her womb where the last ache had come and gone. As for the baby . . .

Her chin trembled. She hadn't felt it stirring today but hadn't thought to pay such heed.

Thor stepped nearer and lowered himself to kneel in the dirt. Before she could react, he touched her waist, something he hadn't done since last they'd last lain abed, his arm circled about her as they slept. Their child had been smaller then and he stronger. Now, having longed for such nearness, she didn't move. 'Twas a taste of heaven amid an hour far from such peace.

Thor bowed his head and firmed his grip. With a deep sigh, he touched his forehead to the front of her belly—his skin against the thin layers of her clothing. He stayed that way for such a long time that tears filled her eyes. He was praying.

Aven gripped his shoulder, her fingers just grazing the ends of his unbound hair as Haakon brought over a chair, asking her to sit. Thor rose to one knee, staying close to her side. Not even the doctor urged him away, and she was grateful.

Stethoscope still in hand, the doctor knelt down. He pressed the long, narrow tube to the underside of Aven's belly. Closing his eyes, he listened. After what seemed an eternity, he rose and moved around to her other side, where he continued his search. Aven's own heart was a gallop in her chest, and she swallowed back tears. This was taking so long.

Concentration pulled the doctor's brow tight, eyes squeezed to thin slants. Finally, his face eased, and he regarded Aven with a smile so beautiful it might as well have been a wing from heaven wrapping around her.

"That's a good, strong heartbeat." He listened again and confirmed his assessment. "The beat is quick, though I believe that's normal." He grinned again.

At the clatter of the wagon, he angled aside, and within moments, Cora was rushing over. The midwife hunched down, taking the doctor's ear scope and pressing it into place at the same spot he had. Her smile was a slow rising of the sun and just as assuring.

"Ain't no mistake. That a fine beat. And from what Jorgan said, you's in labor." She felt the side of Aven's belly as a new pain tightened it. "A right good labor, and as happy as that little one be in there, I think someone's aimin' to meet Mama and Papa now."

TWENTY-TWO

HAAKON WISHED HE COULD SAY THAT HE
didn't know how hard women fought to bring babies into this world,
but he hadn't traveled the globe halfway over without witnessing a few
things in his travels. Throw in his mother's own death, and his hands
could scarcely hold the jar of beans he was trying to unlatch for Thor.

With the very man seated on the porch in near despair, Haakon
braced the jar to his middle and forced the lid off. He set the makings
of supper aside and went back out to fetch the rest of the freshly delivered goods. Just inches from the crate sat Thor, who hadn't moved
in hours. Haakon toted the box inside and set it on the old table. As
much as he was fighting panic, he still had a job to do and that was to
see Thor through the next hours. He could do nothing for Aven, but
he could ensure that Thor wasn't alone.

With a deep breath, he rummaged through the latest delivery.
In company with the warm crock of beans were two thick squares of
buttered cornbread. Peter had brought the meal over just minutes ago
along with the news that Aven was in the thick of laboring. The farmhand had also declared that the doctor had stayed to observe Cora's
methods and offer his assistance should it be of use. Peter had ended
his report explaining that by Cora's estimation, the baby wouldn't

come until sometime in the night. Perhaps even after dawn. The early evening light streaming through the window declared that Aven had a trial in store.

With a sigh that held more weight than he knew how to deal with, Haakon went to the cupboard where there now lived two wooden bowls, two cups, and a pair of utensils that he kept washed and stored for this routine. The table wobbled as he shifted things around. Along with the beans and bread, there was a tin of tea herbs for Thor. Haakon was far from domestic, but he'd gotten good at boiling water, steeping the herbs, and making sure Thor had three strong cups a day per Cora's bidding.

Thor was probably hankering for something a lot stronger, but he didn't complain.

Haakon caught sight of him through the window again. Did the need for a drink still plague him? Thor lowered his head to his hand, and though he would never hear the sigh released, the sheer sound of it broke Haakon's heart. He wasn't entirely tender over his brother, but a throbbing in his chest marched right over every time they hadn't seen eye to eye.

The kettle spewed out steam, and Haakon reached for a rag, only to knock a roll of paper from the back end of the table. It skidded aside and fell, landing with a soft thud. After filling a bowl with steaming water and adding in a pinch of herbs, Haakon crouched down. He reached back, snagged the roll of paper with his fingertips, and, rising again, set it on the table.

Something had him hesitate. He knew this paper and that frayed corner that peeked out at him. Haakon unfurled the roll to reveal the map that had once hung above his bed in the attic. His hand swiped down the center, brushing across the Atlantic from the north—a vast lay of waters that touched the distant coasts of Iceland, Greenland, England, and even the North of Africa. Across the coordinates lay Canada and the United States. But what caught his attention the most was Norway. It jutted into the Atlantic, courageous and sure. Unapologetic and even a little daring as it reached into waters that were frigid and unpredictable. The tip of Haakon's thumb grazed the lowest shoreline where a tiny dot marked the town of Kristiansand. A place on the map he had lain under and dreamed under most of life without really ever noticing it existed.

He swallowed hard as an ache swelled in his chest.

Leaving the tea to steep longer, Haakon headed up the stairs. Upon reaching his pack, he yanked back the flap, tipped it over and dumped out the contents. Everything he owned fell out, last of all a fold of paper. This one not so different than the map awaiting him downstairs. Haakon unfolded the single page to see the drawing given to him by one of the widow's boys. The same one who had run across the clifftops of the fjord while Haakon mended their garden fence against gusting sea winds. The lad had talked constantly in a language Haakon could only somewhat comprehend, but he understood hunger when he saw it. Not only for more plentiful meals but for a man's guidance and attention.

As deep a need had dwelled in Widow Jönsson's blue eyes as he'd set a humble gift for her of the same vibrant color on the table. She had smiled at him, and it was brighter than the sunset over the water. He'd sat there, keeping her and her children company, even as he pondered all the ways he could get exactly what it was he'd wanted from her. She'd been in mourning, and regardless, he'd been a fool to expect a woman to offer over what was sacred and meant for marriage—all for his own satisfaction. Something he'd done time and time again, to his growing shame. She'd done what was right, honoring her husband's memory and her faith, and Haakon had left so disappointed he hadn't even said goodbye.

Haakon lowered his head. The clifftops of Norway now a distant memory, he folded the paper and tucked it safely in the pouch around his neck. The past threatened to punch him in the gut, so he focused instead on the future—the hours to come. Not wanting to leave Thor for long, he stomped back downstairs and outside.

Thor still sat with his head lowered in his hands. His breathing was steady as he stared at the ground. A good time for words of comfort, but Haakon didn't know what to say. What he did know was what his brother had to be thinking. Haakon himself had thought it nearly every day of his life. Their mother had eventually succumbed to the childbirth bed. Instead of rising the third time around, it was Haakon's life that had taken her own.

It took all of Haakon's strength to rally his heart as he sat on the bench at the far end of the porch. Thor pressed calloused hands together, slowly forcing them back and forth. A funeral march was peppier than that rhythm, so Haakon picked up a twig from beneath the bench and tossed it beside his brother. It was enough for Thor to look over at him.

"You should eat some of what Ida sent over."

With a slow shake of his head, Thor went back to staring at the ground.

After chewing on the notion, Haakon tapped the heel of his boot against the floor a few times, hard enough to garner his brother's attention again. "Your tea is almost ready."

Thor made no response. His following sigh was deep—same as Haakon's.

There was nothing else to do now, so Haakon simply sat with him. He was supposed to meet up with Sibby's husband tonight but couldn't leave now. It'd put a damper on finding Jed, but that was just going to have to wait. Sibby's husband, Orville, was a mild-mannered fellow and one who would understand. After having ventured to his moonshine still the other night with Peter, they had all begun to hash a plan as to what to do about Jed and Harlan Sorrel. It was murky yet, but they'd hone it in soon.

Thinking the tea ready, Haakon went in and strained out the

spent herbs. He filled a tin mug with the strong brew and drizzled in honey. Thor probably didn't notice or care, but Haakon had sipped a taste the other day, and the concoction was something awful.

The act of fixing tea always made him think of Aven and how he'd watched her do it dozens of times in the past. He tried not to think of the agony she was in, fighting for her child just as the last woman to give birth in that attic room had done twenty-five years ago.

Worry coursed through him in rivulets, pounding inside him the need to panic. Haakon heaved in a slow breath and blew it out with equal measure.

Back outside, he offered Thor the drink, and with nothing to do but while away this torture, Haakon stepped to the bench beneath one of the windows. For the first time in a long while, his thoughts returned to the Bible page Tate had torn out for him. Maybe it was time to stop ignoring it. He sat, meaning to fish out the thin sheet, when something lumpy jabbed against his leg. Haakon reached into his pocket and pulled out the toy he'd found. The one that had been on the ground beside the wagon.

Leaning forward, he rested his forearms on his knees and turned the ship in his fingertips. He grazed a thumb along the coils and twists that Jorgan had fashioned with the skill of his blade and the patience of time. Then, at sight of his brother striding this way, Haakon set the carving aside and went to stand. Jorgan signaled for him to stay put. Haakon eased back down. Thor spotted his approach, and his eyes went wide in wait of news.

Men would always march into battle to protect what they believed in, and women would always endure the pain of bringing their children into this world. It was the way of this life, no matter the time or land, and yet in some instances, the battle wasn't with swords or with shields—it was between hope and fear as the woman a man loved fought not only for her own life but for the life of their child.

Twice now Jorgan had been through this, and he'd likely be

facing the torment again. Making it all the more consequential when Jorgan sank to one knee in front of Thor and whispered that Aven was doing well. Haakon knew that if Jorgan could, he would have gripped a hand to the back of their brother's neck and pulled that brewing burden of tears to his shoulder. As it was, he spoke in soft murmurs. One need never be loud with Thor. It was only in the sincerity that Thor grasped the words. Only in a person's willingness to mouth what needed to be said. An exchange as potent as any conversation could ever be between a man and those who knew him.

Haakon watched his brothers as a burn tightened his throat. These two faced down something he understood only through the wretchedness of his own birth. Haakon didn't know much of his mother, but he knew that she'd been generous and kind. That her hair had been dark like Thor's and that she'd held Haakon with pride the few minutes she'd been able to. Haakon had always imagined her peaceful in that moment. Her Nordic beauty captivating his da as she held their third-born son. Their last.

If Haakon could fight for her now he would.

If he could lay down his life for her he would.

That's what Da had taught them. To guard all those in their care. If Haakon could turn back the clock to shield the women in his path, he would. Da had raised them as sons of this wild mountain, but Kristin Norgaard had been raised as a daughter of the north. An heiress to woodlands and the plunging blue of mighty fjords. She'd surely run as a girl along the rise of cliffs that pierced skyward to where the Northern Lights held dominion over a vast and breathtaking land. Until the day she'd sailed here to America, just as Aven had.

A flash of blue filled his memory—young Widow Jönsson opening up the folded shawl he'd set on the table in a cottage about this size. The same woman who had brought five children into the world. Five little souls who had lost their da soon after.

Haakon shifted his boots that hadn't been patched by himself—they'd been patched by her. Taken from where he'd set them before falling asleep beside her that night some three thousand miles away. She would have woken in the dark to see to the task. A gift from her to him when she should have been sleeping and when she had nothing else to give. Each stitch strong and placed with loving care by a light that could have only been the moon. To say nothing for the biting, Norwegian cold. If he thought the gesture anything less than an utmost tenderness, he was still a fool.

Bending, Haakon ran his thumb against her neat stitches, then, straightening, watched his brothers. How he longed to overhear what was being said. But when it came to the details of Aven's labor and safety, the telling was for Thor and Thor alone. Aven wasn't his wife. To his rising regret, no woman was. And with all the growing up he had left to do, three thousand miles might as well have been a million more.

"You stay with me, Aven." Cora's sharp voice ripped Aven's focus from the foggy haze of pain. "You stay with me."

Knelt on the mattress, Aven clutched a grip of bedsheets. Her nightgown hung down one shoulder, and the bottom portion was pulled up around her thighs, soaked with the waters that had just broken. Tess rushed in with a fold of towels and helped her mother tuck them all around. Tess's yellow head covering bobbed with her hasty scrubbing, and when she looked to Aven, her eyes were filled with compassion. Against the far wall stood the doctor, who was taking a brief reprieve from pacing to write down more notes. Beyond that, Aven felt Fay's gentle kneading of her lower back, but the pains were coming fiercer than any ministrations could ever counter.

As another round of agony seized her, Aven moaned and fought the urge to cry again. As it was, she'd already given in to weeping. Already vomited over the side of the bed. Already cried out for Thor, and more than once she'd bit back screams as Cora worked to help settle the baby's head farther into place. The only reprieve against these waves was the rock of comfort that was her baby's heartbeat. Strong and steady. Cora had declared it time and time again, and each instance gave Aven something to brace against amid stormy seas.

Yet as pain had a way of doing, she was drifting in and out of despair. Since the spilling of waters, so had intensified the spasms. Now she was losing her breath to them, her body near to tearing apart at the seams.

"I don't know that I can do this anymore," Aven panted when another spasm finally ended. Sunset had long since come and gone. She knew not the hour, only that the women around her would have been deep asleep had they been given the choice. The only female to slumber in this house was young Georgie, whom Cora had settled for the night on the downstairs sofa. "I can't do this." Aven nearly choked on the words.

Ida nestled a pillow against Aven's hip, and though Aven couldn't speak, she was grateful for the support.

"Aven," came Fay's gentle voice. If she was weary, it showed not. "You are being so courageous and brave. You are stronger than you realize, and you are doing this beautifully. It may seem as if you're making little progress and as though the pain will never end, but this child is coming soon." Lantern light glowed warm against Fay's face as she pressed Aven's hair away from her sticky forehead. "You are doing a marvelous job. It won't be much longer now and you will know the sweet face of your child."

Aven's body clenched again, and she let out a sob. It melded into a cry of despair the longer the throbbing lasted. After swiping the back of a wrist over her glossy-brown forehead, Cora instructed Aven to shift farther to the side of the bed, but she couldn't move. Pain was the only thing to fill her mind. It filled this whole room with no beginning and no end that she could ever recall. It just was, and it was ripping her to pieces.

Boots sounded in the hall, and after a gentle knock, Jorgan called through the closed door. "If anyone can be spared a moment . . ."

Aven knew not who stepped away until Ida slipped out the bedroom door. It closed softly.

"Aven," Cora's voice was calm as she brought another lantern nearer. The light that had been mellow and sleepy now brightened. "This baby's wantin' to come now, and I need you to scoot this way. Fay and I'll help you. We gonna get you on your feet."

When Aven insisted that she couldn't, Fay and Cora came around, each took hold beneath one of her arms, and pulled her forward. Aven sobbed as pain lanced in places only owing to childbirth, but suddenly her feet were on the floor and she was standing best she could on trembling legs. She nearly collapsed with the agony of it, but they braced her well.

Cora switched places with Tess, who moved in to support Aven on one side. Cora knelt, shoved back the bottom of her nightgown, and checked for the baby's head. "It's comin'. I want a good sturdy push with the next tightening. It gonna take some time, but we'll ease into it, ya hear?"

When the clenching surged through her, Aven bore down. The longer Cora urged her to keep the pressure, the longer she fought to do so. Finally Aven gasped for air.

Still supporting half her weight, Tess squeezed one of her shaking hands. "You doin' such a fine job, Miss Aven. Such a fine job."

Nausea rising again, Aven cried for a dish, and it was brought to her just in time. She gripped the chipped porcelain bowl with shaking hands even as she realized it was the doctor who supported it. Tess held back her hair, and when the sickness passed, the doctor took the bowl away. Fay adjusted her support of Aven's weary frame, offering more words of assurance, and Dr. Abramson returned, offering her a cool sip of water. Though a window had been opened to the breeze, the room crushed down on her with a stifling heat. A hot tear slid down the side of her cheek, and she hadn't the strength to swipe it away.

Suddenly Ida returned and, with a touch of Aven's chin, lifted her gaze. Ida's limp hitched as she took a small step closer. "Aven, Thor's just downstairs. He's waitin' outside, below your window."

A little cry slipped from Aven's lips, and her vision blurred again.

"He's right there, dear. He's waitin' for you, and he's prayin' for you. You ain't alone."

Choking back more tears, she nodded.

"He walked himself all the way over here without anyone knowin' it." Ida's steely dark eyes held the depth of his efforts. "He sent me to tell you that he's right proud of you. Right proud of you. He also said he ain't movin'. Not the whole night through. He'll be there."

Tears pooled and fell. While Aven scarcely had the ability to wipe them away, a new strength was rising up.

"Ease her back onto the bed," Cora demanded. "Swift as can be done! Aven, you gonna feel more pressure, but don't be afraid of it, ya hear?"

Though every movement was agony, Aven did as told. She squelched a rising scream as she inched herself back onto the bed. Fay looped her unbound hair aside, tucking it well out of the way. Cora pushed her feet up as well so that her legs were bent, and from behind, Fay held her propped up. The doctor moved himself into the corner, where he sat and watched quietly.

"You're almost done, sweet one," Fay whispered.

Gritting her teeth against the pain, Aven nodded.

Sweat beaded on her forehead, and Tess dabbed it away with a blessedly cool cloth. "You's as strong as any mama I ever seen."

"A good push now," Cora said in a rush. She called to Ida for a steamed cloth, which she applied with firm pressure.

Aven did as told and pushed with all that was in her. Time seemed to stretch on. It drew itself out until it became nothing more than a series of pushes, the women's reassuring voices, and the growing pressure of her coming child. Between spasms, Aven panted against Fay's hold and looked to the dark window where just below she knew Thor had stationed himself.

Each of Cora's commands had been steady, but now her pitch rose as did her posture when she came up from a crouch. "This be it, Aven. This be it. Steady pushes now. Easy like. Don't let up, love, keep it comin', keep it comin'."

Aven crushed her chin to her chest and pushed with all she had to muster. She'd never been old enough to ask her mother about birthing, but as she bore down, she knew her mother would have told her that the pain would soon end. It would soon end. Aven groped the mattress as if to find her mother's comforting touch and instead caught hold of Fay's hand. These women who had walked with her and cried with her and now labored with her. Women she would never know had her own mother not sacrificed so much for her to survive. Had Aunt Dorothe not sent letters of hope across an ocean, bidding Aven come to America.

And as Aven gave one final push, a new female came tumbling into her life. A beautiful, slick baby girl that Cora caught with a shout of joy. The only daughter to ever draw her first breath in this house.

The midwife flipped the round infant over and made quick work of swiping her mouth clear of liquid. She patted the baby's backside, causing her to wail with abandon. Cora's face was awash with the same delight that surged through Aven. "Oh, yes, little darling. We hear you. We hear you!" Grinning, she turned Tusenfryd over and nestled her plump, wet form into Aven's shaking arms.

Then came Tess's cry of delight as she nestled a blanket around the baby. "Oh, little Tusie! I think you's tryin' to get even your papa to hear you!"

"She givin' it her all," Ida said, beaming. "But seein' as she'll need a bit of help, I'll go tell him right now." With pride shining in her face, she grabbed up the lantern, moved to the open window, and leaned down with the light. "It be a girl you have, Mr. Norgaard! An awful pretty one, and she givin' her papa a right fine hello."

TWENTY-THREE

THOR COULD FEEL IT NOW—THE CRUNCH OF snow beneath his boots. The motion of the sled over deep drifts. He would rosin the blades to ride smooth and tug the line sure and steady. And it would be there that he'd look back and see her bundled amid furs and thick, woolen blankets. A wee girl sitting in the crook of the sled he'd fashion from the softest of spruce. A hood of white fur cradling a round face and rosy cheeks. A little woodland nymph who knew him as *Da*. Eyes as bright as her mother's and shining the same pleasure to be with him.

Off on an adventure they'd go. On an outing. Her not feeling the cold because she was made for it—born and bred from ancestors of the mountains and of the ice. The tiny, white flakes would be her crowning joy. Evergreen boughs her places to hide and giggle. He could see her there in his mind, just old enough to waddle about in boots he'd fashion with the utmost care from the finest leathers and a wool coat, embroidered by her mother on autumn nights.

He was a father. A protector. A friend.

And he had a daughter.

At someone shaking his shoulder, Thor sat up to the early light of morning, colliding into the stone wall that was Haakon. Having

200

woken him, Haakon moved back and, with fingers spread open, tapped a thumb to his chest for *Fine. Baby fine. Wife fine.*

Thor shot out a breath. Next came a rush of gratitude to his brother for knowing that assurance was the first thing he needed upon consciousness. Still kneeling on the porch beside him, Haakon continued. *T-U-S-E-N-F-R-Y-D.*

Thor's chest hitched at the first time her name was fingerspelled by another. Of all people, it was Haakon. "She's here to see you." He thumbed toward the window.

Thor rose to find Fay standing at the glass. A smile lit her face, and her usually neat bun hung loose, wisps of it catching the air as she tipped her head down, telling a tale of last night that no words could. The ache to see Aven made it a battle to stand his ground outside this house, but all frustration quieted when Thor saw the tiniest, most perfect version of her in Fay's arms. Bundled in a knitted blanket, Tusie was sound asleep, pink lips pressed in a milky pout.

It took an awful lot to get him to make sound, but the moan that slid from his throat was impossible to halt. When sight of his daughter blurred, he swiped a sleeve over his eyes and stepped closer. She was stunning. Plump, pale, and looking as soft as anything he'd ever seen.

Fay feathered her fingertips against Tusie's tuft of light-brown hair. "It shines auburn in the sunlight."

Thor grinned. He bet it did. On instinct, he touched his palm to the glass.

Reaching into the blanket, Fay freed a tiny arm from its cocoon. After pressing her shoulder against the window, she lifted the baby's hand so that it met the window. The baby's fingers were folded in and so miniature that when Thor pressed the tip of his thumb to that very spot in the glass, he could see them no longer. Fay waved for his attention, and Thor watched her mouth.

"She has brown eyes, and you should see these ears." Angling some, Fay loosened the blanket to give Thor a better view of ears that were squished and pointed in the oddest of ways.

He felt a chuckle slip from his chest. He touched the window again, aching to hold her.

At a shadow beside him, he looked over to see Haakon observing the baby. Haakon's eyes were fixed on her face like a ship set on the North Star. He placed fingertips to the glass, working his thumb back and forth as if wanting to touch one of those silken cheeks as well.

Thor dropped his gaze back to his daughter, and his longing intensified. It was a hunger inside him, and by God's grace one he had more time to savor. Still stunned that his and Aven's child was here and safe, Thor inquired as to how much she had weighed. How much had Aven endured?

Fay looked to Haakon for clarification, but Haakon was still staring at the baby.

Thor tapped his brother's arm to get his attention. *Baby weight. Ask Fay.*

He felt the inquiry muffle against the glass as Haakon spoke it.

Nodding, Fay answered them both. "Nine pounds, one ounce."

Thor shot out a breath. Though two pounds slighter than he had been, that was no small baby. *Aven well?*

After Haakon's assistance, Fay's eyes shifted between them. "She's doing very well. Cora's taken good care of her, and the doctor has offered his aid as well. She's resting, but she's right as rain, Thor. Couldn't have done any better or been any braver. She took good care of this one." Fay's blue eyes shone. "You should see them when they're both sleeping. It's hard to tell them apart when they're nestled together that way." She winked.

Ardent was his longing to see such a thing, but this in itself was a gift beyond measure. Thor peered down at his daisy-petal some more, and when Tusie stirred in her sleep, tiny mouth working for milk, he gave Fay his sign for gratitude.

She smiled. "I'll get her tucked back in with her mama."

Thor nodded and didn't so much as move as he watched Fay climb the lower steps and out of sight. He waited there, counting the moments until he knew Fay was in the attic—likely lowering Tusie into Aven's arms. Thor pressed his forehead to the glass and closed his eyes to savor the notion. He stood that way for some moments, then remembering that he owed his brother a thank you, Thor lifted his head. It was Haakon who'd woken him and Haakon who had helped bridge the gap of understanding and assurance just now. Thor turned to express his gratitude, yet there was nothing beside him but an empty porch.

Haakon wasn't sure if he should walk hushed or simply charge up this hillside. Undecided, he called out to make his presence known as he ducked past the spring-loaded branches of oak saplings. Orville had said this would be the spot, confirmed when Haakon smelled chestnut wood smoke. A type of wood to burn when a body didn't want to draw attention. The still for making moonshine had to be around here, and he aimed to find it. Seeing that baby had sealed something inside him. It was one of the fiercest torments and joys he'd ever known, and while he'd been unsure as to the final details of his plan with the moonshiner, the last piece had fallen into place while looking at her.

He'd known for some time what needed to be done. He just hadn't wanted to face it.

It wasn't until he'd stood on the other side of that window scarcely an hour ago, looking down upon one of the loveliest creatures he'd ever beheld, that he knew what the coming days would require of him. A depth of cunning and concentration to rival that of the great sea serpent. Did he have it in him? To see this through . . . he had to.

There was nothing easy about what he was about to do in the days to come, but he had to be courageous enough to press on with the plan.

Birds chirped in the green canopy of treetops. With it warm enough for copperheads and rattlesnakes, Haakon kept an eye out as he waded through waist-high weeds. Sticks snapped under his boots, which wasted any wondering of how best to walk. Orville had probably set up camp in this spot for that very reason. It took little effort to hear a person coming.

From nearby rushed a creek, a necessity for making corn liquor. Haakon pushed past a bramble of weeds, and all at once he saw the still. It wasn't much more than a turnip boiler, old barrels, and copper piping, all banked with clay and rocks—but it smelled the way a good still did from sweet corn mash and the chestnut smoke that trickled through the rickety pipe. Empty sacks from sugar and ground corn were piled up on one side, and opposite that sat a rough mound of gathered wood. A low tent was barred across the entrance by a clothes-line where two dingy socks hung drying. Compared to this operation, his and his brothers' liquor business had been downright stately, yet all a man needed to make a living was right here.

At the click of a rifle, Haakon froze. Orville wouldn't shoot without good reason, so he didn't move as the shadowed man stepped from the weeds, gun aimed.

Suddenly the firearm lowered and its marksman cursed. "You wanna let me know next time you plan on comin' up here in the middle of the day?"

Lowering his hands, Haakon strode through more tall weeds. "See, I got me an idea."

"I *bet* you do." Orville sat and settled his firearm beside him on a low, flat stone.

Certain that was enough of a welcome, Haakon pushed his way into the clearing that spread beside the creek. Water weeds and branch lettuce grew in thick patches, which likened a choice spot for setting up such an outfit. Clean, cold water was the first step in good corn whiskey. Haakon had little experience with moonshine, but he knew enough about liquor to see why Orville's drink kept growing in popularity.

"You know . . . You wouldn't have to be so all-fired tense if you learned to pay taxes." Haakon sat on a squat log. He eyed Orville's rifle, and if he wasn't mistaken it was from the War. Judging by the scope, designed to take out officers during the War at an immense distance. Good thing Orville didn't have an eager trigger finger.

"You sound just like Sibby. I swear she's half sheriff sometimes." Orville smiled a fondness for his wife, then wedged a dried weed into the fire and used it to light a tobacco pipe.

The man looked to be about twenty. His beard was so thin that Haakon could see through to his neck, which bore the same pockmarks that pitted his cheeks. His eyes were like a ground squirrel's—dark and narrow. Sibby was quite fine to look at, and Haakon might have questioned why she'd ended up with such a misfit, but since meeting Orville, Haakon had learned that he was both savvy and good-natured. Even patient. No doubt a breath of fresh air for a Sorrel girl.

A crate sat half filled with jars, and Orville puffed smoke as he finished filling it. When he did, he held over a remaining quart.

Haakon accepted it with a nod of thanks. "Why were you in church the other day?"

"Same reason you woulda been." Orville sucked in a long drag before speaking around his pipe. "Didn't know it'd be so noteworthy."

"It got around. You should be more careful."

"Well, Sibby was wantin' to go, and she asked me to come along." Using the bottom of a tattered boot, Orville pushed the crate aside.

It had been awhile since he'd had a proper drink, so Haakon unscrewed the cap and took a swig. Like Thor, he'd never taken to the coarse taste of moonshine, but this was awful smooth. He took a second drink, then held the clear liquid up to the light. "That's some fine whiskey."

"This was a good run. Got me another one to make right after."

"Business that good, huh?"

"Someone had to pick up when you boys shut down." He smirked as though grateful for all the business they'd inadvertently sent his way. He carried the crate to the back of a wagon just as Haakon had done over a thousand times outside the cidery. It had always been his job to ensure deliveries, and he'd rather liked that side of the business. Dangerous work, but that's why Thor had often ridden shotgun.

When Orville sat again, he stirred a pot of beans that steamed atop the makeshift furnace of the copper still.

"Sibby's pawpaw won't be here tonight if that's what you came for." Orville slid his pipe from his lips long enough to taste from the wooden spoon. "The general was here last night, and I don't expect him to return for a couple days. The only way I made sure he'd be back was by sellin' him no more'n four quarts again. He didn't like that much, and I ain't gonna be able to keep that up."

"Next time he comes, send somebody for me," Haakon said.

"I ain't got no one to send. And this ain't a fetchin' service."

"No, but if we can pull this off, I'll pay you well."

"How well?"

Haakon had learned better than to consult the pouch around his neck in times like these, so he'd already counted out several coins that were now in his pocket. He pulled three out and set them on the rock beside the moonshiner. Not exactly US currency, but gold was gold. A mighty fine sum, and an amount he was reckless to offer up, but if he was going to do this, he had to go all in.

Orville studied one of the ornate coins as he spoke. "I still can't send for you. Sibby used to keep me company here, but now that her pawpaw's around, she steers clear."

"Don't worry about that. Just keep Jed here long as you can next time, and I'll think of a way to keep up on his whereabouts."

"And what if you don't show up?" Orville asked.

"Then sell him as much as you want, even if he doesn't come back. I promise I'll be here."

"Like you meant to be here last night?"

"Somethin' came up." He decided not to mention the birthing or why he'd needed to stick around. It was hard to explain what it was like living alongside Thor. Haakon had responsibilities that few people could comprehend, and the danger of this budding plan made him uneasy to bring talk of Aven into it. "I promise I won't miss the next time."

He explained the development of his idea while Orville scraped a plate clean of beans. Though the moonshiner didn't seem certain the plan could be pulled off, he didn't argue against it either, and finally he pocketed the coins.

Orville pushed his hat farther back on his head. "To be truthful, when Peter told me you'd need my help, I didn't have you pegged as that sort."

Was that relief? Or worry? "Well . . . next time Jed comes, I'll be here waiting, and I'll tell him what he needs to know. Harlan, too, if he comes." Haakon couldn't believe he was saying such a thing, but the time had come. Just as it had come for the sea serpent who wanted more than to hold the seas at bay. Haakon wanted more from this life too. He thought of his brother, and if it was a fight with the mighty Thor that Jed and Harlan wanted, it was a fight they were going to get.

TWENTY-FOUR

LEANING BACK AGAINST THE PORCH SWING, Aven closed her eyes. Tusenfryd was asleep in her arms, her two-day-old daughter curled up tight as though still in the womb. A cloudy sky loomed overhead, so Aven nudged up the baby's blanket to cover her well. Though the late May day was mild, she had quite a mind to keep those wrinkled little feet and hands as warm as could be. There was no need to set the swing in motion. Just sitting here, still and quiet, holding her daughter, was all the comfort she needed. All that was missing was Thor.

Instead, she saw Haakon. He walked with a long stick in hand. The only shirt he wore beneath his suspenders was that of his winter underwear, and around the waist of his dark pants wrapped a low-hanging belt that held a long knife sheath with a blade as ominous. Behind him Sigurd skipped along and Bjørn waddled on chubby legs, struggling to keep up.

"This way, ciderkins." Haakon led them to the center of the yard. "Let's put an end to the questions once and for all. This . . ." He dragged a tip of the stick through the dirt. "Is how big a whale is. Let's say . . . an orca, though we can go bigger if you want to talk blue whales." Dragging the stick beside him, he made a long curve across the yard, then shaped another section before returning the way he'd come. "An orca can rip a seal to shreds in seconds." At the end, he fashioned a lopsided tail. An artist he was not, but the boys stood captivated.

Aven watched as well. Clouds shifted overhead, painting the ground in dappled shades of sun and shadow.

"There." Haakon tipped his head to the side and studied his efforts. He stepped to the center of the drawing and added a flipper, then crossed to the top to make a long, curving fin. "That should do it. Who wants to get eaten first?"

Sigurd jumped up and down, pleading for it to be him, while Bjørn waddled forward as volunteer. Using the stick, Haakon rigged it just beneath Bjørn's pinned diaper and hefted the toddler up from the ground. Aven gasped, but Bjørn just laughed. Haakon carried his nephew that way until he carefully deposited him in the center of the whale.

"You, too, Sigurd. In you go."

Sigurd hopped over the drawn line and stood inside the whale, where he lay down on his back and stretched his body out straight. "I been eaten by a whale!" he cried in delight.

Never one to be left behind, Bjørn followed suit and, once he was sprawled in the dirt, tried to babble the same.

Aven had to smile.

Fay stepped onto the porch and gave her a cup of tea. Aven thanked her sister-in-law. While Aven was managing to get around, the birth had taken its toll on her body, which made Fay and Ida's thoughtful care all the more cherished.

Fay shielded her eyes from the morning sun. "Breakfast is ready if you're hungry, Haakon."

"Thank you," he called back. "And Thor?"

While the doctor had advised Thor take precautions for a short while longer, he'd agreed that careful visits were good and right.

"Jorgan and the doctor are there now with the wagon to bring him back for a spell," Fay answered. "We'll fix him something when he comes." She paused and surveyed her splayed-out children. "What is this?"

Haakon smirked. "Your sons have become food for the fishes, I'm afraid."

Chuckling, Fay stepped back toward the kitchen, lightly grazing Tusie's hair with the back of her hand as she did.

"Alright, ciderkins, how 'bout a shark?" Haakon asked.

Much cheering sprang from the boys. A shark was soon drawn in the dirt, as was a squid, both of which devoured the children. Still chuckling at the boys' antics, Haakon strode to the front of the cidery, where a large metal box made a makeshift bench. The sun was chasing away the shade there, so he sat beneath its brightness and waited as Fay bustled about the kitchen. In the yard, two blond heads bobbed up and down in imaginative play.

Haakon watched with clear contentment, and when Fay brought out a cup of coffee and a plate of food, he rose quickly and met her halfway in the yard. He was just walking back toward the cidery when Fay exchanged an idea with Aven. At Aven's agreement Fay called out to him.

"There's good shade here on the steps, Haakon. If you'd like to sit, that is."

Aven seconded the notion with a small nod. 'Twould be much easier for him to get the second helping he'd soon be needing.

Haakon looked to her then to Fay, and as though not meaning to waste a kindness, he carried his plate over, thanked them both, and sat at as far a distance as the porch steps allowed.

Aven thought again to the reverend's sermon that Sunday. She'd meant to give Thor the notes but with Tusie's impending birth had mislaid them. She would need to find them soon and retrace the story of the prodigal son herself. The notion filled her with the same warring emotions—those of sorrow and those of grace. Laced through it all was the tenderness she'd once had for the sailor on the steps.

It had been but a taste of the love she had for Thor and yet real all the same. The smallest hint of romance in her earliest days on this farm—but as she had slowly discovered that it was with Thor that her heart was the safest, she'd turned instead to a friendship with Haakon. A friendship she had cherished. She had only wished he'd forged the same path for them. She prayed that he was able to now and sensed, deep within, a rising hope for such a future.

"Tell us, Haakon, of your time away," Fay said, surprising Aven as much as Haakon, judging by the way he paused with his cup nearly to his lips. She sat on the steps across from him.

Haakon drank, then lowered his coffee. "Well . . . I was at sea, which you might already know."

"What places did you visit?" Fay inquired.

Aven grazed the back of her finger against Tusie's silken cheek.

"I saw most everything surrounding the North Atlantic. England. Parts of Spain. Much of the Caribbean. And of course Norway." He forked into his biscuits and gravy. "Also a fair number of places along the western coast of Africa."

"My." Fay laced her hands together and placed them within the folds of her striped skirt. The tan and white lines were a stark contrast to her black leather shoes. "And you worked in the ice trade, correct?"

"Mostly. When it was the off-season, we moved other exports."

"What was it like?"

"At times, busier than you can imagine. At other times, we were so bored we almost lost our minds." Haakon set his plate aside and grabbed the napkin Fay had brought with it. He took his time in wiping his hands as he spoke. "If I were back at sea, it would be time for watch. Instead of sitting here eating this fine meal, I'd be climbing the mast and into the rigging to take place at the lookout. The wind beats so hard there it takes your breath away. And there below would be the wind on the water, moving across it like a cat walking along a quilt."

Aven drew in a quiet sigh. Oh, how she remembered that beauty. While her own sea crossing was an experience she'd not wish to repeat, it had been a rough and wild voyage that was as vivid as the picture he painted.

"It sounds very adventurous," Fay said before glimpsing that his coffee was still full. "Of all the places I've been in this country, I've yet to be on the sea."

Haakon gave her a brotherly smile.

"And did you not think to take a wife amid all those travels?"

Aven widened her eyes at her sister-in-law, but Fay seemed more intrigued with teasing Haakon as a sister might. Haakon grinned as though knowing as much.

"It seems you would have met your fair share in all the places you've visited."

Haakon's own pleasure faded some. "It didn't seem wise to take a wife without some place for her to come home to." He turned his coffee cup and gripped the handle for another sip. His gaze lifted to the horizon, lingering there before falling to the empty place at his side. A place that might have been taken by a woman whom Fay and Aven would know as *sister*, and for this man, *beloved*.

Fay's expression was soft with compassion. They all knew that Thor and Jorgan were keeping the deed to Haakon's land under lock and key for the time being. "Perhaps that might be different in the seasons to come."

"I hope so."

Aven did too. She wished she could express it, but no words seemed fitting. Perhaps it was for the best that matters of Haakon's heart and longings were not addressed by her. But she could pray for this man and his growing peace. Hope for a good and steady future for him.

In the yard Bjørn squealed and crouched low as he watched Sigurd draw a fresh picture in the dirt.

"They're good boys," Haakon said, watching them. He rubbed at the edge of his patched boot where neat stitches bound the leather together. "And soon they're gonna have another little ciderkin to play with." He glanced back at Tusie, and when he smiled, his blue eyes lifted to Aven.

"What is this about 'ciderkin'?" Fay inquired.

Haakon swiped a hand down his light beard. "Well," he motioned with his fork toward the cider barn. "Ciderkin, as you know, is the second batch of drink. Made from the dregs of the pulp itself. So since they follow you and Jorgan, they're rather like the second batch." He watched as the boys ran circles around the squid's twisting body. "That makes them ciderkin."

Fay chuckled again, and Aven gave in to one of her own.

"That means you're cider too," Fay said to Aven.

Aven adjusted Tusie's blanket again, taking care to keep it nestled over her tiny head. "You and your imagination, Haakon."

He looked back over his shoulder, and she realized it was the first time in days that she'd addressed him.

Harnesses jangled in the distance. From the direction of the woods, the team ambled nearer, Jorgan on the driver's seat. Thor wasn't beside him, but on more patient inspection, Aven saw him sitting in the back, legs dangling over the end where the backboard was turned down. She couldn't contain her smile at sight of him. Haakon rose and headed back into the yard with the boys.

Jorgan pulled the wagon to a stop in front of the house and climbed down just as Thor did. Thor's movements were strained, but he looked more like himself, skin returned to its soft shade and his eyes clearer. As Thor approached, Aven rose and stepped to the railing with their daughter. On one arm he held a plaid blanket. Reaching them, he beheld Tusenfryd's face, and his own lit with awe. He studied her for some time, taking in every feature and tiny movement. When his head lifted, his eyes met Aven's. There was a contentment about him—a sweetness of homecoming. He motioned for her to come down the steps. She did, and once at his side, he led them down the length of the house.

The walk was slow, but it only gave her more time to enjoy this visit with him . . . the way he was so near. It had been far too long since she'd had a reason to peer up and smile.

At the garden, he circled around the humble fence and stopped at a place where spring grasses grew. Unfolding the blanket, he spread it out and waited for her to sit. Aven did, beaming at him when he settled beside her. His breathing was labored, but any worry that afforded was bolstered by the knowledge that he would be well. As for the baby, Dr. Abramson had asserted that Tusie showed no signs of illness. It was too soon to know for certain, but he was optimistic, and Aven clung to that.

"Has the doctor said when you might return to us?" she asked.

Thor's chest expanded with an inhale. *I home two weeks.*

"Truly?"

He was serious as he added, *Kiss wife. One week.*

A little laugh slipped out. "He told you that?"

I ask.

Aven smiled. "Did you, now?"

Thor nodded. His brown eyes sparkled, and if his longing for such was half of what hers was, 'twas no wonder he'd inquired.

"Well, I look forward to it." More than she could say. There was a uniting between them that would go far beyond words, and she looked forward to that moment with all her heart.

Flashing a shy smile, Thor lowered his face. A dark strand of hair came unbound from its leather cord and fell against his face. Her fingers longed to be able to tuck it behind his ear. He did it himself, and with his gaze falling to Tusie, he watched her with a tender longing.

In a soft rustling, two of Dotti's kittens scampered along the side of the fence, batting at one another in play.

Thor shaped a single question. *Baby well?*

"Very well. She sleeps most often, and when she's awake, she nurses with ease. Though she doesn't like her nappies to be dirty. It keeps me busy, but I wouldn't have it any other way. Fay and Ida have been such a help that I feel positively spoiled."

He grinned and then his expression quieted. *You well?*

While Aven didn't imagine herself as brave as everyone insisted she'd been, she was relieved to be through the ordeal and thankful to have brought a new life into this world. That it was Thor's own child was a joy that softened the recollection of pain. "I am mending. 'Twill be slow, but Cora assures me that it's steady and sure."

He nodded his understanding. His hand moved, to touch her own, but he slid it forward on his thigh as if to force himself not to. He surveyed the grass at his side and with his thick fingers plucked up a tiny flowering weed and then another. One he laid beside Aven's wrist. He carefully placed the other against the folds of Tusie's blanket.

Heart swelling, Aven touched the tiny bud nearest her. It would last but a day, so she would press it into the pages of her journal tonight. Tusie's also.

With gentle mews, the kittens wedged themselves between the garden fence, startling two finches that had been perched on a bend of willow. The birds fluttered away in such a fuss that Tusenfryd trembled. Her wobbly little hands flew wide, and Aven made a cooing sound to settle her. She nestled the baby's arms back into the blanket with care.

Finished, she righted the folds of Tusie's knitted bonnet. "Poor little dear." Aven fetched up the dropped flower and looked over to see that her husband's face was drawn, sorrow sweeping across his brow.

"Thor?"

Lowering his head, he ran a hand over his face as if to return the pleasure that had been there only moments ago. He regarded first the baby and then her before signing a phrase slowly. Each word shaped as if he wished he didn't have to. When he finished, Aven closed her eyes. Though her vision was dark, she could still see the torment in him. A disappointment that was chased heavily by guilt. She hadn't remembered to check, and now the deed was done.

Thor set his mouth firm, and in his face lived the bitter reality. The flailing of Tusenfryd's arms . . . the way she'd startled at the ruckus . . .

Of those on the farm who would hear the world through its colors and shapes, shadows and light, of those who would declare hopes of heart through their hands or form expressions so poignant they went beyond what words could say, Tusenfryd would not be one of them.

Instead, Thor's child could hear.

TWENTY-FIVE

THOR AIMED DOWN THE ROAD TOWARD THE orchards, and by the time he reached the first rows of trees, a soreness affirmed that he was pushing himself too hard. In the distance hills rose beyond the farm in varying shades of blue and gray. He went only a dozen more yards before his gait folded into a limp. He finally slowed. If he didn't ease up, he could land right back where he'd been—flat on his back in a bed.

With the house out of sight now, he struggled along as spring branches drew him in. If only he could flee his guilt as easily.

He'd meant to linger longer with Aven and Tusenfryd, but with his chest in knots and Tusie having wet a diaper not long after her waking, he'd walked Aven back to the house for her to go inside and tend to the baby, promising to return to them before dark for another visit. It was an excuse—they both knew it—and that Aven graciously watched him step away was her own gentle way of upholding his need to absorb this realization. No doubt she would too.

Was it a victory for her right now? That she need only struggle alongside one Deaf person in her life? As soon as the thought came, he cringed at how unfair it was. She'd never been anything but heartening about his lack of hearing and would have been the same with their child.

Closing his eyes, Thor inhaled deep of the orchards. He slowed and, sinking down to a crouch, lowered his head and gripped the back of his neck. When he closed his eyes, the whole world emptied of life. No sight, no sound—just him and this black, vacant void. Was that what he wanted for Tusie? For this to be her reality upon drifting off to sleep at night? Of being woken by others in a start, or snuck up on when she couldn't sense people coming? Of not being able to go to school due to efforts at speech that only invoked taunting because, like her da, she stam-stam-stammered and couldn't get anything out?

How could he have entertained such a life for her?

The reality of it singed from the center of his heart. Deafness was not something he would ever wish upon another, but should it have come to pass, he would have welcomed it, bittersweet as it would have been. Should his daughter have been Deaf, he wouldn't have been alone but instead had a soul who understood this existence. The silence he dwelled in would have welcomed another. He would have had someone to teach and raise in the ways of life as he knew it. He would have something to truly offer. Instead, it would be Haakon to teach her how to whistle and Aven to teach her to sing. Jorgan would hear her questions, and all the others would shape her voice in a way Thor didn't know how to.

Because his baby girl could hear. God bless her, she could hear.

The Lord had been merciful. She would speak and go to school. She would know the melodies of music and the calls of the forest. She would know Aven's laugh—something he craved above any other sound, the longing being rivaled only now by the little babbles Tusie would soon make.

Thor rose and, veering from the path, aimed for Haakon's cabin. He'd rest a spell and visit Aven by suppertime. There was so much to be thankful for. So much. He needed her to know that gratitude stemmed from the very depths of him. It was hard not to walk right back for the house, but wanting Aven and the baby to be able to rest, he'd tarry an hour before knocking on the door.

The walk back to the cabin was strenuous, but he eventually made it to the doorway. Thor worked his way slowly up the stairs, and at the loft landing he saw Haakon seated near the window. The kid was in his usual chair, and with his boots propped up against the wall had the chair tipped back on its hind legs. He turned a limp leather pouch in one hand and in his lap lay a child's drawing. Haakon seemed so engrossed with studying the picture that Thor didn't dare disturb him.

Settling on the edge of the bed, Thor watched his brother lift a jar of clear liquid from the floor and sip. A body might assume it water, but he could smell the moonshine from here. Thor grunted to get Haakon's attention, and when he glanced back, Thor gestured the twisting on of a lid.

"Oh, yeah." Haakon leaned forward, picked up the metal lid and ring, then screwed them on snug. "I wasn't thinking."

Thor nodded his gratitude, but with the scent lingering, he reached over and opened the window. A single whiff of liquor and he could suddenly taste it on his tongue. Suddenly remember the way it warmed his body, making his troubles smaller and further away.

While Haakon didn't seem to have that kind of problem with it, Thor sensed something else amiss with his brother. It had to do with that pouch in his hand. The one usually hanging around his neck. While Thor didn't know what to call the leaves that Haakon kept in there, he reckoned them a severe need for Haakon. With the pouch limp and nearly empty, perhaps that's what was burdening his brother.

Thor's attention slid to the Yellowboy rifle leaning against the wall. Haakon had mentioned the picked-at lock and windowsill, and not only had Thor investigated it himself that morning but he had a sense that was why Haakon stuck around now. He owed his brother a vast measure of thanks. While Thor wasn't afraid, Haakon's allegiance against such foes was yet another reason Thor had gotten to sit by his wife and daughter today. Thor whistled to get his brother's attention, shaping his mouth and forcing out air in the way Haakon had once taught him.

Pressing both hands flat to his chest, one higher than the other, Thor circled them in the sign for *appreciate*. He pressed a palm out toward Haakon for *your*, then finished with the sign for *help* by pounding a fisted hand to his open palm.

Haakon squinted at him as if unworthy of the gratitude. "Sure." When he dropped his focus back to the picture, it was to fold the paper up snug.

Suddenly remembering a different sheet of paper, Thor reached for the letter on the windowsill from Washington, DC. How had he forgotten? He tore inside, pulled out the single page, and noted the date from a few weeks back. A missive from one of the very men who had shaped his education as a boy.

April 29th, 1895

Mr. Thor Norgaard,

Your letter came to me by way of the postmaster. As your inquiry was addressed to the Bureau of Research and Resource for the Deaf and Dumb, the powers that be have delivered it to The Alexander Graham Bell Association for the Deaf and Hard of Hearing. It would seem that the two associations would be allies, but unfortunately, and as far as the United States Postal Service and myself are aware, the bureau you sought to contact does not exist.

I conversed this morning with several professors from the Columbia Institution for the Instruction of the Deaf and the Blind here in Washington, DC, and they, too, expressed a void of familiarity with such a bureau. As far as those knowledgeable within the field, there are none more learned than my fellow colleagues who have assessed your letter. I'm sorry if this news is dismaying, but I offer it as response to your inquiry and the troubling incident you found yourself subject to. In addition, I have never known there to be any links to the Deaf-Mute makeup within the blood-stream itself, but that's not to say the science behind it is ultimately false. Simply that those who obtained your blood likely have been.

With other Deaf-Mutes being at risk to such subterfuge, as well as your own family and community, please contact me at this address should I be of further use to you.

Very Respectfully,

Alexander Graham Bell

Thor lowered the letter so quickly it fluttered to the bed. The bureau didn't exist?

Rising, he searched for the missive that had summoned him for the interview, only to recall that it was at the house. Tromping through his memory was the doctor's familiarity with Sign Language, including use of correct terminology and theories. Not to mention the detailed questionnaire and blood draw.

That was all fraud?

Why would someone go through that amount of effort to deceive him?

For the Sorrels to have been present that day shot alarm through his veins so fiery hot he could scarcely think of what to do next. Thor fetched his boots back up, folded the letter, and summoned for Haakon to follow as he started for the stairs. They were going to need to saddle both horses. And quickly.

TWENTY-SIX

WITH A TUG ON THE REINS, THOR ANGLED the mare's head to the right. She lunged up the south hillside at the edge of the farm that rose to the Sorrels' plantation. Beside him, Jorgan rode at the same pace, pulling ahead just as Thor slowed his mount to sidestep a fallen log. In his saddlebag rested the letter Jorgan had retrieved from the house—Jorgan being at his side now due to Haakon's insistence.

Thor might have questioned that, but there hadn't been time. In truth, if only one man were to be left to guard the farm, he'd prefer it be Haakon. Jorgan was more than capable, but no one was so dangerous when unleashed than Haakon, and they needed that type of defense right now. As for Aven, she was well in the company of Fay and Ida, so Thor decided to lay any worries about her and Haakon to rest for the remainder of the day. This had to be done, and there was a time when he had to fully leave his wife and child in the Lord's hands and *trust*. It wasn't a reckless kind of trust, but going with his gut, and his gut told him to ride up here. He had bigger fish to fry than his little brother.

Based on the tracks surrounding the cabin the other day—about six or seven of them.

When they crested the hill, Thor spotted the old white mansion in the distance. Where once elegant trees led up the formal drive, now rutted stumps lined a patchy dirt lane. The War hadn't been kind to Jed Sorrel's plantation, but the bones of it were still here even if they were rattled to the core. Strung from the porch to a nearby oak hung a limp clothesline, and rising onto her tiptoes to hang a damp sheet was the younger Mrs. Sorrel—Harlan's wife. Nearby, her grown daughter, Sibby, bent over and fetched another.

The fair-haired women turned at the horses' approach. Thor gave a polite wave. He hadn't known if he could make it on his own, and few could translate for him so well as Jorgan, so he was more than grateful for his brother's presence. Jorgan dismounted first, and Thor followed. They left the mares to graze beside the house, then crossed over to greet their neighbors.

Harlan's wife didn't stop in her chore. Thor doubted she had time with many to look after and no husband to help. For Sibby to be here this afternoon—a married woman with her own house to manage—attested to Mrs. Sorrel's need for aid. The matriarch of this land, Jed's wife, had passed away the summer before, and now her daughter-in-law was the heiress of this estate and keeper of the remaining family within its corridors. Though Thor had given them free use of his orchards, the apples scarcely put a dent in their suffering.

Mrs. Sorrel tugged a pair of girl's stockings from her wicker basket. She straightened and shook them out. "Afternoon." A lace kerchief covered her hair that was streaked in silver.

Jorgan greeted her in return. While they'd always been on amiable terms, social calls with the Sorrel women had been with Fay and Aven. Because of that, Thor signaled to his brother to state their business right off so as not to set anyone ill at ease.

Jorgan spoke, but Thor was more focused on watching their re-action. After a minute, Jorgan tapped Thor on the arm and pointed to the women. Thor handed over the letter that had summoned him for the blood draw as well as the correspondence sent from Washington, DC. As Mrs. Sorrel read, Sibby emptied the basket of laundry.

"I'm sure Peter's made you aware of what's been going on." Jorgan added further explanation, describing the situation at the train depot and their suspicions surrounding it all.

Mrs. Sorrel nodded as she skimmed the first page. "He has. The girls and I fixed a fine dinner for the sheriff and his deputies."

Thor tried to hide his surprise. He doubted Harlan would have been pleased to know that—and maybe he already did. The Sorrel women had never been ones to shy away from their men. They'd taken a stance once and for all some years back and were sticking to it. Thor commended them for that, but he hoped no trouble would befall them.

Having finished both letters, Harlan's wife scrutinized the first again. The one that Thor suspected was Sorrel doing. She squinted against the bright light of afternoon and with her attention still down, spoke to Jorgan. "Can you ask your brother what the doctor looked like?" Faint lines creased her forehead.

Having already understood, Thor gave a tug at his hair, then indicated to Jorgan that it had been red. Next he stroked his moustache and made the sign for same. Mrs. Sorrel observed his gestures, and Jorgan spoke as Thor tapped the top of his shoulder to show the man's height. About a few inches shy of six feet, he surmised. While stalky, the man's handshake had been strong.

When Mrs. Sorrel heard the last of it, she drew in a slow sigh. "Might you remember the needle? Anything distinctive about it or perhaps the case?"

Thor's brow pinched as he thought back to that day. He searched his memory for the way the doctor's hands had held the case in his view . . . pulling the lid ajar . . . revealing the contents inside. Everything was mottled and blotchy.

Then it flashed through his mind's eye as though he were right back on that train.

Thor drug his index finger across his forehead.

"He's saying it was black," Jorgan said, then to Thor, "What was black?"

L-I-N-I-N-G. Thor folded his hands together, then opened them like the hinge of the needle's case.

Jorgan described that in English, and Mrs. Sorrel's mouth pinched tight. Her fingers held fast to the letters, clutching the top page beside Alexander Graham Bell's name.

She scanned the hills around them, then folded both pages with haste. "Come with me." She offered Thor the papers and clutched up the front of her checked skirt. Thor and Jorgan followed her lead down the dry pathway to the side of the house where several out-buildings stood. Made of rough-hewn logs much different than the stately plantation home with its summer kitchen and carriage house, he guessed them to be old slave quarters.

At the farthest down the line, Mrs. Sorrel pulled a ring of keys from the waistband of her skirt and pressed a rusted one into the lock. She struggled with the tightness of the knob, and Jorgan stepped in to help, shimmying it until the door creaked ajar. They waited for her to step in first, and when they followed, the inside was as still as a cave.

Slats of light striped the floor from where chinking had worn thin in the western wall. In place of narrow beds for slaves sat dusty benches around the room as though meetings had taken their place. On that same wall, a width of cloth hung pinned between two heavily curtained windows. The emblem in the cloth's center was a crudely drawn white cross, squat and square. On the opposite wall hung white hoods that were as dusty as everything else.

Mrs. Sorrel had brought them here for a purpose. One that had first taken seed between their two families since it was just Jed Sorrel and Jarle Norgaard facing one another at the property line. Thor watched Mrs. Sorrel. Had their mother been alive, she might have been close in age to this woman who knelt to roll back one end of a dingy rug. She worked to loosen a floorboard, and when her grip slipped, Thor flipped open his knife and wedged it into the nearest gap. Together they had the board lifted off and set aside. Mrs. Sorrel reached inside and pulled out a tin. Instead of prying off the top, she clutched it against her skirt and tipped her face to Jorgan.

"Tell me of your brother's wife. Has she delivered the baby?" Her compassion-filled eyes found Thor in what appeared more concern than neighborly conversation. Thor glanced to his brother to follow his answer.

"Just a few days ago," Jorgan asserted. "A girl. Good and healthy so far as we can tell."

Thor gave a sturdy nod, and the tension in Mrs. Sorrel's face softened. Wondering if she might know something about this matter, he signed a desperate question to his brother.

"Thor's asking if there's a way to know if his wife and daughter are out of danger with the illness."

Mrs. Sorrel hesitated, and Thor sensed they were wading into uncomfortable waters. "I'd say that so long as he kept his distance from his wife during the worst of it, they should fare just fine." Her eyes were grieved as though she'd never known the same courtesy.

A heat rose under Thor's collar, but it was with relief that he confirmed that he had. For Mrs. Sorrel to affirm an understanding on the matter deepened his hope. Here she was aiding them with grace. Such kindness from a woman who had known very little of it in her life.

She set the tin between them on the floor. So warped was the metal box that the lid scarcely stayed closed, but when she slid it off, there inside lay small glass bottles, all with identical labels.

Morphine.

"He used this often. As did some of his brothers. Got hooked on morphine during the War, Jed did, and the liking of it trickled through his son's tastes as well. Needle's long gone. That went with them." Her eyes found Thor's. "Lined in black, that case was. Make no mistake that it was the very one you saw that day, and I suspect that's the reason behind your ailment, Mr. Norgaard."

Just as the doctor had explained.

"As for this man who deceived you by posing as a doctor come to help, I fear that may be Roald. Harlan's brother. He ain't been around here since you were boys. Goes by Red mostly. The law got him a fair time back, and I ain't seen him since. I thought he might have been dead, but ain't it just like one of Jed's sons to live to tell the tale?" Her eyes, the same soft blue as Sibby's and Peter's, widened in what could only be a fear at knowing the worst sort of person. "Red's cunning as they come and worked as a medic for the army some years back. He'd have been the one put up to the task of trickin' you."

Since Bell's declaration, Thor had searched his memory of that winter's day at the depot. He realized now that Aven had interpreted all the Sign Language. Thor had fingerspelled N-O-R-W-E-G-I-A-N directly, but Red Sorrel would have known their heritage with or without the answer. No wonder he'd written it down.

Thor gauged his brother, whose gaze was steely. Looking back to Mrs. Sorrel, Thor tried to catch up to what she was in the midst of saying.

". . . somethin' else I brought you here to show you." She rose and pulled back one of the curtains to reveal that a window had been shattered. "This building was broken into a few weeks back. Peter noticed it first. Perhaps he mentioned it?"

He'd spoken of an outbuilding that had been busted into, but they hadn't known which one. Jorgan examined first the shattered window, then the one beside it that was still unharmed. Thor had a way of reading folks, his brothers in particular, and when Jorgan turned he could tell that he was surveying first the width of the room and then the purpose behind it.

Focus landing on a far corner, Jorgan stepped that way. "What was in this cabinet?" He touched the door that hung ajar.

Mrs. Sorrel put the box back, and Thor watched her mouth as he helped her replace the board. "Some of Harlan's old things, though I don't know what. I never had a key to that lock."

Thor angled back to see what his brother's response would be.

"Was it always open like this?" Jorgan asked.

Mrs. Sorrel shook her head.

Jorgan stepped nearer, reached a hand inside the empty space, and drug his finger along a back corner. He studied his tainted skin—the black powder now darkening it—and Thor didn't doubt that they were ascertaining the same thing. Gunpowder. Knowing Harlan, this cabinet had once housed a heap of ammo. And worse yet . . . the firearms to go with it.

TWENTY-SEVEN

STEPPING FROM THE CABIN, HAAKON BLINKED against a morning that was far too bright. Made worse by the fact that there was only a single, tattered leaf of coca in his possession and not a single woman to court in miles.

As for a woman, all he'd need to do was venture out a ways, but that would mean one less man to guard the farm. And even an indulgence of female companionship wouldn't distract him for long to the fact that the pouch around his neck was nearly empty of anything that had the potency he needed. Right now it was the one pitiful leaf, a Bible passage, and the child's drawing. He didn't see how that would be enough to get a man through a day, but it was all he had.

Haakon drew in a slow breath as he left the porch of the cabin. He was just going to have to try and think about other things. Nearly impossible, though, since sleep continued to evade him in the night. If he went to search out any sign of the Sorrel men, he was a wreck of worry for leaving the farm, and if he stayed in the cabin, he remained awake to be the ears Thor lacked. If for any reason dreams claimed him, he awoke to the memory of the young widow's voice in his head. A sound as tender as the way she'd cared for him and her small children. He needed to lay such a memory to rest with the same determination that had gotten him on that ship.

Yet as hard to forget as that lovely voice was the way her children used to follow him about, trailing after him like a line of ducklings, giggling their delight in a language he hardly knew. While he grasped only a few of their words, those smiles and the brightness in their eyes had been telling enough as they'd traipsed along the rise above the fjord. The frigid North Sea air gusting against them all.

With thoughts such as those, Haakon's chest ached with a throbbing he doubted a man could live long through, and it was getting worse the more determined the sea was in refusing to fold up and bridge the two worlds that had claim to him.

Whenever he saw Fay or Aven pinning laundry to the line, chatting away as they did, he imagined Widow Jönsson there too. Barefoot and lovely beneath the Virginia sun. And whenever he tried to slumber on his palette, he couldn't shake the wishing for her to be close against his side. That he knew the way back to her made the longing all the more severe. Made worse that he didn't know how to forget her son's words . . . *På gjensyn. We meet again.*

But that wasn't going to happen because when all of this was said and done, he was going to hitch up the wagon and get himself to church where he'd find a wife good and close and proper.

That's what he was going to do.

The pull of mind and spirit only intensifying, Haakon ached for coca, but with two ciderkins bounding his way on the path now forged between his cabin and the great house, he didn't reach for his pouch. With a wooden sword in hand, Sigurd skipped closer, and Bjørn lagged behind with one side of his nightshirt tucked into a loose diaper. A crust of bread was in hand, and he crammed a corner into his mouth as he waddled forward on pudgy legs.

"Let me guess . . ." Haakon raised his suspenders into place as he crossed the near end of his own yard. "I swept wong again."

Waiting for him among the trees, Sigurd hopped up on a low boulder that brought him closer to eye level. His white-blond hair was askew from slumber. Bjørn tried to climb up as well, but his little legs weren't much help. Haakon reached him and with the toe of his boot gave a gentle nudge. It helped Bjørn reach the top, and he scrambled to a stand beside his brother.

With Thor mending and with himself showing no signs of the sickness, Haakon had a hunch it was fine to touch them, but it seemed better to be safe for a mite longer.

Their smiles were so cheery that he smiled back, finding it as bolstering as the leaves he'd been longing for a moment ago. Maybe—if he was willing to admit it—more so.

Across the way, Jorgan carried an oiled saddle toward the horse barn. Haakon lifted a hand in greeting, and needing to find Peter, he thumbed for the boys to follow him. He borrowed Sigurd's sword and indulged them in a story as they crossed the yard. In his best Barbadian accent, he described what it was like to split open a coconut with a machete and eat the sweet flesh inside. When he finished, they'd reached the top of the road that wove down into the orchards. Sigurd bounded from one foot to the other, soliciting another tale. Bjørn just begged for a "coco-wut."

"I need to go now and help Mr. Peter with some work in the orchard." Haakon slowed as they did and gave the sword back to its owner. "You boys run on up to the house, alright?"

"Can we come?" Sigurd pleaded.

This really wasn't the best time, otherwise, he'd happily toss Bjørn up to his shoulders and march the little fellow there. Instead, Haakon looked to his brother for help.

Jorgan called out to his sons. "Why don't you run along and ask Aunt Aven how Tusenfryd is doing, then report back to Uncle Haakon around dinner time?"

"Great idea!" Haakon seconded.

Sigurd gave his father a salute and dashed off. His brother waddled after him, quick as those stout legs would allow. Sigurd dropped the sword near the porch among a pile of Bjørn's wooden blocks before rushing up the steps. Bjørn fell but rose. He brushed little hands together and hurried on.

"You said you were searchin' for Peter?" Jorgan called when his sons had run inside. "He'll be down at the compost heap."

"Thanks."

"And Haakon?"

Having started off, Haakon angled back.

Jorgan lowered the saddle some. "You doin' alright?"

Since his return, Haakon had been answering inquiries of Thor's well-being, so it was strange for someone to ask after his own regard. Though he had a thousand fears and hopes and even stories bottled up inside, he didn't know how to respond. The fact that Jorgan inquired now humbled him.

"I'm well. Thanks." A thin way to answer, but he decided not to uncover that mine.

Looking skeptical, Jorgan steadied his grip on the saddle and watched him turn away.

Haakon aimed toward the apple groves, over a hundred acres of them bathed in morning light. After a few dozen yards, he reached what had been his favorite tree as a boy. Ida had long ago implied that the gnarled McIntosh resembled a woman bent over as though to fetch water from a well. If Ida had known what such a comment would do to a bunch of lads who'd lost their mother, she might not have mused aloud so. As it was, Haakon used to come here as a child and sit in its branches, letting the curves of applewood hold him as a pair of arms might have. Then again, maybe it was the very reason Ida had sparked their imaginations. Knowing it would be a seed of comfort to hearts hungry for such.

It had been years since he'd visited this spot, but as much as he wanted to pause and contemplate it, Haakon simply ran a hand along a rough branch as he walked. A blackbird flew from his path—as much a part of this land as the roots of Thor's trees. Haakon breathed deep as he walked, drawing in air that was drenched in the scent of dried blossoms. A sight to behold as well.

Was it difficult for Thor to walk here? For him to toil on this land that supplied the key to his very addiction? Haakon couldn't begin to imagine how his brother had kicked the longing for a drink, but maybe that was it; maybe the desire wasn't gone. Maybe Thor just understood that a man ought not to consume more than his share in this life. To not take more than what was right or fitting. The weight of such a thought trudged with Haakon down to the lower orchards where Peter stood in the back of the wagon, shoveling manure onto the compost pile.

Haakon grabbed a spade from where it leaned against a tree. "Came to lend you a hand." He rammed the blade into the muck and turned it.

"Thanks." Peter climbed up into Da's old farm wagon and scraped out another load. Messy business, but Peter not only kept the horse stalls clean, he maintained several aspects of the farm including the compost heap that lived here at the far end of the Baldwin grove. It was honest work and labor Peter had a right to be proud of.

The wagon had always had a few missing boards, but upon closer study, they'd been replaced. "Things are lookin' real fine around here," Haakon said.

Peter scraped another scoop down. "I'm glad for the work."

"I know they're glad for the help."

They labored in silence for a while, and Haakon paused only to roll back the cuffs of his shirt. After swiping sweat from his forehead, Peter paused also and rested gloved wrists on the top of his shovel handle. "So what did you really come here for?"

Good gravy, Peter was sharp, especially since he'd let Haakon get plenty filthy before inquiring. "Uh . . . actually, I was wondering if there was any chance you can head into town for me tomorrow?" He could just as soon go himself—and a day in society would certainly clear his head—but something had him wanting to stay.

"I 'spose so. What for?"

"I need to get a couple messages to folks. One in Eagle Rock and another over in Grayson County." Part of his evolving plan with the Sorrel men and one he hoped would work. Time to end this wild goose chase with Harlan Sorrel once and for all. "'Bout how long do you think that would take? For a message to Grayson."

"By mail? Maybe a week or two."

He didn't have that long. At sea, mail was difficult to get delivered due to danger, carelessness, and the changing of course. Letters often passed from vessel to vessel, sometimes traveling the world over before making it to where they were meant to go. If they didn't get lost before then. The mail system at sea was like a spider web of connection, risk, and loss, all woven together by sailors desperate for word to and from home.

The more determined a body was to get something somewhere, the more likely it made it. Which got him thinking about Cora's son. If anyone was invested in the whereabouts of the Sorrels, it would be Al, whose own mother and sisters were in danger. "Where's Al livin' these days?"

"Over on some balds down in Montgomery. Works on a cattle farm about a day's ride from here. Cora and the girls are plannin' a visit next month, I think."

"Would you say it's about another few days' ride from there to Whitetop Mountain?"

"Where?"

"Grayson County."

"Yeah, I'd say so."

"If I hire you a horse, could you get a message straight to Al tomorrow? If I do your work here?"

"You wanna do my work tomorrow?"

"I'll do it the next day, too, while you're riding back. If you could just get a note to Al, I think he can help us. With your pawpaw and all. The other message is for the sheriff."

"You don't need to hire me a horse. I already got one." Peter skidded his square shovel across the boards of the wagon, causing the last of the muck to fall. "I'll have to check with Jorgan, but I don't think either of us will mind you shovelin' manure."

Haakon smiled. "It's a deal. If I pay you extra, can you leave this afternoon? I know that would mean riding through the night—"

"I don't need you to pay me. If it's important to the cause, I'll do it."

This was a good man. "It's extremely important." The fact that Peter didn't inquire about the contents of the messages made the gesture more humbling. A trust and a faith that Haakon didn't deserve. With Peter's willingness, he was tempted to send him all the way to Whitetop Mountain, but Peter needed to get back. He was a good shot and kept careful watch over Cora and her girls, which was needed more than ever right now. Haakon promised to look in on them during Peter's two days away.

"I wouldn't go elseways, so thank you," Peter said. "Do you want to talk to Jorgan, or should I?"

Regretfully, the time would come for Jorgan to witness the inner workings of his mind, but that day wasn't today. "I'll do it." It would take a little extra explaining to appease his brother right now. "I'll talk to him then come back and let you head off. I'll have those messages written up too. If you could also stop in at the bank in Eagle Rock and change some coin for me, I'll bring that as well." Haakon didn't mean to fuel a fire beneath this all, but he wasn't going to make it many more days without proper sleep. If he could land a face-to-face meeting with the Sorrel men, then he could arrange a treaty of sorts. Surely they were the kind of men who could be reasoned with. Haakon just needed to offer the right prize . . .

And he knew exactly what it was they wanted.

After Haakon explained all that, Peter gave a sure nod and tossed his shovel down before hopping to the ground himself. Haakon shook his hand, then started back toward the farmyard with a renewed hope that this might just work after all. While no man should crave violence, and while he certainly didn't now, sometimes the choices of one man had a way of forcing another's hand.

If the messages he crafted got where they needed to go, things could fall into place. Or . . . this whole plan could crumble by week's end. He was relying on many others right now, and it meant an awful lot of risk. Too much of his plan hinged on those messages arriving and the fact that he not miss Jed and Harlan in passing tonight should they arrive at the still. And now that he was thinking about it, he had a little something that Sibby Sorrel could aid him with. A way to ease this burden just a little bit more . . . if she was willing. He needed to find her, but right now too many eyes were watching him, so it would all just have to wait until dark.

Time to say another one of those prayers. The kind he'd muttered when the sails had finally filled with wind off the coast of Africa. He didn't mean to test the Lord again, and he certainly hadn't earned any favors, but this hope wasn't for him, so he'd pray that God might understand.

TWENTY-EIGHT

THE ROCKING CHAIR CREAKED AS AVEN EASED
it back and forth, keeping the baby content. The chair had been Ida's
domain for a good many decades, and now it was happily lent to
nursing mothers. Aven was grateful for the smooth, soft wood and the
gentle haven on quiet afternoons. With the boys asleep upstairs, Fay
and Ida moved around the first floor with quiet efficiency, though in
truth, they'd much more earned the rest than Aven, so boisterous the
lads had been that morning.

Near the light of the open window, Fay saw to the last of the
week's ironing. Beside her, Ida folded and stacked, keeping a household of laundry in careful order. For all the weeks he'd been home,
Haakon hadn't brought them so much as a scrap of laundry to scrub
even though Fay inquired each wash day. This morning Fay had
marched over, demanding he let them help. He'd finally consented,
and so his own things were freshly dried and awaiting him.

Fay ironed two more shirts and had just pressed Thor's last pair of
trousers when Tusenfryd fell asleep—tummy full of milk and thickening cheeks declaring her fondness for it. Aven righted her bodice,
a juggling act with her daughter snug on one arm. Made easier when
Ida stepped in and scooped up the infant.

"Would you mind keeping her while I see along Thor's things?" Aven asked. It had been too long since she'd been able to visit with him at the cabin, and while the doctor was allowing him to return home soon, the thought of stealing a few moments with him was as tempting as the warm sunshine outside. She couldn't have been more thankful for these days abed with Tusenfryd, but now that strength was returning and a comfortable rhythm of feeding and caring for her daughter had been discovered, a short excursion to see Tusie's papa was sweet on her mind and heart.

Ida pulled up Tusie's knit blanket from the arm of the rocking chair and bundled it around the baby's little nightgown.

Fay watched the gesture with a sweet smile. "Off you go, Aven. You'll not be getting her back for a few hours, even if you were to plead."

Ida chuckled and seconded that notion. "Enjoy you a stroll. We got this one well in arms."

Aven retrieved Thor's stack of clothing, then, recalling Haakon's belongings, fetched that low pile as well. She carried it all out the door, clutching the soft bundles close. Haakon was working in the orchard for the day. Peter off on an errand. She didn't see Jorgan about, so with no one to walk with her, Aven took stock of the narrow stretch of trees that separated the two plots of land. Seeing naught but birds and squirrels, she edged nearer. To continue on alone would go against the creed Thor had asked her to agree to. Aven was just about to turn away when she heard voices through the glen. A man and a woman's. It took but a glimpse through the leafy branches to see the source. Haakon. And Sibby Sorrel.

Aven knew not her married name, only that the young woman stood beside Haakon, who tipped his head near and spoke in a hushed manner. 'Twas such an intimate sight that Sibby's bare feet only amplified their familiarity. Haakon's suspenders hung around his hips, and his shirt was disheveled. Like spun gold Sibby's hair was, and it hung nearly as long and loose as the amber dress she wore.

After nodding to Haakon's soft words, Sibby squeezed his hand.

Aven looked away, glancing back as he withdrew a fold of money. Upon receiving the offering, Peter's sister rose to her tiptoes and kissed his bristly cheek. Lowering back down, Sibby gave him a sad smile, then turned away. Haakon stroked a hand down his beard as he watched her go.

Before Aven could think to move—before she could take a step forward or, better yet, a step away—Haakon turned the way of the grove, spotting her. His hand slid behind his neck, which he arched back in a manner fraught with tension. Though shock heated both limb and lung, Aven knew she couldn't very well remain here holding laundry forever.

She crossed through the trees, and he approached the cabin porch as she did. Aven kept all focus on the folded items as she reached up and pushed them beneath the banister. "For Thor." Her voice sounded fragile, as though it might crack. "And some is yours."

His own was quiet. "He's not here. He's at the spring."

"I—I thought you were down in the orchard."

"I was. Just came up here for a spell. Peter's back, but I'm going to head down and help him finish the chores."

Aven clasped her hands together. She wasn't Haakon's keeper, and she certainly wasn't Sibby's either. But when she thought on Sibby's husband—the man with the dark hair and roughened face—her heart hurt.

"Haakon . . . ," she whispered.

"That wasn't how it looked."

"No? May I ask what it was, then?"

He swallowed and, looking past her to open timberland, gave no response.

She should have known that would be his answer. Was there ever any shortage on heartache? First there'd been the loss of her mother within the workhouse walls. A death that had been sudden and real.

Then, just as Aven had dared to open her heart again, Benn had crushed it when he'd changed her from bride to widow. Last of all, it had been buried in deep by Haakon. When it came to the end of her naïveté, death and the devil might have dug the hole, but it was Haakon who had placed the stone.

"Is there not enough grief in the world yet that you need to be adding more?" she asked.

"It's not what you think. I promise."

"Then tell me what I should be thinking."

"Will you believe me?"

Silence was all she could offer.

"That's what I figured."

Aven turned away, this time in the direction of the spring. With Jorgan's insistence that none of the women or children wander off alone, 'twas no surprise when Haakon kept pace at her side.

Ignoring him, Aven tried to quicken her steps but was weak yet and nearly faltered. Haakon seemed about to steady her but kept his distance. It was a shorter jaunt to reach the spring by a pathway that ran along the back side of the cidery, so she followed its ambling course through thick woods. Haakon was silent beside her. Birds darted from their path, and more than once he pushed wayward branches out of her way.

"Can you please leave me alone," she whispered.

"Not until you reach the spring."

"I can make it there on my own."

His eyes shifted to the east where unkempt acreage grew thick and shadowed. "You don't know what's in those woods."

"Jorgan explained it."

As if just now realizing his suspenders were out of order, he tugged up one and then the other. "Not well enough or you wouldn't be here." When the path narrowed, he led the way, and she saw the handle of a revolver holstered at the back of his waist.

Aven slowed, knowing he was right. 'Twas foolish of her to head off alone—no matter her upset. "Will you please tell me, then?" Jorgan had mentioned there was danger due to Jed's and Harlan's whereabouts, but not in great detail.

Haakon started on and she followed. "Jed Sorrel is wanted for three accounts of murder. Harlan two. In addition to that, they're both wanted for assault many times over." He stepped over a dry-rotted log, then waited as she managed on her own. "Some of the cases involved women in a way that I won't even describe." His gaze dropped to the lace of her petticoat, which she tugged away from the rough bark. "So when we tell you you're not safe in these woods, you're not safe." His hand moved back to the waistband of his pants where he pulled his shirt over the handle of the revolver to better conceal it.

If he wanted to frighten her, it had worked. If he wanted to ensure her heart was broken for those who had been harmed by Sorrel men, the cracking was now complete. Aven heaved in a breath, wishing for a way to lay her own battle down when so much was at stake for so many. When others had lost much more than she. For that alone she slowed and faced Haakon again.

Though he came no nearer, his voice was as soft as it must have been for Sibby. "Remember when Peter first started working for us? The day after he was throttled by his kin?"

Aven nodded slowly, recalling Peter's deep bruises.

"That's just the start of what they can do. Aven, there are sheriffs after them in every county from Botetourt to Clark. Did Jorgan tell you that?"

He very well might have, but she'd been so caught up in Thor's illness . . .

"Good and well that the sheriff aims to help, but we all know there's not much the law can do up here. It's too vast. Too untamed. A man could vanish here if he wanted to. We all know it's not so simple, so we're going to do everything we can to keep you all safe."

Her heart lurched at the sincerity in his eyes. 'Twas so different than the Haakon she'd known when last they had stood in this wilderness alone.

"Even more, to try and find them." Pulling up the pouch from beneath his shirt, he lifted it off. "I've got a message out to the sheriff myself, but there's no way to guarantee the Sorrels' whereabouts."

"You are trying?"

"I am." He drifted across her path, smelling of the cidery and just a hint of the sea as though something on him was yet unwashed from his voyaging. "But for right now I'm gonna walk with you until you reach Thor. And when you do I'm gonna let you go."

Standing so near to him, she realized he had scarcely aged. The freckles across his nose weren't as distinct, and his beard made him appear as commanding as his husky voice, but it was the same face she'd known. All save his eyes, which told the story that his soul was older. Loosening the drawstrings of his pouch, he pulled out a single dry leaf and folded it in half and then half again. She'd witnessed him place such a concoction in his cheek once before—much as a man chewed tobacco. Aven didn't know if this was the same.

Overhead, a blackbird swooped down with a cry. Haakon glanced up as it soared past, speaking as he did. The breeze crackled in the greenery of young saplings, nearly crowding out the hush of his words. "Sibby's gonna come to you one day with something very important to say." His gaze fell back to hers. "When that time comes, please believe her, Aven. Believe her with everything inside you." His fingers fiddled with the folded leaf, which he returned to his pouch, looking frustrated as he did. He backed away, directing her around the bend in the trees where just beyond dwelled the spring. "If you don't put a shred of stock in anything I say from this day forward, please put stock in this. For you and Fay and Ida, and those children . . . believe Sibby. Please."

After another step away, he hesitated. "And Aven? I'm the furthest thing from a saint, but however it might have appeared with Sibby, I promise you I don't dabble with married women."

She gave a small nod, aching to trust him. As needful was to believe well of Sibby, who had showed them naught but a sweet nature over the years.

"In fact, there's . . ." He wet his lips. "I mean, in *Norway*, there's . . . Well, *she's* . . ." His eyes searched the ground with as much ardency as he struggled with words. All at once, they widened as though he'd just realized something. With a sharp inhale, he took a step back, and the vulnerability that flooded his face emphasized a need to end the discussion. "You better head on."

Not knowing what else to do or say, Aven whispered a thank-you and continued down the lane.

He didn't follow, so it was when she reached the farthest reach of the bend that he called gently to her. "Do you see Thor?"

Aven assured him that she did.

Dipping his head, Haakon trudged back the way they'd come, and she waited the minute it took for his footsteps to fade into silence. So far off that she knew he wouldn't linger. He'd said he wouldn't, and somewhere deep inside she wanted to believe him.

Turning away, she continued on down the rutted lane. Such a lengthy venture it had been that her steps were now ginger and her breathing labored. Though her strength was renewed, 'twould be weeks yet before she was fully healed. While she looked forward to lengthy strolls, 'twas a uniting with Thor that outshone any other longing. Fay had confided that while the separation was difficult, and while the new child helped serve as a dear distraction, the time apart was most trying on a man, who hadn't the sweet comfort of a babe in his arms most hours of the day.

When Aven neared the spring and better saw her husband, she dearly needed such a distraction.

He crouched down against the rocky crevice, his thick pants

already soaked through from the spring, while his shirt and boots had been cast aside on a nearby rock. He bent lower for the swell of water that seeped from the stone, further wetting his torso and hair that, since her knowing him, had often been bound. She had a sense he always meant to be as tidy as possible, but whenever she caught him in this manner, her heart soared for the beautiful wildness that was her husband. The same wildness from her very first glimpse of him that day they'd met among hundreds of his apple trees.

Seeing her, Thor stood and swiped his hands through his hair, shoving it to lay back. His manner was easy, but his brow rose just enough to reveal surprise. She might have worried for the danger of others catching him unawares if it weren't for the shotgun laying beside his things. He could reach it in a moment, of that there was no doubt, so she was glad that her presence required naught but a smile to ensure her safety.

After absorbing the sight of her standing there, he smiled too. Looking past her shoulder, he surveyed the path behind her. *Come alone, you?* His pleasure faded to worry.

"Haakon walked me here." She needn't wonder if he was as surprised by that as she. 'Twas more than clear in the steady drive of his gaze that lifted past her and up the path. When his attention returned to Aven, she spoke. "He worried for my coming alone. I'm sorry to say that I was bent on finding you."

Thor drew in a heavy breath and signed for her to take care. With having trusted Haakon? Or with risking such to be here now?

When he observed the bend in the trees again, she waited until his gaze returned to her. "He's gone."

Thor nodded soberly and with both hands mimicked the shape of plucking petals off a daisy.

"She's well with Ida and Fay."

Nodding at that, and as if determined to lay aside worries for this moment, he invited her to sit. Aven raised her hem from the dampened earth and treaded to the low boulder he'd gestured to. Thor wet his thick hands, then splashed water onto his face, rubbing well. The gush of the spring was mild at most, but safer a choice than his venturing to the pond alone. Aven sat beside his things and where moss grew in patches, making a comfortable perch. She pulled her knees up and tucked her skirt well around so that the hem touched the tops of her shoes.

Bending forward, Thor wet his hair one final time, and when he shoved it back again, the long dark strands hit the tops of his shoulders, where they dripped, pooling water along the dips and rises of his shoulders and chest. There was no towel in sight, so he swiped at the moisture and, coming around to her side, sat at a fair enough distance for her to stay dry.

Rather wishing he hadn't, she inched closer. His face was tilted down, but the smile that formed there was unmistakable. His moustache lifted, and the sides of his eyes creased. How she longed to lean nearer and kiss that appled cheek, but she would wait until he sensed it safe.

For his initiating, she would wait. Just as when he'd first courted her.

As it was, his fingers grazed the lacey curve of her petticoat that peeked from beneath her skirt. He ran his thumb against the ivory threads where the lace brushed at her ankle. His gaze fell to the shotgun now at his side. Beside it rested an entire box of ammunition. Sunlight glinted off the strong planes of his torso, and she knew it would take much for him to ever be defeated. She'd witnessed his abilities against foes before, and while even those instances had him outnumbered, what if the odds tipped too far against him? If this amount of danger was indeed stalking him, it could come down with even mightier a blow than before.

He looked past her, studying the length of the ridgeline, and when his gaze locked with her own again, there lived in his eyes the same unease that Haakon had shone.

"Thor . . . ?" Aven touched his arm—risky perhaps, but there were greater ones afoot and she dearly needed him. "What are we to do?"

In a rush of comfort, he moved his arm around her, pulling her in to him. He tucked her head beneath his own as he always had, and she closed her eyes tight. He held her that way for what she wished was much longer. When he released her, it was to shape an answer as though to seal a resolve.

Send away. He pointed to her, then formed the letters of many names—all save his own, Haakon's, and Jorgan's.

Did they mean to place themselves in harm's way for the family's safety? While she longed for peace—most especially for the children—to think of safety coming at so great a cost . . . "Thor . . . you are coming also?"

He indicated that he would follow, but as Aven peered up at him, she had a startling worry that of the two men she had spoken with this afternoon, Haakon wasn't the one who had just lied to her.

TWENTY-NINE

SEATED ON A STURDY BENCH, HAAKON USED his foot to pump the treadle of the grinder. He lifted a bucket of water and poured it over the moving sandstone to wet the gritty surface and to keep shavings from getting into the wheel, which cranked toward him at so slow a rotation he needed to ramp up the speed.

But he could scarcely focus on the task, because her name was Kjersti.

It had come rushing back to him as he'd stood speaking with Aven and now he was holding on to it awful tight. Mrs. Kjersti Jönsson. He meant to remember that.

Gripping up the ax from the floor beside him, he pumped the treadle quicker, took careful hold on the back end of the iron head, and pressed the sharp edge to the turning sandstone. A grating sound filled the cidery as he tipped the head from side to side, pausing only to hold the bucket by its rim and splash more water onto the operation.

Only in rare moments could he recall her face now, and even more distant was the recollection of her voice that came to him when he least expected it. When both faded in full, he would have nothing to remember her by. Perhaps then this dogging on his spirit would cease, and thoughts of the woman from the north would plague him no more.

Brow furrowed, Haakon leaned the weapon against the nearest wall, unsheathed his knife, and tried to concentrate solely on the challenge before him. When the hinge on the treadle stiffened, he rose in search of oil. Growing stronger was the longing for the wife that Fay had nudged him to consider. Not a woman in his memory or in a distant land, but one who was here. A wife to live beside him. Perhaps even on this very farm. A few pretty faces from town flitted to mind, but he swiped each one away because they paled in comparison to the one belonging to the name now sinking deep into his heart.

After all that Kjersti had loved and lost, he wouldn't begin to imagine their friendship had been as potent for her. To say nothing of the way he'd been living his life with the loosest of morals. Her hand was more than he deserved, and she had to have known that. Likely she'd married again by now. Few men could overlook such a woman, and he'd be a fool to assume she would wait for an aimless sailor who had left her as abruptly as he'd come.

Frustration mounting, Haakon nabbed a can of oil from beneath Thor's workbench. He uncapped it and dabbed grease onto the hinge with his finger. After wiping his skin clean on the side of his pants, he sat again and sharpened the opposite side of his knife. When that was good and done, he bettered two more blades. These knives were rarely kept on him, but he'd have each one well concealed on his person before hiking back to the moonshine still tonight.

But a few hours ago, Sibby had come by inviting the women and children to the Sorrel mansion for tea in two days. From what Haakon had witnessed of Fay and Aven's recounting of it, the invitation had been graciously accepted. Perhaps Aven was heeding his urging after all. He desperately hoped so. This was the beginning of the end, and he needed her to trust Sibby in full for it to go as planned.

He worked until the dim air marked the time a plate would be ready for him from the kitchen. Cora and the girls were staying over for supper. Peter, too, but none of them would think much of Haakon taking a plate and heading off as he'd gotten accustomed to doing. In fact the added distraction to the family would help him slip out of here unnoticed.

After angling his blade up and down one more time against the stone, Haakon ran the base of his thumb over the warm, sharp steel. Satisfied, he let the wheel still. It was with a strange sense of calm that he folded the last knife, pocketed it, and rose. Having brought his pack along, he set it on Thor's workbench and through the nearest window spotted Jorgan and Sigurd heading for the house. Supper would be ready, and while Haakon wasn't in the mood to eat, it would be best to get something in his stomach before he headed off.

He rifled through his pack and fished out the letter he'd written. One he meant to leave in his absence. Should he not return, it would be found come morning. At the latest, in a day or two when someone visited the workbench. Except the trouble with having stuffed the letter into his pack earlier was that he'd also found the six coca leaves he'd stitched inside the canvas while still at sea. Six new coca leaves that were now in his pouch where they belonged.

At the sound of footsteps, he spotted Cora entering the cidery. She carried a plate in hand and a cup in the other. Both she set on the workbench at his elbow while she eyed the letter in his hand. Haakon checked his watch and absently thanked her for the meal. When Cora pushed the plate closer to him, he lowered the letter to the wooden surface that was roughened and stained with a few decades worth of cidermaking. He drank a gulp of sweet tea, then checked his pocket watch once more.

"Have you got somewhere to be, Haakon?"

He looked at her properly but didn't answer.

"If you's in a hurry, I can walk with you."

To deny that he was going somewhere would be a lie, so he dragged the plate closer, forked into the slice of meat pie, and crammed the bite in his mouth. He chewed quickly, then chased it with another drink of tea. "You better get on back to the house, Miss Cora."

"Nonsense. If you got somewhere to go, I'll walk with you."

He shook his head. He was going where she couldn't. "You need to go back to the house."

"Well, it too fine an evening for a body to be walkin' by themselves, so at least let me accompany you to the edge of the yard."

He'd learned long ago that there was no sense in arguing with this woman when she was bent on an idea, so Haakon scooped one more bite into his mouth and nodded. "To the end of the yard, then."

After patting his knife sheath and his left pocket to verify the contents, he stepped away from his toiling. He was as ready as he would ever be. Cora moved to his side and looped her hand around his arm.

Her smile was gentle. "I ain't walked out with a man in far too long."

"Then you ought to more," he said distractedly, glancing back to make sure he hadn't forgotten anything.

"Maybe I shall."

Her head rose no higher than his shoulder, but there had once been a time when he'd been small enough to run into her arms. Small enough to show her the cuts and bruises on his knees and for her to pull him onto her lap for a hug and a trace of her healing salves.

The late evening air was cooler than that in the cidery, and as they edged around the back end of the building, he spotted the first star overhead.

"The last man I walked out with was my Albert," Cora said as they strolled beneath it. "Did I ever tell you that we met over a row of potatoes? Just two days after he been sold to Jed Sorrel. I was sixteen and he just a couple years past that."

"No, ma'am, I didn't know that."

"Did I ever tell you how long I was a slave for?"

Haakon shook his head. It would have begun upon her birth, but he'd never done the math.

"Nearly twenty years, child." She lifted the hem of her homespun skirt as they passed over thickening grasses. "Nearly twenty long years."

His chest rose with grief at the thought of it. "I'm awful sorry."

She gave his arm a slight squeeze. "That was all them years of me belonging to another. Of Mr. Sorrel ownin' me and my loved ones by law and liberty. But you know what?"

Their pace slackened as she released his arm. The air around them was dimming, and this was where she'd promised to go no farther.

"I was more free for every one of them years than you is this very night."

"What do you mean?"

"I mean the bondage you keep yesself in. The freedom that marks a soul from the inside out ain't got a cost that you can pay. It been done paid long ago for you and for me by a man on a cross. And still ya ain't takin' hold of it. You's less free standin' on this hill as a white man than my Albert ever was kneelin' over another man's potatoes."

Haakon slowed to a stop.

"Instead, you's *choosin'* to be a slave. You's walkin through a swamp, cryin' out in pain, and freedom be right there on the road." Stepping closer, she squinted up at him. "Have you sought the Lord's forgiveness for what you did them years back with Aven? Maybe even for other ways you put your own wants above what was right?"

He wasn't sure. He had apologized to Aven—but while there was so much he regretted, he'd never sought the Lord's forgiveness. Not directly.

When he stayed quiet, she nodded slowly. "That's what I suspected. If you's wantin' a fresh start, Haakon, then you gotta step into it. It right there . . . and that sweet Aven, she done helped pave the way, but it was the good Lord who cut the road to be walked. So why ain't you takin' it? Why ain't you enjoying the freedom—and a right fine view—from that higher road?"

He swallowed hard.

"I've a sense it be due to you not wantin' to be owin' to anyone. Not even to a Mastuh as good as the one who died for the savin' of others. But what you ain't seein' is that you's livin' by a different mastuh. You be *'yes, sir'n'* a mastuh of your own makin'. One that can't offer a shred'a hope and one that sure can't set you free. Not now and not ever." Cora reached up and brushed a coil of graying hair away from her forehead. "Do you remember the day my Albert walked with you down to the pond?"

The day Cora's husband had led him to those murky waters where, with Da watching on with pride, Albert had lowered Haakon beneath the surface with a prayer. Having been baptized as infants, Jorgan and Thor watched from the shore, but upon their mother's death, Da had never taken Haakon to church. Not until it was some years later, and it was Albert who had offered to see Haakon baptized—*"If the boy wants it,"* Albert had said.

Cora smiled up at him. "You ran the whole way there and was the first one in the water."

His eyes stung at the memory.

"Albert waded in after you, and once he'd dunked you down and lifted you up for your new breath, there were tears in your da's eyes and a smile on your face like no other."

Haakon blinked away a building sheen all his own.

"And you wanna know somethin'?"

Desperately.

"Your da and I . . . We done had this same talk. All them years ago it was him standin' here instead of you. He promised he'd get you boys back to church, and up until the very end, he did."

Haakon's chest throbbed with the hope that his father had made his peace with the Lord before his death.

"Much like with him, there always been a zeal about you, Haakon Norgaard. Once upon a time it was for somethin' good. What might you say it be now?"

If he were honest . . . "I'm not sure."

Stepping nearer, she touched his heart, and if she felt the pouch beneath his shirt, she gave him only a gentle smile. "I been prayin' since the day you was born that you'd have a zeal for all that was good, and I'll be prayin' for you this night."

Not knowing what to say, he searched her face that was as loving and sincere as the day he first remembered her.

"I'll head on back now." Reaching up, she cupped the side of his face. "You keep yesself safe now, child, and know that wherever you go, I'll be prayin' always. So long as I have breath."

Unable to speak, he gave a nod. Her eyes glistened with unshed tears as she turned away. With dangers about, Haakon watched until she was safely to the house. When she'd stepped onto the porch, he turned away and continued up the hillside. He climbed higher, and his breathing picked up, as did his nerves. It was a good thing he'd eaten only a little. His stomach wouldn't have handled it.

When he was a good distance from the farm, Haakon slowed to a stop, placed his hands on his waist, and tilted his head to the sky. Just sighting a few more early stars before closing his eyes. He searched his heart, and though a prayer was there, his words felt insufficient. Instead, he lifted the small pouch from beneath his shirt and loosened the strings. Practiced fingers pulled out the newly discovered coca. He had them all now—lined up in his hand like small soldiers for a battle. But what side they fought for, he didn't know.

His pouch still open, Haakon removed the torn Bible page and, with light dimming, unfolded it. Dark was falling quickly so he read with the same haste. A desperation that had been living in him for weeks now, and truthfully, years.

Really, his whole life.

With two sides of printed scriptures on the single sheet, he didn't know which part Tate meant for him, so he absorbed the cluster of psalms in a few blinks, searching for anything that caught his eye. *"And as the flame setteth the mountains on fire; so persecute them with thy tempest, and make them afraid with thy storm."*

He had no idea what that meant.

But he'd also known the might of God amid a raging sea. He knew a fear of being lost. Haakon squinted in the dim light, and something else caught his eye. *"Blessed is the man whose strength is in thee."* Desperate for more, he turned the page over, skimming to nowhere in particular. Night was falling and he could scarcely read. *"For a day in thy courts is better than a thousand. I had rather be a doorkeeper in the house of my God, than dwell in the tents of wickedness."*

His eyes lifted up the hill, and though he could see no more of the text, the final words he'd glimpsed moved like an echo through him. *"For the* LORD *God is a sun and shield."*

An ache pinched the back of his throat. A shield. He needed it. They all did. If he was truly to do this, a hammer was about to fall on their land, beginning this night with his very own life. The sunlit verse fresh in mind, Haakon folded the page in the dark.

He tucked it away, as well as all the leaves, grateful for the moon that cast its glow along the path. It carved out the way up and the way down, and though the direction was yet for the choosing, this had to be done. It had been less frightening to walk with Cora by his side, but he had her prayers, and that was more a comfort than any numbing he could leech into his body.

Reminding him that it hadn't been so long ago that he'd stood on the cusp of another dark night. That one holding not many lives in the balance—only his own—as he'd climbed atop the railing of *Le Grelotter.* He'd been at sea scarcely a year, and it had taken much less time to discover that there wasn't a woman beautiful enough or a drink deep enough to drown out what he'd been running from. Not even the coca he'd sampled had brought him enough relief, and so it was with a rush of despair and a plea for peace that Haakon had launched himself over the edge and into the frigid Norwegian Sea. It was the worst choice he could have possibly made, and for God to have waded with him to another sunrise was a mercy like no other.

The last thing he'd seen in his mind before striking the hull and nearly blacking out was the face of his mother. The very first person he'd wounded.

She'd have been fifty-four this year. Her dark hair would have been laced with silver, and she'd have had more children to her name. But instead it was Haakon and Haakon alone to stand here now on this stretch of mountainside—his mother in his heart and his father's courage sliding up his backbone, making it firmer even as his spirit softened with loss and longing.

She'd have loved Tusie. Haakon didn't have to remember anything of Kristin Norgaard to know that. She'd have fussed and cooed over her granddaughter, making much of every sound and wiggle from the babe. Though all secondhand, memories of his mother rooted in deep, and though brand new, a hope for Tusie's future watered it all until there was a rise of determination in his chest that wouldn't be pulled free. No matter how afraid he was.

For his mother and Tusie he would do this. For all the others including the good woman who had walked with him to this hillside, he would press onward. He prayed for strength, pleading to God to rally it inside him as he climbed by memory. And he prayed to God to forgive him for the selfish choice he'd made that long-ago night. He was called to do better with the life granted him, and while he was certainly walking into danger, he meant to leave it alive. If God would but grant him another mercy. Should the outcome be dire, he prayed that God would welcome him to peace.

The moon bloomed nearly full, but so tangled were these woods that the glow wasn't enough to ensure his footing. Haakon winced as a ripping at his forearm told him he'd stumbled into a blackberry bramble. He pulled the thorny branch free of his skin and sleeve, then veered to the left, finally hearing the call of the creek that would lead to Orville's camp.

He almost tripped on more briars but managed to stay upright as he clamored as quietly as possible from the thorny patch. Once clear of it, he walked until the water gurgled down into a quiet pool and in the distance glowed a low campfire. Millions of stars shone down now just as they had done at sea, yet the shadows that stretched long weren't those of masts but spindly trees. And he had no map for this. No guiding course save truth.

THIRTY

SO AS NOT TO STARTLE ONE ANOTHER AGAIN,
Haakon and Orville had arranged a signal last they spoke. Picking
up two dry sticks, Haakon snapped them in quick succession, then
waited. In the distance, two more twigs snapped one after the other.
Safe to go forward. He waded through more weeds and into the
clearing. Face lit by the light of the fire, Orville's eyes were small as
glass beads while he watched Haakon draw near. The man's stringy
hair fell against his face as he lowered his head to scoop stew from a
wooden bowl to his mouth.

"Thought you'd be here about this time." Orville gauged Haakon
around a strand of hair as he chewed. He raised his bowl a smidge.
"Want some? Sibby made it."

"No . . . thanks."

"You look like you're about to bolt."

Mouth dry, he gulped. "Do I?"

"If Jed shows, he won't be here for a good hour, so you might as
well get settled. And for Pete's sake, breathe natural." Orville passed
over a quart of moonshine.

Haakon accepted it and, not wanting to take any handouts, flipped
a half dollar into Orville's hand. He would have unscrewed the lid but
was too nauseated for anything other than a gulp of air.

Orville tucked the coin in the band of his hat. Taking up his fork again, he stabbed a bite of meat. "You thinkin' of changin' your mind? Ain't too late, I suppose."

"No." Haakon rubbed at his forehead with the heel of his palm. "I just need to sit for a minute."

"Well, ya got plenty of 'em. Did you get word from the sheriff?"

"Peter brought it just this morning. We're all clear." Tucked deep in Haakon's pack back home was the sheriff's assurance that neither Haakon nor his men-at-arms would see the inside of a jail cell over the rumble that was about to rock this mountain.

"Good."

Haakon set the jar on the ground beside him, and while Orville ate, he considered their plan. When the void in his stomach became too much to bear, he accepted the tin can of stew Orville passed him. Orville dumped more into his own bowl, scraping the pot clean with a fork. The moonshiner stayed quiet, so when Haakon heard a steady rustling, he surveyed the dark slope.

"You hear that?"

"Right on time," Orville said, then more softly, warned Haakon to keep a level head. "None of this is gonna work if you panic now."

Haakon blew out a slow breath and with it forced aside fear. He inhaled determination, because walking toward the campfire were six men. No white robes. No pointed hoods. Just gruff faces and gritty clothing. The man in the center was burdened with an uneven gait, and even in the moonlight Haakon made out a crippled hand. No need to count the fingers. It was none other than Jed Sorrel. His gray hair had thinned with age, but it was the same man through and through. The old general limped on a leg as stiff as wood. His bum knee had to cause a great deal of pain, but Jed didn't so much as grimace. Behind him lumbered a taller brute. Broad of shoulder, thick in arm, and with a glare fixed right on Haakon. A smirk lifted one side of the man's wiry blond mustache.

Harlan.

The very reason Thor had been so ill and why Aven and Tusie had been in danger. Haakon gripped the rough log beneath him as tension heated his back.

Finally Jed spoke. "Looks like we got company." A tattered patch covered his missing eye.

One of his men pulled forward a pistol, and Harlan hitched a long-barreled rifle up over a shoulder that was just as daunting. Haakon doubted that was how they usually approached Orville's camp.

When they all stopped a dozen yards from the crackling fire, Orville waved them forward. "He won't cause no harm. Just sold him some whiskey's all." When the Sorrels didn't move, Orville tipped up a bewildered expression that was worth its weight in gold. Exactly how much it had cost. "Y'all know each other?"

Jed's eyes narrowed, distrust flickering in those dark depths. All the men regarded the general, who finally spoke. "Your brother around?"

"No, sir," Haakon said. "But I'd like to speak to you about that."

"Sir?" Jed spat. "*Sir?*" The aged general limped forward. The snap of twigs cracked underfoot, echoing through the smoky air. Jed's hands grappled with his firearm, knuckles taut around the short barrel as he lowered a fierce glare on Haakon. "You done blown up my barn and nearly kill one of my granddaughters, and now you're sittin' here jaunty-like callin' me *sir?*" He came all the way up to Haakon, stuck his face in Haakon's own, and spoke. "Don't you 'no, sir' me ever again."

Since politeness wasn't an option, Haakon went with, "If you like."

The back of Jed's fist smacked a burn across Haakon's face. Pain throttled his skull, and grateful it hadn't been the handle of the pistol, Haakon angled away to spit out a shot of blood. All of Jed's men had guns drawn now. Four were aimed at Haakon, the other at Orville, who suddenly held his bowl of rabbit stew midbite.

Jed's single eye bore into Haakon's, breath rank with sour drink. "How about you only speak if asked a question."

Haakon said nothing as Jed took two hitching steps back. The general called for one of his men to bring him something to sit on, and a massive stump was hefted over by none other than Harlan. Finished, Harlan planted a wide stance behind his father, solid as a grizzly and just as mean. So slight that Haakon might have missed it, Harlan rubbed his side—just as Thor had done when in pain. And like Thor, Harlan looked to be mending from whatever illness he'd harbored and passed along. A man couldn't lift a log that heavy without being near to full strength again.

A few retorts came to mind about the stunt Harlan had pulled, but they would all be on Thor's behalf, so Haakon silenced each one.

Sitting, Jed hitched his injured leg out in front of him, the sole of his shoe nearly worn through. "Now. Why don't one of you explain to me why we have so much company tonight?" His gaze drilled into Haakon before sliding over to Orville. "And I suggest it be you."

Choking down his bite of stew, Orville set the bowl aside. "He came to buy some moonshine."

Jed signaled to a cohort, who cocked the pistol aimed at Orville.

"*And* he came to tell you something." Orville pulled his hat off as though reverence would help. That Harlan seemed oblivious to the fact that Orville had eloped with his daughter was why Orville was still alive just now. A bold risk by the moonshiner, which bespoke his fidelity to this cause.

Jed's expression never wavered in a stillness not so different than the quiet before a storm. "That so?"

"Yes," Haakon said. Everyone looked at him. Well . . . it *had* been a question. "I came to talk to you about Thor. And a deal you might wanna strike." He licked the inside of his lip, resisting the urge to spit out the taste of blood.

"Just seemed a good night for a parley, huh?"

Haakon nodded. No sense in pretending.

"Your brother what brought you back to these parts?" Jed asked, and Haakon could see that he wasn't going to buy an ounce of this easily.

"Somewhat. I came back for my land—what my father left me. Thor's been holding it hostage, so . . ."

"Can't handle your own fight," Jed finished.

He could handle them just fine, which was why he was sitting here sorely outnumbered. "I was just thinkin' that maybe we could come to an understanding that pleased everyone. Unless I'm mistakin' that you boys have been after Thor."

Challenge for challenge. Like honey to a hive with men like these.

He could practically *feel* Cora's hand to his cheek, pleading for him to be careful.

So quiet the Sorrels were that the air might as well have drained from the hollow. A stoic kind of calm that was their way of inducing fear. A control they had strived for decades to incite.

It took all of Haakon's determination to keep it from working. He wasn't afraid of the Sorrels, not for himself, but he knew what they were capable of and didn't want to invite danger onto the farm until it was good and time. Because of that, he needed to be downright clear. "Thor's staying at the cabin on my land. He's been unwell so is alone unless I'm there." They already knew that, but Haakon didn't want to let on. "I come and go, but tomorrow night I'm headin' off well before light. Let's say by two in the morning. Thor keeps a few firearms near, but I'll make sure they're cleared away before I go."

Orville didn't so much as move as he spoke, and Harlan's gaze on the man was just as steady.

Pulse racing, Haakon continued. "There's a key to the door, and I'll leave it in the chinking on the top of the jamb." He rose, aiming to walk out of here like he owned the place.

Harlan blinked at him, and the rest of Jed's men stared with the same blank scrutiny.

Needing to tip the scales farther his way, Haakon added, "As you know, Thor can't hear a thing, so getting in unnoticed is easier than it seems. Really," he examined each of Peter's kin in turn, "It's downright simple."

Jed shifted and when silence stretched on, Orville rose, fetched two jars of moonshine, and passed them over. Firelight glinted on the glass offerings. Harlan's study of him mellowed, and he accepted one.

"And why would you do such a thing?" Having spoken for the first time, Harlan's voice was deeper than the well he'd probably crawled out of.

"Let's just say it's time some justice was served." Haakon watched as Harlan unscrewed the metal lid. "As you know, Thor's the one standing in the way of our liquor production. If he wasn't around, I don't see why someone else couldn't start that up again while ensuring that distribution was . . . better spread." Someone who knew the ins and outs of it all, even Thor's production methods. Haakon had worked at his brother's side for as long as he could recall, which was an advantage few possessed.

They all understood that Jorgan was too good to betray Thor. But as for Haakon . . .

These men knew firsthand that he had risked his neck for lesser things.

"And in exchange?" Jed said coolly as he filled the jar cap with moonshine. He laid the metal ring on the ground between his feet.

Orville rose and dropped in a pinch of gunpowder to verify the proof.

"There's a lot of women and children on our land, and they'd need to stay awful safe," Haakon said.

"Sacrificing one ram for the whole flock?" Harlan pulled a brass match safe from his pocket and with his thumb flipped open the hinged lid. "Right shame, your terms, 'cause I rather fancied them ewes of yours." He struck the match and stepping around his father, lowered it to the dish of whiskey. The gunpowder sizzled and flamed. "That fair-haired one got somethin' to her. Though the one belonging to your tongue-tied brother is awful fine as well. A little feisty, but that's its own kind of nice." He winked.

If Haakon had a cannon, he'd have lit it. Instead, he forced himself to stay calm.

"You boys sure know how to pick 'em." After dropping the smoldering match in the dirt, Harlan referenced Tess next with a brass-and-curdled term. One Ida had raised them never to say. "Why Pete fancies her . . ." Harlan shook his burly head. "She don't need to be tended to. She need to be taught a lesson."

One the brute would have managed had Peter not stood up to him that long-ago night, risking limb and life to protect her.

Haakon stared at the man who had once pummeled his own heir and who'd left Cora's son in a ditch for smiling at his daughter, Sibby. Al had scarcely survived the beating by Sorrel men, and Harlan's disdain was far from spent. Something had to be done.

The reason Haakon was here. But with Harlan still leering at him . . . "I suppose there's no sense in strikin' a deal, then." He kept a cool demeanor as he nabbed up the jar of moonshine that he'd paid for.

Orville sat still as ever—nothing moving but his dark eyes that ricocheted between them.

Haakon squared his shoulders, and though he stood at ease, he was tall enough to acknowledge Harlan eye to eye. He wasn't afraid to handle Peter's father. Haakon knew what it was to be wicked. He'd spent his whole life heeding his own desires. While he was trying to veer far from that path, he was ready to clink glasses with the devil once more. But this time, he wasn't going to swig. "I thank you for your time. Sorry we won't be able to sort somethin' out." He shifted the jar to his other hand and stepped wide of the fire.

The Sorrels exchanged silent appeals. Norgaard brew had been one of the finest drinks to ever stem from these parts, and they all knew it. Thor's liquor hadn't blown up their barn by being weak.

"You just expect me to forget what you did?" Jed asked from where he sat.

"That was a long time ago, sir—Mr. Sorrel."

"Not long enough."

Here it was. The moment he'd been sick over all day. Really, since this whole plan had begun. "Then since we can't bury the hatchet, while I walk down that hill, why don't you go ahead and take me out. And if not, you know how to find our farm come tomorrow night, and I'll have everything cleared away in the cabin." A downright truth. Then to Harlan, "And if you so much as touch any other soul on our land, I'll see that you spend the rest of your life regretting it."

With that, Haakon stepped away. Though no more than a click, the priming of a shotgun was loud to his ears. His whole body surged with heat, and he braced himself for the trigger pull. Breath tight in his throat, he walked until the dark swallowed him up. He pined with the need to glance over his shoulder, but fixed the notion from mind. No sense appearing weak now that the deal was practically sealed. The last time he'd turned his back on Jed and his men, bullets had pelted his path, and Thor had fought through a wall of Sorrels to save him. And now? Even as he braced for buckshot to tear through him, there was nothing but silence as he walked down the slope toward home. As clear an agreement as any other that the men on this mountain had accepted his terms.

THIRTY-ONE

THOR LIFTED THE DRIPPING SCRUB BRUSH
from the pail and rammed sudsy bristles against the cabin floorboards. For too long these stains had lived down here, so it was with
relief that he sloshed water onto the wood and scoured the droplets of
Haakon's blood with all his might.

Last he'd knelt here, it had been atop Haakon as he'd taught him
the fiercest lesson he could. While time did nothing to diminish the
wretchedness of Haakon's intentions, it tended to a different kind of
work. One built on the foundation of Haakon's renewed behavior and
Aven's growing peace.

As for Haakon being allowed to stay, Thor still had the deed to
this cabin. He knew the importance it had for his brother. Where
Jorgan had been given the house upon their da's death, Thor had
inherited the orchards. This cabin and the surrounding acreage was
perhaps less grand when assessing the different realms, but Haakon
had never complained. This place might as well have been a castle for
all the time he had spent caring for it.

Thor still needed to consult the others, but if they were agreed,
this deed could be placed in Haakon's hand again. While the property would be for him to do with as he wished, Thor couldn't shake

the desire for it to not be sold off. He couldn't imagine what it would feel like to watch Haakon leave again. It had broken him then, and it would do just the same now. Perhaps worse. In that instance, it would be Haakon's call, and for now, Thor had a floor to restore.

Finished with the nearest boards, he leaned back on his heels. The old wine barrel was at his elbow now, so he shoved it farther away and in doing so caught sight of someone in the doorway. He expected it to be Haakon, but it was a dark-haired man wearing a floppy hat. His beard was stringy, face pockmarked, and Thor knew the moment he saw him that it was a moonshiner from high up in the hills. Thor knew little of courtships in these parts, but he'd heard that the moonshiner and Sibby had recently wed.

He'd never spoken to the man and certainly hadn't tasted his liquor, which made it all the more a shock to see him standing in the doorway holding a filled case of quart jars.

Thor sucked in a breath and rose. The scrub brush still in hand, he dropped it in the bucket. Reactions clattered inside him—one being to step away, another being to step nearer and inquire as to what the man sought. But panic riddled him from the inside because something wasn't right. Aven, Fay, and the boys were due to have tea this afternoon with Sibby. An unexpected invitation that Thor hadn't questioned, but now . . . Was something wrong?

Before Thor could reach for his notepad, the man lowered the crate of moonshine into the open doorway. "This is a little something from your brother." His eyes met Thor's as he did, and before he straightened, he lifted a center jar, one buried in as much straw as all the others. But instead of holding clear whiskey, it encased a fold of paper. The man gave a subtle nod and Thor returned it to show he understood.

"A pleasure doin' business with y'all." The man pulled off his hat, then clapped it back on.

He stepped away, and just as unexpectedly as he had come, he was gone.

Thor stood unmoving, trying to make sense of what was going on, but knowing he had to face whatever was in that note, he moved nearer to the crate and lifted the only jar he was going to touch.

Desperate for Aven, Thor approached the house and rapped on the door. When it opened, his wife stood there in a gown she'd tailored from a glossy evergreen fabric. All of them were due to leave for Sibby's, but he needed a moment with her first.

"Thor!" Her surprise showed in the sweetness of her smile.

Much less open about his emotions just now, he coaxed her out with a beckoning of his finger, and when she paced into the yard beside him, he pressed a hand to the small of her back, urging her to follow him. She smelled of honeysuckle, and the Sunday-best dress was like silk to his fingertips.

Aven laid a hand on his sleeve and spoke when he looked at her. "They're all to leave in a minute."

Thor nodded to show that he knew. She could catch up.

In urging her on, he pressed more firmly to help her understand his wishes. When she peered up at him, he saw the same startling he'd felt in Orville's presence. On the walk over here, Thor had prayed she would do as he asked and knew he needn't doubt for a moment as she kept stride with him. Her steps taking two to his one, he slowed some as he led them to one of the outbuildings, this one a shed where they'd stored much of Aunt Dorothe's old things, fabrics, boxes, and the like.

Thor opened the door for her.

The last time they'd stood in this shed together, they'd been combatants and not lovers, him frightening her senseless in the dark because he couldn't speak and her stabbing him in the arm with those stupid scissors she'd been holding. Now he had the scar *and* the woman. Which was saying something. For years since, they'd had privilege to one another, and as much as he'd relished it, never had there been an instance in their marriage when he'd been so needful of his bride or more on the cusp of losing her.

She could have just as easily paused to question him, but she entered. Following, Thor left the door ajar. In the shadows she turned to speak, but he touched her waist, guiding her behind the door where, for the first time in far too long, he kissed her.

Her gasp was cut short by his urgency. The doctor's missive had directed that such a joining not occur until tomorrow, but Thor doubted a few hours would make the difference.

For a fragment of time, he feared she would reject him—heed lingering cautions as was wise—but she cupped the back of his head and pulled him as close as her temperate strength allowed. Aiming to help, he pressed her farther back until a tall stack of trunks lent her support. Though his manner was fervent, he could feel her welcoming of it as her fingertips grazed the side of his beard. Not wanting to be forceful, he took care to savor her with softness. She kissed him with an ardent drive, and it made him feel alive again, this piece of his body and soul that had been missing.

It was to just be a few stolen moments, so when she started on the top buttons of his shirt, he closed a hand around her own, stilling her fingers. He broke the sweetness of the kiss to lift the inside of her wrist to his lips, equal parts savoring the renewed liberty while longing for it to be more. She tried for the buttons of his shirt again, this time with quicker persistence as if fearing he'd stop her. Losing the battle with himself, Thor pressed his hands flat to the trunk on either side of her and lowered his head, yielding. The pause allowed him to catch his breath and regain his wits.

She needed to go. And it had to be now.

He pulled away, taking a step aside. The separating had to be immediate before he lost his nerve. Before he longed for more and more of this and forgot what the night ahead would actually hold.

Not long-awaited pleasures but a grim reality. With hasty fingers, Thor crammed his buttons back into place. How he wished he could speak to his wife as he did, but he had to pause to do so. When he did, he looked into a face wrought with the same regret he felt.

S-I-B-B-Y. Tea.

Aven's brow furrowed. Yes, the outing was that important. Haakon's message from the jar had made that more than clear, and his own instincts reinforced the urgency. He added *Now*, and when her confusion deepened, he stepped nearer again, cupped the side of her face and spoke her name as best he knew how. "Av—"

Her eyes widened, and in Sign he added, *Trust me.*

Slowly, she nodded.

S-I-B-B-Y now you go.

Her confusion made her trust more potent. She was following his lead though she knew not where it voyaged. His sweet wife. He'd vowed to protect and cherish her, and this was that promise at its most zealous.

He touched fingertips to his lips and lowered his hand in *Thank you.*

She nodded again. "I'll see you in a while." If her voice was soft, he couldn't tell, but he sensed it might have been, so faint had been the avowal on her lips. Did she believe in those words? Was she trying to rally herself? Or did she simply know how desperately he needed to watch her say them?

With all the bravery he knew she possessed, Aven slipped from the shed as quickly as she'd come, stepping out into the sunlight that shone like melted copper on her hair. Ida, Fay, and the boys were already on the path that would lead to the Sorrels' plantation. Thor watched as Aven called out to them, breaking into a faint run to catch up to the group. Aven accepted the lacy umbrella that Fay held for her. In Ida's arms lay Tusie, and Aven shifted the umbrella to shield the pair before turning back to glimpse Thor. If she sensed this was him saying goodbye for now, she was being courageous about it.

Still in the shadows, he stepped to the doorway so she might see him better, praying it wouldn't be the last, and watched until they were well on their way.

Needing to keep moving, he started across the yard to the cabin when he realized he'd not finished the buttoning of his shirt. Two at the bottom hung undone. He fastened them with haste, looking up to ensure that Aven was well along with the others. That's when he saw that Haakon was striding across the yard with a sack of grain on his shoulder, bound for the barn.

As Thor continued toward the cabin, he finished minding his rumpled shirt. Haakon glanced to the shed where Aven had appeared from, then back to Thor, who'd done the same. Last, Haakon rolled his eyes, but as he turned away Thor caught a trace of amusement that underlined everything he'd come to hope about his brother's acceptance of Thor and Aven's marriage. Maybe people really did change. In fact, he now knew it to be so.

THIRTY-TWO

SEATED AT THE GREAT ROOM TABLE, HAAKON blew out a slow breath. It was agony sitting here waiting. Well past midnight, the house was dark and quiet, and while it had been years since he'd been in this room, it didn't hold the ceremony he'd once imagined his return would. A lone candle burned on the bare table, and while it was enough light to see by, the way it danced and trembled served as a reminder of how easily a single light could be snuffed out.

Heavy with the burden of this night, Haakon lowered his head. He didn't need to glimpse his pocket watch again to know the time.

By now the key would be sliding into the lock. It would click, but Thor wouldn't hear it. Then footsteps on the stairs. In Haakon's mind, he slowly counted them until he was sure that whoever had come for Thor was on the second level.

Haakon closed his eyes, pinching them tight. He thought of his brother and the summer they had built the treehouse. Of how he couldn't yet write his name, but how using the tip of his knife, Thor had scratched it for him into the trunk of the maple. It was that same night that they'd first bunked out there. The three of them, free as birds under the stars. Haakon had snuck a loaf of bread from Ida's kitchen, and Thor had snitched a jar of jam. Jorgan had offered up a whole bag of taffy, and together they'd made themselves fat and happy as the wind played in the leaves and the heat of summer melted into air so soft it lulled them to sleep like babies.

The next day, they'd woken early and swum at the pond. The morning fog had barely lifted by the time they'd started a game of king of the hill. Haakon always lost, but he never minded. If only his brothers had known how much he just wanted to belong. How much he craved their time spent with him. To teach him.

He'd walked in their shadows not because he had to but because he'd wanted to.

Time had changed him, though, and in striving to be what he thought was a *man*, he'd lost sight of that. He meant not to do it again. It was for that reason—and a million others—that Haakon opened a box of .44s. He stuffed several into the magazine of his levergun, then, reaching over, handed a box of shotgun cartridges to the brother beside him. Thor accepted it.

Haakon showed him his watch. The Sorrel men would be at the top landing of the cabin now, and upon discovering Thor nowhere to be found, they'd be furious.

Thor shook his head, pulled out his own pocket watch, and offered it over in comparison. They were an hour apart.

"Huh?"

Your time wrong.

"Well, I'll be," Haakon muttered. He couldn't remember what continent he'd been on when he'd last set his timepiece, but since coming home, he'd apparently been operating in the wrong time zone. No wonder he was so tired. "I guess we can all sit at ease a little longer, then." No sense in ambushing men who weren't there.

Thor's mustache lifted as he pocketed his own watch again.

All of Haakon's life, he'd wondered what Thor might say if he could truly speak it. Partly because Haakon was curious, and partly because he wished the opportunity upon him. To hear the sound of one's voice was like knowing the beating of one's own heart. Thor would never know that, but what he did know was something that Haakon longed for. Thor knew what it was like to walk with integrity. To lead in a way that others followed because they knew they would be safe.

Of all the things Haakon wanted in this life, it was finally that very trait. It hadn't happened suddenly, but he'd learned it in unnoticing ways. First with his family, who had been more patient with him through his self-centered adolescence than he'd deserved. Then afresh through Tate Kennedy, who led the crew the same way: humble but fearless. Last, he'd seen it in the women in his life—in more ways than he could ever tally.

When he'd first looked at Tusenfryd through the glass, it had amplified his longing once and for all to protect those in need. Haakon wanted Aven's daughter to know—without a shred of doubt—that just as with her father, she would always be safe at her uncle's side. Bjørn and Sigurd too. That they could look upon him and, regardless of what life handed him, he could teach them in wisdom.

That he could learn to be even a small portion of who Thor was.

Thor was worthy of everything that Haakon had once wanted to strip from him. To his shame, that hadn't been so long ago. Haakon couldn't undo that, but as Aven had demonstrated, and as Cora had reminded him of, there was forgiveness. Haakon had sought such a newness in the barn earlier, alone save for the horses and the sack of grain he bore. One burden he'd laid down right there against the stall, the other he'd laid down because he couldn't make it any other way. Now he meant to walk forward in a way that did right by that kind of freedom. It wouldn't be easy, but that's what made it important.

Thor's eyes were down as he opened the action on Jorgan's double-barrel Remington. Every firearm had been so well cleaned that there wasn't a speck of dust on the barrel. With those meaty hands of his, Thor pushed the release to open the barrel, then crammed two shotgun shells into place. He closed the gun and handed it over to Jorgan, who stood waiting. Jorgan's gaze was steady on the windows. Was he thinking of his wife and sons just now? His family, who—thanks to Sibby's help—was tucked safely away in another county.

The women wouldn't have known when they ventured to Sibby's for tea that the friendly pastime had been a diversion. Upon their arrival, they would have found Sibby with a wagon, ready to whisk them farther to safety. Haakon knew they were gone because when Peter had checked just an hour ago, there was nothing in the Sorrel household but a table laden with strewn dishes and a ticking mantle clock. Even the Sorrel women and children had sought secret shelter with a neighboring family for this night. Peter had seen to it.

Haakon watched as Thor took up his shotgun from the table, opened the action, and fed a casing into the chamber, then three more into the magazine. Some time back, Thor had emptied brass casings of buckshot and refilled them with .20 gauge pumpkin slugs and black powder. Those iron balls were hefty enough to take down a rhino, and they kicked like a son of a gun, but if anybody could handle ammo like that, it was Thor. He slid a second handful into his pocket for reloading.

The great room stretched all around them, an empty cavern that sighed and creaked as the night cooled. The second floor was empty, the house void of all its occupants except the five of them here. Thor and Haakon sat at the table. Jorgan paced slowly in front of the windows, where Jed and his men had once shattered the glass. Peter stood with his arms folded across his chest and a keen eye on the yard.

Near the kitchen door, Al straddled a bench, silent as all the rest. Haakon watched as Cora's son turned the trigger guard of a pistol slowly around his finger. Al's eyes were trained on the floor between his boots. He'd survived a beating by the men they'd face this night, but it wasn't revenge in his hunched posture, it was grave calm. A regard that his abusers didn't deserve, yet one Al extended because he respected life. He also respected justice, which was why when Haakon had explained this plan through the note Peter delivered, Al vowed to be here this night.

Two light taps sounded through the front door, then a familiar voice. Al looked to Haakon for direction, and Haakon gave a firm nod. The young man moved to the main entrance of this house, unbolted the door, and opened it. Orville stepped in with a rifle in hand. He tugged his hat off, spat a stream of tobacco juice back out the door, and asked what the holdup was.

"We're waitin' on the sheriff." Haakon leaned back in his chair.

Thor thumbed toward the newcomer and inquired if his watch was wrong too.

Haakon smirked as he pulled the last few bullets from the nearest container. He slipped the ammunition into his shirt pocket. This was no occasion for humor, but the quips loosened the tension in his shoulders. Worry was weighing on his mind like a brick. "Everyone squared away?"

"As I live and breathe," Orville assured. "Sibby got them all off without a hitch."

"She have enough for the tickets?"

Orville adjusted the scope on his sniper rifle. "Said you gave her plenty. Train even left on time."

"Perfect."

Since Thor wouldn't understand Orville from across the dim room, Haakon confirmed to his brother in Sign that his wife and child were safely along with the others.

Thor nodded his gratitude.

It had been the last of Haakon's savings that Peter changed to bills at the bank for him. The same bills Sibby accepted that day in the meadow when Aven had witnessed the exchange. Four years of risking his neck at sea were now six train tickets. He wouldn't have it any other way, and it brought immense relief that the women and children were well away and safe until this blew over. The orchestrating of it all had been a time, though. If it weren't for Sibby's assistance, Haakon didn't know how he would have gotten them whisked away. Then there was Peter's help, and Orville's. Not to mention trying to lure the Sorrels to come this night.

His brothers would have helped him work out the details, but it had seemed unwise for them to show such unity with the Sorrels watching on.

Haakon hadn't expected his brothers to side with his scheme so smoothly, but they had already concluded that something had to be done to see the Sorrels brought to justice. While Jorgan probably preferred more warning than half a day, he had confirmed his gratitude that Haakon had gotten the women and children well away from this place beforehand.

Exhausted from so much preparation, Haakon ran a hand over his face and beard. He had needed to be in so many places at once, he'd scarcely slept flat for a week. He'd sent messages, procured supplies, and saw to just about everything else he could think of. He'd even sharpened the ax that was well hidden in the cidery should it come down to the need of it. He hoped not, but with men such as the Sorrels, there would be nothing predictable about this arrest. There couldn't be too many weapons on hand, or too much preparation.

As for the women, Haakon hadn't wanted to be secretive with them, but their lack of knowledge was for the sole purpose of their protection. They knew nearly nothing of what was about to transpire, and that seemed safest, not to mention less panic inducing.

Orville slid his hat back over his dark, stringy hair. "Where's the sheriff?"

Haakon consulted his newly adjusted pocket watch. "I don't know. He said he'd be here by now."

"You sure he got your message?" Orville asked.

"I delivered it myself," Peter said. "Put it right into his hand before headin' off for Al's. Sheriff read it, and gave me one in return. Both Haakon and I looked it over, and he promised that him and his men would be here tonight."

"You don't think they got lost, do you?" Jorgan asked.

"Let's hope not." They needed them. "Sheriff knows how to find us and assured me they'd be here." They were going to have to trust in that even though they were only six men strong just now and none of them trained soldiers as some of the Sorrels were.

When the sheriff did arrive, the lawman would have the assurance of all six of them standing with him to bring Jed and Harlan to justice, and the men in this room would have the same surety of the law on their side. None of them meant to go to jail over this. Haakon tried not to think about what would happen if the sheriff didn't show.

Al shifted his boots. Jorgan coughed into his shoulder. Peter began to pace again.

With most of an hour to go, Haakon decided that in the chance he were to be killed, this was a good time to get a few things off his chest.

"Your wife kissed me the other day, Orville. On the cheek."

Sibby's husband chuckled from his end of the room. "She told me. Said she felt sorry for you."

He didn't doubt it. "And Jorgan, I really am sorry I didn't tell you sooner about Whitetop Mountain."

Jorgan conceded with a nod. While no one but Haakon knew who Tate Kennedy was, Haakon had vowed that the family could not be safer than in the protection of his best sailing mate. Living at the southern end of the state in Grayson County, Tate had welcomed the message, and Al had brought back the guarantee that all was in order.

Looking like patience was getting the better of him, Jorgan sighed as he sat. The sheriff *was* taking awfully long. Haakon trained his ears for any sound from outside. It had only been a few minutes since he'd last checked, which meant one of two things. Either the Sorrels would wait until two o'clock like Haakon indicated, or . . .

"What are the chances they'll come earlier?" Peter asked. "Ambush Thor and his know-it-all brother at the same time? Get to the cabin before you have a chance to split like you said you would. Or worse." Peter's gaze was steady. "What if they didn't for one moment buy what you sold them but are coming to raise Cain anyway?"

Thor squinted at Peter, but in the near dark wouldn't understand him.

Haakon leaned forward to better see the moon through the uppermost windows. "I'd say it's a pretty good chance." He checked the nearby boxes of ammunition to make sure they were emptied, then indicated to Thor in Sign what the others were speculating.

Thor nodded his agreement.

No matter what the Sorrels had or hadn't been convinced of, the men would be coming to bring destruction for all and any who stood in their way. Instead of prowling around, they now had an open invitation. A quicker, cleaner blow. Riskier for everyone in this room but safer for the women and children. Safer even for those in this land and nation.

"The sheriff ain't here." Al angled to the kitchen door. "But what's to say they're not already at the cabin?"

Everyone looked to Haakon, and it humbled him. That his direction mattered. "I'm startin' to think we don't have any more time to burn." He pulled forward his leather pouch, loosened the drawstrings, and shook the contents onto the table. Half a dozen leaves floated down. A stimulant that would make him as fearsome as the berserkers who fought in the tales of old. An elite sect of warriors who knew no fear and no pain. And he had enough of a supply for everyone in this room should they wish.

Feeling Thor's gaze on him, Haakon stacked the brittle leaves, counting them as he'd done out of habit for too many years. While

Thor wouldn't know exactly what they were, it was plain enough how taken Haakon had become with the leaves. It was also plain as day that the man beside him had overcome a turbulent battle in and of itself; sobering had been no easy task for Thor, and yet he'd fixed his mind and heart on it, letting go of a crutch that he refused to pick back up to this day.

Haakon turned the leaves in his fingers. Coca was an asset this night. A steady calm that would fortify a body for the challenge ahead, and he'd be a fool to assume the Sorrel men didn't have their own kind of elixir on hand. Harlan probably had enough morphine in his system to blow through a brick wall and not even notice. But Haakon regarded his comrades in turn who didn't rely on such an influence. He could suggest such, but he knew what they would say.

All of them were watching him.

All of them about to stand on courage that couldn't be paid for.

These men were prepared to draw only from valiant hearts. Was that not drive enough for a man? It should be, and for too long Haakon had forgotten that.

Though it pained him, he folded the leaves but didn't cram one in his cheek. Instead he rose. He could put them away, save them for trials to come, but with Cora's words fresh in his heart, he ducked into the kitchen and grabbed the iron lifter. He wedged the tip beneath a round cover in the stove top and raised the lid to the glow of coals beneath. He wanted to know what the road was like that she spoke of. Where the view was fine and where freedom was there for the taking.

His cheek throbbed for the tonic, but Haakon dropped the leaves in.

They smoldered and blackened. The faintest hint of their potency wafted to his nose, then they and their scent were gone. The only thing in his pouch now was the Word of God and the drawing by a little boy who didn't know he was being fought for across the sea. For a home—this land—that Haakon longed to share.

Shooting out a slow sigh, Haakon replaced the iron cover and returned to the other room. "Well, I think it's time. The sheriff will show, and if he's late, we'll just have to stall our friendly neighbors some." He pointed at Al and then Peter. "You two head through the grove along the east of the clearing. Stay low and keep a cover on the yard and cabin. Nobody fire unless you have to. We're only aimin' to stall them. Watch the main house, too, for any trouble coming this way. Sound an alarm if need be."

He shifted toward the others. "Jorgan and Orville, you two go around by the north end and do the same." Orville with his sniper rifle could cover them from a massive distance from the safety of the far ridge. Jorgan knew the lay of the land, so the pair would be better together.

Haakon's gaze locked with Thor's. "You and I will go to the cabin." The most dangerous of locations.

Thor gave a firm nod.

If this was a trap, it only seemed right that the pair of them be the ones to walk into it. It was he and Thor who had fueled this war at their own times. Everyone else was just along for the ride.

Thor's chair creaked as he stood. Orville followed suit.

Turning some, Thor aimed a finger at Al, who promised to be careful. Thor gave Peter a silent appeal as well.

"I'll stick to the plan," Peter promised.

Though he scarcely knew Orville from Adam, Thor gave him a nod of comradery.

Orville rested the sniper rifle on his shoulder. "Sibby's menfolk tormented her enough in this life, and I'll do all I can to help y'all get them behind bars." He dropped Haakon's coins on the table and stepped back.

"That's yours to keep," Haakon insisted.

Shaking his head, Orville pushed them farther away. Thor confirmed his appreciation. Haakon did too. Brow furrowed, Thor stepped to Haakon, gripped the back of his head, and pressed their foreheads together. Thor leveled him with a warning look.

"I won't do anything stupid," Haakon promised.

Thor nodded. He didn't do the same to Jorgan because there was only one fool-headed brother in this family. Instead, he clamped a hand on Jorgan's shoulder, gave a reassuring squeeze, then started through the kitchen.

The floorboards groaned beneath Thor's weight as he aimed for the door. His boots moved solidly over the floor—a sound that announced him wherever he went and one never tempered. Not only was Thor unable to hear himself but he had no cause to sneak around. He walked without reservation and lived life with the utmost integrity to justify such. People knew when he was coming, and it was right that way. Haakon pitied the men who would face him this night. If it was a fight with Thor they wanted, it was a fight they were going to get, and never again would Haakon fuel a doubt that he wouldn't be there to stand beside him.

THIRTY-THREE

THOR OPENED THE DOOR AND, BEFORE HE finished crossing the front porch, smelled smoke. He signed to Haakon to see if he noticed it as well, but his brother shook his head. The scent had to be faint to normal senses, though that didn't ease Thor's worry. This wasn't oak, which they stocked beside the kitchen stove. This was pitchy. Something more like pine.

Haakon's cabin was built of pine.

Ducking low, Thor hurried toward the trees that divided the two plots of land. Haakon followed at his side. Peter and Al broke off, heading north and keeping to the eastern side of the clearing while Orville and Jorgan aimed farther still to take cover among the trees skirting the graveyard. The moon was waning but offered enough light to see by, casting dusky shadows across the open meadow. Thor neared it in stride with his brother, and it was like moving through a dream as they stepped low through the narrow stretch of woods.

Haakon crouched down just short of the clearing and Thor saw the glow of flames lighting the upper floor of the cabin.

No.

Smoke leaked from the cracks in the chinking and walls. It trickled from the frames of the closed upper window, a telltale sign that it had just begun. Haakon's face was drawn in despair. The Sorrels retaliation lashed as yellow flames against the nearest panes of glass.

Thor scanned the open yard where two of Jed's men stood, watching the spectacle. With another man charging away from the smoking structure, it made three. Neither appeared to be Harlan nor Jed, so their count was higher—but to what number, he wasn't sure. Haakon had suspected that there were six or seven of them, but no one knew for sure.

Thor slung the strap of his shotgun over one shoulder and, keeping low, started forward. Haakon groped at his arm for him to stop, barely getting hold as Thor yanked free. They had to get that fire out. Thor gripped his brother by the shirt front and with his other hand pointed toward the well.

Haakon shook his head. "It's not worth it."

But Thor knew otherwise. That cabin was everything to Haakon. And not at risk of a life, but so close was the cabin to the trees that ambled alongside the great house and cidery that embers could just as soon have the entire farm up in smoke. All reason enough for Thor to survey the dark. Sensing it clear, he rushed to the back side of the cabin and paced along the nearest wall. A few yards off stood the old well. Smoke hazed the air around him, and he was just nabbing two buckets from the back stoop calculating the steps to water when a bullet whizzed into the sidewall. Thor dropped, and needing to get to water quick, he rushed for the well, crashing behind the low stone wall just as another shot slammed past.

This wasn't happening.

Haakon chambered a bullet, freed the safety, and ran for the cabin, keeping as low as Thor had and following the same path. At the end of the structure, Haakon sank to a knee and pressed his back flat to the wall. Thor was still there on the other side of the well and, so far as Haakon knew, hadn't been hit. Shooting out a breath, he pressed his trigger finger into place and glanced around the side of the house. A rifle blasted through the night, and he slammed back against the wall as bits of it shattered. Alright, then. This was how it was gonna go.

What he wouldn't give to be able to call out for Thor to make sure he wasn't hit. Since hollering in that direction was pointless, he'd try elsewhere.

"You don't want to do this!" Haakon shouted toward the meadow, where at least one of Jed's men was hunkered down in the tall grasses. The others had dispersed to a more distant reach, but he didn't know where.

Two rounds cracked into the side of the cabin.

Haakon pressed the stock of his Winchester to his shoulder, hitched in a breath, and angled around the corner of the building. He fired, chambered, and fired again before leaning back out of range. He tried to think of how long ago the fire had been set loose upstairs. Five minutes . . . maybe a few more? There wasn't much fuel up there, but with the smoke still in the air, it had to have reached the walls by now. He and Thor didn't have much more time, and the Sorrels knew that.

When more shots slammed his way, Haakon stepped from behind the house and fired three of his own. A Sorrel volleyed just as many, and when it ceased, Haakon leaned back around and fired until his magazine clicked empty. Something had hit somebody because he could hear a man groaning. He didn't know who he'd struck, and it was a sobering grief that Peter's father could be one of the men out there, falling in plain sight of Peter himself. But Harlan's son was all in and not only standing up for the safety of these lands but for his ma and sisters. Cora's family too.

Groping a hand into the pocket of his shirt, Haakon yanked out a fistful of cartridges and reloaded. When gunfire rattled the corner of the cabin, he ducked farther away. Wood and chinking splintered. Dust flew and smoke drenched the air, making it harder and harder to breathe and see.

Within the veil of smoke, Thor rose, set his shotgun on the top stones of the well, and fired one of the largest rounds a man could shoot. The force kicked his shoulder back and tore through the clearing as two more shots cracked from the woods from where Orville and Jorgan were hunkered down. Haakon braved a look around the corner to see that another man had fallen. That was two down—one of whom looked dead.

He hated this.

Making it a wretched relief when the remaining Sorrels ran westward toward the far stretch of woods. Haakon aimed again, this time firing in a way meant to wound. He and his comrades weren't here to kill. They were here to ensure arrests. Where was the sheriff? Using the light of the moon all he could, Haakon fired again. Then, with the men leaving range and nearing the safety of the trees where the rest of their menfolk had to be, he slung his gun over his shoulder. More shots cracked from where Orville and Jorgan hid.

Haakon took the opportunity to dash for the well, which was shielded from range on the backside of the cabin. Water. Now. And lots of it. Thor had the same idea as he dipped a bucket and crammed it into Haakon's grasp. Doing all he could not to spill the contents, Haakon kept low and ran for the back door of his cabin. It was locked so he kicked at it. The door wouldn't budge. Haakon fired twice at the knob before Thor loosed a deep cry.

Haakon moved clear. With one hand, Thor took aim on the doorknob and unloaded another lead slug. Haakon rushed forward, kicked the pulverized section, and the whole side broke away. Smoke wafted out. He didn't know how quickly his home was being destroyed, but the glow of the fire showed that the lower stairs weren't burning yet.

Haakon raced forward, splashed water onto the upper steps, and turned to swap buckets with Thor. Flames clawed at the loft, the smoke burning his eyes and stinging his throat. He tossed water higher up, then ran out with his brother to refill pails.

Their second trip inside got the flames out on the stairs, enough for Haakon to race up and check the damage while Thor went back to the well, his run hitching to a limp when he reached it. As Haakon ran upward with a bucket, he feared for the main house but decided Al and Peter would keep watch over it.

Coughing on smoke, Haakon neared the top landing and saw that the loft was only half burned. The other half was damp, protected by Jed, whose pistol sent a bullet ripping through Haakon's shoulder before he'd even reached the top. Haakon fell back, crashing down to his knee a few stairs from sight. Pain jarred him from end to end, but he stayed low on the wet steps, swung his rifle forward, and fired up into the smoke. Another bullet struck the wall behind him. He should have expected nothing less than such a tactic from the general. No one else was this amount of crazy.

When his rifle clicked empty, Haakon gripped it with his left hand. Blood oozed down his arm, wetting his fingers as he gripped the barrel. With his right hand he reached for the revolver at his back. There were six rounds in the handgun, so he crept up the stairs and, keeping low, reached the top. Smoke gusted every which way, ripping the air from his lungs. He should go down. Let the fire do its work. Jed wouldn't last much longer. But it would also mean the destruction of the cabin.

Gritting his teeth, Haakon crushed the front of his shirt against his mouth, heaved in the best breath he could, and rose high enough to fire into the burning haze, bracing himself for an opposing bullet to his flesh. Jed was gone from sight, so Haakon rammed back the trigger, aiming at every smoke filled corner, and when the revolver clicked empty, he charged back down the stairs and rushed outside.

He had no idea if Jed was down, so Haakon pressed on as he holstered the revolver. Where was Thor?

His brother wouldn't hear the gunfire. Did Thor know to get out of range?

He needed to warn him. Haakon heaved for air, then grimaced as the pain in his shoulder burned like the hot lead that had torn through it. A hissing smacked the ground beside him as a shot was fired from behind. Haakon scrambled forward and, flinging a look over his shoulder, saw Jed stumble from the house. The man had a handkerchief tied around his mouth and the pistol in his hand. The latter of which was trained on Haakon as he fired again. With no cover, Haakon staggered into the dark, praying it would suffice even as his gaze tore around for sight of Thor.

Another shot fired. Haakon couldn't load his rifle or revolver like this. Not without time and cover. Where was the well? So thick was the smoke now, and the dark, that it was a hellish haze he was trapped in, and Jed was still firing blind.

With a burn in his throat that wasn't owing to smoke, Haakon crawled forward until he felt the underbrush of the woods. Having made it to cover, he scrambled over a fallen log and dropped behind it. Every movement was agony as he pulled fresh ammunition from his pocket using fingers sticky with blood. He hadn't an endless supply of bullets, so it was only two that he chambered into his rifle. Slinking against the log, Haakon clutched the barrel to his chest to catch his breath. Smoke still gusted from the cabin, but there was enough air here in the woods to breathe by.

Despair and darkness threatened to drown him, but something else rose up beyond it.

A sun and a shield. That's what the promise offered. He was unworthy, far and away, but it was extended all the same. A light in the darkness that was more than he could ever deserve. Haakon reached up with a trembling hand and gripped the pouch that dangled around his neck. The leather was soft to the touch, no crackle of leaves or clank of coins, but the little sack held as much value as it could ever carry.

He closed his eyes, chilled from shock, and fought for consciousness. His back pressed against the coarse bark of the fallen log. He didn't know where Thor was. Or any of the others. Were they safe? Had any of them gone down? Where was Harlan all this while? A breeze gusted past, pushing smoke in the opposite direction. Tilting his head back, Haakon heaved in the cleaner air. There were no stars overhead, only the tops of trees, all laden with drifting sparks as his cabin burned.

Pain wrenched at his shoulder, and his vision blurred.

What he wouldn't give to be on a ship now. What he wouldn't give for that kind of speed. That amount of wind in his sails. Lord knew they could use that much water.

Haakon sucked in another breath and at the sounds of fresh gunfire lifted his head. What was happening? Shots crashed through the night one after another, popping from both directions. Amid it all, one of Thor's slugs fired, which announced as loud as anything could have that he was alive. Haakon nearly collapsed with relief. His chest heaved as he thought of his brothers and friends still out there. They weren't giving up, and he had no right to either. He still had two bullets in his possession. Time to make the most of them.

Shifting around, he moved onto his stomach and searched the hazy clearing for sight of men from any side. Jed was nowhere in view. Now and again a spark flashed in the dark as a musket fired from where some of Jed's men lay hidden. From the back of the cabin, Thor rushed out into the moonlight with two empty buckets in one hand and his shotgun in the other.

What was he doing?

"It's not worth it," Haakon called, but with focus riveted elsewhere, Thor couldn't see him. "Thor!" He knew better than to shout at his brother, but a different kind of instinct was taking over. One to protect him.

Though it would blow his cover, Haakon stumbled to his feet and waved his good arm overhead. Thor spotted him and to Haakon's relief took stock of who it was without taking aim. Ducking low again, Haakon lumbered toward him, pointing to the center of his rifle as he did. He flashed two fingers for the amount of rounds he had left. Thor dug in the pocket of his shirt and pulled out three .44 Rimfires. He handed them over.

"What about you?"

Blinking quickly, Thor shook his head in that way he did when he couldn't understand. His face was filthy and sweat slid down his forehead. Thor wiped a sleeve over his eyes and blinked at Haakon again in desperation.

Haakon rammed a finger to his brother's chest and pointed to the bullets again.

Thor tapped the barrel of his shotgun that was still strapped over his shoulder. *L-O-A-D-E-D.* Then he knocked the Colt holstered at his hip that used these same .44s as Haakon's rifle. Thor fingerspelled that his revolver was also loaded, and with that assurance, Haakon snatched the ammunition from Thor's sooty palm and crammed them into his rifle.

All was quiet again. He wanted to shout for Jorgan and Peter to know that they were all right. Al and Orville too. But there was only one way to find out. Haakon thumbed back toward where the others should be, and Thor nodded.

Crouched low, they picked their way in that direction, taking care to stay close to the wood line and out of the shadows that the moon made. While not a strong glow, it was enough to detect the shape of a moving body. Smoke singed the air thicker now, which had Haakon glance back to the cabin, expecting it to collapse, but flames no longer glowed. Instead, smoke seeped from the building as it did when its fuel was well soaked. Thor's doing.

Hope and gratitude pulsed inside him even as Haakon trained

his eyes on the meadow and surrounding areas for any sign of movement. When they reached the portion of woods where they'd all parted ways, he cut deeper into the trees, taking just yards before he sank down. Thor did the same. Gripping his shoulder, Haakon pulled them nearer to one another so Thor would see him mouth the words in the near blackness.

"You go in search of Jorgan and Orville," he whispered. "I'll look for Al and Peter."

Thor nodded once, gripped the side of Haakon's head, and gave a firm squeeze. Haakon stumbled away, holding onto every shred of hope that he'd see that calm, courageous face again.

THIRTY-FOUR

JUNE 2, 1895
WHITETOP MOUNTAIN, VIRGINIA

WHEN A TINY HEAD OF SILKEN HAIR WRIGGLED against her own, Aven looked over to see Tusie stirring amid the bundle of blankets they shared in the night. Tusie was unswaddled now, but well warmed in her linen nightdress and this snug cabin. While much of the floor was covered in blankets and slumbering people, the Kennedys had welcomed them with open arms and a cheery spirit. With Mr. Kennedy bunked down in an outbuilding to make room for all the women and children he housed, Aven unbuttoned the top of her nightgown and pulled Tusie close to nurse with no fear of immodesty.

The early hour of morning was lifting the darkness to a soft, gray light as she nestled a light blanket around them, creating a cove of warmth. With six hours of travel and a bustling night of settling in behind them, Aven closed her eyes and nearly drifted off again.

In the quiet of her heart, she thought of Thor and the dangers he and the other men were facing. Were they well? Had they confronted the Sorrels? Aven whispered a prayer that had become one of many in the night.

At the sound of stirring coals, she looked over to see Mrs. Kennedy adding fresh wood to low embers. The young bride smiled at Aven as if having known she and the baby were awake.

"Don't let me disturb you." Scarcely nineteen, Mrs. Kennedy's voice was gentle as she pushed a brown braid back over her shoulder. "I've just come to put the kettle on. I'll have hot tea and coffee ready before long."

Aven felt a swell of emotions rise up. Though so simple an offering, the gesture was anything but. This woman and her husband had welcomed them in with scant warning, and yet their hospitality showed no end. Mrs. Kennedy even gave up her bed in the small bedroom to Cora, Ida, and Georgie. Tess slumbered on the floor beside it, and out here in the main room, Fay and the boys were asleep amid mounds of blankets and quilts. Dear Sibby had slumbered on a padded window seat while Mrs. Kennedy had dozed in a rocking chair.

After slipping an arm beneath the baby to support her weight, Aven cradled Tusie close and sat up some. "We cannot thank you enough for your kindness, Mrs. Kennedy."

"It's our pleasure. But please, call me Wren." Smiling, the young woman's manner was as gentle as her woodland namesake. She angled an iron pot closer to the flames and reached aside for a wooden spoon. "Fret not, for in truth Haakon sent along funds to secure extra provisions, and his message lent me yesterday to borrow extra bedding from neighbors." She winked. "Since his return from sea, my husband has spoken much of your brother-in-law and their adventures together. It's a joy to meet his family."

Aven smiled. She could only imagine how colorful life had been alongside Haakon amid the distant shores and tides of foreign places. "The pleasure is ours." She regretted knowing little of this man, Tate

Kennedy. Aven hadn't inquired of Haakon's years at sea or considered where he'd been. Lord willing, there was still time to discover such.

On the wagon ride to the train station, Sibby had informed them that with the sheriff's help, the men planned to confront the Sorrels once and for all. At wondering how the men would find the Sorrels in the first place, Sibby confessed that Haakon had devised a carefully thought-out plan to lure them to the farm. While Aven didn't know what that would entail, she prayed that the men would take care. For her husband to be among them made the prayers all the more fraught with longing. As much as Aven desired freedom and a future for her daughter, to think of it being at the loss of their life with Tusie's father was a grief she couldn't begin to bear.

Haakon hadn't meant to slumber, but having hunkered down beneath a rotting log to try and staunch the flow of blood from his shoulder, he'd closed his eyes just briefly as pain pulled him in and out of consciousness. He'd risen to a dark sky yet, so hadn't been gone to the world for long. He struggled to his feet, and though his stomach clenched for food, he continued his search for Al and Peter. Were Jorgan and Orville still safe on the ridge? Had Thor found the others yet? Haakon strode through the tail end of night, each quarter hour graver than the one before as his search proved empty.

All was so quiet and still that he wondered if others were asleep. He didn't want to imagine any other purpose for the silence.

Perhaps all the men in these woods knew there wasn't much sense in firing at one another in the dark. Daylight would not only make aiming more efficient but twice as deadly. As much as Haakon longed for the sun, he wished it away all the same.

He kept to the trees, and soon dawn woke on the horizon, hazed by indigo clouds and lingering smoke. Still there came no sign of them. Haakon scanned the woods around him for any signals of life. If his men had scattered, they could be anywhere. Gun at the ready, he traipsed through underbrush and with each step prayed he'd come upon his men in one piece.

Suddenly two shots fired. Not from the woods on either side of the meadow, but from the cidery toward the house, judging by the spray of dirt just shy of the front porch. Haakon didn't know who was firing at whom, but if one of his men needed help, he'd be there.

Ducking low, he trekked back toward the farmyard. The dark and his searching had blown him well off course, and now that light was lifting, he realized just how much ground he'd finally made up. One of the windows of the great house was smashed in and another raised halfway. At the edge of the trees, Haakon crouched and searched the open yard where Bjørn's wooden blocks still lay scattered beside Sigurd's forgotten wooden sword.

It was a good hundred feet from here to the house. Haakon glanced around. How many of Peter's kin were still out there? At least several, and whoever had broken into the house might have had company. It was foolhardy to go in by himself, but if the Klansmen were on a mission to torch another building, he couldn't stay here and watch. Haakon was deciding how best to approach the structure when the front door opened with a clatter.

Al stumbled out. His hands were raised and a man strutted behind him, pressing the tip of a pistol to the back of his head.

"It's empty!" Al hollered, and the moment he did, the man beat the pistol across his skull.

Al fell and struggled to stumble away. The other man pulled a knife and rushed after him. Still crouched low, Haakon raised his rifle and centered the bead sight on its target. His finger flew to the trigger, but a split second before he pulled it, a handgun blasted from somewhere else, and the man dropped, groaning. A second round fired, and the Sorrel stilled.

Al ducked as he ran for the woods. Wanting to be seen, Haakon stood, and Al raced that way. Cora's son sank behind a tree, soaked in sweat and heaving for air. It glistened on his skin, and blood matted his coarse hair to the side of his scalp.

Haakon knelt and yanked out a handkerchief. "What happened?"

Al pressed it to the side of his head. "I was searchin' the house when they outnumbered me."

Haakon scanned the cidery where those two shots had come from. "What of Peter?"

"I think that was him who just fired."

"Have you seen Jorgan and Orville?"

"No."

"The others?"

"Nothing."

Haakon shifted a leg forward, trying not to collapse with pain and exhaustion. Panic was keeping him upright just now. It was starting to terrify him that no one had seen Jorgan. "How many are left inside?"

"I think there's only one of 'em now. Two are down in the meadow, and I think Orville might have gotten another from where he's hunkered down."

"Who's in the house?"

"Peter's pa. They've used up all their ammo. There wasn't even a bullet in that pistol. The fella was just usin' me as a decoy to get back to cover. He sounded like he wanted to split. That's the only reason I made it back out. That other fella got a hold of me and told me to start walkin'."

Haakon blew out a heavy breath. For Al to have risked his life like that . . .

"Jed was hidin' in the cider shed through the night, but I don't know if he's there now. Peter thought he saw him come out, but it was too dark to know for sure."

Haakon looked that way, weighing the dangers.

Al eyed Haakon's bloodied shoulder. "What happened?"

"Bullet went through. Bleeding's slowed, I think." That was his assessment based on the fact that he hadn't passed out yet. His shoulder hurt like the dickens, and the more he thought about it, the more he noticed the pain. Haakon lifted his gaze to the house. The sun was still low, sky a blazing pink, but there was enough light to see well now. "Where's Harlan?" He gauged the dead man sprawled in the yard, but as Al had confirmed, it wasn't Peter's father.

"He's upstairs. From what I overheard, he's the one who started the fire. I was worried he was after doin' it again, so I followed."

Haakon owed Al a great thanks. With Harlan still on the loose inside, someone had to go in, and that someone needed to be him. "Wait here and cover for me. If you see anyone, try and round 'em up. We'll do better now if we group in." Really, he didn't know if that was the case, but he was desperate to find everyone.

Al nodded. Suddenly someone hurried along the short end of the cidery. Peter. He ran low, aiming straight for the house, a shotgun in his grip. If Peter didn't know who was in there, he was running straight into a shootout with his own father. Before he could think, Haakon darted off, reaching the stairs a step behind Peter and using the force to ram him into the wall. They hit hard, and Haakon grabbed him by the collar. "No!"

With no way to tell friend from foe, Peter threw a punch. Haakon ducked against it, and Peter's face, covered in dirt and sweat, went slack with shock.

"It's your old man in there." Haakon said, breaking them apart. "Let me go in."

"You can't. You're shot. You can't fire a rifle if you're shot."

"Thanks for that bit of sense. I got my pistol."

"It's empty, or you'd be holding it."

Dagnabit, was Peter always so observant? "Then give me yours."

"There's nothin' in it." Peter reached for the doorknob. "It's my responsibility. I'll do it."

"Listen to me." Haakon switched his rifle to his good arm, which was fortunately also his shooting shoulder, but it took every ounce of strength he owned—and some he lacked—to chamber a bullet. As he did, he felt a tearing inside the muscle that told him he wouldn't be chambering any more bullets for a good long while. By sheer will he kept a groan from escaping. He hitched in a breath. "See. I got it." Enough of a truth. Any other man he'd ask to come with him, but not Peter. His head swirled with the pain, and he blinked quickly to try and steady his vision. "Go take cover. Better yet, find the others and bring them to help. 'Specially Thor."

Peter knew as well as Haakon did that Thor was their best shot. Not only that, where Haakon was cunning, Thor was composed. A mixture they needed because Harlan Sorrel was lethal as they came. The truth of it showed in his son's taut face.

"And Peter, I think there might still be one of them out there, so be careful." Haakon scanned the woods, and while he saw nothing, he had a hunch there'd been seven of them. Not just six. From what he'd learned from Thor and Jorgan, the doctor who had drawn Thor's blood was much more deadly than Thor would have ever realized that day at the train station. Red Sorrel hadn't been present the night at the moonshine still, but Haakon couldn't shake the worry that the man had never been far. A tactic pulled to confuse others of their exact numbers and one Jed would be clever enough to ensure.

"There's also Jed unaccounted for," Haakon cautioned him.

Peter nodded his understanding.

It was a risk sending Peter off with danger still present, but it had to be safer than sending him inside. "Stay low and find Thor." Haakon almost promised Peter that they'd get the sheriff and his men here and take Jed and Harlan down to the jail proper-like, but with the sheriff yet to show, he couldn't guarantee it. "I'll stall your pa best I can."

Nodding, Peter hurried off, keeping well away from the front of the house as he ducked back into the woods. Haakon trudged inside and shoved the door closed behind him. He was making as much noise as a bat in a basket, but it didn't really matter at this point. Peter's father was in here somewhere, and they were going to find each other one way or another.

He crossed through the kitchen, one he'd scarcely stood in since returning. Everything was as he remembered—Ida's touches, and Fay's and Aven's—all of it *home*, which made it all the worse that an intruder was here.

Haakon's passage through the great room was blessedly without incident, and he moved with caution up the first set of stairs. Upon seeing that the hallway was vacant, he took careful survey of Jorgan and Fay's room before moving to the next. He leaned in, gun raised, and saw that Aven's old room was empty. He had a sense the third room would be the same, and it was. Haakon's gaze lifted to the attic stairs that wound up. He trained his ears for any sounds above and heard nothing.

The last time he'd gone up a stairwell, he'd gotten shot, so he held his gun ready and stayed close to the wall. Al had said the remaining Sorrels were out of ammo, so Haakon hoped Al was right as he swung up toward Aven and Thor's room.

Something small and hard slammed into him, and Haakon crashed down against the wall. Glass shattered. What was left of the oil lamp clanked as shards below. Kerosene dripped from his shirt.

Well. Now he knew where Harlan was.

Next came down the glass kerosene jug. Haakon ducked out of the way, and it shattered across the hallway, oozing into the boards. Glimpsing movement in the doorway above, Haakon lunged up and fired. The last bullet he had access to ripped through Harlan's thigh. The man stumbled. He spat out a slew of curses, and a box of books came crashing down next.

Haakon pressed his back to the corner of the stairwell to avoid being clobbered. "Now we're even!" he shouted.

Why he hadn't just taken Harlan out, he didn't know. He supposed it was because the man was unarmed, and as reckless as it was, Haakon didn't take to killing an unarmed man.

Unable to chamber the last few rounds, he opened the brass slider and shook out the bullets. They hit his palm, and he crammed them into his pocket for safe keeping. The nearest hiding spot was Dorothe's old bedroom. Haakon charged in to find it much changed, but all he cared about was a place for the empty rifle. No sense leaving it around to be found should Harlan have any kind of ammo left. Haakon crammed the gun behind a wingback chair and threw a blanket over the muzzle. Next he whipped off his leather pouch and stashed it there as well.

Stepping back into the hallway, he unsheathed his knife. "You gonna come down here, or do I need to come up there?" He reeked of kerosene, and not liking how flammable he was, nor the likelihood of Harlan having another match, Haakon ripped the buttons from the front of his shirt and yanked it first away from his good arm, then his bad. He wadded up the garment and pitched it aside. The top of his winter underwear had a good soaking of kerosene as well, and with no way to take it off, he spliced his knife into the fabric and tore the top away from his torso.

At sight of Harlan coming down the stairs, Haakon rushed to finish—ripping the cloth away and readying his knife again.

Just behind Harlan trudged Jed.

Haakon's blood cooled at sight of them together. Jed's clothing was singed, face streaked with soot, meaty hand clasped around the handle of the ax from the cidery. He dragged the sharpened blade behind him in what had to be sheer will. Eye patch gone, the sewed-over hole of his missing eye was rutted and scarred—stating just how much he could endure.

Harlan had his own knife drawn. Behind him he pulled a sturdy chair. The wooden legs clanked down the stairs with each step he took. Blood spread in a wide patch along the top of his pants leg where a dark hole furrowed through. If Harlan felt pain, it wasn't showing.

"You don't have to do this." Haakon lowered his stance and fought the urge to back away. "You can come with us to the sheriff's office and have a proper trial. The both of you."

With a growl, Harlan hefted up the chair and slammed it down the hallway. Haakon ducked but it rammed against him. Seeing stars, he shook his head and stumbled to right his stance. "Don't you think there's been enough killing for one day?" Haakon turned the knife handle, keeping his grip light and ready.

From the table at the end of the hallway, Harlan picked up a pitcher of dried flowers and hurled it down the hall.

Haakon ducked again and it struck the wall, shattering. He slowly rose. "Really, now."

Jed watched from the stairs.

"Do you always let others do your dirty work?" Haakon called to the general, then to Harlan, "Your own son is out there." He stared at the man who bore the same coloring as Peter. The same tall height. Both of them had thick, cropped hair of wheat yellow. Even their shirts were the same cut—narrow in the waist, broad in the shoulder, and rendered from sturdy flannel, as though fashioned by the same woman years ago. "Your son is fighting for his life against his uncles and cousins. Do you really mean to do this?"

Lunging away, Harlan dragged forward the narrow table. He hoisted up the hunk of furniture and, with the legs poking outward, charged forward. Haakon grabbed up what was left of the chair and slammed it at him. Everything collided, and Harlan crashed past. One of the table legs rammed Haakon in the gut, jarring air from his lungs. Harlan's knife flew from his hand, skidding down the hallway.

Heaving for breath, Haakon ran back for it and scrambled to grab the weapon before it reached Jed.

A blade in each hand, Haakon centered himself in the hallway and tried not to collapse.

Or panic that there was a Sorrel on each side of him now.

His stomach throbbed from the blow, and he sucked in the deepest breath he could. Broken glass crunched under his boots.

Kerosene reeked in his nostrils. He prayed Harlan didn't have another match.

"Seein' as you got that out of the way," Haakon panted, "let's do this nice-like." Flecks of blood mottled the bare skin of his side in a rough scrape from the table leg, and he spat out more blood from his mouth.

Jed pulled the ax forward, planting the handle in both hands. The kind of stance a man took when gauging where to strike a tree.

Haakon weighed his odds, and as poor as they were, he was faster than the old general and perhaps less injured than Harlan, who limped something fierce now. Harlan's pants were sopping with blood, the floor sticky with it. Likely some of it was Haakon's own now that the hole in his shoulder was oozing again. It dripped down the length of his arm, slicking the knife handles before falling in crimson drops to the floor. That side of him nearly useless, Haakon cradled both knives in his numb hand and used his good arm to drag a portion of the shattered table closer. After snapping off one of the broken legs, he held it like a club.

Without warning, Jed limped forward, ax raised. Haakon charged him, swung the table leg as hard as he could, and crashed it against the ax handle. Jed stumbled back, and Haakon swung again, this time knocking him in the side of the skull. Harlan was coming—the pounding of floorboards announced it almost as loud as his breathing. Haakon waited as long as he dared, then ducked and rammed his back up just as Harlan collided into him. It flipped the man away, who crashed into the ground. Remembering the ax, Haakon scrambled aside as Jed swung it past him and into the wall.

This was where he was going to die.

Haakon stumbled back, fighting for his feet. Fighting for consciousness. Fighting for the belief that these men couldn't do this anymore. Not to his family and not to other innocent souls in this nation. If he blacked out between this father and son, that would be the last of him, and while he could dart into Aven's old room, slam and bolt the door, and escape through the window, he wasn't going anywhere. He was going to stand here until either he or they couldn't anymore.

Haakon faltered, but managed to straighten. His left eye was swelling shut, and he blinked quickly as his vision blurred again.

Gripping the doorjamb at the far end of the hallway, Harlan was trying to rise as well, but with blood still leaking from his wound, he made slow progress. The man's face was paled, highlighting the yellow hue still darkening his eyes. Thor's had brightened to white again, but Thor had been resting and heeding a doctor's advice. Who knew what Harlan had been up to.

The man still wasn't up yet, so Haakon turned the table leg in his good hand. Jed's weapon might have been fiercer, but he was stronger and faster. With that bolstering, Haakon charged Jed again, swinging the hickory rod into him with all the force possible. The ax clattered against the wall as Haakon rammed him. He gripped the smooth handle, desperate to wrench it free, but Jed's hold was solid. More than Haakon could manage with a one-sided pull and loss of lifeblood. Haakon stumbled back, and as the pain of his bullet wound throttled his mind, his vision hazed almost to black. He blinked, desperate to hold on.

"Behind you," Jed called.

Haakon looked that way just as Harlan heeded the warning meant for him. Thor was stepping into the hallway from the top of the first flight of stairs, soot stained, sweat drenched, and with a shotgun aimed at Harlan, who stood but feet from him.

Haakon owed Peter the biggest thanks of his life.

Hunched in pain, Harlan backed deeper into the hallway toward Haakon, stopping when he was centered between both of his foes. It was the four of them now—stretched along this hallway like pints lining a shelf. Panting, Haakon doubled over and wiped perspiration from his eyes with the back of his hand. He took care not to lose sight of Jed on his left as he did. The man looked exhausted. As weary and broken as everyone else here. Finally able to straighten, Haakon rammed his knife into its sheath and held fast to the other. He had to brace the table leg to his side with his bad arm, and while it was a struggle, he managed to shape enough Sign to ask Thor how many rounds he had left.

Thor lifted his finger from the trigger just long enough to indicate a single one.

"I think he's just got the one shot," Harlan said.

Despite everything, Haakon stared at him. He had to be bluffing. There was no way Harlan could know what Haakon had inquired in Sign. Then again, maybe Harlan had observed them over the years more than they'd realized.

"Then you can't kill us both," Jed said.

If Jed thought it was buckshot in that firearm, then he had some fair reasoning. He was also standing in a decent spot. Two men removed from Thor, Jed had enough obstruction in front of him to block most if not all of the pellets. Except there was one major problem with that kind of thinking.

Thor hadn't loaded buckshot.

He had a lead ball the size of a fat acorn in that barrel of his, and enough black powder to send it to the next county.

"I'm telling y'all, you don't want to do this," Haakon said. "You come with us, and we call it quits. We'll take you down to the sheriff, and nobody else has to die today."

Harlan spat. His face twisted in anger as he turned his profile to glare back in Haakon's direction.

The count on their crimes was so high that political justice bore an extent Haakon couldn't fathom. Death would be easier on them—one of the reasons he didn't want to grant it.

Angling sideways to better see them both, Harlan swayed but didn't fall. "That little lady of yours have the baby?"

Haakon realized he'd spoken to Thor. Glaring at Harlan, Thor made no response.

"Or did something go amiss?"

Haakon stared at Harlan's yellowed eyes and sallow skin, then it clicked in his mind like the links of a rising anchor. Harlan and the needle. The illness. The epidemic hadn't been strong enough to take Thor down, but maybe Harlan had known that. As for Aven and the baby, it had posed the greater risk. Peter's father hadn't been after Thor. He'd been after Thor's heir.

His daughter.

More brutal a blow to Thor than death itself.

Harlan smiled, and Haakon craved for more than a table leg in hand.

Thor's shoulders were heaving now. Sweat slid down his forehead, and he blinked it away.

Though his hands shook with fury and exhaustion, Haakon signed to his brother again, asking if he remembered those two squirrels on Hickory Ridge from when they were boys. The time Thor was testing out the rifling on a new .22. Understanding filled Thor's eyes, and with souls on the line and not wild game, he gave a somber nod.

Touching the side of his finger to his lips, Haakon lowered it in the sign for *sure?* It was a lot to ask of a man.

Thor's gaze drilled into Harlan. He confirmed with another nod.

With slow, unthreatening steps, Haakon centered himself in the width of the hallway, directly behind Peter's father so that Jed was no longer shielded. Thor could take the leader now if he wanted to, and knowing as much, Jed moved—on instinct, no doubt—until Haakon was flush between him and Thor's shotgun again.

"I'm tellin' you now to come with us," Haakon said for the last time as he peered past Harlan, straight into the barrel of Thor's firearm. The last place he ever wanted to be, but this was the only way. The stench of kerosene still wafted from the floorboards as Haakon shifted his boots over the glass. "This doesn't have to end here." They were all centered now in the long stretch of hallway, each of them straight as a cannon blast.

Jed turned the ax handle over his hand once and then again. "And I'm tellin' you to shut up."

From the pocket of his shirt, Harlan pulled out a brass match safe, eyes surveying the oiled floor beneath them all. Thor's finger eased over the trigger.

Haakon lifted his gaze to his brother's, and at Thor's resolute nod, he dropped flat, slamming to the ground as fast as he could. Thor ripped the trigger back, and Haakon didn't have to lift his head to see the jolt to Thor's shoulder from the force, the hole he'd blown in the distant wall, or to know that both Sorrels had just gone to meet their Maker.

THIRTY-FIVE

HAAKON HAD DECIDED LONG BEFORE THIS
moment—long before he rose, feeling like death warmed over—that
if one of his men were to not make it this night, it needed to be
him. There was just no other outcome that was fair or right. Haakon
himself was the one who had shipwrecked upon this farm—boards
warped, jagged, and utterly raw. He was the one who had lured their
enemies here once and for all, and he was the one who had the least to
lose. He had no family.

Not the way the others did. Not Al or Orville, who had wives,
nor Jorgan or Thor, who also had children. And not Peter, who was
a beacon of hope and strength for his ma and sisters. Even for Cora,
Tess, and Georgie.

But as Haakon and Thor made their way down the stairs, Haakon
feared that fate and he weren't going to see eye to eye. Maybe it was
the calm in the air . . . the call of birdsong. The way the wind moved
gently in the trees in the yard.

Or maybe it was because when he heard footsteps in the underbrush, he knew it wouldn't be so clean a draw as for him to be facing
their final foe. Instead, he saw Peter running nearer. Al was right on
his trail, soaked in sweat and looking nigh unto passing out.

The young Sorrel called out that Orville had been hit. That he was down and wounded something fierce, but that Jorgan had been with him, keeping him alive. And there in that moment, Haakon was filled with fear. A fear that told him this had been too easy. Not the fight itself, but the fact that every life he valued in this place was still pulsing.

That's when he heard the firing of a gun. Haakon dropped the same instant the others did, pulling Thor down with him behind the porch railing. Three more shots pummeled the porch. All Haakon could think of was Thor needing to live. Peter and Al needing to live. But when he unfolded and stumbled to his feet, it was Peter who had skidded to a halt in the dirt. So quick that the young man almost fell as he turned and ran in the direction of the gunman. Haakon shouted for him to stop, tearing after him with a force that nearly buckled his knees, but what kept him from stumbling was the sight of a red-haired man trying to cram another round into the firearm aimed at Peter and Al. With Peter running toward him, the man dropped the unreadied pistol and brandished a knife.

Peter pulled his blade with the same speed and crashed into the man, sending him flying into the base of a tree. They flipped over one another, and in a motion that Haakon had dreaded since this all began, the man swiped his blade across Peter's middle just as Peter's knife sank into his chest.

Haakon was trying to run but he was falling. He was falling, and it was black, and it was cold, and it should have been him at that tree and not Peter.

Both men crumbled, and Haakon caught himself, fighting for his feet. He reached them and rammed the man aside even as he saw that the life was leaving Red Sorrel. Thor heaved him farther back, and there was a knowing in Thor's face that had him shoving the man down with a great and terrible force.

"Peter!" All Haakon could think about was finding something to staunch the flow of blood from Peter's abdomen. He had no shirt to rip off, but Al was already done with his own. Cora's son wadded up the flannel and pressed it to Peter's middle where blood had already soaked his own shirt. Peter was trying to speak, but nothing was coming.

Haakon gripped the back of Peter's neck, easing him down as Peter sank lower against the tree. "Look at me," Haakon demanded, and when Peter did, he added, "You just breathe." Haakon inhaled slowly to try and guide him along, and to his relief, Peter drew in a breath. The young man nodded as though avowing to stay calm.

Peter's hands came around Al's own to help staunch the flow, but his fingers could do nothing more than tremble. Deep crimson streaked Peter's wrist, and all hope drained from Haakon—funneling right out of him and onto the ground that was being soaked by Peter's very life. Though Al's skin was a glossy brown, his hands were darkened further with what could only be too much blood.

Having kept guard against Harlan's brother, Thor came around and knelt behind Peter's head. The red-haired man was still as death. Thor eased Peter's head away from the tree roots and against his lap.

Shaking with shock, Peter coughed. Blood tinted the inside of his lips. He grimaced, as though sheer will were keeping him conscious. Haakon sucked in a breath. Peter lowered his hand to his side, and the tremor of it shook against Haakon's knee. Haakon gripped it, holding with every assurance he could offer . . . But what was he giving?

"We need a doctor." The words fell from Haakon's lips, so distant it might have been someone else. "Someone go for a doctor!"

Thor gave Haakon a silent appeal to drop the notion. Al eased up the bloodied cloth to show the width of Peter's wound. The severity.

Haakon nearly turned away, not because he couldn't handle the sight but because he didn't want Peter to see the last glint of hope drain from his face. As it was, it had already drained from Peter's own. The man's skin was the faintest of whites, lips tinting blue. His eyes were still open, though not as alert.

Reaching over, Haakon used his other hand to grip Peter's shoulder and spoke to Thor through a haze of despair. "What do we do?"

Thor's face was grave as he cradled Peter's head in his lap.

Still applying pressure, Al shifted closer to Peter, who had his focus tilted toward his uncle. With slow movements, Peter turned his head back to Haakon. Gripping Peter's hand tighter, Haakon gave as firm a squeeze as he could manage so that Peter would feel it through what had to be a growing numbness. He moved closer and bent forward for his face to be square to Peter's own. So near that Haakon felt the faintest traces of breath.

"You hang on, you hear? It's gonna be fine." He didn't know why he was saying this, and while he wasn't about to offer up false assurance, he was going to extend every comfort he could think of until Peter made it to a place of lasting peace. "We're right here, and your ma and sisters are safe. They're right safe."

Peter's darkening lips quivered.

Leaning back on his heels, Thor sucked in a breath. He tipped his face toward the sky, and though his beard was thick, it didn't hide the fact that his chin was trembling beneath it.

Haakon squeezed Peter's hand all the firmer. It was growing weaker, and he didn't want it to go limp. "You're doin' right fine . . ." He could barely whisper through the clench of his throat. Tears were coming now, and Haakon swiped them against his upper arm.

Peter's mouth worked in the faintest of breaths, whispering for Al.

Al leaned nearer, and Peter's eyes searched through what might have been a void. Still applying pressure to Peter's wound, Al spoke. "I'm right here."

Blinking quickly, Peter seemed to still be searching for him. The hand in Haakon's was going slack. Al leaned closer and, letting go of the bloodied cloth, gripped the top of Peter's head. "I'm right here. Ain't goin' nowhere." He put his hold back into place though it wouldn't do for long.

With Al looking near to collapsing, Haakon moved to help. Thor stopped him and motioned to Peter's hand still gripped in Haakon's own. Thor kept Peter's head in his lap and, reaching around, took over the compression. Hands freed, Al shifted lower to Peter, who was trying to speak. The very man that Peter had once pistol whipped tilted his head to the side and with tears in his eyes bent to listen. What would he hear? For so long Peter had stalked behind Al in what had seemed like only hate, and in the seasons since Peter had been making amends for that. Peter's mouth moved so faintly that Haakon couldn't hear it, but whatever was said made Al's face go slack.

Thor lowered his gaze from Peter's mouth in what could only be a gentle and silent knowing for what he'd read there. Thor bowed his head.

Straightening, Al looked down at the young man and nodded quickly. "I'll be sure to tell her. I promise."

The hand in Haakon's own was cold. Haakon tried to chafe warmth into it. Although it would do little good, he didn't mean for Peter to die without having done everything he could for him.

When Peter tried to say more, Al leaned nearer again. After a few moments, his attention lifted to Haakon. "I think he's askin' after his pa."

How forthright should he be? Haakon looked to Thor, who gave a small shake of his head.

Nodding, Haakon leaned nearer. "All is well, Peter. They won't be around to hurt anyone ever again. All is well."

Peter tilted his head back and gave a weak nod. Between ragged inhales, he managed the faintest of words not meant for any of them to answer for. The softest whispering of Tess's name. Peter heaved for another breath as a single tear slid down the side of his face and into the dirt.

His skin was as ice now. Grief welled up in a way Haakon didn't know how to contain. How could he bring this man comfort? Haakon had never lived so well by faith, but because of those around him, it was rooted in the furthest reaches of his memory. He meant to do better by that now. And for Peter . . . "Our Father who art in heaven. Hallowed be thy name."

Peter's eyes searched for him as though following the voice—the promise—in a haze of darkness.

"Thy kingdom come, Thy will be done. On earth as it is in heaven."

Peter blew out a slow sigh. His face eased in what seemed more peace than pain now.

"Give us this day . . . our daily bread. And forgive us our trespasses . . . as we—" Face skewing in agony, Haakon couldn't speak anymore.

"As we forgive those who trespass against us," Al said, his voice soft then growing stronger as though he knew Peter was fading fast. "Lead us not into temptation, but deliver us from evil."

The hand in Haakon's was still now.

Al's voice tremored with sorrow. "For thine is the kingdom . . . and the power . . . and the glory forever. Amen."

The lines of Peter's face had softened, and his eyes were closed. On the other side of him, Al lowered his face to his knees, draping both arms over his head, and folding his body in as if to keep it from coming apart with grief. His shoulders shook. Thor gripped the earth beneath his hands as though trying to pull courage into a body that was drowning.

Haakon heaved for a breath amid those same waters.

Peter wouldn't be standing anymore in the orchards lit by the sun. He wouldn't be making jokes that were funnier than everyone wanted to admit, and he wouldn't be smiling over at Tess as if she were his most cherished friend in all the world.

Bowing his head, Thor let out a sob. Haakon looked to his brother and the tears pooling in his eyes, and when he peered back down at Peter, he saw that their friend was gone.

THIRTY-SIX

CRADLING A BASKET FILLED WITH SPRING greens, Aven stepped from the Kennedys' garden and latched the willow gate. She towed up the hem of her skirt and started toward the water pump. Behind her, Cora and Ida knelt in the soft soil, tending the small herb plot—all hands eagerly aiding the Kennedys for their kindness and care. With many mouths to feed and as many beds to make up each night, all were eager to pitch in. 'Twas busyness that settled hearts eager for word from the men.

Having waited four years for Tate's return from sea, no one understood so well as his new bride. Wren had scarcely stopped doting on Tusie, and as it was the babe lay nestled in the crook of Wren's arm as she drizzled water onto porch flowers from a tin can. Combined with little Georgie's fervent help, Aven had cradled her daughter only for feedings and slumber during their four days here.

Across the meadowland, Sigurd and Bjørn stood beneath a lofty hemlock, peering up where Tate straddled a thick branch as he lashed a rope into place. Having promised them a swing, he had nearly completed the task. After knotting the rope well, the man climbed down, hefted up the youngest Norgaard lad, and brought him closer to test its strength with a mighty tug. When Tate had finished, Bjørn clapped pudgy hands, then reached over to try and pilfer Tate's spectacles. The man chuckled, tossed the lad into the air, and Bjørn let out a belly laugh.

"Methinks we have a thievin' pirate in the making!" Tate rumbled in a playful brogue.

Sigurd hopped up and down and began a recitation on what he'd learned of pirates from his uncle Haakon.

Setting the basket beside the pump, Aven lifted and lowered the handle. The first trickle of water had just poured from the spout when she noticed a wagon in the distance. Straightening, she shielded her eyes. With sunset not far off, the yellow glow lit the wagon from behind, making silhouette of both horses and driver impossible to distinguish until Aven saw that reining in a team of grays was a lean man whose black floppy hat shielded a face only a few shades lighter.

The driver lifted a hand in greeting. "Evenin', Miss Aven."

"Al!"

He touched the brim of his hat, the gesture so solemn that Aven's heart plummeted. "What has happened?" As the words fell from her lips, others gathered around.

Al surveyed them all before looking back to Aven. "Thor's well, Miss Aven. And his brothers."

Relief for those safe waterfalled down—lit by the sun that Thor was among them—yet with others unaccounted for, the lingering silence crashed upon rocks of worry.

Al glanced to Sibby and spoke as he climbed down. "Orville's taken a bullet. It was quite a landing, but he'll mend. He's askin' after you and is eager for you to be by his side." He came around and gripped one of the grays by the bridle, eyes down. "But I have to tell you that Peter . . ." Al's voice broke on the name. "Peter . . . He didn't . . ."

Sibby's quick intake of breath was so sudden that Tess glanced from Sibby to Al in shock. When all Al could do was shake his head, Peter's sister bent over, falling to her knees. Fay rushed to her side. Even as Al cast a look of utmost despair to Sibby's hunched form, he reached for his own sister, who was still standing in stunned silence. When Al pulled her closer against him, Tess moved as though wood being forced to bend to winds rushing in.

Tugging off his hat, Al pressed it to his chest and spoke in words that were soft and low. Tess shook her head. Taking a step back, she shook her head again. Another breath had her knees buckling. Al was swift to steady her, pulling her in to rest against him. Tess buried her face in her brother's chest, and the wrenching of her tears sent a huddle of birds flying from the rooftop.

Aven knew that cry from when she'd lived beside Norway's raging seas. 'Twas the cry of a love lost.

Peter was gone.

Agony coursing through her every limb, Aven laid the basket aside and followed Cora over. They helped Tess into the house where she huddled down on the bed. Aven hurried back to the doorway to check for Sibby just as the young woman sank against the side of the tree where the swing now hung. Fay sat with her, stroking her hair as Sibby leaned down to rest her head on Fay's lap. Sibby's cries were the same wrenching pleas as those coming from the bed.

And here beneath this roof, two hearts surrounded Tess's own—both of whom had once stood beside a beloved's grave and mourned. 'Twas a crossing-over that Aven wouldn't wish on any woman, and yet Tess was upon its murky waters in the worst of ways. Her own aching over Peter spilling down, Aven could scarcely stem tears, but for Tess she rallied best she could, knowing that she would mourn the sweet man in the days to come when the loss of him found itself in every corner of the farm and in so many traces of her memory.

While it was surely much longer, it seemed only minutes later when Wren brought a hungry Tusie in to nurse. Aven tended her daughter, then Wren took the slumbering baby back to watch over. Tate saddled his horse and left soon after to escort Sibby to the train station, where she was determined to be at Orville's side come the morrow and no doubt to comfort her mother and sisters with the news that, by Al's explanation, Jorgan had already delivered.

As dusk crept in, and with Cora's wise leading, Aven gave Tess the gentle administrations that Farfar Øberg had once given her. A smoothing of her hair. A hand to squeeze when it was needed. Soft murmurs of comfort or a listening ear when the only sound worthy of that moment was the cry of the brokenhearted who needed to know *why*.

Laced through it all was every prayer Aven could spirit toward heaven and, of equal importance, being a source of strength for Cora, who was not only bearing her own grief but trying to hold that of her daughter's as well.

In the hours that followed Al's news, the smallest things became surreal. The light streaming in through the window. The way it shined on the table setting that was still set for the noon meal. The way Tess's hand rested on the quilt where the same golden warmth streamed across it. When her tears were spilled from the first wave of devastation, Tess traced her finger along an eight-point star of creamy calico, pausing only to wipe her eyes as new tears fell.

Aven knew that from this moment onward, grief would come in currents, swelling around Tess, Sibby, and Peter's mother in the weeks and months and even years to come. It would rush in, forcing its way where it was least invited, and yet it would do a washing that only grief could do. One that cleansed away a fragile sort of rest so that what remained was the courage to seek joy and peace in the arms of the Lord amid a storm. 'Twas a time Aven well remembered, and 'twas a current that still swirled around her at times, even to this day.

Leaning against Aven now, Tess curled her hand around a damp kerchief and let out a shuddering sigh. Aven thought afresh to what Al had assured Tess of but hours ago.

Peter had loved her.

Aven's own tears brimming, she bent just enough to kiss the top of Tess's curls. "Peter will be missed," she whispered against that sweet head of ebony hair. "He will be so dearly missed."

THIRTY-SEVEN

THOR STOOD AT THE FAR END OF THE BALDWIN grove, and while a compost pile was a strange place to come apart from chores, that was Peter's shovel still leaning against the farm wagon, and those were his boot tracks in the dirt surrounding it. Thor gripped the sideboard of the wagon and drew in as steady a breath as he could manage.

Having just returned from Orville and Sibby's, Thor had taken the long way home. With memories of Peter now fresh to mind, it was a half mile worth walking. Though a heaviness dwelled in his heart, it was the communing with others that was lifting it. And it had been right good to see Orville and Sibby.

While unable to speak above a whisper, Orville's color had returned, and with the doctor's regular visits there, Orville was in the best of hands. Thor had brought them a box of food stores from the cidery and two skinned hares. He'd brought the same offerings to Mrs. Sorrel, and while the visit there had been as bittersweet, her tender and courageous heart over Peter bolstered Thor's own steps back down the mountainside to where Peter would no longer be waiting.

During both visits, Thor had left them with assurance that Peter had showed little degree of pain. While his wound had been severe, shock had taken over so quickly that Peter's calm was an unmistakable mercy and one that he hoped his family would find comfort in. It wouldn't lessen their sorrow, but there was solace in knowing that Peter's final minutes were restful.

Pulling himself away from the edge of the Baldwin grove, Thor aimed for the road that would lead the women and children back to the farm. What he wanted to do was sit in the shade of his trees and watch for their return, but with it too soon for them to arrive, he headed back toward the house. It would take at least two days for them to return from Whitetop Mountain by wagon with Al, so he wouldn't see his wife and daughter until close to nightfall.

He ached for that hour.

With heavy steps, Thor climbed the porch, and when he reached the kitchen, Jorgan was there cutting up another skinned hare.

Thor slid two fingers past his eyes for *Haakon*.

Jorgan was sober as he turned the piece of game. "He's not doin' so well."

Thor started up the stairs, aiming for Aven's old bedroom where Haakon was laid up. He expected to see his brother abed still, arm bandaged and kept in a sling, but instead Haakon was seated on a chair in the center of the room. His head was down, eyes on the floor, but Thor didn't need a solid view of his face to see how pale his skin was. Nor that Haakon's free hand where it rested on his knee was shaking slightly. Bandages wrapped his palms, and a square of paper sat folded between his tremoring fingers.

After fetching a stool from the corner, Thor placed it across from his brother. Exhausted from digging graves as much as he was from grief, he sat, his knees nearly touching Haakon's own.

Haakon blinked at the floor, then straight to Thor. Shadows rimmed his eyes, and his mouth looked parched.

Thor made the hand sign for *water*, but Haakon shook his head.

As for morphine, Haakon had declined that as well. Out of need, Haakon had stated. That he was enduring this amount of pain without medication was something, and for him to be getting along without those leaves he'd been so fixed on had to be intensifying the matter. No wonder his brother was trembling so.

Thor well remembered these days. The wretched days of an addictive tincture cleaving to mind and body even in its absence.

Haakon's breathing was labored, jaw clenched in a way that when he spoke, Thor couldn't understand. Haakon tried to sign it, but his hands didn't cooperate. Wanting his brother to be understood, Thor lowered his head and watched his mouth again before signaling him to repeat himself.

Looking relieved, Haakon spoke again and seemed to be asking if there had been any word from the sheriff.

Thor nodded. *P-A-P-E-R-W-O-R-K done.* As for what had happened here that night, the sheriff had given assurance that not one of them would be seeing the inside of a jail cell. Haakon looked as relieved as Thor felt.

The morning of the shootout's end, the sheriff had arrived while they were all still gathered around Peter. He'd assisted them at once, explaining that he would have come when expected, but the Sorrel men had ambushed them first. Having left his brother, Red, to watch the sheriff's comings and goings, Harlan and his men had known when to move in quick to disrupt them along the way. From the ramshackle state the lawmen had arrived in, escaping with their lives was a feat. They'd only managed by taking cover in an old trapper's cabin. Though only wounding one of the deputies, the Sorrel men had headed off, preserving ammunition and dispersing the lawmen's mounts as they did. The sheriff and his deputies who could walk trailed them on foot.

The hindered lawmen hadn't reached the Norgaard farm until nearly dawn and had come upon Jorgan and Orville first. Orville had been shot after taking down one of the men at the far tree line and was alive today because a deputy had taken a horse and raced for aid. Jorgan confessed that he was certain it would have been the Sorrels to find them and had been resolved to the likelihood, but refused to leave Orville since it would have meant the man's death. The sheriff had guarded Jorgan and Orville until gunfire at the house sent him that way. He'd found them all around Peter.

Later Dr. Abramson confirmed that there would have been nothing else to do for Peter other than offering him courage and comfort for the passage home.

Lowering his head, Haakon rolled it from side to side. He was dreadfully quiet when awake, and when he managed to sleep it was restless. While Thor couldn't hear what Haakon murmured in his sleep, Jorgan admitted to it being about a woman.

They didn't know who, but in Haakon's furrowed brow Thor saw regret.

With the square of paper still folded in Haakon's hand, Thor gently reached for it. His brother allowed him. Thor opened it with care. He didn't know where it had come from but had seen Haakon study it so often of late he didn't doubt its value.

With it splayed open, Thor studied the picture. High on a cliff stood two figures, one tall, one small, and just below crashed waves of riotous color. What looked like a ship was moored in the distance. All in deep indigo and charcoal gray that were still so soft, the chalk had smeared along the page, making the storm even more vivid. A compass had been drawn in the bottom corner as though to show someone the way.

Thor lifted his gaze to his brother's face. *Who?* The sign was simple, but it didn't make the inquiry any less weighty.

Though a tremor still coursed through him, Haakon's focus was steady on Thor's own. "It's a little boy. In Norway. There's a couple of them. Children, that is." Still shaking, Haakon set his jaw as if to steady himself. "Their father died last year, and I was acquainted with their mother. I was thinking that . . ." He drew in a slow breath. "I was thinking that . . ." He tried to wet his lips.

Thor would have fetched him some water then and there but didn't want to miss what his brother needed to say.

"Thor. That cabin's charred through."

Had Haakon been thinking to put a family in it? *We fix cabin.*

Defeat and hope warred in Haakon's eyes—the blue of them muddied with the suffering he endured. Perhaps for promise of that very future.

We fix, Thor repeated. He needed his brother to know how much he meant it. Between the three of them, they could get it done. They'd tackled harder things than that before.

Haakon slid his hand forward on his leg, and with care Thor gave the drawing back. As he did, he sensed that if hope won out, Haakon would be leaving them again. He didn't blame him. Not for one minute. A man was made to have a mate—a wife, a beloved—and the Good Book induced a man to find one. It was a task that was both terrifying and rewarding and one Thor had longed for because God didn't place His sons on this earth without also placing His daughters to walk by their side. Womenfolk were a precious part of this world and one more lovely and more mysterious than any other, to Thor's way of thinking.

He didn't know who this woman from Norway was but she had affected his brother most deeply. Thor meant to bolster Haakon closer to her side. *Name?* he inquired.

Haakon spelled it with a gentle regard, his wounded hand shaking with resolve and perhaps a trace of longing. *K-J-E-R-S-T-I.*

Thor nodded, committing it to mind to share with Aven, who would knit it into her own heart for prayers of the utmost sweetness and strength. While he hated the idea of his little brother leaving again, to aid Haakon in any way would be his honor. If there was something he could do to help Haakon onto such a journey, he would.

THIRTY-EIGHT

JUNE 16, 1895
BLACKBIRD MOUNTAIN, VIRGINIA

AS HAAKON EXAMINED THE STAIRS OF THE
cabin, they seemed sound. Still, he ascended the half dozen nearest
the top slowly, testing each one to be sure. Rather how the last week
and a half had gone—each hour as uncertain as the one before. By
sheer grace they were all making it through.

At the top landing, Haakon stopped. Shoulder sore, he pressed
against the bandage and gave a small roll of the joint to try and ease
it. He'd learned that the bullet had ripped through the muscle just
beneath his collar bone. He'd come to on the surgical table, and while
the pain had been mind numbing, based on what he knew of this
doctor's methods, there was no cause to worry about infection.

So far, Orville was showing a steady recovery, and fresh word had
just come this morning that he was mending well. Haakon was more
than thankful. There had already been such loss. As it was, upon
Tess's return, Haakon had met her in the yard, and though still weak,
had walked her over to Peter's grave so as to show her the way on land
she'd never journeyed upon before.

323

Haakon rubbed fingertips over his forehead. Having climbed this far, one more step seemed fitting. He pulled himself up into the loft that, while stable, was charred beyond saving. While the fire hadn't burned through the thick walls of his cabin, the damage to the logs would be irreparable. The roof made it through with only a portion collapsed, but with walls needing to be rebuilt, not to mention the floor, the roof was going to have to come off anyway.

What little furniture had been up here was ash.

Haakon picked up the sooty remains of a glass jar. He didn't know where to begin.

Then again, he'd learned of late how to take one small step and then another. Over time, it always added up. It had to. Over the days of his recovery, when the quiet of a bed had been his one domain, he'd imagined bringing her here. Her and her children. In fact, he worried that he'd been talking about it in his sleep. Now that he saw the extent of the damage, he didn't know when or how anything could be done. As he'd once told Fay, wanting a wife and having a place for her to live were two different things.

Waiting another year could afford enough time to repair this building, but he'd also learned in the last week that a man only had a short time on this earth. Maybe the days granted him should be made the most of. Should another year go by . . . what would he return to Kristiansand to find? Something told him he needed to go and that it needed to be before winter.

It was a little reckless, but the currents were just begging to be taken.

The cabin wouldn't house a sizeable family for long—but if he could enlist some help in piecing it back together, it could do for a start. Already his brothers had offered their service. It was with that assurance that Haakon turned away and started back down the stairs.

Da had raised them to walk in the footsteps of the Vikings of old. That meant valor and fortitude. Fearlessness and family pride.

All noble traits, but for too long Haakon had tried to blame his past behavior on a lineage of pilferers and plunderers. Thor and Jorgan hadn't done it that way. They'd wooed their wives and guided their families with a different side of Viking mettle. One of courage, resilience, and protection.

Because of that, Haakon had crossed *bloodline* off his list of excuses for his sins, right next to *last born*, *orphan*, and *unwanted*. Leaving nothing left but a bunch of marks over the deceit he'd bought into. The crossing out was a process as painful as any other, but now in the aftermath stretched a voided and purged cavern in his chest ready to be filled with something of richer make. He meant to fill it along that good and higher road Cora had reminded him about.

Outside, he found Thor and Jorgan waiting for him in the yard, where they stood assessing the crumbled roofline. Haakon gladly joined them in that, and once they'd pieced together a plan, they walked toward the great house, where by the smell of it, something fine had been fixed. On the porch, Fay was moving chairs into place and Jorgan stepped up to aid her.

With only a few moments left for the chance this evening, Haakon tapped Thor's arm. When his brother slowed, Haakon spoke what needed to be said.

"Thank you."

Already thank.

"Well I'm thanking you again." If it hadn't been for Thor, Haakon wouldn't have walked away from that hallway. While he had aimed to give Harlan and Jed a time of it, he didn't think he would have been able to beat them both. Not in the condition he'd been in. He owed Thor his life. Peter too.

Never as a boy would he have imagined that it would be his honor to have known Peter Sorrel. One of the greatest honors he'd ever been given. And as for Thor, Haakon wished it hadn't taken this long to know the privilege he had in getting to live life alongside this man.

He wished it hadn't taken four years, as many continents, and a night of fire and brimstone to realize what he should have realized so long ago—the man standing beside him wasn't his enemy. His brother was his best friend.

"Oh, that's such wonderful news." Aven took the empty basket from Ida. 'Twas a juggling act with a sleeping Tusie burrowed in the curve of her other arm.

Having brought over a freshly baked pie to Cora and the girls, Ida closed the kitchen door. "Al and his wife are stayin' for the week, they said."

A fine notion, that. A way to band together on this horizon even as hearts clung to those so dear. "I'm so glad they've come."

Ida spoke on, and Aven listened of Tess and how she was faring.

"I've a sense that Al's wife means to take Tess back with them for a spell," Ida said, checking on the second pie cooling on the table. "Sometimes an outing do a person good. We'll see what the child decides."

"Aye." And in the meantime Aven would continue to pray for Tess's comfort and for the washings of sorrow to work a good in her life. The Lord promised that very assurance, and Aven herself knew it to be true.

At sight of the men near the porch, Ida fetched the pie, and with Tusenfryd nestled close, Aven helped carry fixings for the small party to the front porch. 'Twas a strange day for festivities, yet with time and lives precious, there seemed no better hour than this. Fay was already out on the porch, moving chairs into place with Jorgan's help, and if Aven wasn't mistaken, there was a look passing between them as tender and loving as any might have been.

When Thor and Haakon reached the steps, Thor climbed first.

He'd scarcely parted from Tusie since his homecoming, and now 'twas no different as he reached for the babe. A kiss he offered to Aven, then another to Tusie's cheek as he folded his daughter into the crook of his arm. He kept her wee sunbonnet well in place, his fingers large and rough to the delicate lace trim.

Haakon admired his brother before shifting to better see the baby. Fading cuts and bruises still staked a claim on Haakon's face and hands. When Aven invited him to sit, he settled on the porch steps as he so often had. The mark of a wayfarer if she ever saw one. He had asked for nothing but the plainest of needs since his arrival. Only a place to lay his head and a chance to make amends. So different from the younger Haakon she'd once known.

Though Aven meant not to pry, Thor had hinted that Tess might not be the only one venturing off. 'Twas a farewell in the making—she could feel it. Bittersweet as it was, there were changes afoot for Haakon, and by what Thor had explained to her . . . blessed ones. Changes that Aven hoped for, lacing the name of this woman into her nightly prayers alongside so many others.

From the kitchen, Aven fetched tiny candles that Fay had dipped for such occasions. *Kinderfesten*, she called it in German. A tradition from Fay's childhood that she had brought to the Norgaard family. The wee flames kindling much merriment as the birthday person made a valiant effort of puffing them out.

And for Haakon this day, 'twas a celebration that had been long awaited.

Ida laid the pie into Haakon's hands while Fay brought over a box of matches. Carefully, Aven pressed a series of the tiny candles into the flaky crust.

When she finished, Haakon lifted blue eyes to her. "Four?" Voice winsome, he seemed to sense what they were about.

"'Tis for each year you were gone. Each year of not celebrating your birthday here, together."

He pulled in a slow breath and turned the pan half about on his open hand. A delay it seemed, for when he glanced back to her, his eyes were damp. A regard that she now knew to be draped in gentleness, braced by humility, and hemmed in friendship. In his words lived his gratitude, but in his face dwelled a thankfulness that administered what words could not.

The most precious gift she had left to give him—her trust—was his.

So dear was the realization that it penetrated every piece of her heart, including the broken places that the Lord had been stitching back together, helping her to see that she was placing her faith in a safe pair of hands once again.

Those very hands still holding the pie, he seemed uncertain of what to do.

Aven opened her fingers to show several more candles. "And however many you might need until we see you again."

A muscle in Haakon's jaw worked. On a slow inhale, he withdrew one from her palm and with a bittersweet resolve, pressed a fifth candle into place.

A whole year? But blessedly, only the one.

"You'll be missed," Ida said, placing her weathered hand to the side of his wrapped shoulder. This woman who had raised him since he was a babe in arms himself.

Though his smile was muted, there lived in his face a thankfulness that matched their own to him. Fay struck a match and instructed Haakon as to what to do. With a sparkle in his eyes, he blew out each flame in a single breath.

Fay dished out pie, and once everyone had a share, Aven settled onto the porch swing beside Thor. Though as wide as Tusie's whole form, his hand patted a delicate rhythm to her back that made nary a sound, so soft he touched her. Each time he leaned his head back to drop a look to Tusie's smooth, sleeping face, he kissed the top of her wee head again.

Haakon watched Thor with such focus that Thor rose and strode to his brother in loud steps. Haakon's eyes widened the closer he came. Gingerly, Thor pulled Tusie away from his chest and lowered her to his brother.

Haakon shook his head, "I've never held—"

Thor gave a nod of assurance. Haakon accepted the swaddled infant, cradling her with a trace of apology as though he were far from worthy.

Desperate to bolster him, Aven moved to his side. "Well done, Haakon." She showed him how to support the baby's head.

Thor watched on, pride shining in his eyes for his brother and daughter.

With Tusenfryd settled, Aven shifted her hand away from Haakon's fingers. Without so much as a falter, Haakon cradled her tiny form. "She's a beauty, she is."

Aven smiled. "Aye."

Thor returned to his seat, and Haakon regarded him as though to concede an understanding of how so small a creature could steal a man's heart.

Haakon shifted his hands, thick wrists flexing with the gentle weight of his niece. "A sun and a shield," he whispered, almost as though in prayer. "Along the only road worth walking." He lowered his face beside Tusenfryd's and brushed his mouth to her round, silken cheek. Her closed eyes scrunched tighter at the brush of his beard, and Haakon smiled. When he pulled away, there was a sheen in his eyes again. "I'd like to give her something. If I may."

"Of course," Aven said.

He cradled the baby with his good arm and used his free hand to reach beneath the collar of his shirt and pull up the leather cord that always hung there, drawing up a pouch of the same make. Haakon grimaced but could raise his injured arm no farther. He struggled again, and even as his eyes beseeched her for help, the tips of Aven's fingers caught hold of the cord, and she helped him lift it off.

"If you'll open it," he said.

She glimpsed inside to discover two folds of paper.

Haakon pulled one out and offered it over. Aven unfolded what was a page torn from a Bible. "You are giving this to Tusenfryd?"

"It's one of my most prized possessions. I don't want it to get lost while I'm away. If she'll keep care of it, I'd be thankful."

If he meant to undo her this eve, he was succeeding. "I promise this will be well cared for." She held the treasure with utmost regard. "And Haakon?"

"Yes?"

"I wish you the greatest happiness. The both of you."

Though his nod was sincere, he blinked back what looked like a trace of worry. Did he fear rejection? While Aven knew not the future, she couldn't imagine this maiden wishing him away. It would be a good and brave man who sought her hand. Yet his uncertainty was clear as he scanned the bottom steps as though to find where he'd dropped an answer.

Aven longed to know this woman who had such an effect on him. She would be captivating, of that there was no doubt.

"How long will it take you to arrive?" Aven asked.

"At least a few months."

She watched his thumb brush against Tusie's tiny ear. "I'll be praying each and every day." That the heart he sought would be readied for this sailor's arrival and that if for any reason the woman was lost to him, God would see Haakon through the unknown.

"I thank you, Aven. For that and much more."

When Tusie started to fuss, his blue eyes lifted as Aven rose. Giving him one last smile—this one a farewell—she gathered up the baby to nurse her inside. Thor stood and opened the door. Aven thanked him, and he braced the small of her back as she stepped into the house. Leaving the door ajar, he took her place on the steps. With a nod, he bid Jorgan to join them. When the three of them were settled, it was soon just the familiar scent of pipe tobacco, the soft cadence of two voices, and the quiet camaraderie of all three.

In the great room, Aven sank into the rocking chair, her arms full of a slumbering joy and her heart full of thanks for this family. Beginning with the hour she had first met them when the shores of Norway had been but a memory and when the warmth of this land unfolded around her, inviting her in, beckoning her to a new and wondrous way of life aside the sons of this mountain. So many courageous hearts that had forged out families, carved together a living, and built a home where the spirit and heart were at peace.

EPILOGUE

HAAKON CLIMBED THE MOUNTAIN PATH ON legs more accustomed to sea than land. A faint snow fell, scarcely worth noting here in Scandinavia. The dusting of autumn flakes speckled his coat, and he buttoned it closed with fingers roughened from life aboard a whaling ship.

After leaving home three and a half months ago, he'd journeyed first to the Rappahannock River with Tess. Wedged into the eastern coast of Virginia, the river had once served as a boundary between the North and South during the Civil War. Al's wife had encouraged Tess to join an organization there that taught freedmen and women to read. A way for Tess to continue a purpose dear to both hers and Peter's lives. Not only for civil rights but in honor of all the afternoons that Peter and Tess had sat together, Georgie's reading primer spread between them.

Haakon had left her standing on the shore of the great, glittering river where she had been farther north than she'd ever been in her life and where he could see in her dark eyes a renewed purpose.

By passenger ship he'd gone farther up the coast to Canada, giving his shoulder the additional weeks to heal. From there, he ventured to Iceland, where he labored with a whaling crew bound for the Faroe Islands, an isolated piece of land once settled by Vikings. There he'd boarded a cod vessel rigged for Norwegian winds that had brought him to this hour. Months of grim labor lay behind, and weeks of procuring cod from Kristiansand's waters still lay ahead, but this uphill walk was the reason behind every frigid mile and lonely night.

On the hillside before him huddled a small herd of goats. Their numbers were sparser than he recalled. What had been a herd of over two dozen had wilted to a scant few. Just west of the livestock stood the widow's stone cottage. So narrow it held only one rough-hewn bed and, if his memory served true, the children bunked in any nook and cranny, from padded baskets for the littlest ones to a makeshift loft for those who could climb the ladder. Even nearer than the cottage spread a garden encircled by a low fence of driftwood and weather-beaten rope.

It was there that he saw her, knelt among rows of undersized cabbages and tattered beets.

Her harvest was as sparse as everything else she owned, and he hoped she had already brought most of it in. He feared she hadn't when he stepped nearer and saw that she was thinner. Draped in a wool cloak of dark evergreen, her slim shoulders bent over a row of carrots as she worked one free. Just outside of the crooked fence sat a wooden cart slight enough to be pulled by a goat. Scattered around were young children, each a mite older than last he'd seen, but few so tall as to reach his waist.

Their mother spoke in Norwegian, directing the nearest boy to dig up a carrot instead of catching snowflakes on his tongue. The lad knelt and tugged a scrawny green top with all his mittened might.

"*Nei*," she chided gently and, sliding over, used a spade to show how it was done. Upon finishing, she gave her son the tool, picked up a stick, and began working her own section by scuffing it against the firm earth.

A petite girl moved beside her and crouched down, so close that the woman opened up her cloak and brought the child nearer. In that, Haakon saw a flash of blue beneath from what could only be his shawl.

He strode closer, and soon Kjersti's eyes lifted to him.

There were any number of women in Botetourt County he might have courted. Women who were much closer and easier to pursue. But voyage he had, doing the harshest work he'd ever known, to stand here wondering what to say to the young mother with the flaxen hair.

She looked at him as though certain it were a dream. As though any minute she would wake from an imagination bent on tricks.

With gentle movements, he opened the gate and crossed into the garden. A few steps from her he knelt and, to her clear astonishment, took her hand in his. It was cold and thin. Shadows pooled around her eyes where once bloomed naught but her youthfulness. While she had only aged the same months as he, life was trying to whittle her away. Alarm spread through him.

Pulling out coins, he handed them to her oldest son. "Go to the village and buy bread and meat."

The boy—perhaps eight—didn't understand. His mother knew some English but she wasn't speaking. Only staring.

Haakon's Norwegian was far from ample, but he knew enough for survival in the lake camps. "*Brød. Kjøtt.*"

"*Ja.*" The boy wet his lips at sheer mention of provisions.

Haakon nodded for him to hurry. "*Rask, ja?*"

Clutching the coins, the little fellow ran off down the lane that would lead to the village, perhaps a mile away. More snowflakes fell—lightly dusting the land. While this day was mild yet, forceful storms would blow in with abandon before long, covering the region of Kristiansand with more snow than a person could walk through.

Looking back to the boy's mother, Haakon noted the steely determination in her eyes. Soil was streaked on her ivory jaw, and her cheeks were reddened and wind chapped. Her hair, a wild tangle of yellow, was pulled back in a tumbling braid as though fashioned with frozen fingers sapped of strength. Her lips, which had once been rosy, now bore a purplish tint that filled him with dread.

"You must stand now," he said, scarcely able to speak through the tightening of his throat. Haakon moved nearer and touched her wrist with a work-worn hand. "Please."

She pulled away. "I am going to get these carrots out of the ground." She spoke low and cool, and while her English was perfect, the Norwegian lilt colored it lovelier.

It bothered him that he noticed something so trivial, but she was stunning to him. It was why he'd been captivated from that first sighting and why he hadn't been able to shake her since. Lord knows he'd tried.

Grabbing up the spade, she crammed it into the near-frozen earth, desperate, hungry, and fighting against a land that was soon to freeze solid. He could have coaxed the spade from her, but he didn't mean to oppress, only to help. Haakon reached for a sharp rock and used it to pit the ground one row over. He did this until he had several carrots dug up. After placing them in the cart, he noticed her watching him. She swiped soil from a gnarled root and set it beside the ones he'd added. Wondering if she might allow him closer now, he rose and knelt before her again.

Both of their hands were covered in soil as he took her own in his. Dirt was wedged under her nails in a way that confessed she had done much digging of late. The scraggly potatoes in the bottom of her cart confirmed it. Wanting her to stand, he began to rise, but she wouldn't be helped up. So uncertain she seemed that he thought of how best to explain his intentions as he knelt again.

"Please hear me. I would like to take you inside and for you to rest." Rubbing his thumbs on the backs of her hands, he gently chafed his warmth into them. "The children can join you and keep watch of the fire. Then I will come back out here and finish harvesting this garden." The cart would hardly be full, but he would pick the plot clean as she had meant to. "Will you allow that?"

She made no response. Her mouth parted in a mix of silent doubt and wonder, fjord-blue eyes on his face as if she'd heard a decree that couldn't be true.

"Please, it's cold," he said again.

And her cloak was so thin. With a careful touch, he reached just past her shoulders and lifted the dark hood into place, covering her hair. Shielding her face from the bitter wind that swept up from the sea. To his relief, she allowed him. Haakon brushed his thumb against the homespun cloth of the shawl, then forced his hands to fall away.

She spoke his name hushed-like, pronouncing it as it was spoken in this land of its origin for the kings of old. "*Hoh-kun*." The sound of his name in her voice, the fact that it sprang to her memory and perhaps had never been forgotten, was a breaking inside him.

"Kjersti." In God's mercy, he'd been gifted it again. He'd been praying it in his heart the three and a half months since. "*God dag*." There was probably nothing good about this day for her, but it was one of the few greetings he knew.

She didn't answer, and rightfully so. To his surprise, she tossed a look out over the fjord below, an inlet of indigo water fed by Norway's lakes and rivers. "You have come to farm the ice?" Her gaze returned to his face. "It is too early."

"No. To fish for cod." He had struck a deal with the captain of a fishing vessel for procuring cod for New York. The hull of the ship was loaded with coarse salt and barrels for brining. In compensation for able seamanship and labor alongside the crew, Haakon had asked only to secure a small cabin for the journey home. He ached to have a reason for his bachelor's hammock to be dreadfully insufficient on the return trip.

Her eyes went steely. "You should go *now*."

"Are you asking me to leave?"

She nodded. "And please do not come back." She regarded her children, who observed him with wide eyes. "I will not stand for them to be hurt again. They mourned you for weeks and weeks. The only grief to surpass that had been for their father."

Her confession was a wrenching in his spirit, and deservedly so. "I'm so sorry I brought them sorrow." He wished he could describe how much.

"Do not offer them any gifts nor tell them any stories. Do not knock on our door, and do not kneel here any longer. You can see the road. Please take it."

With a glance back, Haakon charted the humble lane that would lead him away from this small farm. Back down to the shoreline where, just beyond, the fishing vessel was docked. The same path he'd taken when he'd first departed this place. When he'd pulled himself from her warm embrace, taking care not to wake her. She had a right to be angry. She had a right to that and more.

Perhaps if he stated himself more clearly. "Kjersti. Please let me take you inside and help you." Haakon shifted to kneel closer. "If you don't mind, I'd like to stay in your barn and tend to the goats and this field and whatever else needs care for as long as it needs it."

Her eyes betrayed her. Shock wasn't so easy to conceal when you were aching for hope.

"Then, if you would allow me one last thing, I would like to take you home. To Blackbird Mountain. It's in America and is good country. I have a cabin there . . ." One that he and his brothers had gotten a good start on just before his leaving and that they had vowed to finish repairing for him. "There's land and a garden and a pond. Lots of orchards. There's family too. Sisters and brothers. Even cousins. I would like to take you there, so that you and your children can live with me and so that I can care for you."

Her mouth fell a little farther open.

"But first, I would ask you to allow me to make you my wife."

The cold, Norwegian light was beautiful on her skin, and it just got lovelier when she turned to peer at the horizon and the tall ship docked there. Masts and sails jutted up from the deck, all strong and tidy with its rigging and oak beams. She looked back to him as though needing another language to speak with. As though neither English nor Norwegian would suffice. He knew just what that language was. One that said more than spoken words ever could and that he'd spent all his life learning.

He slid his hands beneath her hood, cupping her face with a featherlight touch. His fingers were still soiled, but this was no time to worry, and her face already bore the streaks of this earthen labor. Certain she would allow him to pull her no closer, he drew himself over the threshold of her fallen spade and slowly, so as not to frighten her, pressed a kiss to her forehead.

Her breath slipped out in a soft rush, and he whispered a single "Please" against her skin.

With that, he pulled away lest he long for more.

"Would you ask me to send my children away?" The determined strength returned to her voice.

"What do you mean?"

"That is what the man from Oslo wanted. He came here and courted me in the summer but was meaning to send them to a far-off school." She pressed Haakon's hands away. "He said there were too many of them. Too many of another man's children to look after. My answer to you will be *no* as well, because I will not send them away."

"Too many?" Haakon leaned back to better see her. "Oh no, madam. I scarcely think there are *enough*."

That pinch of surprise betrayed her again.

He'd asked himself over and over during the journey here—why couldn't he shake her from his soul? Because he knew what it was like to be left behind. The passing of his mother had quaked his world, and he'd grown up on uneven ground because of it. The same would be for this woman and her children after their own wretched loss. Something in him longed to soothe that brokenness just as he'd once needed. It wasn't charity, nor was it a wiping away of memory, but instead a deep-rooted thirst that had him yearning to care for her more and more with each passing day. To protect her and love her as he had been longing to do for a woman for as long as he could recall. He hoped—with all his heart—to have her love in return.

After inching himself farther back, he pretended the need to count the children. First the nearest boy, who stood in quiet observation, scarcely taller than the low garden fence. Then the oldest girl, perhaps three, still squirreled away beneath her mother's cloak. Third was a stout boy of about seven who had a dirty face and a wondering expression as he sat on the tongue of the cart. Fourth was the strapping bit of courage who had gone off to the village.

"That's four, then. Might there be one more?" Haakon rose enough to trudge over to a wide basket beside the goat cart. The thickly woven lid was ajar just enough that he was quite sure those were two curious eyes watching him. "It's quite a large farm I live on, and would be awful empty without just *one more*." He lifted the lid to find a wee stowaway peering up at him.

She was the smallest of all, her blonde curls topped with a knit cap and her cheeks so rosy with cold they were as pink as the tip of her nose. Her dress was embroidered wool, same as her coat, and her brown stockings were wet in the knees.

"I thought there had been five," he said victoriously.

She smiled at him, and he smiled back. She looked to be the same age as Bjørn, though not nearly as plump, and that alarmed him.

"Now this is more like it." Haakon crouched down to see her eye to eye. "Forgive me, I've forgotten your name, little one."

"Hana," her mother said softly. "She doesn't speak yet."

"No? It is lovely to see you again, Hana."

The girl bent down, picked up a rag doll, and showed it to him. He took that as the finest of hellos. Haakon touched the red-and-white plaid of the doll's dress.

"While I was hoping for more, I suppose *only five* will do." He reached over to shake each of their small hands. Then he winked at the babe in the basket, who was lifting the front of her dress to try to show him her belly button. "Especially you."

He glanced back to Kjersti to see a wet sheen in her eyes, pooling liquid against the vibrant blue of them. He'd always been told his eyes were rather fine, but he'd known the moment he saw her that he had met more than his match.

He thought of her that night—that night in the barn when he'd finally been alone with her. So frigid was the winter that she had fetched a pile of furs, causing his hopes to rise. But one had been for the young goat and two others for each of their shoulders. Kjersti's children and nursing infant had been left in the cottage with an old neighbor woman for the evening, their young mother taking a few hours away to ensure another little creature made it until morning. Haakon had stayed, offering to help her, but ever since his wretched behavior with Aven, he always took great care not to coerce a woman beyond what he sensed made her comfortable. When Kjersti expressed her pleasure in his presence in no manner other than the brightness of her eyes and the depth of her kindness, his hope dwindled. As the hour wore late, she'd kept them both awake with conversation, pausing only to chafe the little goat or ensure it was able to feed from its mother. His disappointment mounting, he'd heard less and less of what she had to say.

He meant to do better about that now.

Haakon wiped dirt from another carrot and placed it in the cart. "I didn't bring any gifts." He had nothing to his name save the strength of his back and a proud piece of mountain. "And I will tell no stories if you wish it."

Her eyes filled with more tears as though she wished for quite the opposite. She was looking at him as if the man from Oslo had been insufficient for yet another reason. One she wasn't about to admit. He hoped it was so.

Looking at her now, he knew she would have done all she could to ensure her children's survival. She was born and bred from the blood of Viking women and knew how to carve life from this land if it was the last thing she did. A woman did not grow up as a daughter of northern shores without such resilience in lands not beholden to mercy.

He also knew that she would have married someone good and willing if it meant saving her children. But though she was strong, he meant to ease her burden and help to carry this load. As for his own burdens of heart, he hoped he might have someone to share them with. Someone to help shape them and spur him to press on with fortitude for this pilgrimage. If she might marry for love . . . if he could even hope that it would be him . . . "If you would allow this, I would like to take you home with me. You and your children. The voyage will not be easy, but I promise that I will be with you." He would do everything in his power to see them safely to the other side.

Wind hit cold from the east, the same wind that would bear them away from here if she was willing to bid her homeland goodbye. It was a lot to ask, and while he was prepared to pursue another way—a life with her here—he desperately wanted her to be a part of his family back home, and they a part of her. "I would like to give you my land and my home. My life and my name." And most of all . . . "My heart. If you would have me."

She heaved in a shuddering breath, wrapped an arm around the girl beside her, and though uncertainty still wove within her every blink, there was a wonder and a yearning that brought him the first traces of hope. The lass beneath her mother's cloak gave him a shy smile, and the lad on the wagon tongue inhaled a deep breath, his own hope abundant in the look of longing he gave Haakon.

"*Mor bedt for deg hver natt,*" the boy said.

Kjersti's eyes went wide at her son's bold announcement, then lifted to Haakon with the same vulnerability he felt in kneeling here.

An understanding stirred in Haakon as he pieced together what the boy declared. "And I felt them," he said in return for her prayers. *Every night,* her son had just admitted. Haakon recalled all the hours he had walked the dark mountainside in search of danger or sat up with a rifle across his lap beneath the stars. All the times he'd thought of her when he should have been dreaming. "Every one."

Haakon rose and stepped nearer to the boy. "Thank you for the picture you drew me. I've kept it close." He pressed a hand to his chest to show how much. "It helped me find the way back here."

Though he didn't know English, the boy's chin trembled. To Haakon's relief, Kjersti spoke in Norwegian, her voice tender and holding as much emotion as her son's face did with each falling word. After she'd translated, the boy gave Haakon a valiant nod. He twisted his fingers together as if in effort to keep from crying. Haakon gripped them in one hold, squeezing assurance and warmth into them.

Rising up from the sea came a rush of salty air—as cold with the season as it was with coming sunset. He turned back to Kjersti. "That's a lot for you to hear at once, so if you'll consider what you might say, I'd be grateful." He had several weeks here and meant to grant her every moment to decide if she wished.

Now it was her hand he took, this one with a different kind of touch. One that had her lashes lifting to his face and their different sides of broken meeting between them.

"*God dag,*" she said softly, answering his earlier greeting.

Haakon smiled. At the very beginning, then, as was a right and fair place for her to start. He deserved nothing more, and that a hope was rising inside him was more than he could ask for. And as for those words that fell from her lips just now, it *was* a good day. It was rather all kinds of perfect even as, with bone-weary hands, he unearthed another carrot. Despite his urging for her to go inside to warmth, she remained across the row from him—the spade passing between them until the soil was purged and smoothed. He didn't push his desire on her further and instead relished her nearness until the cold of dusk had her coaxing her little ones indoors.

He didn't follow, as it wasn't his place, but she returned a spell later with a lantern for his work, a slice of bread for his trouble, and a gentle smile that he savored on his walk back to the ship by starlight.

Meaning to tend to all the chores he could, he came back the following evening and each one after until the weeks ashore had passed and he'd spent every waking hour hauling in cod and passing warm evenings in Kjersti's cottage, eating the stews she served him and savoring the stories the children treated him to—each finer than his own.

Until the morning came that the ship's berth could hold no more catch. It was that same dawn that Kjersti stood beside him in a stone church. The children sat along a front pew, their polished shoes not touching the floor, as they watched their mother receive a ring onto her finger once more. Kjersti's face was awash with joy as Haakon slid the humble band into place. Wrought through him was all the gratitude a man could possess and the consciousness of just how many precious lives were in his care. As she accepted his own heart in return, it was an exchange more powerful than any he'd ever known. A changing inside him rivaled only by the forgiveness and hope that had come to him from above.

In Kjersti's promise lived her own kind of hope. One he meant to honor. And with her hand inside his own that day, so came into his life a Mrs. Haakon Norgaard. He scarcely knew how to reckon with that kind of blessing. A sobering gift it was, and one he meant to honor.

In the cottage that night, he told as many stories of home that he could think of to blissful and bleary-eyed children. Kjersti listened on with a quiet contentment, and when the last child was well asleep, Haakon understood a cherishing with his wife that he would have missed in any other fashion. There, amid pine-drenched starlight, he discovered a wholeness that he hadn't before comprehended. One that told him that life wouldn't always have cause to bring them joy, but that it was worth finding and protecting all the same.

The following day when she knelt beside a distant grave with five little ones, he waited . . . giving them all the time they needed. When she rose, she brushed soil from her hands and allowed him to walk her down the hillside where they both carried cherished memories for those lost. It was there that he led her onto the ship as his wife—a homebound future up ahead and their children following close behind.

A NOTE FROM
THE AUTHOR

MAY I TELL YOU A SECRET? NOW THAT YOU'VE reached the end of *Daughters of Northern Shores*, I have one more piece of the story to tell you . . . and it's why this novel is in your hands and perhaps why your heart is beating with the same span of emotions as my own has been.

Upon my first imaginings of *Sons of Blackbird Mountain*, before words were even on the page, I knew several things: Thor was going to love Aven. Haakon was going to think he loved Aven. And in the end, when it came to those bullets Jed Sorrel fired as young Haakon scampered up the hillside, Jed wasn't going to miss. Instead, Haakon was going to fall and not rise. The boys were going to carry him home, and Aven would be there in his final breaths.

I knew Haakon's death as vividly as I knew the love story. I could see the scene in my mind, the heartbreak laced with redemption as he made amends in his final hour, ushering in healing and restoration for the hearts involved. It was the most vivid scene in my mind. There would be no real need for a second novel.

But then something happened.

As flames raged through the Sorrels' barn, and as Jed fired that pistol in Haakon's direction, that young man looked back over his shoulder, and I'm telling you, he looked right at me. It had nothing to do with his charm or even the color of those remarkable eyes. It was the raw and real peering into someone's soul. A pleading— straight from Haakon—to have a second chance. That if I could trust him, and more importantly, trust the seeds of redemption within him, that something new, rather like the sun over that hillside, would brighten the land. And in that moment, I couldn't let him fall. Because of that, he made it to the top of the hill, into the sun's glare, and out of sight.

I didn't mention this in the author's note of *Sons of Blackbird Mountain* because it didn't seem the time yet. I tell you now because it's what sparked the pages of *Daughters of Northern Shores*.

When it came to this second novel, less and less went according to plan than ever before. Never—with any book yet—has there been such a glaring difference between my vision for a plot and the pages that you just ventured through. Stories have, for the most part, gone to plan, but not with those on Blackbird Mountain. I've spent nearly as much time trying to make sense of the *why* of this as I have in writing the books themselves.

Perhaps this had to do with the characters—their hearty spirits and vibrant passions. The bold way these men walk their land and protect their families. The courage of the women who share life at their side. Even the dangers that have come their way.

Perhaps it's had to do with the wilderness and the vast terrain that breathes from its very center a place known as Blackbird Mountain. A place where legends ring true in a way that permeates every rise and hollow of a farm that few have ever ventured to.

Or perhaps it's the fact that I intended for this novel to be so, so different. The plot I had conjured up for this second installment? You read only fragments of it. Most elements changed course with the same energy that lifted the sails of Haakon's ship. The determination that stirred the grasses and had Aven lifting her eyes to the sky, wondering what might be coming.

As an author, this was a difficult place to be. To admit to that is probably harder.

Deep down I have craved safety. Yet it has been the tumultuous waters that asked to be sailed instead. The call of adventure is not always an easy one. As the pages of this novel unfolded, I felt like Bilbo in my hobbit hole, not wanting to step away from the calm. But in that is where the abundance lies. I am so thankful I did not write the story I had planned. It would have been gentle, yes, but I don't believe it would have been as honest.

As for those daughters of northern shores, I have come to realize that perhaps the reason this season has been so challenging is so that I get to be one of them. It's very likely that you are there, too, in a place of uncertainty. Perhaps we've watched the sea together, awaiting that ship to come in. Perhaps we've knelt in our garden as a storm raged all around, determined to make beauty come from dust. Perhaps we've said goodbye to the gentle, easy way, and have come to know the need to draw courage up from the wellspring every hour of every day.

Perhaps you know, as I now do, the meaning in Cora's words: *It a gusty place to stand, but it only mean that the Lord be all the nearer.*

The Lord be all the nearer.

Perhaps that's why this book took the twists and turns I never saw coming. So that it could be not by my strength but by His. That in my uncertainties, the Lord is all the more able to fill the gaps with His glory. That by changing course, by seeing the world through new eyes, by laying dirt on Peter's grave, God is more present. His goodness is here, even in the hurting or the frailty.

To all His daughters and sons, let us hoist the sails into the grand unknown. May we hold sweet memories in our hearts while facing the vast waters with hope. May we love much and believe deeply and sacrifice well.

To each of you who has journeyed with me to these shores, I thank you.

DISCUSSION QUESTIONS

1. Which original characters from *Sons of Blackbird Mountain* were you most excited to see again in the sequel? Of the brand new names and faces, who did you most enjoy meeting?

2. This book traveled to several distant lands by way of *Le Grelotter* and her brave crew. Of the different places that Haakon and his fellow sailors traveled, which place would you be most curious to visit? Any stops you'd wish to make along the way?

3. How did you see Thor and Aven, the leading characters in the first book of this series, grow over the last four years and during this second novel? Which traits of theirs did you find lasting? What elements of their love and personalities seemed new or different?

4. When Haakon returns to the farm after four years away, he anticipates change within the family, including the possible passing of loved ones. What do you sense life was like for people in this era before the ease of communication with modern technology? What would it have been like to harbor uncertainties or longings when word between loved ones was sparse?

5. The plot of *Daughters of Northern Shores* takes several twists and turns along the way. Were there moments when you thought the story was going to turn out differently than it did? In what ways?

6. When Thor opened the letter from Washington DC, were you surprised it was sent by Alexander Graham Bell? With *Blackbird Mountain* having hinted at tension between Thor and this notable forerunner of Deaf education, how do you think this strain might have changed after Mr. Bell was the one to respond to Thor's inquiry in *Northern Shores*?

7. Of the three brothers, Jorgan leads the most discreet and stable life within the pages of this series. But what sort of issues do you think arose for him during the story? What conversations do you think he and Fay might have had behind the scenes? What sort of courage or determination do you think Jorgan was leaning on when facing the final scenes of this book?

8. When Peter goes to battle against his father, uncles, and grand-father, what do you think this meant for him? With similar instances of family division having arisen during the Civil War some forty years prior, do you think this was an unexpected con-cept to Peter, or do you feel it was a choice he was prepared to make long ago?

9. There are several women who have small but significant roles within this novel including Tess and Fay, as well as Mrs. Sorrel and Sibby. Which of these women stood out to you, and what types of character qualities did you most admire within them?

10. Depicted on the cover is the young widow, Kjersti Jönsson. With her only present in two chapters, did it surprise you that she has such a prominent place there? In what ways, do you see her as a quiet heroine of this novel? What purpose did she serve in Haakon's life while he was in Norway? How did this compare to how she affected Haakon while they were apart?

11. For Sigurd, Bjørn, Tusenfryd, the children sailing in from Norway, and those yet to be born, what do you think life would be like for them growing up as children of the Norgaards in Appalachia? What do you think their heritage will mean to them? Their home

on Blackbird Mountain? The freedom their fathers fought so hard for?

12. The title *Daughters of Northern Shores* is meant to symbolize not only the women who love and care for the men in this novel but how the *Sons of Blackbird Mountain* have vowed to protect them. Though immersed in a rugged environment, these women embrace life and care for others with courage and grace. In what ways did you see this reflected? Were there additional ways that you saw the title symbolized?

ACKNOWLEDGMENTS

MY SINCEREST GRATITUDE TO MY EDITORS at Thomas Nelson for their guidance with these novels: Jocelyn Bailey with *Daughters of Northern Shores* and Amanda Bostic with *Sons of Blackbird Mountain*. Your insights and ideas made the pages above and beyond what I could have done on my own. To the whole team of editors, designers, marketing, and sales. You truly are a wonder!

A heart full of thanks to my agent, Sandra Bishop, for believing in me and my stories from the very first one. Thank you for your wisdom and support and for the box of groceries when the cupboard was bare. You are more than an agent; you are a gem.

To my critique partners and writing pals Amanda Dykes, Kara Swanson, Jocelyn Green, and Jody Evans. You all are dears through and through, and I am so grateful for the chance to talk story and do this writing life side by side. May your words always be blessed!

To author Sigmund Brouwer who believed in my writing even when it was risky, I thank you. The Blackbird Mountain books would not be published today if it weren't for your daring.

To my family, you are cherished beyond measure. And to the sailor on the ship . . . I look forward to the day you might become the sailor on the steps. May the sea hold you safely until then.

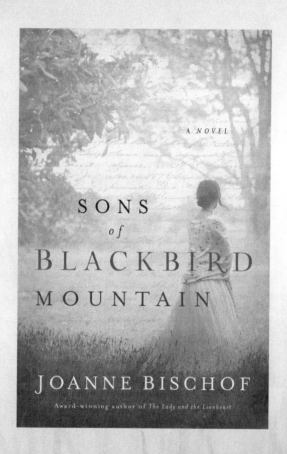

ABOUT THE AUTHOR

Mike Thezier Photography

JOANNE BISCHOF IS AN ACFW Carol Award and ECPA Christy Award–winning author. She writes deeply layered fiction that tugs at the heartstrings. She was honored to receive the San Diego Christian Writers Guild Novel of the Year Award in 2014 and in 2015 was named Author of the Year by the Mount Hermon conference. Joanne's 2016 novel, *The Lady and the Lionheart*, received an extraordinary 5 Star TOP PICK! from *RT Book Reviews*, among other critical acclaim. She lives in the mountains of Southern California with her three children.

Visit her online at JoanneBischof.com
Facebook: Author, JoanneBischof
Instagram: @JoanneBischof

DISCARD

356